Fenris Unchained
By Kal Spriggs

Copyright 2020 Sutek Press

This is a work of fiction. Names, characters, businesses, places, events and incidents are either the products of the author's imagination or used in a fictitious manner. Any resemblance to actual persons, living or dead, or actual events is purely coincidental.

Books by Kal Spriggs

The Shadow Space Chronicles

The Fallen Race
The Shattered Empire
The Prodigal Emperor
The Sacred Stars
The Temple of Light
Ghost Star
*The Star Engine**

The Renegades

Renegades: Origins
Renegades: Out of the Cold
Renegades: Out of Time
*Renegades: Royal Pains**

Angel of Death

In Death's Shadow
A Quiet Death
For Love of Death

The Star Portal Universe

Valor's Child
Valor's Calling
Valor's Duty
Valor's Cost
Valor's Stand

Lost Valor
Stolen Valor
Hidden Valor

Fenris Unchained
Odin's Eye
Jormungandr's Venom

The Eoriel Saga

Echo of the High Kings
Wrath of the Usurper
Fate of the Tyrant
*Heir to the Fallen Duke**

CHAPTER I
Time: 0815 Local, 01 June 291 G.D.
Location: Dakota, Dakota System

A yellow light began to flash on the control board.

That was nothing new, not aboard the *Kip Thorne*. Warning lights lit up half the panel. It was a Christmas display of yellow caution lights, flashing priority lights, and red danger lights that gave the board an aspect of impending doom.

The pilot didn't look over to the panel to see what was wrong. One of the red lights indicated a malfunction in the auto-pilot system. That meant that the tall, blond woman had to bring the *Kip Thorne* down by hand.

Not a difficult a task for an experienced pilot. She enjoyed flying, enjoyed it more than anything else, really. She didn't enjoy thirty-six hours of flight time spent awake on stimulants while flying a ship that needed far too many repairs.

She shot a glance at the panel, and then flipped on the intercom. "Rawn, take a look at the starboard thruster." She shook her head. Tried to push thoughts through a mind that seemed turned to mud.

The intercom crackled and hissed, his voice difficult to make out. "Uh, Mel, we might have a problem."

The light ceased flashing. She sighed in relief, "No, it cleared up here, good job whatever you did."

The ship bucked. The alarm light flashed red. A moment later, so did six or seven other warning lights. "What the hock did you just do, Rawn?!"

Mel fought the control yoke, eyes wide, and she half-wondered if she were talking to herself, "Rawn, was that the starboard pod going out?"

The ship yawed over as she overcompensated and she fought it back under control.

"Rawn, you'd better get that thruster back online."

She heard a squeal from the bridge access hatch as it opened behind her. It had always reminded her of a ground vehicle's brakes screeching just before an accident.

She tried not to apply that metaphor as some sort of warning to her current flight. Her brother spoke from behind her: "I'm going to pack the escape pod. Anything you want me to throw in?" he asked.

"What?" Mel craned her neck to look at him.

The ship spun sharply and threw her against her straps and

tossed her brother into the bulkhead. She bit off a curse and struggled with the controls for a moment. It seemed to take an eternity to fight the ship back under control.

The radio crackled, "Freighter *Kip Thorne*, this is Dakota Landing Control, you broke out of your landing queue, return immediately, over."

"We're going to lose the other thruster. The port thruster is in worse shape. What do you want me to put in the pod?" her brother asked.

His calm voice made her clench her teeth.

"We are *not* abandoning ship," she told him sharply. "I can land this thing." It would be hard, though, with just one thruster. They couldn't engage their warp drive in atmosphere, not without disengaging safeties that were there to prevent anyone from doing just that. *Even if we had time,* she thought, *it would be a stupid thing to do.* The warp drive field would tear the atmosphere around them and if they hit anything solid in their path, the difference in relative velocity would not only kill them but quite possibly wipe out Dakota's biosphere.

She forced her mind to focus. When she spoke, her voice had the calm tone that she emulated from her father: "Dakota Landing Control this is Freighter *Kip Thorne,* we just lost our starboard thruster and are requesting immediate assistance, over."

"Freighter *Kip Thorne,* is this some kind of joke?" The speaker's nasal, officious tone suggested she wasn't amused.

Rawn snorted. "I know the safe combo, I'll grab our cash and some keepsakes. I'll clear out your desk too." He pushed his way back off the bridge.

"Get back here—" Mel clamped her jaws shut. *One thing at a time.* "Negative Dakota Landing, this is no joke, our starboard thruster— "

Her voice broke off as another yellow light began to flash, the warning light for load limit on the other thruster. "Our starboard thruster is out and we're about to lose our port thruster, requesting assistance, over."

"Negative, *Kip Thorne,* you'll have to break off your descent and return to orbit," the nasal voice answered. "A repair craft can be sent to you there."

"Dakota Landing, this is an emergency. We lose our port thruster, there won't be anything keeping us up here." Mel snapped. They had already begun their descent and the thruster didn't have enough delta-v to keep their intended flight path, much less boost them back into orbit. "We don't have enough thrust to get back into orbit, and you don't have time to—"

"*Kip Thorne*, break off your descent or you will be intercepted by our customs cutter. Over."

"Dakota, I hope they got a tractor," she answered. "Because—" The ship shuddered and the other thruster went dead. "We just lost our other thruster. *Kip Thorne,* out."

She turned off the radio and sat in the chair for a long moment as the small freighter bounced. Soon it would begin to tumble, she knew, without the guidance from the main thrusters.

"Six years, six years I kept her goin'. Dad, I did my best."

She wiped her eyes; now was not the time to cry.

The ship fell now, without anything to slow its descent besides atmospheric friction. Superheated air flashed across the hull and cast glowing flames across the cockpit glass. The station-keeping thrusters were stopping any kind of spin, but as the temperatures climbed, they would fail soon enough.

Mel sighed. She kissed her finger tips and touched the control yoke one last time, then unbuckled and left the bridge. She didn't look back.

* * *

Time: 1720 Local, 1 June 291 G.D.
Location: Dakota City Detention Center, Dakota System

Marcus looked over at his companions.

"Don't be so gloomy. They're not nearly so angry with us as they are with whoever crashed that freighter." He ran a hand through his brown hair and gave them a shaky smile.

Brian didn't lift his head out of his hands. "You were carrying ten kilos of rex. Do you know how illegal that is? We'll be lucky if they only confiscate our ship and give us a few decades in jail."

Strak spoke from where he sat, cross-legged on the floor. "That's overly optimistic really; rex dealers don't get good treatment in jail. Most of the inmates know someone who's OD'd on it."

Marcus winced. Not that he feared jail, or death, really, but that kind of death wasn't the type he had imagined for himself, so long ago, when he started on this path.

"Look, I'm sure I can get us out of this." He was, too. There'd be an opportunity to come up, he knew. He had played the odds before and he knew, one way or the other, he could find a way out of this scrape. *Though the price might be a bit more than I'd like to consider...*

Rex was a performance drug, and it was the most illegal and the most common illegal drug in known space. Rex's addiction was both chemical and psychological because it gave a person something that was priceless.

A rex junkie didn't act like any other druggie, because rex didn't distort your senses or give you a euphoric feeling. People on rex were confident, their thoughts were clear, they were able to make quick, well thought-out decisions. The most shy, nervous youth could become the self-assured center of activity with a single dose of rex.

Marcus had been hauling ten kilograms of rex tertius, hidden in a compartment beneath his bunk. Tertius was the third level, the cheapest. It only affected brain activity. Secundus and primus Rex chemically modified the body.

Primus was the highest level, the most addicting. Secundus heightened the senses and stimulated the central nervous system, giving a person greater control over their body. Primus did all that and also lent strength, streamlined metabolism, and heightened reaction speeds.

Of course, if rex's benefits were heaven, its side effects were hell. The withdrawal symptoms were even worse, but Marcus would really rather not think about that just now.

They sat in silence for a while and Marcus studied his two companions. He'd signed on as crew aboard their ship, the *Varqua*, six months ago. A crew of five, including these two. The *Varqua* was a tramp freighter, a Stout-class, one of thousands that plied the edges of Guard Space, serving the smaller colonies.

Brian Liu was the owner of the ship. Marcus figured he had good contacts out here on the edge of Guard Space. The *Varqua* had been a profitable ship, unlike most that plied their runs. A short, stocky man, clearly of Asiatic origins, Brian was a decent enough boss, though he came off as aloof and arrogant often enough. Marcus couldn't fault him that, though it often felt like Brian saw him as less than human sometimes.

Strak was something of an enigma. Quiet and unassuming where Brian was arrogant and cold, overweight and slow where Brian was muscular and bird-quick. He had held a sort of general maintenance job aboard the *Varqua*. In reality, he served as an adviser for Brian, and a watchdog over the rest of the crew. Getting anything past the old man was more than difficult, it was nearly impossible. He seemed remarkably loyal to Brian, and Marcus got the feeling that they shared some kind of history.

Marcus hadn't ever felt unwelcome... just the outsider.

"Everything would have been fine except for those pirates," he muttered.

The door at the end of the cell block clanged and then groaned open. Two prisoners led the way, followed by two guards. The first prisoner was in his late teens and he wore a ragged set of coveralls. An unruly mop of blond hair hung above a face covered in dirt and oil.

The other prisoner was a tall, statuesque blonde, with dark brown eyes. She wore an equally ragged cut of clothing. As they came past, Marcus blinked in surprise. "Mel?" He asked as he moved close to the bars.

She turned, hearing his voice. Her eyes went wide in recognition.

Before he could register what was happening, her fist snapped out and slipped between the bars to strike him full in the face.

Marcus dropped like a stone. She kicked through the bars, hitting what she could, punctuating each word with a kick, "You owe me ten thousand dollars, you free-booting piece of—"

One of the guards cuffed her to the ground and then drew her to her feet and pushed her into the cell opposite the other three prisoners. Both of the guards and most of the other prisoners were laughing at them both.

Marcus sat up, touching his nose and winced, "I think you broke my nose!"

Mel shook her head, jaw clenched in rage, "Too bad I didn't break your neck."

Strak laughed, "Sounds like she knows you fairly well, Marcus."

Marcus sat on his bunk, holding his nose with one hand. "Well, now that you worked that out of your system, do you want to talk?" he asked in a calm tone. He felt hot blood run down his face and the salty copper of it in the back of his throat. It didn't bother him all that much, he had tasted worse things before.

Mel shook her hand, flexing it a bit. He'd warned her before about striking a man in the face with a closed fist, she'd be lucky if she hadn't broken a bone with how she'd hit him. "Sure. You still owe me ten thousand Guard Dollars. You're still an awful person." She took a seat on one of the bunks in her cell. "What more do we have to talk about?"

Marcus stared at her for a long moment. There was something

more here besides his theft. Granted, Mel had a tendency to overreact at times. "Five years hasn't been enough to cool your anger?" He couldn't help a glance at her brother, but Rawn just stared at him, his blue eyes cold. Neither of the siblings answered.

Brian looked up, "That waste of oxygen destroyed your lives, too?"

The boy spoke, his voice was calm, but his eyes were cold. "Marcus Keller is not a man to be trusted."

"A little late to tell us that." Brian's voice filled with bitterness. "He had ten kilos of rex stashed in his room."

"Wow, I knew you were awful," Mel stopped flexing her hand and looked over at him in shock, "but dealing rex? That's sick, that's really sick." She smiled sweetly. "I hate to think what they'll do to you in prison."

Marcus held his nose, though that just meant more blood ran down the back of his throat. He didn't say anything. There wasn't anything he could say. He looked away from her angry dark eyes and met those of her brother Rawn. *She has every reason to hate me,* Marcus thought grimly, *and her brother, too.*

***

"Hey, boss, got a couple possible recruits." His underling set a couple of file folders on his desk. He could have easily provided digital files, but Mueller, like most Guard Intelligence Agents, didn't like to leave digital tracks. They were too easily tracked, whereas archaic paper was easier to hold onto and to securely destroy.

Agent Mueller looked up from his paperwork, "Not interested. I wouldn't even want to pick up the other two to get our man if it weren't for the package deal." Dakota was a backwater world, but the United Nations Star Guard had a large presence here of late, mostly to squash some of the inter-sector smuggling that had begun to erode their authority. Agent Mueller didn't care about smugglers, though. He didn't even really care about the Dakota System. If it had suited his purposes, he would have sacrificed the one marginally inhabitable planet without a second thought, along with its entire populace.

He was here to recruit a couple of wayward agents back to the fold and to eliminate a real threat in the process. In suiting with such important business, he'd appropriated the local military commander's offices while he finalized the paperwork he needed to initiate his plan.

"One of them is a pilot. Her brother is certified engine crew." His first recruit seemed enthusiastic, but he'd been burned by Guard

Intelligence for failure to achieve assignments, so it only followed that he wanted to make up through enthusiasm.

"Oh?" Mueller raised an eyebrow. Skilled technical support was always in short supply, particularly those who could be reliably leveraged to serve his purposes. "That could be useful, but this is a recruitment mission—"

"Both of them lost their parents to a GFN terrorist attack."

The Guard Intelligence Agent picked up the file, he browsed both folders quickly. He began to smile slightly, especially as he read the note from the investigating officer. "Interesting... All right, you've convinced me. Tell the magistrate I want them."

***

"The accused will step forward."

Mel stepped forward into the courtroom. The only occupants were a pair of guards and a man in Guard Fleet uniform. "Sir, I want to—"

"You will be silent or you will be held in contempt of this tribunal," the uniformed officer cut her off. "The tribunal is now in session."

There was a faint hum as recording equipment turned on.

"Certified Pilot and Ship's Owner Melanie Armstrong of the Century System is charged with Criminal Negligence, Reckless Endangerment, and Willful Disobedience of Traffic Control Commands." The tribunal officer sounded bored. "How do you plead?"

"Uh, sir, that is—"

"Accused pleads guilty to all charges. Evidence is amended to tribunal recordings."

"Hey, I didn't say—"

"The tribunal finds the accused guilty of above crimes and also for contempt of the tribunal. Sentence for conviction is fifteen years hard labor. Convicted is remanded to Guard Custody for duration of the sentence."

The officer flipped a switch. The hum cut off.

"Hey, wait, you can't do this!" Mel shouted. "That wasn't even a trial! I demand to see a lawyer—"

One of the guards grabbed her by her collar and dragged her out.

***

Time: 1100 Zulu, 11 June 291 G.D.

Location: Female Block, *Justicar* Prisoner Transport

The cold, dark ship's sole purpose and design came from the need to transport the maximum number of prisoners with minimal difficulties. Cells were just that, cells of solid steel that ran down the length of the ship, each door secured by a digital lock whose combination changed every time the guards opened it.

They separated Mel from her brother and put her in the female block. There were only three other women in the block. Apparently the Guard didn't get many prisoners on this run.

She didn't talk to them. They didn't talk to her. The silence was almost companionable. Her food arrived via a tray slid under her door, twice a day, delivered by a female guard who never spoke.

On the third day, her door opened.

There were two female guards. One of them gestured. "Out."

They took her out of the cells, past the security checkpoint and into a sterile room. "Shower's there," one gestured to a door.

"Clothing's there." She gestured to a neatly folded pile of clothing on a table.

"When you're clean and dressed go through that door." She pointed at a second door.

They left without another word.

It was the first moment of privacy Mel had had in days. She wanted to cry. Instead, she went to the shower. It was an experience she wanted to savor, but she also didn't want to be dragged out of it. She suspected that or worse would happen if she lingered too long.

She hurried and then got dressed quickly. It was normal, comfortable civilian clothing; it even fit her fairly well, though it was bland and unremarkable. It felt alien after the prison smock she'd worn for what seemed forever. A part of her mind whispered that it had only been a week. She didn't want to imagine the longer period of imprisonment ahead of her.

The second door opened into another sterile room.

A long mirror covered one wall. A man sat behind a table with a slim folder on it.

"Have a seat," he said without rising. He was a bland, boring-looking man, in an average-looking suit.

Mel sat. She knew this was some kind of game, knew she was being manipulated. It should have made her angry, but somehow it only made her feel more helpless. Over his shoulder she saw her reflection. Her face looked pale, blond hair lank, eyes shadowed.

The man opened up his folder. "Melanie Armstrong, born 266 to Anne Marie and Hans Armstrong on the planet Century, of the same system."

His voice was empty and cold, "Your aunt and uncle were archeologists on Century, they and their youngest child were killed in a pirate attack on Century, leaving only your cousin Jiden Armstrong alive. Your grandmother, Admiral Victoria Armstrong of Century's Planetary Militia is something of a local war hero. You got your pilot's license at fifteen, qualified for entry into the Harlequin Sector Fleet Academy at seventeen, rather than joining Century's Military Academy. You were in the top five percent of your class for three years. Two months before graduation, your parents died in a Guard Free Now terrorist attack. You resigned and took guardianship of your younger brother. In the six years since, you managed the *Kip Thorne* as captain and owner until a week ago when it broke up above Dakota."

"I suppose you even know my calculus test grades from my plebe year," Mel joked weakly, "So what is this about?" She didn't like that he was dredging up the past.

The man smiled thinly, "You got excellent marks, your teacher put in a recommendation that you be sent to further schooling in higher level mathematics." The man stood "Do you know what your sentence is?"

"Penal colony I'd guess." Mel answered.

"Fifteen years on Thornhell." He stood up and looked down at her. He wasn't tall, probably ten centimeters or more shorter than Mel, but he seemed to loom over her.

Mel couldn't help but swallow nervously, "I heard there was a war on there." What she'd heard of the planet left her feeling faintly sick. Some kind of uprising on a hot, jungle planet where the dominant lifeform was a plant that grew spines up to a meter in length.

The man shook his head, "Not anymore. Not that it matters much. You'd be working in the mines. Fifteen years is ten years longer than the survival rate on that planet."

"It's not fair!" Mel snapped. "I did the best I could, I didn't even get a fair—"

His voice cut across hers like a knife, "No, it's not fair. The universe isn't fair." He smiled a cold, reptilian smile. "Think on this though. How fair would it be if your freighter had landed on someone, rather than smashing into some wilderness on a backwater planet?"

"That didn't happen!" Mel shook her head.

He smiled wider at her response. "No, it didn't. But your next stop was Salvation. Think for a moment what would have happened if your thrusters went out there. Something similar happened on Expo just last year. Over fifteen hundred dead when one battered freighter crashed into a residential block in the middle of the night. No warning; definitely not fair to them, eh?"

Mel looked down at her hands. "If we'd made that run, we could have paid for the repairs we needed."

"No, if you'd made the run, you would have needed to make several more to pay for the repairs you needed. We reviewed your logs and analyzed your cargo versus your maintenance bill. Even with some kind of loan, you weren't going to pay for it all." The man answered.

Mel looked up, anger in her face. "What's this about? I'm going to die on some crappy, worthless world, I failed my brother and I failed myself. Is that what you want to hear?"

She gestured at the mirrored wall, "Is that what they want to see?"

The cold man smiled. "What do you know about the Second Sweep?"

Mel's jaw dropped at the complete change in subject. She shook her head while she tried to get her bearing. Finally, she answered, "Started a hundred years ago. Bigger war than the War of Persecution. We almost lost."

"We very nearly were *exterminated*." The cold man spoke softly. His eyes seemed distant and there was a tone of reverence to his voice. "The Culmor were at the front gate. Fifty million soldiers and sailors died. Over three billion civilians wiped out. The entire Sepaso Sector razed; half of Harlequin sector exterminated."

He caught Mel's gaze with his own cold and calculating eyes.

"That certainly wasn't *fair* to them. That didn't stop it from happening. You wrote a paper about the automatons." He paused. "Tell me about them."

Mel stared at him for a long while, "Uh, the Preserve and Triad ran low on trained personnel. They made fully automated vessels for the fighting." She frowned. "Most had small crews to run them, some were controlled entirely by computers: Artificial Intelligence, supposedly limited by programming to think only within tactical orientations. They weren't supposed to think outside of the mission perimeters."

The unknown man picked up a copy of her paper, she could follow along as he read the instructor's comments scrawled on the top, "A decent paper, excellent research but you didn't touch very much on the reasons the ships were discontinued."

Mel shrugged. It seemed a strange topic of conversation, but... "They behaved erratically in combat. Mission perimeters were vague in many cases. They were amazingly effective as rear-area raiders, or serving as suicide attackers against Culmor bases. While in formation with human ships, though, they sometimes targeted friend and foe, went berserk. Some took damage and went haywire."

She was slightly surprised at all she remembered after several years. Then again, it had been an interesting topic in history. The subject had been all the more intriguing for the fact that most people didn't like to talk about it.

Her interrogator finished for her, "And then the war turned, we didn't need them anymore. Triad and the ships were discontinued, most of them were scrapped."

Mel nodded impatiently, "Right, they weren't designed to carry crews, the weapons, plants and engines had none or minimal radiation shielding, the ships didn't have life support. It was easier and cheaper to scrap them than to refit them for human use."

"Don't worry, this all has a purpose." The cold man smiled, took his seat. "That history is something of a fascination of mine; also, it's part of my job."

"Which would be?" Mel asked.

The man removed a wallet from within his suit, "Guard Intelligence."

Mel pushed back from the table, as if he'd transformed into a venomous snake.

He grinned broadly, "No need to fear, I'm not hunting you or even here to harm you. As bad as it may sound, I'm actually here to help you."

Despite his words, he clearly enjoyed the effect he'd had on her, Mel saw. The light to his eyes and the smirk on his face marked him as someone who cultivated the persona.

Mel knew that she should stay quiet and shouldn't provoke him. Even so, she couldn't help but snort in derision, "Right. As in 'I'm from the government, I'm here to help you.'"

The spook's smirk vanished and his eyes narrowed in irritation. "Some agents believe that coercion is sufficient to gain service from those they need. I do not believe so. Believe me when I tell you this: I will lie to you, I will use you, but I understand that I must give you some incentive if I want you to assist me."

He stared at her in silence for a long moment and Mel could tell he had second thoughts about that offer of his. It would be far too easy for him to wave a hand and have her dragged back to her cell.

Good job, Mel thought to herself, *piss off the guy who holds your life in his hands.*

Even so, she couldn't help a spurt of irritation with the man. He wanted her to feel this way, wanted her to second-guess herself. He was building towards something and he wanted her off balance and uncertain. She fell back on the fire that had gotten her through the Academy and she felt her back straighten, even as she clenched her teeth on the spike of anger at this continued manipulation.

"What do you know about the Wolf-class battlecruisers?" He demanded.

Back to the games, Mel thought with a sigh. She took a moment to think. Part of the Academy had dealt with ship identification, with a basic overview of every Human military ship made in the past three hundred years. The Wolf-class had stood out to her because of the paper she had written, so she remembered more than she otherwise would have.

"The class was designed for heavy combat. Fully automated, some self-repair capabilities. Only ten or twelve of them even begun in construction, I don't think any of them ever saw combat."

It was the sum of all her knowledge. She'd been far more fascinated by the smaller ships while at the Academy. *I wanted to be a fighter pilot,* she remembered. That part of her seemed very distant, in many ways as dead as her parents.

"Three Wolves commissioned, two of them went on missions, the third went to the breakers within a month of completion," the agent stated flatly, all emotion gone from his voice.

"The *Romulus* went against a Culmor dreadnought squadron at Baker in order to delay its attack on Harlequin Station. That mission cut the war short by an appreciable margin. It destroyed three of the squadron's four dreadnoughts, and the fourth was destroyed in a follow-up run."

Mel blinked. A *battlecruiser* destroyed three dreadnoughts?

"The other ship, the *Fenris*, departed on a separate mission three weeks later, in March of 193. It first attacked a troop transport convoy, sighted at Bell, then against a captured deep-space station serving the enemy as a raider base. Its final target was to be the center of the Culmor advance in this sector: Vagyr."

Mel frowned, "Wasn't Vagyr captured intact nearly a year later?"

"It was, by 'auxiliaries' that were, and are, little more than pirates," the agent replied.

"The *Fenris* never arrived at Vagyr. It intercepted and destroyed the convoy, scouts confirmed the destruction the raider base, and that was it. Guard Fleet presumed it destroyed in the fight at the raider station. Significant debris clouds suggested a considerably larger raider force at the station than intelligence had suggested." He shrugged. "Logic, therefore, suggested the autonomous ship was destroyed in combat."

"I assume we're having this conversation because it wasn't?" Mel snapped, her patience at a ragged end. The history lesson grated, particularly given the fact that her future seemed tied to this random bit of history.

"Indeed." The agent smiled. "In fact, you are quite right."

"Two weeks ago, a merchant ship suffered a minor warp drive failure. Their FTL warp drive kicked off in what was supposed to be an empty, barren system. While undergoing their repairs, they spotted activity in the inner system. They also detected military transmissions in the system. Like any merchant with something to hide, they quietly got their ship repaired and left. Someone aboard talked and one of my colleagues collected their sensor data as a precaution."

"And it was this missing ship?" Mel asked.

"That took confirmation by a cruiser squadron we sent to investigate. They were extremely fortunate: the *Fenris* queried them for identification and accepted their modern codes."

"So the ship was damaged and hid in some backwater system. What's the problem?" Mel asked. Some part of her whispered that she would be better off trying a more helpful tone... but everything about this Guard Intelligence agent made her back go up.

The agent closed his eyes, sighed slightly. "I've had to tell this story twenty-seven times. Do let me finish at my own pace." He opened his eyes and peered at her somewhat inquisitively, "I don't think you want to make me angry."

His gaze reminded her of a snake that had just eaten, regarding a mouse it might make room for. Mel shivered.

"Guard Fleet dispatched a courier ship with the proper clearance codes and query data to order the ship to power down. Upon receiving the query codes, the vessel replied that makeshift repairs were 98% completed, and that the mission would continue. Upon receiving the codes to power down, the ship did something it shouldn't have. It ignored the codes and replied that the mission would be completed.

Then it engaged its strategic warp drive."

"And you have no idea where it went." Mel sat back.

"On the contrary. We know exactly where it is going.

***

Time: 1500 Zulu, 11 June 291 G.D.
Location: Solitary Confinement, *Justicar* Prisoner Transport

Agent Mueller stepped up near the bars and dropped a chair outside. He settled into it backwards, arms crossed over the back, "Leon, you look awful."

The prisoner didn't look up from where he sat, huddled in the shadows at the rear of the cell.

"Trying to ignore me? You got pretty good at ignoring many things, Leon, but you never could ignore me." Mueller entwined his fingers and rested his chin on them.

"What do you want?" The voice was only a whisper.

"My friend, my mentor, what do you think I want? I want you, the famous agent, I want you working for us again." Mueller let the sincerity drip through his voice. It was easy enough, after all, because it was the truth. They needed him, and men like him, especially now.

"That will never happen," Leon hissed back.

"Come now, never is an awful long time." Mueller replied. "I know you've still got family back on New Paris. For that matter, I'm sure I can find someone a little closer to… focus your mind."

He hated to use threats, not because they weren't effective but because it seemed so dirty. *Why do people continue to make me threaten them,* he thought, *just to do what needs to be done?*

"What do you want?" The whisper was faint, difficult to hear. It was enough.

"I need you on this one. It's bad, I won't lie. Has the potential to be extremely bad. Entire planet annihilated, not a good thing to have happen on my watch, you understand." Mueller shrugged, as if to say it would be an unavoidable tragedy.

"I get the point, what do you want me to do?"

"Don't cause problems. I've talked your friends into helping us. Go along with it. They'll come through this fine; you'll come through this fine. Maybe I can even get you some treatment—"

"No. I have my own ways for dealing with my demons."

The agent shrugged, "Have it your way. It's a shame you left. Yours are hard boots to fill."

"What, the killing, destroying and murdering boots, or the scheming, plotting, manipulating boots?" The prisoner scoffed. "I'm sure you're doing just fine."

"Thanks, Leon, you always knew just how to cheer a fellow up," Agent Mueller smiled. "I must say though... I did learn from the best."

"Get out of my sight before I kill you," the voice of his former mentor showed some echo of real anger. That surprised him a bit, he thought it would take more than that to break through the man's shell of self-pity.

"Oh, you wouldn't want that to happen, Leon. If I die, well, let's just say you wouldn't want certain other deaths on your already heavy shoulders." Despite his languid words, the man rose quickly and left. He'd already set the hook, no need to further bait the tiger.

***

Time: 2000 Zulu, 11 June 291 G.D.
Location: Security Offices, *Justicar* Prisoner Transport

"It may be a mistake trying to rehabilitate two agents at the same time." The overweight man reclining in the office didn't look important; he looked like a middle-aged businessman. His name was Daniel Feinstein, and he was the Harlequin Sector's Chief for Guard Intelligence.

He was supposed to be headed from the Ten Sisters system to Harlequin Station on an appropriated civilian courier. Which was why he checked again at his watch; he had a limited time before he had to catch the military courier with its faster FTL warp drive.

If he missed that departure, then people might start to wonder where he'd been if he *hadn't* taken the civilian courier. It was unlikely in the extreme that anyone could connect his brief disappearance with this project. Given the potential repercussions, however, it wasn't a risk he wanted to take.

"One of them is willing. He was cast out over something that wasn't really his fault." Agent Mueller said. "I interviewed the others, they're all suspicious of each other anyway, I doubt the subject of past involvement with espionage services will come up."

"It's your call." The Sector Chief shrugged, "I think you know what you're doing. Operation Rising Wolf is approved," he stamped his seal on the final operation order. "You obtained a ship?"

"One of the converted Lotus Blossoms."

The older man snorted, "Terrible name for a ship class."

"The designer was somewhat eccentric. The ships do their duty, that's all that matters,"

Mueller stared at the stamped orders. Months, if not years of work had culminated in this moment for the ambitious agent, Feinstein knew.

"Have you talked with Agent Scadden?" Feinstein asked.

"Did he have some additional information in regard to this project, sir?" Mueller's voice was polite and level. Feinstein hid a smile with practiced ease. Evidently the other man didn't want to admit that Scadden had tried to warn him off.

Even so, Feinstein gave him a level look, "Don't forget, even the best lose sight of why we do the things we have to do sometimes." Feinstein pushed himself to his feet.

"He'll remember on this trip," Mueller said.

The younger agent took his copy of the operations orders. Feinstein knew that they essentially gave him the power to take any action he saw as necessary. It was a heady amount of power for any man, Feinstein well knew. He operated under those orders, subject only to the authority of the Guard Security Council.

"Has the Fleet got any chance of stopping it?" Agent Mueller asked the question absently, almost as if he didn't really care about the main mission.

"No. Nothing in position at any rate." Feinstein cocked his head in consideration as he answered. Agent Mueller's ambition was well known, as were his obsessions. It wasn't unthinkable that *he* had lost sight of the bigger picture.

"Was the populace warned on Vagyr?" Agent Mueller asked.

"No, if it looks like we knew this was coming, it will only focus suspicion on us." The senior agent spoke after a slight pause, "You think the convicts will prove malleable?" Feinstein asked the question levelly, but he studied the younger man's face for any signs that he had become unreliable. *If that is the case,* Feinstein thought, *I'll terminate this project, regardless of the potential ramifications and the resources allocated.*

Agent Mueller met his gaze with a look of professional confidence. "They'll do their jobs. They won't ask too many questions. When things start happening, they'll do as I tell them, out of fear or greed. Doesn't much matter which."

CHAPTER II
Time: 0800 Zulu, 12 June 291 G.D.
Location: *SS John Kelly,* Expo System

Mel looked the unfamiliar cockpit over with a critical eye. She'd seen a couple of these ships before, though never from the inside. The Lotus Blossom class were somewhat infamous. A far fancier name than was entirely necessary, she thought. The ungainly and actually rather ugly ship had little in the looks department to compare to most small freighters. It wasn't really a freighter at all, more of a military light cargo transport.

Marcus stepped in the door behind her, "Should have known I'd find you here, already. Studying a bit early aren't you? We still have six hours before departure."

She didn't answer him at first. It took her a few seconds to squash her anger so that she didn't erupt from her chair to attack him. He would expect that, she knew from the overly relaxed tone in his voice. He wanted to provoke her. "You're a manipulative son of a bitch, you know that?"

"Mel, I'm hurt... *really*." His innocent tone didn't fool her. Marcus took a seat in the copilot seat behind her.

"Don't you have something else to do?" Mel asked.

"Why? I'm only familiarizing myself with the systems, just like you," Marcus flipped several switches and rattled his fingers on the controls. She didn't have to look over her shoulder to see the insolent smile on his face.

She sat there for a long while, concentration broken by anger. She hated this man, hated him with every ounce of her body. "Why'd you do it?" She asked finally.

He didn't answer for a moment. She expected another off-handed joke. Instead, when he finally spoke, his voice was gruff. "You wouldn't understand."

"You're right. I probably couldn't understand how a betrayer thinks." She answered. "I don't think I'd want to anyway."

"Things aren't always what they appear, Mel." His voice was sad, somehow. "Keep that in mind when you work with Agent Mueller. Sometimes things aren't what they appear to be."

"His name's Mueller?" Mel asked.

There was a moment of silence. "Yeah, Adam Mueller. I caught his name when he flashed his badge." He cleared his throat, "If you hadn't been too busy taking bad deals from the guy, you might have caught his name, too. You've got to realize that things aren't what they look like with him."

"And sometimes people are exactly what they look like," Mel snapped back instantly. She didn't want to think he'd had any motivation besides self-interest. Those thoughts robbed her of her anger, left her only with pain.

His seat creaked as he leaned forward to speak softly in her ear. "Don't trust anyone on this ship."

With that he rose and left.

***

**Time: 1400 Zulu, 12 June 291 G.D.
Location: *SS John Kelly,* Expo System**

Mel completed the undocking procedure and drew away from the prison ship. She looked out the canopy, gazing with distaste at the prison vessel. "LMV *John Kelly*, clear of your drive, *Justicar*." She couldn't find it in her to wish them a good journey.

She heard a dark chuckle from behind her. "I'd love to be able to take all the prisoners off and blast that ship out of the sky."

"I'm sure you would, Marcus, but you won't be doing that." Agent Mueller said from behind them both. Marcus muttered something about who he wished was aboard the prison ship when he did it.

Mel smiled in spite of herself.

Her smile broadened as she looked across the indicator panels and saw only two yellow lights. She took her time as she swung the bow around and inserted the coordinates for the warp engines. There was joy in a ship that responded so readily to her touch. There was happiness to be found at the yoke of any vessel, even if it wasn't home. *I have no home now,* she thought, her joy darkened with sorrow. She had lost the last thing she had left of her parents. Her only family left was here on this ship and back at her parent's homeworld of Century.

"Warp coordinates uploaded. Strategic drive active in thirty seconds," Marcus acknowledged.

Being reminded of his presence killed the smile. It didn't hurt nearly as much this time, but it certainly didn't feel good.

She watched the countdown timer. Most such maneuvers were routine; the good thing about warp drives was that they worked or they didn't. The drive rings that circled the ship did their job unless they suffered actual physical damage, at which time the ship reverted immediately to normal space. *Though they can function at lower levels of capability,* she thought.

Watching a ship go into warp was a sign of how well a ship worked. A ship in top shape engaged smoothly, because its drive was properly aligned. Most civilian ships were slightly misaligned, not enough to cause damage, but enough to cause slight nausea to those unfamiliar to the experience. Slower than light warp drives, often called 'tactical' warp drives utilized only one ring so noticing any motion was difficult. The faster than light warp drive, often called strategic drive by the military, utilized both drive rings on a ship and so any issues with alignment were more easily detected.

As she'd expected, the drive was very smooth. "Minimal misalignment."

"She goes as smooth as a—"

"If you finish that statement, you're going to wish we had a doctor aboard." Mel stated flatly. She'd heard a variety of coarse phrases before; the last person she wanted to hear it from now was him. She opened the intercom to the engine room. "Rawn, how are things down there?"

"No problems, sis." She could almost hear his shrug. "Strak is monitoring the power plant, and that Giran guy is keeping an eye on the control panel."

"Thanks, Rawn."

She heard the door slide closed, and flipped on one of the internal cameras to watch the Guard Intelligence agent walk down the corridor, toward the hangar bay.

She felt Marcus looking over her shoulder. "Getting a little suspicious of our good friend and boss?"

"I have far less reason to trust you. Shut up." She spoke without force, though. Why the Guard needed to rely on seven convicts to do this job she didn't know. She didn't trust those reasons at all. This was a job for a skilled team of salvagers or mercenaries, not for an ad-hoc assemblage of convicted criminals.

She flipped on the receiver for the hangar bay intercom. Two of the other crew members were there, Brian, the third and last member from the *Varqua*, and Stasia, who seemed to be a hacker of some sort. The hacker seemed to have a large number of boxes to sort through and as Mel watched, the woman opened up a box, drew out some computer components and then checked them off an inventory.

"Everything good down there?" Agent Mueller asked.

"Da, seems good." Stasia was a short, skinny woman with

mousy brown hair and a thick accent. Her face had a pinched look and she seemed to squint at everything nearsightedly. Mel had spoken to her briefly; she'd seemed very distant, as if her mind was elsewhere.

As Stasia returned to sorting through her boxes, Brian gestured toward three black crates. Each was long and narrow, roughly the size and shape of a coffin, banded with metal strips. The security camera didn't have a good angle, but Mel zoomed in and was able to read bright orange numbers written on the top of one of them.

"Three crates arrived for you just before departure." Brian spoke. There was an unspoken consensus by the crew that no one would refer to the agent as 'sir'. He hadn't earned any kind of respect, and he gave them that minor victory. That they followed his orders seemed good enough for him.

"Only three?" the agent asked.

Brian held out the inventory list, but Mueller waved it away. "Have them put outside my cabin."

"That crate is carrying MP-11s," Marcus said from behind her. He pointed at the first crate. As the agent turned, the other two crates were clearly visible. "That one is a case for a MG-144, and that is a—" He cut himself off, looking at her.

Mel stared at him for a long moment, the obvious question unasked. Marcus was a smuggler, a thief, and a general scumbag. There was no reason for him to instantly recognize the coded label on a military weapon crate.

Movement on the screen caught her attention and she saw that the Guard Intelligence agent was headed toward the bridge. She cut the camera feed and brought up data on the warp drive just as the door opened.

"I trust everything is well in hand?" He asked.

Mel didn't trust herself to face him without revealing too much. Marcus saved her by unbuckling. "Everything's good here. We can probably go to autopilot for the rest of the trip. Good computers – equipment, too – for a freighter. Where'd Guard Intel come up with it?"

"There will be a briefing in five minutes in the lounge. I trust you'll both be there."

The agent turned and left without saying anything.

"Fishing for information?" Mel asked.

"Trying to distract him. Agent Mueller is a very perceptive man. I thought it best to give him some false lead as to what we were doing in here during his absence."

That sounded a little weak to Mel, "Sounds to me like you

know something about this GI agent."

He snorted, "Sure I do. *I* know *he'll* know we're up to something if we aren't on time for his little briefing."

Mel opened her mouth to retort, but too late. He had slipped through the hatch before she could come up with something suitably acidic.

"I *hate* him," she growled. Even she wasn't sure which one she meant.

***

The eight of them met in the lounge for the first time.

Agent Mueller stood next to a holo-projector. Brian and Strak had taken one couch, Mel and Rawn the other. Marcus, Stasia and Giran were seated at the lounge's lone table.

"As most of you can easily guess after our conversations, we are going after the *Fenris*." The agent smiled. "I believe we can dispense with the pleasantries and get straight down to business."

He had a smirk on his face, as if he expected them all to laugh at his turn of phrase. When none of them responded with so much as a smirk, his face went cold. "First: payment." The agent ticked off his fingers as he addressed each item. "All of you will be pardoned for your crimes. Easy enough for me to arrange, I assure you." He shrugged. "Second: each of you receives a bonus for completion. In addition to your freedom, each of you will receive ten thousand Guard dollars to help you start a new life."

The seven ex-prisoners eyed each other. Mel judged from the suspicious looks she received that the others trusted her as little or less than she trusted them.

"Each of you has talents that I may find useful." The agent spoke on, "Stasia is our computer expert. Hopefully she's learned her lesson regarding illicit hacking and will not stray. Melanie and Marcus can serve as pilots, Brian and Strak as general crew, Giran and Rawn as engine crew. All of you have other abilities that may come in handy. And all of you were conveniently present when I needed volunteers." He said the last in a light-hearted tone.

Mel didn't feel any surprise when no-one laughed at his joke.

The holo-projector came to life, where it displayed an external view of a ship. "This is the *Fenris*. You all know what it is. We are going to shut the vessel down, before it strikes Vagyr. A task force is preparing to meet it in orbit, should we be unable to stop it."

No one looked at him; they all had good ideas what the price of failure would be: a digital pardon was very easy to 'misplace.' *For that matter,* Mel thought darkly, *he could easily have us all killed or marked as escaped prisoners.*

"What should happen is that we catch up to it at one of its navigational stops, and we shut it down via external command. If that proves ineffective, we have to board it. That will not prove to be an easy task." The projector changed, flashing through a deck-by-deck overview. "The entire ship is covered by a security system, which allows the AI to send in security robots, close out sections of the ship, and do all sorts of nasty things."

"You're giving us all this, just for playing taxi?" Rawn scowled. Mel wanted to kick her little brother for being the one to ask the question out loud, even though she'd been about to do the same thing.

There was a long, empty silence. The GI agent was silent, his face impassive.

Strak said, "He's using us because we're a cut-out. If this doesn't work, the Guard won't take the blame." The old man stood slowly and shrugged his shoulders, "Probably lots of evidence will point to a salvage ship, us, having activated the ship in the first place."

Everyone looked from him to the agent, Mueller smiled. "A clever idea, but one that is entirely excessive. The Preserve built the *Fenris*. The AI system was produced on Triad, ten decades ago. The forces we're positioning in Vagyr show that the Guard is doing our best to avert tragedy. We don't need any kind of cover-up."

"So," Mel asked, irritated by the agent's smug attitude, "Why do you need us?"

"Because you are expendable," he shrugged. "No reason to send highly trained professionals to deal with a semi-berserk battlecruiser, not when a handful of criminals can do the job just as well. Also, you were easy enough to recruit, whereas mercenaries or professional agents capable of the job would take longer to assemble."

"You said this would not be dangerous." Stasia protested. Muscles in her right cheek twitched nervously as she spoke.

"I also said I'd be paying you ten thousand in Guard dollars and giving you your freedom. If you're looking to question the terms, by all means, we can discuss any changes right now." They all rapidly got the impression that changes would include first, removing the payment and second, putting them back in their cells.

He's all by himself, Mel thought. *It should feel like an empty threat, but who knows what resources he can call on? And for that matter, who says he doesn't have a ringer? Any one of the others could be an undercover agent to keep an eye on us all, just in case anyone tries to mutiny.*

"Excellent. The *Fenris* needs to drop its drive field in three locations to make navigational checks on the course we believe it is taking. The ship has an older version of our warp drive, meaning our ship has twice its speed. We should have sufficient time to catch it at its second navigation check."

"What command will we be sending?" Stasia asked.

"I've got the authorization codes and copies of its core programming. There wasn't time to put together a program to shut it down before we left. That will be your job, Stasia."

Agent Mueller pointed at Rawn and Giran: "You two will be checking her code and making sure that it has no flaws. Our trip should take twenty-six days, including two navigational stops, one at Expo and the other at Salvation. Our rendezvous is located in the Crossroads system, two light years to the galactic west of the Bell system. We should arrive between twenty and thirty-six hours ahead of the *Fenris*. Data on the ship is in the computer. Disabling that ship is our objective, through any means necessary."

Mel shivered at his words. She wondered if she'd have been safer on Thornhell.

***

A battlecruiser, even a battlecruiser designed as an automaton, was filled with access corridors, passageways and the like. Mel spent her time paging through the maps included in the technical readouts of the vessel. The raw firepower aboard the ship amazed her. It massed slightly less than a modern battlecruiser and yet it carried more weapons than a modern dreadnought. *What it could do with modern upgrades is terrifying.*

What stunned her after looking through the ship's layout was what wasn't strictly in the specs. The ship's design called for a fully autonomous role without any crew at all. Nevertheless, it had a small crew bunk room, a kitchen, and numerous corridors designed for human access, along with sufficient radiation shielding to make an auxiliary crew possible.

A soft voice spoke from behind her, "Interesting vessel, eh?"

Mel nearly started out of her seat. She turned to see Brian Liu in the cockpit with her, leaning on the back of the co-pilot's seat.

"Yeah, I guess. More interesting than setting here doing

nothing, anyway." Mel answered. As a pilot, she had little to do while the vessel was in warp.

She had little to do the rest of the time as well, for the *John Kelly* very nearly flew herself. She'd tried to spend some time assisting her brother in scanning through the code they were going to upload to the rogue AI ship, but she quickly bogged down in the 'simple' tasks he gave her. She half suspected he just wanted to one-up her.

Giran, she had found to be more than a little creepy. He and Rawn seemed to get along fine, but... He had a way of simply staring at someone with cold, emotionless, eyes that seemed far too similar to Agent Mueller. Rawn might not see that as disturbing, but Mel found the empty space outside the window of the cockpit far more welcome than the tiny room where the two scanned the upload materials.

Just as something struck her as creepy with Giran, she found something to be slightly off with Brian Liu's public appearance.

She thought that it was just that: an appearance. Mel believed in straightforward honesty; to the point of bluntness, if necessary. She didn't doubt that most of the others had their secrets. Even so, something about Brian's personality was... off, to her. She just couldn't put her finger on why. He was outwardly cheerful and brash, even flamboyant. Yet he couldn't hide the intelligence behind his eyes... or the calculation in his voice.

Brian nodded as he leaned against the co-pilot's seat. It was a relaxed, pose, almost as if he didn't have a care in the world.

"I've got little to do either, but I browsed the data earlier. Did you see who the principal designers were for the vessel?" Something lurked in his tone; possibly just an edge of real interest, possibly some slight sense of anger.

Mel looked down at the screen, "Andrew Takagi and Sarah Takagi?"

"Doesn't ring any bells?" His smile was friendly, but again, there was an edge of something else.

Mel looked at the names again, she could rattle off ship designs and specs, but she'd always had problems remembering the names of people. "Uh... not really."

He shrugged, "The Takagi clan's one of the best and brightest scientist families. The founder, Michelle Takagi, designed the warp drive we still use today. A lot of scientists still don't understand the math she used to do so. They're also famous for the fact that she and most of her associates sought asylum in the Preserve for safety from the government of New Paris." His tone was hard, almost as if he disapproved.

New Paris had a seat on the Guard Security Council... but Mel had heard dark things about the day-to-day life of common people there. It was a democracy, she knew, but one where the people voted in lock-step with power blocs, and where the bureaucracy had hands in everything.

Still, she didn't see what that mattered to their current mission. "Wasn't that nearly two hundred years ago?"

Brian shrugged, "She lived to be a hundred and fifty. She had two daughters and three sons. Two of which were working on this while she was still alive. Do you honestly think she wasn't involved in at least some aspects? Think about it. The best scientists in human space were designing this ship from the bottom up. They didn't just design the higher systems, they designed every aspect, from the waste systems to the highest areas." Brian pointed at a list of drawings. "That ship isn't just a relic; it's a work of art by great minds. Walking its halls would be like speaking with the Takagis."

"Well don't get your hopes up. Even if this works, they won't let us anywhere near that ship." Mel sat down in her seat again. The man's strange fascination with the ship was odd. Certainly it was a significant work, but... "Can't be that great a work of art if something went so wrong that it's going to annihilate a world full of people."

Brian shook his head. "Art can always be corrupted by men for evil ends. Tragedies like that are common throughout history." He straightened, looking tired. "Sometimes I hate the human race."

"You say that like you aren't human," Mel snorted. "We do some pretty good things sometimes. Aren't we trying to stop this thing?"

"Should we be?" he responded. Mel looked up to see the look of calculation in his eyes again. "Vagyr is all but an outlaw system. Pirates kill thousands in the Harlequin Sector every year. This ship is headed to destroy the shipyards and shipping in the system. Is that a bad thing?"

"It is for the innocent people in the wrong place at the wrong time." Mel answered sharply. It didn't matter if it was a 'pirate' world to the bakers, clerks, and mechanics. They were just people trying to make a living. She shivered as she imagined that ship going on a similar course to Century and how powerless her family's homeworld would be against it.

"Someone's always in the wrong place at the wrong time." A voice said from the doorway. "Feeling depressed again, Brian?"

They both turned to face the old man, Strak.

Brian smiled. "Always. How you holding up back in the engine room?"

"Good enough. Wondering if you wanted to grab a bite to eat, I've some down time, wanted some company." He looked over at Mel, "You can come too if you want." Strak made the offer without much enthusiasm. Strak kept to himself, with the exception of Brian.

Mel gave him a polite smile, even as she cursed his presence. She wasn't sure where the conversation with Brian Liu had been headed, but it at least had held her interest. "No, thanks. I'm going to finish up here and then probably get some sleep."

|***

Mel stopped in the mess room later that night.

Unfortunately, she found she had company. "Marcus." She gave Stasia a friendlier nod, which the mousy woman returned.

Marcus started, looking up from his food. He looked tired, unshaven, and depressed. "Hello, Melanie."

She took a seat across the table from him, not really knowing why. "You still have three hours before you're on duty."

He shrugged, "Thinking about things, trying to figure people out."

"People are easy enough to figure out." Mel responded.

He raised an eyebrow. "Oh really? Here's one for you. You're all set up at the Academy, you found out your parents were murdered by terrorists. Why didn't you stay? You could have had a chance at justice, maybe even finding the perpetrators yourself. Instead, you left, you took up your parents' career."

Mel gritted her teeth, all appetite forgotten as rage boiled up inside her. "How dare you ask me that question? You seem to think I ran, like you did, from responsibility. I never ran away. Some things are more important than vengeance."

He recoiled from her anger. "Sorry." He got up from the table and held up his hands, seeming to realize that he'd crossed a line. "No, seriously, I am sorry, Mel, that was something I had no right to ask about." He picked up his food tray, dropped the remainder of his food in the disposer, and moved to the sink to wash his dishes.

Mel stared into her food for a time, her appetite completely gone. Stasia's timid voice intruded: "What was he talking about?" The mousy woman's thick accent made her w's sound like v's.

Mel looked over, and for a second, she had to fight the urge to lash out. She let out a harsh breath to shake the irrational anger off; her decision to answer was more from guilt at the homicidal urge than any desire to talk.

"I went to the Fleet Academy at Harlequin Station. My parents were killed by a Guard Free Now bombing in a restaurant at the Veleca system." She shrugged. "I was... pretty angry. I still am, about that and a lot of *things*," she shot a glare over to where Marcus still washed his dishes. "I couldn't continue what I was doing. If I went to the Fleet, I might have found the people who did it, or even the people responsible. I didn't want that to happen."

"You didn't want to catch them?" Stasia's voice was incredulous.

"She didn't trust herself to get past the anger, to seek justice and not revenge," Marcus answered from the galley. His tone was resigned, as if he had heard her statement so often that he recited it from memory. *Well,* Mel admitted to herself, *it was a topic that came up a few times before.*

Mel shot another glare over at him and then turned back to Stasia, "I would have done something violent and bloody. It wouldn't even have mattered to me if the people were really the ones who had killed my parents, or if it just looked that way. People would have died. I would have become little more than a weapon. I would have been no better than the ones I was after."

Stasia leaned back in her chair. "That is a lot braver than I think I could be."

Mel snorted, "It wasn't all that. My brother decided to go after the people himself, at the ripe old age of fourteen. I had to go and sit on him to prevent him from getting himself killed. We didn't have anyone else but each other." That wasn't entirely true. She could have taken him back to Century. Their imposing grandmother could have kept him locked down, probably could have done a better job at raising him than Mel had. *But it wasn't just about him...* "I think we kept each other sane. He still looks. Every planet we hit, he disappears, questioning people, looking for information."

"The people were never caught?" Stasia asked, puzzled.

"They caught a few dupes. The man who built the bomb, another who actually put the bomb in place. The man who planned it and his superiors, there were no real leads." *They all vanished like smoke.* She didn't know anymore if she was angrier at the Guard Free Now terrorists who had planned and executed the attack or the Guard authorities who had been so incompetent to fail at tracking them down.

Mel pushed the food around her plate, her interest in eating gone. In her mind, she saw again the recordings and pictures that she had reviewed countless times: the shattered building, the bodies, and the ragged crater only a few meters away from where her parents had sat down for dinner.

"But your brother still hunts and you still anger." Stasia shook her head. "Tragedies that they would well understand where I come from."

Mel heard Marcus leave the compartment behind her.

"How does he know so much about you?" Stasia's voice held a note of interest and maybe something more? Mel wondered if the hacker fancied Marcus. *Best to warn her off, if that's the case.*

Mel shook her head, "A mistake on my part. I needed someone to help with the ship, another pilot and someone to lend a hand. My brother didn't have everything together at the time. I needed a partner. He showed up at the dock in the Foster system, looking for work. His background seemed to be perfect."

"From the anger you bear, I guess he was not?" Stasia gave her a friendly smile.

"He knows shipboard work backwards and forwards. He's a good pilot, and a cool head in a fight," Mel answered. "Within a year I considered him a good friend." He'd been more than a friend to her, but she wasn't about to discuss that with Stasia. *I don't want to think about it myself,* she thought. "Then a year and a half after I took him on, he skipped off the ship, took our entire savings out of the ship's safe. Ten thousand Guard dollars, everything we had." Without that savings, the *Kip Thorne* had begun to fall apart, she hadn't been able to keep up with maintenance and docking fees, she hadn't been able to pay bond for valuable cargoes... it had all been downhill. "I still don't know why he did it. It doesn't matter. I'll never trust that man again."

***

Rawn pulled her aside as she headed back towards the cockpit. "Mel, watch yourself around those two."

"What?" She blinked as she stared at her younger brother.

"Giran was able to pull up her prison file. That woman cracked software networks since she was five. You can't trust her any more than you can Marcus." He shook his head, "I've found little additions to the coding she's given us. I can't figure it out, but I don't like it."

Mel stared at him in shock. "You think she's trying to hack the AI, maybe slip something in?" It seemed bizarre, especially given how dangerous the ship was.

Rawn's eyes narrowed, "Maybe, I don't know. But keep your distance. You're too trusting. If she's up to something, the last thing we want is to be caught up in it along with her."

"If she's up to something she might let something slip. This is bigger than us, you know. There's a whole *system* depending on this working," Mel scowled. Messing around with the lives of millions, if not billions, of lives was not something she took lightly.

Rawn waved a hand. "She's not going to slip anything in that Giran and I won't notice. Vagyr may be a wretched place to live, but that ship isn't going to blast anything in that system." He sighed, "I can think of some other systems that I wouldn't mind letting it slip away to, though."

"What, you know of some mysterious Guard Free Now headquarters world?" Mel scoffed. Her voice went somber and she saw, again, the images of the explosion that had killed her parents. "No one deserves to have death delivered upon them without warning or reason. That's what this ship is. Letting that happen to anyone is as random as our parents' deaths were."

"That's saying our parents' deaths were *random*." Rawn snapped. "Not everyone fears the things they may do to others. Some people use innocent lives as bargaining chips, view civilian lives as pawns in a chess game." His voice was tight, his eyes filled with hate.

Mel frowned. She didn't like where his words headed. He'd gone off and gotten himself in trouble before. She wasn't about to let him do that again, "All right, Rawn. Cool it."

"Just stay away from those two. Especially Marcus, he can't be trusted at all. I don't want you hurt when something happens." Rawn turned away.

***

Time: 1900 Zulu, 12 June 291 G.D.
Location: Crossroads System

There were many star systems which could be classed as high value. Harlequin Station was one such, with two life-bearing worlds, three metal rich asteroid belts, and gas giants to provide hydrogen for power generation.

If Harlequin Station was high value, then Crossroads was definitely low value. Its only value was to serve as a way-point for ships on their way to bigger and better places.

A number of small, icy rocks orbited the cold, tiny star... along with one large starship that emerged from warp exactly where the Guard Intelligence Agent had said it would be.

Mel felt a tingling along her spine. Reading about all the firepower that ship had was one thing. Knowing it might be aimed at her was quite another.

"It's *Fenris*," Marcus stated. "Right on time."

"Unidentified craft, transmit identification codes or be fired upon."

Everyone started at the voice. It was the voice of a man, gruff and gravelly. It didn't sound like the soulless machine they'd all expected. The sound was dangerous and slightly sinister, but somehow also carried the overtones of irritation at the interruption and perhaps even a sense of boredom.

Agent Mueller nodded at Mel, "Transmit the codes, prepare the upload."

Mel did so and then waited for what seemed to be an eternity.

"Identification codes accepted, *John Kelly*." Perhaps it was Mel's fears talking, but the voice of the AI sounded slightly disappointed that it couldn't open fire. "Transmit your data upload when ready."

"Do it." Mueller said. He had a smile of triumph on his face.

"Transmitting." Mel said.

She watched as the laser transmitter made connection with the receiver on the other ship. As it began downloading the program, she released a sigh of relief.

"Orders have been updated. Receiving programming update." The voice modulated, changed. There was no boredom in its next transmission, only pure hostility: "Security protocols have been engaged. Primary programming cannot be compromised. This vessel will *not* be hijacked."

"Detecting the warp drive powering up." Marcus yelped. "We're being hit by targeting sensors."

Agent Mueller looked around frantically, "Did the upload go through? What happened?"

Mel brought up the communications system on her screen. Her eyes widened as she realized someone else had also accessed the program from the engine room. The other user began to delete the upload as she watched.

She saved the file to a drive on her console, then opened the intercom to the engine console. "Rawn, someone's trying to delete the program, stop whoever it is!"

"What?" he answered. "What's going on up there?"

"Just stop them, lock the console."

She brought up the security camera for the engine room, caught a sight of Rawn yelling something to Giran, and then Agent Mueller stepped in front of her view. "Was the upload complete?" he demanded.

"It wasn't. I can't tell how complete it was either, because whoever tried deleting the file wiped the record of the transmission from the computer first." Marcus said angrily. "It got the opening packet for certain, but I'm not sure beyond that." He looked up from his console. "The *Fenris* just went into strategic warp."

Mel pushed Agent Mueller out of the way of the screen. She felt her stomach sink and her throat seemed to constrict as she forced the words out of her mouth, "We've got a bigger problem. Does anyone know where Giran got a gun and why he has it aimed at my brother?"

CHAPTER III
Time: 1930 Zulu, 12 June 291 G.D.
Location: Crossroads System

In under five minutes, Brian, Stasia, and Strak had joined Mel, Marcus and Agent Mueller in the cramped confines of the cockpit. Mel explained quickly what had happened. She didn't mention to anyone that she'd initiated a security lock-down on the engine room access doors and consoles. Giran wasn't going anywhere.

Agent Mueller began to speak, "Look. There is nothing to worry about, the upload may well be complete. It may require a short time for the program to take effect—"

"We don't have a copy of the program that vas sent, then?" Stasia interrupted. "Giran deleted it, da?" Her accent thickened under the stress of the situation, Mel noted.

"We have this," Mel told her. She held up the drive on which she'd saved the program.

Agent Mueller reached out, "I should hold onto that—"

"No, maybe you shouldn't," Marcus's voice was flat with anger and distrust. "Maybe we should try and figure out how Giran got a gun on board without you knowing."

"Who cares? For all we know, her brother was the one who was messing with the connection and Giran tried to stop him." Mueller snapped back. "Now, you will return to your duties—"

"No. We are going figure out what is going on," Mel snapped. "There's no reason for my brother to have messed with the program. Giran is an unknown. Stasia, you're the only person we have who can look at this—"

"I know something about hacking, I'll help." Marcus said.

Mel scowled. "I don't trust you."

"You don't have to trust me, you can watch Stasia and I do it in here," Marcus answered. He took the drive out of her hand and inserted it into his console.

"There's no need to look at the program. As I said, get back to your stations," Agent Mueller said. "Whatever went wrong, I will handle it. Nothing any of you did was wrong. I looked over the program myself right before the transmission."

Everyone stared at him for a long moment. "That's right. You looked it over before we transmitted it. You could have made any additions you wanted to right before we sent it." Strak's voice was thoughtful.

"And if you wanted Giran to have a pistol, you could have given him one." Mel said. She felt her stomach drop as she started to think through some of the implications.

"You're accusing an Agent of Guard Intelligence of something that sounds like treason," Mueller snarled. "More than that, you're accusing the man who holds your pardons."

"No one mentioned treason besides you." Marcus answered slowly.

Mel wasn't sure where the pistol came from; it seemed to magically appear in the Agent's hand.

"Now, let's all just calm down a bit." His cold gaze fixed on Marcus, and his weapon pointed in the same direction. Agent Mueller didn't see Brian until it was too late.

Mel barely saw Brian move. One moment, Brian stood near the rear of the cockpit, just inside the door. The next instant, Brian had the Agent pinned to the floor. His pistol skidded across the floor to stop at Mel's feet, and an icy feeling passed through her gut as she picked it up. Brian patted him down for any other weapons. No one else moved.

"Let's look at that program." Mel said. She tucked the pistol into her waistband.

Stasia shook her head as she began. "He's changed the formatting, added a copy of the orders we were given. And there are additional things here, like layers of code within the program I wrote."

"Can you figure it out?" Mel asked.

"Maybe... if we pull it apart, sort through the additions. We don't know what was added or who added it." Marcus said. "It looks like at least two separate people put in their own codes."

Mel pulled the drive out and tucked it in her pocket. "Save your copy and get to work." She didn't want to leave Marcus and Stasia alone. She especially didn't want Marcus out of her sight, but there was something more pressing.

Mel looked down at their former captor. She felt slightly sick to her stomach. No matter what happened, she felt there would be no going back now. "Agent Mueller, you Brian, Strak and I are going to get that gun away from Giran." Brian pulled the agent to his feet. "Now are you going to cooperate?"

His narrow eyes held only calculation. "There's nothing you can do now. If you cooperate with me, you'll still get your pardons and your money."

Brian shook his head. "Strak, get something to tie him up. We'll lock him in the galley for now."

***

"You move pretty fast," Mel said to Brian. She watched Strak drag the trussed up Agent down the corridor.

Brian shrugged; "Good reflexes."

Mel frowned. "Combat reflexes, it looked like. Do you know how to handle guns?" It would be convenient if the man knew how to handle himself in a fight.

Brian didn't turn his head to look at her, "I have, once or twice."

"Marcus said that those crates in Mueller's room are guns." Mel began.

"MP-11s, an MG-144, and a crate of ammunition." Brian answered quickly.

"Am I the only one on-board who can't read military inventory codes?" Mel asked.

"This is an exercise in futility. His room is locked, and we have no access code for his door." Brian answered. He waved at the locked door that Strak had just passed

Mel sighed. She stopped before the door in question. "Observe." She pulled out a red key and inserted it into the slot above the keypad. The door clicked open. "Emergency key, kept on the bridge at all times. Unlocks any door on the ship; it is built into the hardware."

Brian snorted, "Safety standards are kept even on spook ships."

Mel recognized the three crates stacked against the far bulkhead. Someone had assembled two MP-11 submachineguns. Both lay on the table near the bed. Next to them were seven equal stacks of money.

"The agreed-upon payment." Brian said, moving up to pick up a stack. "Hard cash, non-consecutive bills, hard to trace."

Mel picked up one of the submachine guns. "With a bullet to the brain if someone asks too many questions. This is an awful lot of firepower."

"The crate has two more MP-11s." Brian said. "The machine gun isn't assembled."

"Leave them." Mel shrugged. "You and I to the engine room, and get Giran to stand down. When he finds out we've got the ship under control, he'll have no choice but to surrender."

She tried not to think about what he might have done to Rawn. Time for worry and panic later.

***

"You're throwing your lot in with them?" Mueller demanded of Leon, his face red with fury. "A bunch of smugglers and worse?" He strained at the bonds that held him in the chair. It seemed absurd that the former ship's captain had taken him unawares. Clearly he had underestimated Brian Liu.

Apparently, he thought, *not as much as I underestimated my former mentor.*

"They haven't killed anyone. I know you have. I think I know why you brought us out here. Why you wanted us to be the ones who transmitted the program. That ship is going to kill Vagyr for certain now, isn't it?" His mentor's voice was cold, leached of emotion, and Mueller recognized the tone as one he had heard before... and it made him shiver a bit.

Best to not show any sign of weakness, he thought. "You know politics," Mueller said, his voice cold. "If you can get that decrepit brain of yours thinking again, think how it will look if a Preserve-built ship decimates the population of an entire world?"

"When someone goes public with records that show that they kept the ship as a secret weapon, when expert witnesses comment on the piracy levels that the Preserve had to lower. The public outcry will force the Fleet to attack the Preserve. None of their allies will support them. Two threats to the security of human space ended with one blow."

"Millions of innocents dead. I swore when I left that I'd never take another innocent life, and now you've made me break that oath." Leon bit the words out, his expression barely under control.

The self-hatred in his voice gave Mueller a sense of relief. As long as this man was focused on his own self destruction, he wasn't nearly as dangerous.

"I didn't make you do anything. Did you really think this was a mission of mercy? Come on, JP. You knew all along. Jean Paul Leon was one of the best agents that ever lived, he realized exactly where this was going, but he was too sunken in self-pity to do anything about it. You understand, don't you? The work we do is essential. It is vital to preserve the security of the Human race." *Give him an out, a cause,* he thought, *and he will see how important all this is, he'll come back to the fold.*

The man who had once been Agent Leon shook his head. "Wheels within wheels." He pulled a steak knife out of a drawer in the galley. "This was a recruiting mission as well. Bringing in potential agents and lost agents in all at once. Nothing like a lot of guilt and a little blackmail to reel in new workers."

"So, tell me what was in that code." The man punctuated the question with a jab at Mueller's arm. "Giran must be a prior agent. Not like me though. Discarded probably, when a mission went bad. What are the other additions to the code?"

"We have to come to an understanding, first. You can threaten all you want, but I know too much for you to kill. And if you don't treat me better, I might just let something slip to the others." Mueller gave the other man a smirk. He knew, despite the posturing, that he was really in charge.

Agent Leon shook his head, "Mueller, you always were a little slow on the uptake."

***

Mel finished loading the magazine of the gun when she heard the scream. She and Brian looked at each other and then rushed toward the noise. The galley was located aft of the cargo bay, on the lower deck. Mel ran down the stairs two at a time.

She and Brian stopped in the doorway.

Agent Mueller wasn't going to be answering any questions.

"Why'd you kill him?" Mel snapped.

Strak looked up from where he stood over the body. "I didn't. I went upstairs to check the engine room door. I was worried Giran was going to use the manual override on the door." He gave a disgusted wave at Agent Mueller's body, "I didn't want a crazy armed man on the loose."

Which was apparently what they had. Agent Mueller had been stabbed with a knife from the galley, a single blow hard enough that it had thrown him backwards, chair and all. The killer had left the steak knife in his chest. From the amount of blood, Mel guessed any kind of first aid would be too late.

"He looks surprised." Marcus's voice came from behind them. "So… which one of you did it? Not that I'm complaining, but this will make getting pardoned a whole lot harder."

***

The five of them stood in the cargo bay. Stasia with a small data pad, searched through layers of code. Now and again she'd stop and shake her head. She also cast suspicious looks at all of them, Mel noted. *Though,* Mel thought, *I can't really blame her.*

"So, one of us murdered Mueller, for an unknown reason. Mueller tampered with the code, maybe with Giran's help. Giran and Rawn are locked in the engine room, Giran is armed. Oh, and a homicidal warship is headed for an inhabited planet." Marcus finished ticking off the points on his fingers. "Suddenly, it looks like we should take the money and run."

"We've got to stop that ship." Mel said.

"How?" Stasia asked, flatly. "I am not even certain what was sent. How does freighter stop a warship?" Her accent had thickened the words to the point that Mel barely understood her.

"First we need to take control of *this* ship. We need Giran out here," Brian said

"Where he can be murdered?" Marcus raised his eyebrows as if suggesting that was Brian's plan.

"Stop." Mel snapped. "First thing. From now on, we stick together. No one goes off on their own. If we've got eyes on each other, whoever the murderer is, isn't going to slip away or do unto someone else."

"Fine thing to say if you are *armed*." Stasia snapped. "I was alone in the cockpit when this happened. How do I know that you all didn't do it together, and want me as some kind of alibi?"

All of them stared at the mousy little woman. "That is crazy." Strak answered.

"True," Marcus shrugged. "Four people can make just as good an alibi as five. If we were all working together, we'd probably have killed you too."

"That's enough." Mel snapped. She cast a dark glare around at everyone. "First thing, we take charge of this ship. There are three more guns in Mueller's cabin. Unfortunately, the engine room is just the place we don't want to shoot up. We have to convince him to surrender."

When nobody spoke, she continued. "What I propose is getting him on the intercom, telling him to come out, surrender. We don't mention what happened to Mueller, that will panic him."

"You don't want your brother perforated," Marcus drawled.

She fixed him with a glare. "Exactly."

***

They once again assembled in the cockpit. The five of them squeezed into the tight space.

Their breathing seemed abnormally loud to Mel's ears. She

frowned. Mel looked around with a puzzled expression. "Something's wrong."

The others looked at her questioningly.

Marcus gave a curse, shifting over to run a hand in front of the air vent. "Giran cut life support."

In the silence, all of them could hear their breathing come quicker as heart rates picked up and fear began to take hold. Mel broke the silence, "We've got time. Every ship's rated for eight hours minimum without active life support."

"This one's good for sixteen hours," Marcus said, quickly regaining his confidence.

"What happens after sixteen hours?" Stasia asked.

Mel shook her head, "It doesn't matter. We capture Giran, one way or another, before then." She looked around at the faces, "We need to appear confident or else Giran won't pay any attention to us whatsoever."

Brian nodded his agreement first, "And then we'd have to do things the hard way."

Mel turned on the security screen for the engine room. There was no sign of Giran or Rawn on any of the cameras. Then again, Giran had certainly had time to position himself outside of view of the sparse coverage of the engine room cameras.

Mel activated the intercom. "Giran, this is Mel, we've got control of the ship."

She started as Giran's voice crackled out of the speaker, "Do you really? You've got the ship's controls, certainly. We're the ones in the engine room. I'm the one in charge, no matter what you think you know."

"Surrender, Giran. I don't know what you thought you were doing with Mueller, but it's over now." Marcus snapped. "No matter what he told you, he'd betray you just as quickly as any of us."

Giran chuckled. "Mueller? I could care less what he thinks he's done. You've obviously taken care of him, and I do hope it was something... permanent." There was a slight pause. "Here are my terms. First, you will tell me exactly how much of the transmission was accepted. Second, you will unlock the engine room door. Third, you will go to your cabins, except for Melanie Armstrong, who will lock down the vessel from the cockpit and fly the ship to coordinates I will provide. If you do those things, you'll be rewarded with twenty thousand Guard dollars, new identities, and you will be dropped off on a non-Guard world, free to go about your lives."

No one spoke in the silence. Mel felt confusion take hold. Giran spoke again, "Oh, and if Agent Mueller isn't dead... make him so."

"Why should we trust you?" Stasia's voice was nervous.

Mel slammed a hand on the intercom, cutting off the conversation. "No way we're dealing with him!"

"Why not hear what he has to say?" Stasia's voice was harsh. "We didn't want to do this in the first place. This will get us out of it. The Guard can take care of this mess, and whoever Giran is working with—"

"Whoever Giran is working with?" Marcus snapped. "Don't be stupid. I really only see two possibilities. Either he's a pirate, in which case he'll probably sell all of us into slavery or he's Guard Free Now, in which case he'll kill us whenever convenient."

Mel's world seemed to stop. "Guard Free Now?"

Marcus shot her a look, "Now is *not* the time to go ballistic."

"We need to know more." Brian Liu turned the intercom back on.

Evidently Giran hadn't realized they had cut him off. "...are your only alternatives. And Thornhell is where they would send us. Besides, you can't really trust anyone else on the crew. I was an agent for Guard Intelligence. Mueller told me there was another one he was trying to rehabilitate. I gather the guy was something of a loose cannon, did things that even Guard Intelligence thought were excessive. Since Mueller wanted to send that ship to Vagyr to wipe out most of a planet's populace, that tells you something about the other agent who's no doubt sharing that cramped cabin with you."

There was a pregnant silence. Minds went to Agent Mueller's body still tied to a chair in the galley. Mel watched her companions search one another's faces in the cockpit as everyone tried to match a face to the described psychopath. Mel didn't see anyone look guilty. Everyone looked scared.

"I don't really have time for a long stalemate, so look, I'll even turn the air back on as a gesture of goodwill." Giran's spoke with a tone of benevolence and civility.

The hum of machinery and the soft hiss of airflow brought the tension down. Even Mel, who had pushed the limits of environmental systems before aboard the *Kip Thorne*.

Giran spoke again after a moment, "Now, why don't you tell me how much of the transmission went through?"

"The orders went through, and thirty percent of the programming upload." Brian said, his eyes narrowed, head cocked. He raised a finger to his lips when Mel's hand went to the switch to cut him off.

Giran's voice went harsh. "What did it say?"

Brian smiled slightly, "It said it would not be hijacked. What does Guard Free Now want with a warship like that?"

Giran's voice was sarcastic. "What do you think we want with a warship—" There was a squelch of static, no doubt as the terrorist cut himself off.

Mel felt anger surge, felt her breathing become ragged. Her brother had hunted for those who'd murdered their parents on every world they visited. She'd very nearly dedicated her life to hunt them from Guard Fleet. She'd stopped because she didn't want to become a person dedicated to vengeance.

That didn't mean she didn't want revenge.

"Thanks for the information, Giran, got anything else to say?" Brian's voice mocked. Gone was any semblance of the brash, flamboyant man, replaced with an almost alien arrogance. At his side, Strak seemed somehow diminished. Brian turned off the intercom and turned to look at the others. "Does anyone feel like trusting him now?"

Mel shook her head. She felt slightly light headed, she figured it was emotional shock. The others looked dazed.

Marcus looked over at Brian, "That was smooth." It almost sounded like an accusation. Mel looked at Marcus and saw an angry, almost betrayed expression on his face. Marcus had served aboard Brian's ship, did the other man's change of personality startle him as well?

Mel frowned; did Marcus think Brian was the other agent? That was impossible; he'd been with her when Mueller was murdered. Unless someone else killed Mueller, she had to acknowledge. The others stared at Brian. She noticed, in a detached sort of way, that they all breathed more rapidly. She put it down as tension at sharing such close confines with a possible sociopath renegade agent.

Brian shrugged, "I'm not and never have been an agent of the Guard or Guard Intelligence. I can give you proof of that quite easily."

Mel tried to slow her breathing, feeling her stomach churn. She couldn't seem to catch her breath. She looked over at Strak, whose hand went to his forehead as if in pain.

Brian Liu blinked, swayed, and then slumped.

Mel's eyes widened and her hand shot for the emergency shutdown switch on the environmental controls. Her lunge turned into a sag as her body failed to respond. Her arm flopped loosely, and her body sagged in her seat. Her head struck the corner of the control panel and her vision filled with stars. She heard dull, muffled thuds, almost as if several objects fell to the deck. She felt warmth run down her face from where she'd struck the panel. She felt pain there too, but the pain seemed distant.

Her vision tunneled out, as even the stars receded. Why were they going away? Where were they going? Why were they leaving her alone?

Why was everything always going away and leaving her alone?

***

The voices seemed to come from far away. Perhaps they came from that same tunnel down which the stars had receded.

"Will she be all right?" The voice seemed familiar, seemed right.

"They'll all be fine. I upped the oxygen content as soon as they went unconscious. We don't have long though." That voice sounded familiar too, but it seemed wrong, somehow. It wasn't a welcome voice at all. "I'll secure them. They don't know you're involved. If things go wrong, you can make sure we get the ship."

What ship? Did they want the *Kip Thorne*? A jolt of fright went through her, shocking her out of her dazed state.

She opened her eyes.

One eye didn't seem to be working, didn't seem to want to open. The other only saw her right arm. It dangled down toward the deck plating below her. Her world was canted crazily, and she groggily realized she leaned over in the pilot seat. Her head still felt disconnected. It took several moments to make sense of the situation.

The memories came back in a dazzling rush. She was aboard the *John Kelly*. The *Kip Thorne* was destroyed. The Guard Intelligence Agent who'd shanghaied her and her brother was dead, presumably killed by a psychopath who might be a renegade Guard Intelligence Agent. Or was that a renegade Guard Intelligence Agent who might be a psychopath?

Another former agent and now Guard Free Now terrorist was also aboard the ship. He'd first bugged the code going to a rogue AI controlled warship that could destroy worlds. Then he'd taken her brother hostage. Finally he'd pumped carbon monoxide into the cockpit, and perhaps the rest of the ship, to subdue opposition.

As her mind connected that last piece with her current position, slumped against the control panel, Mel realized that something pressed into her side.

It wasn't the seat restraints, she fuzzily realized. She hadn't worn them, which was why she'd hit her head. The seat didn't have arms, so it couldn't be those. What had she tucked into her belt?

She heard a grunt behind her, and that same familiar but wrong voice from before. It was the voice of Giran, she realized.

"Not so smart now, are you?" She could hear the strain in his voice as he lifted something. "Well, I was going to keep you all tied up, but your reputation precedes you. Not to mention, you've put on some weight, what with your addictions. So, Marcus, I think I'll dispose of you before things get too inconvenient."

Her mind still struggled with what was poking her in the side as she heard the sound of a pistol being cocked. That sound brought her back to Brian Liu when he tackled Agent Mueller when he'd drawn his pistol. The GI Agent's pistol had slid to her feet. *I picked up Agent Mueller's pistol,* she thought.

There was a Guard Free Now terrorist standing behind her. He had a pistol. He was about to kill Marcus, who she didn't hate so much anymore. In fact, she wasn't sure she really hated him at all. Giran might have already killed her brother. Giran might be the one who'd killed her parents.

Mel didn't push herself up. She didn't struggle to her feet. She surged to her feet. Mel pivoted even as her dangling hand pulled the pistol out of her waistband. She moved in one fluid motion.

The pistol, which had seemed so large before, felt absurdly light as she raised it.

The tip of the barrel was only inches away from Giran's face when she pulled the trigger. The cramped cabin seemed to collect the noise and concentrate it into her ears. Each time she squeezed the trigger a concussive wave of force seemed to pillow her head, and bash its way down her ears and into her brain.

She kept the pistol aligned with the terrorist's head as he fell, squeezing the trigger with a clean, smooth and mechanical trigger pull. She didn't know how many rounds the pistol held.

She did know that she didn't miss once.

As the pistol clicked empty, she stood there for a long moment. She stared at the red ruin that had once been a face. She felt hollow and empty. She lowered the pistol. Mel ejected the empty magazine and set the pistol down on her vacated seat.

"What was that?" The voice came from Marcus, who tried to push himself up from the floor.

Mel looked around the rest of the cabin. Evidently, Giran had pulled most of the others out of the room already. Only she and Marcus remained, probably because they'd been the ones furthest in. "I killed Giran." Mel's voice was flat, disconnected. Later she would be sick, would be angry. Right now, she felt at peace.

"Oh. Good." Neither of them interrupted the deafening silence. "I don't suppose he told you anything useful?"

"I was a little rushed," Mel snapped. "He was about to shoot you out of convenience."

Marcus pushed himself off the floor. He winced at the mess that the pistol had made of Giran. "Well in that case..." He looked over at Mel and hissed: "What did he do to you?!"

He wrenched open the first aid kit and pulled gauze and other supplies out, his movements almost frantic.

"Marcus." Something in her voice stopped him. He looked up and for once he met her gaze without his normal barriers. His eyes seemed sad, almost haunted.

Mel spoke softly and slowly. It was very important that he understand what she had to say to him. "I don't hate you." Then she fainted.

***

"Mel, Mel, are you all right?"

Mel opened her eyes, "Rawn!" She sat up quickly, seizing her brother in a tight hug. "I thought that he had killed you!"

"What? Oh, I'm fine." Her brother's voice seemed almost bitter.

"Giran had him locked in a storage closet in the engine room," Brian said. "We found him quickly enough."

"Where's Marcus?" Mel asked, looking around. Someone had set her on a chair in the galley. There was no sign of Mueller's corpse. They'd also cleaned up the blood. She hoped they hadn't cleaned and replaced the knife.

She felt Rawn stiffen, and he pulled away from the hug. "He's with Stasia, going over the code." His voice was cold.

"Strak's making sure that there aren't any surprises in the engine room left by our little saboteur," Brian said. He stood, filled up a cup with water and brought it over to Mel. "How's your head?"

"My head?" Mel asked, hand going to her temple. Probing fingers felt sealant in a line across her forehead, running into her scalp.

She pushed herself off the table and swayed to her feet to look in the tiny mirror next to the door.

She winced. Someone had obviously done what they could to mop up the blood, but she still looked a mess. A crooked gash ran up from her left temple across her forehead and into her hairline. A lot of blood had run across her face, and her left eyebrow and eyelashes still had crusty flakes of dried blood. Streaks of blood still splotched the left side of her face.

"Scalp wounds always bleed a lot." Brian said, pressing the cup into her hands.

Mel sighed; "Who patched me up?" Whoever it was had done an adequate job, though she would definitely have a scar.

"Marcus did." Brian said.

"After he killed Giran," her brother snarled.

"Marcus didn't kill Giran." Mel snapped back at him, irritated by his sullen attitude. He should be grateful, but it was just like him to be angry with Marcus for something he hadn't really done. *They never got along,* Mel thought sourly.

"Oh, sure, is that what he told you?" Rawn snorted. "He almost definitely fragged Mueller, and now he's killed Giran. Don't let your sympathetic nature get the best of you. Marcus is a killer, and we can't trust anything he says."

"Giran was working for Guard Free Now. He was a terrorist. He was probably going to kill us all." Mel said. She kept her voice calm only by reminding herself that now was not the time to hash out some sibling issues.

"Oh, and did Marcus tell you that? Did he say that before or after he killed Giran? Did Giran even have a chance to defend himself?" Rawn's face was drawn back in a sneer of derision.

Brian looked from brother to sister. His eyes flickered back and forth, an odd, fascinated expression on his face. Mel bit back an urge to tell him to get lost.

"Marcus didn't kill Giran," Mel repeated.

"How would you even know? You were unconscious; head wound, remember?" Rawn tapped his own temple in emphasis.

Mel's hand slapped the table. "Because I killed Giran!"

"YOU WHAT?!?" Rawn stared at her in shock. "No, you couldn't have. You're just trying to cover for him."

"Listen to me Rawn!" Mel snapped. "When we… restrained Mueller, he dropped his pistol. I picked it up, I tucked it into my belt. When I woke up in that cabin, Giran was about to kill Marcus. God only knows who he was going to kill after that. I drew the pistol and shot Giran."

Rawn stared at her for a long time, his face filled with shock. "I don't believe this. You have no idea... You really have *no* idea." He shook his head, and strode past her, out the door.

Mel stared at the empty hatchway for a long moment, "That went poorly."

"I'd heard that Guard Free Now terrorists killed your parents. I would think that your brother would applaud your actions." Brian's voice was puzzled.

"I think Rawn hates Marcus as much as he hates those terrorists. Giran's dead, so he can focus his ire on Marcus now," Mel sighed.

Brian frowned, "If you say so."

Mel shot him a dark look, "Yes, I say so. What's this with no one trusting what I say? I know what I'm talking about, he's my *brother!*"

Brian held up his hands, "All right." He frowned, "I didn't realize siblings would fight so much."

Mel felt her face flush, "We don't, not always." She frowned at him, "You don't have any brothers or sisters?"

Brian cleared his throat. He looked slightly dismayed, almost as if he felt he'd said too much. "I, uh... didn't have a normal family life."

"Adopted?" Mel asked. She wondered if she'd ever get a chance to find out why he'd worn a different personality.

Brian's face went wooden. He spoke without emotion, "Something like that."

Mel took a calming deep breath. No point in anger, not when she had other, more pressing issues than Brian Liu's family troubles. "Let's go see if Stasia has turned up anything worthwhile."

***

"What do we know?" Mel asked, a few minutes later. They all sat in Agent Mueller's cabin, as it had a combination of the most space and the best equipment. Stasia had several portable computers linked together running various programs, positioned around the room, taking up most of the empty space.

Marcus had taken a seat near the desk. He began to assemble the MG-144. Mel hoped he was doing that just from a need to do something with his hands, rather than any particular foresight.

Stasia spoke hesitantly, "There were two, possibly three

modifications to the code we sent."

"Mueller, Giran and who?" Brian asked.

"Good question." Marcus answered. "Maybe you could tell us? You moved pretty fast in taking down Mueller. You aren't acting like the flamboyant kid any more, either. You even had me fooled back when I worked for you."

"Says the man who smuggled and dealt rex." Strak said, his voice gruff. He seemed to have regained some of his lost energy but even so, his posture sagged and he had a grayish tone to his skin.

"I wasn't going to sell the rex." Marcus said, his voice calm.

"What else was it for?" Strak snarled. "You can't have that much and not be either a dealer or—" He stopped, his mouth wide.

"Or a user." Mel said, her voice soft. "You're a *rex* addict?"

Marcus looked away. "We all have our demons. Rex keeps mine at bay."

"Uh, how are you coping without it, I mean, withdrawal's supposed to be a particularly awful." Mel asked.

Brian stared at Marcus for a moment. "You aren't showing any signs of withdrawal."

Marcus smiled slightly and tapped the side of his head. "Cranial implant. I stocked it before the pirates hit us. I've got some time left."

Stasia stared at him for a long time. "What level?"

"Rex tertius… now. I was a prime addict once, but I kicked that habit six years ago." Marcus spoke calmly, his voice steady despite any dismay at having such a secret outed. As it should be, Mel realized, if he was a rex junkie.

His confidence, his self-assurance, was a lie, brought on by chemicals. Was everything about him a lie? "How long?"

Mel knew that over time, rex brought a procession of paranoia, delusions, and psychosis in a self-replicating spiral. Mental deterioration of the simpler form of rex was mirrored in physical deterioration in the higher levels. Chemical imbalances and over-use of the body led to arthritis and muscle scavenging. Over-stimulation of the nervous system eventually burned out nerve centers, leaving areas of the body paralyzed. Like most poisons, the dosage and usage determined the rate of deteriation.

Marcus faced her, "I quit, completely after… well, before I met you." He shrugged, "I started up again last year. I needed something… extra, something to keep myself going."

Mel shook her head and looked away.

"Back to the subject at hand," Strak said, "what did our late unlamented friends send to the potentially psychotic warship headed for an inhabited planet?"

"That is the thing. I think it *wasn't* headed for Vagyr," Stasia snarled.

"Wasn't?" Mel asked. She her stomach sink. She *really* didn't like the sound of that.

"No. I thought the order packet at the front was a confirmation of previous orders." Stasia typed quickly on the nearest computer and after a moment brought up a copy of the orders. "Instead, they are an update. Vagyr wasn't the final target, but after that packet… now it is."

"So, Guard Intelligence used us to send that ship to Vagyr to kill millions?" Brian's voice was almost absurdly calm. "We are *so* dead."

Stasia grimaced. "Da."

"What about Giran's code?" Mel asked, somewhat hopefully.

"We think Giran and Mueller were working together, at least initially, and that Mueller didn't know that Giran had completely gone off the deep end." Marcus scratched at one ear. "But Giran wanted to hijack the ship. He modified the orders packet, slightly, and then he started splicing the code that we thought was to shut the ship down. The stuff Mueller gave us as the base code never would have worked anyway. Giran didn't know that, so he tried to piggyback his code into ours and jumbled the whole thing."

"Wait, our code wouldn't have worked?" Mel asked.

"Da. Mueller gave us wrong keys from start. Guard Intelligence never had key codes for Wolf-class ships. Those ships were made by the Preserve, and war or not, they didn't give codes out to former enemies." Stasia stood and paced nervously, "If we had correct codes, then *Fenris* would have powered down."

"Well, actually, then Giran's codes would have worked and the ship would have gone into warp and made rendezvous with Guard Free Now terrorists," Mel said bitterly.

"Instead we don't know where it went." Brian said, impatiently, "And it's still headed to kill a planet."

"Well… that's the thing. We have one chance to intercept it." Marcus pushed the now-assembled MG-144 to the side. He began to type rapidly on a handy datapad. "The updated orders packet was modified by Giran. Mueller wanted the ship to go straight to Vagyr. Apparently, Giran wanted it to go to these coordinates and stop along the way."

"Why would he want that?" Strak asked.

"Probably as a backup, in case he botched the code." Brian mused. "He didn't have anyone to check it and he wasn't sure how much Mueller trusted him, so he modified the orders to send the ship through that star system. There's got to be a force waiting there to seize the ship."

"Right, because the order packet states a maintenance crew coming aboard." Marcus confirmed. "The timing is such that we could get there around the same time as the warship, given the route it'll be taking."

"We can't let those terrorists have that ship." Mel snarled. Her own energy startled herself. "We have to stop it from hitting Vagyr." It seemed so clear to her now, even as she felt a grim resolve fall over her. She hadn't managed to do anything right as the captain of her parents' ship. If she didn't change that trend, millions of people were going to die.

Brian looked over at her, "You understand what you're saying? What that means for us?" She heard surprise in his voice to mirror her own.

Mel nodded. "We have to board *Fenris*."

***

CHAPTER IV
Time: 0430 Zulu, 12 June 291 G.D.
Location: SS John Kelly, On Approach to Igen System

Humans couldn't watch the stars in faster than light warp. Instead, a sphere of flickering ghost fire surrounded the ship, cocooned by the warp shell from the rest of the universe. It was a beautiful sight, to Mel, one that showed both creation and destruction as the exotic energies wrapped the ship in its own little pocket of space.

Marcus sat hunched in the pilots' seat, staring out the window with eyes sunken from either stress or lack of sleep or both. He hadn't moved since she'd shown up, had ignored her pointed comments that his shift had ended. He finally spoke, "We don't have to do this, you know."

"Yes, we do." Mel answered, her voice sharp.

"You know, if this goes wrong, no one will even know *why* we died." Mel would almost describe his voice as insanely calm. It had to be a result of the drugs, she knew, but that knowledge didn't prevent his tone from unnerving her.

"Thanks, I really wanted to hear *that*." Mel gritted her teeth. Why did the man have to make such statements? She felt nervous enough as it was.

"Coming out of warp in thirty seconds," his robotic voice answered.

Mel let out her breath, and her hands caressed the ship controls, bringing it out of warp like a mother waking her child from sleep. She smiled slightly as she did so; despite her discomfort, she still took pleasure from the smoothly functioning ship.

They emerged from warp and Mel brought up the sensors. She performed a full sweep. They emerged from warp on the very edge of the Igen system, far outside of sensor range of the inhabited world.

The *Fenris* transmitted to them before it even registered on their sensors. "Courier vessel *John Kelly*, any further attempts to transfer viral attacks or corrupted data will classify you as hostile." The grating voice came as no surprise this time.

The surprise lay in the AI controlled warship that waited only a scant thousand kilometers away from their emergence point. That kind of pinpoint accuracy bespoke either total coincidence or a very cold calculation.

"What is your mission?" The gravely voice made it plain that an incorrect answer would bring rapid destruction.

Mel scanned the sensors and picked up the second ship an instant before Marcus highlighted it. "Fenris, this is acting-Captain Melanie Armstrong. You received falsified orders from a traitor on our crew at our last rendezvous. We are here to correct that." She held her breath.

"What authorization?"

Mel tapped in the code and waited, still holding her breath..

There was a long pause, "Those are the same codes you sent last time. Your vessel has given two sets of conflicting orders with the same codes." The warship's tone was one of sorely tested patience, Mel noted. She made mental note that Brian had been correct, the programming on this ship was a thing of art, in that an emotionless computer could imply so much emotion.

Mel spoke cautiously, "We have, but as I explained, the initial orders were modified by the trait—"

"Why would a human betray humanity to the Culmor?" Fenris interrupted.

"Some humans betray others for ambition. The Second Sweep ended a hundred years ago. Vagyr is a human world again." Mel clenched her hands on the armrests till her knuckles turned white.

"Verification of that information is notably lacking." The dry tone selected by the computer suggested that it had at least some grasp of irony.

"Look, in addition to all of that, the other ship is hostile. They belong to a terrorist organization known as Guard Free Now, and it was one of their agents aboard this ship that tried to hijack you." Mel's voice was desperate.

There was no hesitation from the AI, "Interesting... they said you'd say that."

Red lights began flashing above the sensor panel. "He's hitting us with targeting sensors," Marcus cursed. "And his weapons are already online. I'm taking us on evasive—"

"NO!" Mel blurted, her hand snaking out to disable his pilot yoke, "That will prove our guilt to him. There's no way we can dodge that kind of firepower at this range." She took a deep breath, then opened com to the ship again, "That vessel and its crew are part of a terrorist group bent on hijacking your ship, to use it against innocent people."

"The other vessel says it is a military maintenance crew, and you are the terrorists. Uniformed personnel state you are a threat," the AI's voice was cold, "Do you have any other evidence?"

Mel clenched her teeth, "I'm transmitting a condensed history backing up—"

"You cannot transmit any data. You tried to hack this vessel once; you will not get a second chance" came the ship's implacable voice.

"He's firing!"

Mel's hands went for the controls just as the ship shuddered under an impact. Alarms wailed lights flashed across the panels.

Then, ominously, the sound and most of the lights died. Mel's continued movement towards the controls caused her to float up against the restraining harness.

"Reactor's out. Backup is down too." Marcus's bitter words cut through the silent cockpit. "We're sitting ducks."

***

"This is a mistake, we should try to fight them," Marcus snarled. He floated across the cargo hold from Mel. All of them gathered there, hovering near the airlock. Most of them faced it as they waited for the GFN ship to dock.

"They could have a hundred men aboard that ship. If we fight them they'll kill us all." Mel answered. "As long as we live, we have a chance of stopping that ship."

"Do you have any idea what those terrorists will do to us?" Brian asked, his voice flat. "You do know that they once executed the entire crew of a luxury liner just to get attention."

"She's right. They won't kill us out of hand." Rawn protested.

"Just like she was right about not trying to evade?" Stasia asked. "We are trapped, now, because of *her*."

"It's too late to change the plan now." Mel said. She kept her voice flat. She was tired of the bickering, of the ship, and of the way that everyone seemed eager to pass blame but hesitant to accept responsibility.

"Why? Is it because you don't want us to fight them?" Strak clenched his over-sized fists.

"No because they're already here." Mel jutted a chin at the airlock where lights were now visible.

The hatch opened and a silhouette threw a small object inside.

"Get down!" Marcus shouted as he pushed forward in front of Mel.

A pulse of intense sound and light knocked Mel to her knees. A wave of something washed across her skin. She clutched at her eyes and screamed at the intense pain; losing her balance she toppled to her side and curled into a ball, her senses totally overwhelmed. Her body tingled, and her mind fought to make sense of what had just happened.

It had to have been a stun grenade. Those were designed to incapacitate, with a strong stunner field. They produced a flash and detonation to disorient those not caught by the initial shock. As her senses returned, she realized that Marcus had taken the full blast, which was why she was still conscious, albeit blind and deaf.

She lay still and slowly counted away the seconds until her eyesight and hearing would return. It wouldn't be long, only a minute or two, she told herself.

It felt like eternity.

"...take that one, he's our man. And take that one too. He has knowledge we can use in the seizure of the ship." The cold voice cut through the buzzing in her ears.

"Sir, should we kill the others?."

"No... not these. They've skills we might be able to use." The man's voice was deep and cold. "Robert, you and Giles restrain the rest of them in our cargo hold. Merric, take your team and extract their core. Our agent said the antimatter was at ninety percent, so it will help us with the warship significantly."

Mel couldn't make out the further murmur of conversation until they moved closer to her again. "If you can, strip the magazines as well. We're strapped for time, though. Get scuttling charges placed as soon as we have the core. First sign of anyone, get back aboard. I'll give you thirty seconds and then I blow the charges."

Mel opened her mouth to speak when a finger was pressed to her lips. She was so startled, she limply allowed her hands to be bound.

"Taking the first lot to the cargo hold, Colonel." That voice came from whoever was holding her.

"Get on with it. I'll be on the bridge."

A voice murmured in her ear a moment later, "Stay limp, for God's sake. If they realize you're awake, it's more than your neck on the line."

She stayed limp, partially from confusion at the words and partially from the lingering effects of the stun grenade. She cracked open her eyes and monitored their progress once they boarded the other ship. Peeling paint and battered fixtures were all she noticed. Plainly the terrorists weren't big on maintenance of their own ship. She hoped they took better care of the environmental system. *It would really suck to suffocate,* she thought, *because some idiot hadn't bothered with basic maintenance.*

Her captor stopped at a hatch and then carried her into a dark room. She opened her eyes wider. Stacks of plastic crates filled most of the room. "Giles, keep bringing them down. Cover for me."

A nervous voice spoke, "If they figure out—"

"Then we're both dead, Giles. You, they'll probably space right off, but me, they'll torture until they find out everything I have to tell them." Her captor leaned her back against the wall and began removing her restraints. "So... go cover for me and stop looking so nervous."

"I'm going," the sullen whine answered. A moment later Mel heard a hatch groan shut.

Mel opened her eyes and stared at the man's face. He had closely cropped brown hair, brown eyes, and the pale complexion of most spacers.

"I knew we had at least one double agent in our crew, I never suspected the terrorists would have one of their own." She wondered if she could believe anything this man said.

He smiled: "And I figured there were only two people I could trust aboard that ship." He shrugged, "I figured the pair of kids who had their parents blown apart by GFN terrorists wouldn't be inclined to join up. Good thing you stand out as being both female, blonde, and cute."

She shook her head, feeling the buried anger flush her face with heat. She ignored his comment about her looks. "Not likely that I'd work with *them*," Mel growled. She looked around until she saw Marcus' prone form. "How'd you know?"

"One of my associates got me a roster of the crew before my... companions and I departed Expo." He shrugged, "It came with all the files on the prisoners. As much as I dislike them, Guard Intel does a very thorough background check."

She started, "You're not—"

"No, I'm... with someone else. We're very interested in stopping GFN from getting that ship." He quirked an eyebrow, "Though I'd be interested in who killed Agent Mueller."

Mel shook her head, "I assumed it was the GFN agent. The surviving one, anyway. Giran was GIA, I guess he had a change of heart."

"Yes, I'd heard. Honestly, I'm not trusted enough to know the names of the two Guard Free Now members that were aboard." He shrugged, "But I know GFN didn't kill Mueller. They wanted him alive for interrogation."

Mel frowned, "Then who—"

The hatch opened. The agent spun and his hand dove inside his jacket, but he relaxed a second later. An grossly overweight man, his face beaded in perspiration, carried Stasia into the room. The agent nodded, "Giles." Mel studied the other man for a moment. He wore clothing strained at the seams. His lank, blond hair looked greasy and unkempt.

Giles just nodded, "They aren't paying attention. Even so, they might notice—"

"I'll expedite." The agent nodded.

Giles deposited the unconscious woman and left. The agent shrugged, "I don't have much time. The others are… well, paranoid doesn't really describe it. They *know* that people want to kill them. Some of them… take it to extremes." He shrugged, "They're extracting the antimatter core from your ship. It's a delicate process, so they're a little distracted."

Mel gulped, "The only people who do that—"

"Are trained professionals and pirates, yes, GFN does tend to attract the worst sort of people." He scowled, "Just be glad the 'Colonel' thought you and your companions had useful skills. Otherwise…" He looked away.

"What now?" Mel asked, clenching her fists. The thought of being helpless while the GFN terrorists did what they wanted to her and the others… *They could have dumped me out an airlock or worse.*

"Now, we finish getting your other companions in here and we find out who we can trust."

Mel thought back on Rawn's words. "I'm not sure we can trust anyone."

He smiled, "Probably correct." He looked over his shoulder as Giles entered. This time he carried Strak's heavy body. The fat man grunted and sweated under the weight. The agent returned his gaze to Mel, "But your terrorist was taken for debrief, along with one of your crew." The man shrugged, "Do you think I can trust the others not to betray me?"

She shivered as she thought about the group. There wasn't a lot to recommend them and she definitely didn't trust any of them. *Well, no one besides her brother, anyway,* she thought. "We've got a rex addict, a criminal hacker, and…" she thought of Brian and his secrets "… I'm not sure what. It might be best not to trust them."

"I didn't plan on it." He held out his hand, "I'm Robert, by the way. Call me, Bob." Bob's crooked smile seemed to dare her not to trust him.

She took his hand in her tingling and clumsy fingers, "Bob, pleased to meet you."

"Mel, take charge of them, get them ready. When the time comes, they need to follow my directions." Bob stood, "Giles, let's go."

Mel looked at Stasia, Strak, and Marcus. She frowned, "Wait, where's my brother?"

Bob glanced at the three unconscious bodies, he frowned thoughtfully, "The Colonel ordered two men taken. I didn't see who they were. One of them must have been your brother."

Mel gritted her teeth as she made the connections, "Brian.. he must be the GFN agent!" It made sense suddenly, "He was with me when Mueller died. He disarmed the agent, he's got some kind of combat training. He betrayed us!" She felt hollow suddenly, "What do they need my brother for?"

The agent shrugged, "The Colonel didn't say. Obviously something important. Was he doing anything vital?"

Mel shook her head, "He was involved in the coding for the first transmission. Maybe the terrorists want to know what exactly was sent."

The agent frowned, "Maybe." He glanced at the agitated Giles. "We need to go, before they realize we're taking too long. I'll try to get to see your brother, but..." He shrugged, "They use us for menial tasks. Giles because he's incompetent and me because I'm new. They won't let us near a vital prisoner." He nodded once more and stepped out.

They pulled the hatch shut and she heard the bolts lock it in place.

She shivered. There was nothing she could do, now, except wait.

***

Marcus coughed and rolled over. Mel saw him shake his head and peer around blearily, "Oh, *God*, I hate those."

"Stun grenades?" Mel asked. She didn't know that anyone might come to recognize the effect. Then again, if anyone deserved it, Marcus probably did.

"No. Withdrawal symptoms." He blinked up at the dim lighting, "Stun grenades too, though."

"Withdrawal?" Mel asked, uneasily. "I thought you said you'd stocked your implant." She looked around nervously. She did not like to think that she was locked in a tight area with a rex addict in withdrawal...

All forms of rex caused permanent brain damage over time. At first this was a slight dulling of emotions. This first part was reparable, if someone caught took care of it quickly enough. Even so, the symptoms were likely to proceed.

She had heard that less than one person in a thousand could walk away from rex forever.

"Yeah, I did." He shook his head. "But that stun grenade did something to my implant."

"That was, what, an hour ago? You're feeling—"

"My body chemistry's been tightly regulated for a long time now. It's off kilter, okay?" He shook his head and then seemed to think better of that and held his head very still, clinching his eyes shut.

"Are you kidding me?" Mel stared, "You can't handle an hour without—"

"Hey, let's not get into control issues, okay?" Marcus snapped, "I'm not the one—"

"Oh, just get a room, will you?" Stasia snapped, clamping her hands over her ears. "Oh, my head. I hate those."

"Withdrawal symptoms?" Marcus asked.

"No, stun grenades." Stasia shook her head, "Though it is almost as bad as withdrawal."

Strak sat up, rubbing a heavy hand across his face, "Nah, withdrawal's worse."

"Uh, am I the only one in here who's never gone on holiday at the pharmacist?" Mel half-joked. She privately downgraded the small value of trust that she had earlier evaluated. *These people are not the ones I want to depend on for my survival,* she thought.

Marcus frowned as he massaged the back of his neck. "Probably... you were always a goody-two-shoes." He looked around, "Where's Rawn?"

Strak looked around, "Where's Brian?"

"*Brian* is a GFN terrorist." Mel snapped, "And the other terrorists took Rawn because they need him to do something."

Strak surged to his feet, "Take that back, you lying piece of filth."

Marcus immediately placed himself between Mel and Strak. "Hold on there!" He turned to Mel. "I think you need to explain yourself."

Mel gritted her teeth. She clenched and unclenched her fists as she spoke. She stared over Marcus' shoulder into Strak's eyes, "The terrorists took two people. I heard them clearly. They said 'take *our* man for debrief, and take that one, we need his knowledge.'"

"You're lying." Strak snapped. "Brian would never—"

"You saw him point at Brian and Rawn?" Marcus asked.

Mel looked away, "Of course not, I was blinded from the stun grenade."

"Then your brother must be the terrorist, because—"

"GFN terrorists killed my parents you sack of—"

"*Enough*!" Marcus snapped, "Mel, you were dazed from the stun grenade, you couldn't see what was going on, you probably could have heard wrong too." He took a deep breath, "I don't want to hear anyone blaming anyone else."

Strak grudgingly nodded once. Mel bit back on her desire to say how she knew exactly what the terrorists had said. Obviously Strak couldn't be trusted, or else he had far too much faith in his former boss.

"Fine." Mel snapped. "Either way, we need to be prepared. They're disorganized right now and they obviously don't feel we're a threat. We should be ready to move when the time comes."

Stasia frowned. "An hour ago you were saying we should not fight, when we had weapons and equipment. And now you want us to fight when we have none?"

Mel shrugged, "Circumstances have changed. Either way, time will soon run out out for Vagyr." She paused, "Also, I heard them talking about taking the antimatter core from the *Kelly*."

Marcus and Strak both nodded. Strak spoke, "Makes sense, a lot of pirates do that with wrecks. They can't count on coming into just any port to refuel."

"Isn't that dangerous?" Stasia asked. The hacker sounded very nervous, Mel noted. Then again, antimatter was, by its very nature, extremely dangerous to handle.

Strak scowled, "If they're stupid, yeah. We wouldn't feel a thing, though, and it would solve our problems." He shrugged, "It's not too hard, though, just... *delicate*."

"You've done it before?" Marcus asked.

Strak looked uncomfortable, "A couple times."

"Was that when you were working for Brian?" Mel asked.

Strak scowled, "No, that was before." He looked at Marcus, "Wanna shut your girlfriend up before I sock her?"

Mel started to her feet, "I'm not his—"

Marcus rolled his eyes, "*Enough*." He massaged his forehead.

Mel sat herself on a handy crate. She didn't know who to glare at, so she sat with arms crossed and glared at the wall. As soon as she got out, she was going to get her brother. After that she was going to stop the *Fenris* and then… then she was going to show those murdering terrorists some justice.

***

There was no sense of time, but it felt to Mel as if days passed before the hatch opened. Bob poked his head in, he shot a glance around, then looked at Mel. "Ready?"

She nodded, "This is our chance, guys, let's move." She jumped to her feet.

The others stared at her, "What's going on?" Marcus snapped, "Who is he?" Mel could hear the distrust in his voice.

"This is Bob." Mel said, her voice honey sweet. "Bob is a double agent. He's going to help us get out of here and stop the Fenris. He is, coincidentally, how I know Brian is a GFN terrorist." She kept her voice honey sweet as she glared at Strak.

"I don't care what he says," Strak snapped. "That's a lie."

Bob looked around, "Look, trust me or not, it is better outside the locked room than inside it." He shrugged, "They've docked with the *Fenris*. Half the crew is aboard already, the other half is racked out or on duty." He tossed a pistol to Mel and then a second one to Marcus. "There's eleven millimeters of trust, each." He threw a heavy bag into the room, "Your environmental suits from your ship too."

Marcus frowned down at the large pistol. "Why the heavy ammo?"

"They're wearing body armor. And…" He pulled an enormous revolver out from inside of his jacket. "I like big guns."

"Either way, we need to go," Mel snapped. She jacked the slide on her pistol and stepped forward. "Let's get my brother."

Bob shook his head, "The boarding party took their prisoner. Their double agent went with them. They left before I had a chance to see if your brother was all right. But I doubt they've caused him any real harm, not when they need him. After that, though, all bets are off."

Mel nodded unhappily. "Fine then. We board the *Fenris*."

Marcus frowned, "I'd be happier taking this ship. We might be able to beat it to Vagyr—"

"And say what? 'Hi, we're aboard a GFN pirate ship, which we hijacked, after escaping GIA custody because one of us murdered the agent in charge.'" Mel bobbled her head back and forth in her best impression of a brainless idiot, "'Oh, by the way, there's an insane AI warship headed here to wipe out all life in the system!'" She treasured the look of irritation on Marcus's face.

Strak gave Marcus a disgruntled look. "She might have a point." He looked like he would rather have admitted to eating children.

"Besides that, they've got excellent security systems aboard the *Liberation*, and the crew outnumbers us four times over." Bob said. "I've got codes that might convince the *Fenris* that we're the good guys."

"Not if they're the same codes we used," Stasia pointed out.

"Either way, let's go!" Mel snapped. "My brother only has so long before they don't need him anymore. And he's not likely to do what they tell him, not with our family history."

Bob nodded. He stepped out of the hatch and gestured for them to follow. They moved down the tight corridors, watchful for any sign of the crew. As they moved, Mel noticed more and more battered features of the ship. She ignored most of them, until she saw an environmental sensor held to the wall with baling wire. "Haven't you people ever heard of basic maintenance?"

Bob looked back at her, "Uh, look, GFN can't just drop in on a place and get a ship repaired, you know."

Mel just grunted. She hated to see a ship, any ship, so mistreated.

It didn't take long for them to reach Giles. The overweight man had stuffed himself into an environmental suit and he stood guard next to an open airlock. He looked nervously back and forth. "Oh, there you are! Thank God, I thought we were all dead!" the fat man sobbed. His fat rolls jiggled obscenely inside his suit.

"Who's he?" Marcus asked suspiciously.

Bob shrugged, "A pirate who had a change of heart."

"I was never a pirate," the man whined, "I—"

"Let's go." Mel said, stepping around him and moving towards the open airlock behind him. She could see the umbilical that joined the other ship.

"There's no guard?" Marcus asked. He looked around suspiciously. Mel could see that sweat beaded his forehead. *Great,* she thought, *he's probably going to start hallucinating and shooting at invisible monsters here soon.*

"I arranged for the Colonel to post Giles and myself for this shift," Bob said, following Mel. "It should be four hours or so before anyone else notices."

"What if the boarding party sends someone back here?" Strak asked.

"Then we'd better be elsewhere." Bob said. "Look, would you rather be back in that cargo hold?" Mel could hear a tone of irritation in his voice, but she wondered, suddenly if this were some sort of trap. *I don't care,* she thought, *this is my chance to make things right, to rescue my brother and to stop the* Fenris.

Marcus frowned, "Honestly, I'm thinking about it." He massaged his forehead. "Slow down, Mel, we don't want to run into anyone."

Mel reached the umbilical and shoved off. She felt the ship's internal gravity cut off. For a long moment, she soared, weightless. Despite the situation, she felt a surge of exhilaration as she drifted across the gap to the far hatch. The armor around the hatch was pitted, but the metal of the airlock itself was new.

Mel landed lightly on her feet inside the open airlock of the warship. She cleared out of the way, and moved deeper into the warship. As the others gathered, Mel stared down the corridors, eager to find her brother.

Piping and power conduits lined the overhead, deck and walls. A mesh grating overlay the lines that ran on the deck. Simple lights spaced every five meters down the corridor. The unadorned metal surfaces had no paint or protective coating, unlike most ships. The corridor had an angularity that spoke of a design for utility, Mel decided. Her parents' ship, the *Kip Thorne*, was designed as a tramp freighter. It was designed as much as a home as a cargo carrier.

The *Fenris*'s only reason for existence was war.

Mel turned, to see the others had followed. Strak knelt, looking at the airlock repairs, "Pretty crude. Someone did that in a hurry."

"Repairs?" Stasia asked.

"Airlock was damaged, probably in the fighting that damaged the warp drive." Mel shrugged, "The ship has automated repair robots. On a warship, aesthetics come in a distant second to utility."

Strak shrugged, "Those 'bots did a good job, even if it's crude."

A gravelly voice spoke from the corridor, "I'm glad you approve."

They all spun, but the corridor was empty. The dry gravelly voice spoke again: "I'm interested in you, now."

Mel gulped, recognizing the voice, "It's the ship, it's Fenris." She felt ice go down her spine as she realized that the computer could see every move they made, hear every word they said, and could think through their actions before they finished them.

"Clever," the dry voice rasped. "Even when you think you're

not being watched, as in that other ship's cargo hold, you stick to your story."

"That's because it's true!" Mel snapped. She knew it was pointless to argue with a computer program, but she couldn't help it, it sounded like a person.

"Wait a minute, how were you watching us on that other ship?" Marcus asked.

"I hacked their computer and took over their security systems remotely."

Mel opened her mouth in shock, "But that's impossible—"

"Lady, I'm an AI that processes data in femtoseconds." The gravelly voice sounded amused. "I can do whatever I want."

"Then you know we're telling the truth!" Mel said.

"No." The voice corrected. "I know *they* were *lying*."

The airlock door slammed shut behind them, cutting them off from the umbilical that connected the two ships. "I also know that ship is a pirate, and I know what to do about that." Further down the corridor, a blast door slammed shut.

Mel felt the slightest surge beneath her feet. "It just engaged the in-system warp drive. We're moving."

Marcus scowled, "For us to feel that despite the warp drive—"

"My warp drive suffered extensive damage and I've been forced to conduct repairs outside of what was ever intended to be done short of a major shipyard," Fenris said, "There are drive field issues that can crop up, including acceleration bleed due to unbalances in the drive field. A section of the hull only thirty meters away from you experienced twenty-four hundred gravities acceleration. Congratulations... you survived."

The group stared at each other.

"What are you doing?" Mel asked. She hated the weakness she heard in her tone, yet she felt powerless. What could she do against a computer that seemed to know everything?

Well, she thought, *everything except that it's following mission parameters that will kill millions.*

"I'm eliminating a pirate." A humming filled the corridor. Mel could feel the vibration in her bones.

"That's the main weapons charging," Strak said.

The discharge came with an audible crack. Marcus threw his hands to his head, and groaned.

"One less pirate," Fenris gloated.

"Did you offer them the chance to surrender?" Mel asked. "Not all of them might—"

"Everyone aboard that ship got what they deserved," Bob scowled. "Don't waste any pity on them."

Giles gulped, but the fat man then nodded quickly. Mel shivered. She imagined the few seconds of panic, the initial confusion, and then how the ship would come apart into vacuum.

"Why did you wait?" Strak asked.

"Curiosity. I wanted to see what you'd do." Fenris admitted. "Now, you and the remaining pirates will be kept until the authorities deal with you."

"Thank you," Mel said, "That's just what we—"

Fenris' gravelly voice interrupted her, "After, of course, the mission is completed. Security protocols demand that."

"Oh, no." Mel sagged.

***

CHAPTER V
Time: 1000 Zulu, 13 June 291 G.D.
Location: *Fenris*, Igen System

A distant concussion caused them all to turn their attention to the hatch that led further into the ship. Marcus cocked his head, "The terrorists giving you trouble?"

Mel couldn't help a slight smile at the bite in his tone. So long as she wasn't the target of his humor, she could admit he could be amusing.

There was a moment of silence, then "They're trying to escape. Internal Security Protocols are engaged." The gravelly voice showed the slightest edge of irritation. *Good programming,* Mel thought, *or maybe something more...*

"What does that mean?" Giles asked, looking around nervously.

Another muffled explosion occurred. Marcus smiled, "It sounds like they're giving this ship a headache."

There were several minutes silence. Stasia looked around, "It would be possible..." She walked over to the closed blast door at the end of the corridor.

Mel followed her, "What?"

Stasia stared at the panel for a second. "I could hack the door," she said quietly. "We could get out into the rest of the ship."

Mel nodded, "I—"

"I can hear you." Fenris's voice spoke from above them. "And I can see you."

"That's easily fixed." Mel said. She drew her pistol and fired into the sensor pod above them.

"If you attempt to escape, I will use deadly force." Fenris grated.

"You're about to kill a planet of people. Do you think I care?" Mel shouted. She waited for a response, but the ship didn't seem to have one for that. "Does that not compute?" she demanded to the silence.

"Mel, are you sure about this?" Marcus asked.

In the distance, muffled by the sealed door, they heard the rattle of gunfire. "Either we sit here and the ship goes to Vagyr and wipes out the planet. Or we sit here and it goes to Vagyr and gets blown apart by the defenses and we die, or we sit here, and the terrorists take control of the ship and they kill us. Or... we get out and stop the ship, stop the terrorists, and we go home happy." Mel took a deep breath. She looked over at Stasia, "Now would be a good time to start hacking."

The gunfire trickled off.

They stood in silence for a long while until Stasia grunted in satisfaction and the door whooshed open. "Done. The programing for the doors is separate from the main system, just tied in through commands. The other doors should go faster now that I know what I'm doing."

Mel stalked forward. She didn't look to see who followed. She didn't care.

***

"I told you to stay put." Fenris said with more than a little irritation. Mel would have found that amusing if she wasn't so angry herself.

"I'm not good at doing what I'm told," Mel snapped.

"Maybe we should go back," Giles spoke.

"Listen to the pirate." The gravelly voice spoke. Mel found the next sensor pod on the wall, and smashed it with the butt of her pistol. "I won't warn you again. My security protocols won't allow you to modify my orders."

"I don't care what they allow." Mel snapped. The others followed behind her, though she saw that Giles stood at the very rear of the group. They paused at the next closed door.

"You don't want that door to open." Fenris said. His tone almost had a note of caution, Mel realized. *We must be getting somewhere he doesn't want us,* she thought eagerly. Though, when she consulted her mental map of the ship, she couldn't think of what might be important in this area.

"How would you know what we—" Mel began, just as Stasia got the door open.

A group of terrorists stood on the far side. The closest three were about to emplace a breaching charge on the door Stasia had just opened. Behind them were ten or fifteen more.

Mel's jaw dropped and she stared at the terrorists, too shocked to even react.

They stared back. The two at the front had expressions of shock on their faces. One of the men behind them went for their weapons. Before Mel could so much as start to move, a huge pistol came over her right shoulder. An even larger revolver came over her left shoulder.

The two pistols fired as one. For a second, she thought her head had exploded.

"Shut the door! Shut the door!" she shouted.

The terrorists scrambled, drawing weapons. The two guns over either shoulder fired again. Mel screamed incoherently and dropped down, hands clamped over her ears. The door slammed closed.

"I told you so." Mel thought she detected amusement or satisfaction in the Fenris' voice. It was hard to tell over the ringing in her ears. She just hoped it wasn't a product of ruptured eardrums.

"You okay, Mel?" Marcus asked and grabbed her shoulders.

"What?" Mel shouted. Her head throbbed and her ears rang. For a second, she saw double.

"Oh, God, don't scare me like that!" He clamped her in a tight bear hug.

She patted his shoulder awkwardly. He released her after a moment.

"We have to move, they'll be through that door as soon as they recover from the confusion," Mel shouted. Her ears still rang. Bob reloaded his massive pistol. She noticed that each of the rounds was a massive cylinder, color-coded.

Mel thought for a moment, thinking back to the blueprints she'd studied. "This way!"

The others followed her hurried footsteps to another sealed blast door.

"This will take us into the service corridors!" Mel shouted. "There should be fewer sensors!"

Stasia opened the door. "I will close behind us."

Mel led the way forward. Just as Stasia closed the door, they heard a sharp concussion. "Just in time," Strak said. He looked at Bob, "You have any more weapons?"

The agent shook his head. "Just those two and this."

Strak grunted. "Next time we run into them, let me try to snag one."

"I need a datapad as well." Stasia said. "I do more with that."

"What?" Mel asked. She didn't see why a datapad was important, not just now.

Marcus laughed, "Supplies, we need supplies."

"Oh." Mel said. "There are store rooms ahead we can use." She didn't know what kind of supplies the ship might have, but it was worth a look.

She began to lead the way, then paused. "Bob, what kind of weapon is that?"

"It's a Magnum Research BFR twenty-five millimeter." Bob

said. She had to read his lips to make out his words over the ringing in her head.

"Twenty five millimeter?" Mel asked, rubbing her temples. "Isn't that an anti-vehicle weapon?" She only vaguely remembered that part of her training at the Academy, but something about the rounds seemed familiar.

"It can be." Bob shrugged, "Guard Marines use it standard in the GMAR."

"They also wear powered armor, mate." Strak said. "That pistol's illegal for anyone but the Marines." Mel could see the disapproval on the older man's face. *Good,* she thought, *it speaks well of Bob that he disapproves.*

Bob shrugged, "If some Marines show up, here I'll gladly turn it over."

Marcus snorted at that, Mel saw, as well he should. If they had some Marines in full powered body armor, they wouldn't be running from some terrorists.

Mel massaged her temples some more, "Take the lead, Bob. Two rights, then a... left, I think."

"You think?" Bob asked, nervously. The tone of his voice made her headache throb. *Okay,* she thought as she rubbed her temples, *maybe Strak was right to disapprove a* little *about the size of caliber.*

"Sorry, I didn't expect to have to memorize the ship's schematics for boarding it while being pursued by terrorists." Mel barked. "Step it out, Bob."

"Yes, ma'am." He snapped to attention and gave a rigid salute.

They started to move down the corridor, taking turns smashing the sensor pods as they went. Behind them, Mel heard a rattle of gunfire over the ringing in her ears, muffled by the closed doors.

"I want to know what they're shooting at." Strak said. Mel saw him wince at what sounded like a distant scream. Mel had a dark suspicion she knew. She hoped she was wrong.

A door to Mel's rear slid open. She spun as something low and lean darted through. Giles shouted and raised his pistol. Twin beams of light lanced away from the thing's head toward him. Someone screamed. She raised her pistol, lined it up on the creature. It spun to face her and froze.

The metallic wolf stared at her for an eternity from over the sights of her pistol. She fired.

The bullets struck the head and chest, their impact knocking the compact robot back and leaving large dents as they bounced off the metal skin. They whined and hummed like malignant wasps as they ricocheted away. She heard them clang off of the metal surfaces of the bulkheads and deck.

The robot fell to the deck motionless.

Mel turned at a gasp. Giles lay on his side, his fat chest heaved in panicked breaths. His right hand clutched over the inside of his thigh. Blood spurted between his fingers. A fine mist of it sprayed out to strike Mel on the face.

"Oh, God," he said, "It won't stop, it—"

Marcus rushed over. He pushed Mel aside. With gentle fingers Marcus pried Giles' hands away, then dug his own fingers into the spurting wound. He tried to stem the flow. "Bob, do you have a first aid kit?"

Mel sank to her knees and clutched Giles hand. "It'll be okay, Giles." Despite her words, she felt her stomach turn over. She knew enough first aid to know it was a dangerous wound, possibly deadly if they couldn't treat it.

Bob hurried over. Mel tuned him out. She stared down at the man she barely knew. "Stay calm, Giles. It will be okay."

"I— I never meant for this to happen," Giles moaned, "I don't want to die."

Mel looked over at Marcus, who shook his head. She closed her eyes, then squeezed Giles hand reassuringly, "You won't Giles. Do you have family?"

"God, it hurts. Oh God, my mother, she told me, she told me... Oh God…" His voice dropped to a murmur and his eyes rolled up. Mel felt his wrist, and found a pulse that seemed thready and weak. She looked over at Marcus, "Can we stop the bleeding?"

He shook his head, "We don't have anything. His femoral is severed. It's pulled up his leg. I could tourniquet him, but then he'll just take longer to die."

"Oh," Mel said. She stared down at the stranger she didn't know, the man who she would watch die. "I hate this ship."

Bob knelt beside Marcus. He looked over at Mel, "It wasn't the ship that killed him." There was anger in the look he gave her, anger and accusation.

She looked over at him, "What?"

"It's a bullet wound," Bob said.

Mel stared at him in horror. The robot hadn't fired bullets. No one had fired... except for her. "*I* killed him?"

"It was a ricochet, it wasn't your fault," Marcus said. Yet his voice was defensive, almost as if he felt otherwise, just didn't want to admit it.

"Momma?" Giles said, his eyes coming open.

"Giles?" Mel asked. She didn't even know the man... yet she had killed him.

"Mom, forgive me. I'm sorry I left," Giles said. "Don't worry, mom, I won't forget you."

"It's all right, Giles." Mel said, feeling hollow. "It'll be all right."

"It hurts, Mom. Why's it hurt?"

Mel felt hot tears roll down her face. She couldn't speak. What could she say?

Giles closed his eyes. His rapid breathing slowed. Then it stopped.

Mel stared down at the man she'd killed. "I'm sorry."

"Is that death?" a gravelly voice asked.

Mel gave an inarticulate shout of rage, and rose. Strong arms grabbed her, restrained her.

"I never saw a man die before."

Bob spoke, "You killed enough of them when you destroyed the ship."

"I did," Fenris answered. "And I thought little of it. They were pirates, I had the option to kill them or let them go. Their deaths were not *real* until now."

"You've tried to kill us just now!" Mel shouted. She fought against Marcus's restraining arms.

"I didn't mean for any of you to die. I tried to herd you to a place I can secure," Fenris said. "I fired at his weapon. I'm not the one who killed him."

"But he is dead," Bob said. He looked down at the prone body, "He was my companion for months. I didn't even really like him, but he deserved better. Think on that, machine. You may not have killed him, but you made the circumstances that ended his life."

Only silence met his response.

Stasia moved forward. She crouched over the robotic wolf. "I will see what I can use off it." She cleared her throat. She pointedly didn't look at Mel and the body.

Mel sagged against Marcus's arms, "Oh, God, I killed him."

Mel took a deep breath, trying to stop the flow of tears. Then she turned and began to vomit. She felt Marcus's hands hold her shoulders as she emptied her stomach. "It's okay. It wasn't your fault."

Marcus' voice was soft and hesitant.

"Thanks," Mel said, standing. He put her arms around her, and she didn't push away, comforted by his warm arms around her. It could easily have been him she'd killed. Or Strak. Or Stasia, or Bob—

God, why couldn't it have been me*?* The simplicity of the thought penetrated her mind. "Why did someone else have to die for my mistake?"

Marcus spun her around, "Look at me Mel."

She couldn't raise her head, couldn't meet his eyes.

"Melanie Armstrong, look at me."

She did. He spoke slowly, "You did the best you could. You did what I or Bob would have done. You saw a threat, you fired. Don't second guess yourself."

She heard Bob's voice behind her, "It was a horrible situation. It was in the middle of our group. We're just lucky no one else died."

Mel shivered. She looked away from Marcus and found her eyes went back to Giles' corpse. Marcus pulled her close against his chest, and she didn't fight him. "I hope Rawn is okay," Mel said softly.

She felt Marcus' arms clench tight around her for a second. "Rawn's tough, I'm sure he's fine." His voice sounded hollow and wooden.

The arms dropped away and Mel wondered what she'd said to anger him.

***

Colonel Frost glared at the two dead men. "You're sure it was Robert Walker?"

His demo expert spoke, "Sir, I was face to face with the woman. Bob was right behind her, and then there was that other guy—"

"You're certain Robert Walker betrayed us?" Michael Frost snapped, his face flushed red with anger.

"Yes sir."

"Colonel, if he's helping them, that'll mean—"

"I know. They'll know how many of us there are and they know what equipment we have. Also, if they get a chance to send a message out, they can report on our base of operations, on our codes, on any number of secrets!"

Colonel Frost slammed a fist into the wall. On top of the ship's robotic defenses, he now faced human opponents. "What's the status of our wounded?"

"Davis and Chu are both dead, from when Bob and the other

one fired on us." Captain Roush spoke after a pause, "Those robotic dog things wounded Smith and Reed. Nothing major, some light burns. They're mostly just shook up. Their weapons are toast though."

"Salvage what you can," Frost said. He ground his jaw and massaged the knuckles of his fist. Things had gone horribly wrong. "What's the status on the prisoner?"

Roush gulped and looked to the side, "Uh, the ship sealed us off from our prisoner and his guards." He cleared his throat, "That's when Smith and Reed got hurt. The sleeper agent said the ship has seven of those things. So far they've been waiting any time we blast a door down."

"I know."

Colonel Frost frowned. The ship didn't seem to view them as a threat. It did, however, know far too much about them. It controlled them, watched their every move. "We need control of this ship before we get to Vagyr." He gave a sigh. "Tell the men to get some rest. That computer seems to want us to stay here, we'll stay here… for now."

He turned his gaze on the bodies of his two men. He turned a basilisk gaze on Captain Roush. "Do not let this happen again. There's no reason our men shouldn't have shot them first. Make sure they all know the stakes."

***

Mel walked in a daze. Marcus warned her to watch her head and she stepped into a low, dark room. The storeroom was totally empty. Somehow, that didn't surprise her.

"We can't stay here long," Bob said. "Security situation sucks. That machine can block us in here and keep us bottled up far too easily. We need to get on the move, and get out of its sensors, somehow."

Mel didn't want to speak, didn't want to think. She spoke, anyway, "There's some access passageways. Crawl-spaces mostly. Fenris won't have as many sensors in those corridors."

Strak spoke, from where he'd begun to strip the fused pieces of Giles' pistol apart, "This ship took heavy damage. I'd bet the damaged areas won't have decent security either."

"I have a working system, from the robot. Give me time and I can tap the security system, and find an area without functioning sensors," Stasia said, then shrugged, "We will probably be killed by the other security robots, anyway."

"If the renegade Guard Intel Agent doesn't kill us first," Strak glared at Mel.

Mel felt too detached to care.

Marcus spoke, "What, you think she killed Agent Mueller? She was with your boss when it happened, right?"

"Yes... and he's conveniently missing. And then there was Giran... do not forget who killed him. And she's got a story how Brian Liu is a GFN terrorist. And now someone else is dead," Strak snapped.

"I didn't mean to kill Giles," Mel said.

"But you did mean to kill Giran and Agent Mueller?" Strak demanded.

"Giran was a GFN terrorist and we have pretty good proof on that," Marcus said. "You seem pretty sure your boss isn't the rogue killer. I mean, he had me fooled this entire time thinking he was some arrogant kid. Who's to say he didn't have you fooled too?"

"He couldn't be a Guard Intel Agent!" Strak shouted.

"Why, not?" Marcus sneered, "They kick him out?"

"They don't take our kind!" Strak shouted.

Everyone stared at him in confusion. Finally, Marcus asked "What do you mean by that?"

Strak cursed and threw the remains of Giles's damaged pistol against the bulkhead. He moved to the door, "Trust me, Brian Liu and I would never be accepted by Guard Intelligence. Let's leave it at that."

"What makes you and Brian so different?" Mel asked. The anger and loathing in Strak's voice broke through the apathy in which she'd wrapped herself.

He shot her a look of pure hatred, "We aren't normal like you, girl. We're different, and they've got tests for people like us."

Bob frowned, "I don't..."

"You're Genemods," Marcus said. "Or you're mutants."

Strak's jaw clenched. "Brian's a Genemod. I'm just a mutie." He used the derogative slang that Mel had heard in spacer bars and on the streets.

The Mutant Act still withdrew all rights from those deemed to be genetic aberrations. Genemods got lumped in with those who mutated due to extreme environmental conditions. Penal colonies like one in the Electra system existed to deal with such 'threats' to society.

"Oh, man...." Marcus took a couple steps back, almost as if he were afraid that Strak's condition might be contagious. "No wonder you two were so nervous back in the jail."

"That's how I know Brian isn't the one who killed Agent Mueller. We hate him, and people like him, but our only safety lies in *not* standing out." Strak's voice was rough and angry.

"I'm sorry," Mel said. She hadn't ever really thought about people like Strak, but suddenly she felt sick as she caught a glimpse of what his life must be like.

"You're sorry? I don't want your sorrow!" Strak yelled. "Try living your entire life in fear, try living on the edge of society because you know that drawing even a little attention can mean the lives of you and your family. Then we'll talk about sorry."

Bob spoke, "It doesn't matter to me what you are."

"It matters to me!" Strak snapped. "I care what I am. I'm *proud* of what I am! My people adapted to a world that kills normals like you. Brian, he's... he's special, even for a Genemod. He's proud of what he is. If all normals weren't bigots, he'd be someone important, not the owner of a tramp freighter!"

"Strak," Stasia said, her voice level. "I don't care what you are. You may call normals bigots, but not all of us feel that mutants are not human. I am an outcast, too. I will never... fit in. I do not hate you."

Strak turned baleful eyes on her, "I didn't ask for your opinon." Stasia recoiled from the anger in his face.

"Look," said Bob, "regardless of how anyone feels, we're already guilty of breaking a dozen Guard laws. We still need to work together. We still need to stop this ship."

He turned to Marcus, "What—"

The room seemed to twist and then fall out from under them. Mel shouted as pressure squeezed her head. She felt her ears pop and felt a dribble of blood stream out of her nose. The twisting sensation repeated itself.

Mel felt her stomach heave. She clenched her jaw, and clutched her hands to her head. As the sensations passed, she pushed herself to her hands and knees.

"What was that?" Bob gasped.

"The FTL warp drive," Mel wiped at the tears that had gathered in her eyes. "For it to have that kind of effect, it must be massively out of alignment." She pushed herself shakily to her feet. "Everyone okay?"

Strak grunted from near the door. Stasia waved a limp hand.

Mel looked at Marcus, then cursed and grabbed one of his trembling hands. "Marcus, you okay?"

His face pulled into a rictus of a smile. "Implant."

"What's happening, Marcus?" Mel demanded.

"Implant?" Bob asked as he moved close.

"He's a rex addict. He's got an implant that regulates his dosage."

"Oh, that's not good." Bob pulled out a folding knife, and snapped it open. "Hold his head still."

"What are you doing?" Mel demanded. She had a sudden mental image of him cutting Marcus' throat like some wounded animal. *Surely there must be some option besides that,* she thought with horror.

"His implant is probably shorting. If he's lucky, it's just shorting out his nervous system. If he's really unlucky, it just dumped all of the remaining rex in his system, and he's going to die very painfully." Bob said as he twisted Marcus's head to the side. "Hold his head still."

Mel clenched her hands around Marcus's head. "What are—" She broke off as Bob slid the blade behind Marcus's ear. "How do you know what you're doing?"

Marcus screamed and his body arced.

"Most rex users have it behind their ear. A little hair covers the needle scars." Bob said, his voice tight. "Okay, I found it. Hold him still."

He pressed with the knife. Marcus screamed again. Mel felt tears roll down her face. "Hold on Marcus. It will be over soon."

"Just a sec." Bob said, his fingers probing the cut. "This is really going to hurt."

"No!" Marcus jerked against Mel, "No!"

Strak moved over and put his weight on Marcus' shoulders. Mel just nodded at him in thanks. Bob tugged and Marcus gave out a shrill scream. He thrashed hard enough to throw Strak off. Bob tugged again and Marcus went limp.

"Oh, God." Mel said, her hand going to check for a pulse. She let out a sigh of relief. "He's alive."

Bob held up a slight ovoid of metal and plastic. "Huh, this is an expensive one. How long has he been an addict?"

"Uh," Mel looked over at Strak, "He said a year. He also said he used to be an addict of prime, about six years ago."

"Hmm, makes some sense then." Bob dropped the bloody implant, and then slammed his boot on it. It crushed with a satisfying sound. "That's an expensive one. Most users who put that kind of money into it never quit. Someone or something must have broken through to him. Too bad he got back in."

"How do you know so much about rex?" Mel said, suddenly suspicious.

Bob met her eyes, "I worked... well, call it a counter-drug operation, for a while. I've never heard of a warp drive doing that to an implant, but the stunners we used would do it sometimes."

"Is that how you learned to cut it out?" Mel asked.

Bob smiled slightly, "Got to leave me some secrets, dear." He jerked his chin at Marcus, "Your friend will live. I don't envy his headache when he wakes."

"I think we miss the problem?" Stasia reminded them.

Mel stared at her for a long moment and then cursed her own stupidity, "Of course. We just dropped into FTL warp. The *Fenris* is on its way to Vagyr."

***

CHAPTER VI
Time: 0900 Zulu, 14 June 291 G.D.
Location: *Fenris*, Six days from Vagyr

"The nearest section without functioning sensors is ten meters that way," Stasia said, pointing down the narrow crawlspace. "I will have to open doors. Ship has locked next set."

"Do humans still believe in an afterlife?" the gravelly voice of the ship spoke.

Mel started. She cursed as she struck her helmet on the low ceiling. The group looked around at each other. None wanted to speak, but finally, Mel opened her mouth; "Some people do. Some people don't."

"I just read the Bible, the Koran, and the Hindu Vedas," the computer spoke. "I find little evidence that humans possess souls."

"It's not about evidence," Mel said, "It's about faith. Some things are worth believing in." She remembered some of what her parents had believed, though she had to admit that she'd lost her own faith with their deaths.

"I believe in my mission. I believe I was made to serve mankind, to destroy threats to humanity."

Mel rolled her eyes. Of course the computer only believed in its mission. It *was* just a computer.

"How are you dealing with killing people? How are you going to justify destroying a world of people?" Mel snapped. Anger replaced her fog of apathy.

"Not well. Machines don't have souls, do we?" There was a moment of silence. "I can't pray for forgiveness. I can't hope for an afterlife better than this one. My security protocols only allow me to follow the mission."

Marcus spoke, "Let me get this straight, you're a machine capable of thinking about souls, but you can't contemplate doing anything besides what your orders require you?"

They moved forward in the silence that followed. Clearly the AI looked for an appropriate answer. Mel wasn't sure what kind of existential crisis the machine was in, but she did know it had to be complex for the lengthy minutes of silence.

She nearly collided with Stasia as the other woman stopped, "Ship's sensors will not function beyond this door. I will have to override it. Ship has done full environmental lock-down on door."

"My security protocols require me to complete my mission,"

Fenris spoke. "They don't let me do anything else. They do not reason, they do not think. There can be no mitigating circumstances." The speakers went silent for a moment. "If I were you, I wouldn't open that door."

"Thank, you." Stasia said. "I do not care for your advice."

"I admire your persistence. Please don't open that door."

"Now he's being polite?" Mel scoffed. "Wow, now I really want to see what's on the other side." *Although that didn't work out so well the last time,* she thought.

"I've got it." Stasia finished before Mel could voice her thought.

The door slid open. A sudden roar of wind blasted Stasia forward through the hatch. Mel grabbed her leg and held on tight, slamming down her environmental suit's face shield. Then the wind tore her through the hatch.

She held tight to Stasia with her right hand. Her left clutched frantically for a hold, and she barely caught an out-thrust projection.

The others hung in the passageway, buffeted by winds behind them. Then the hatch behind them slammed closed.

Mel floated for a moment. She took deep, calming breaths. She looked over at Stasia, half afraid the other woman wouldn't have had the sense to close her helmet. She let out a gust of relief, seeing Stasia's faceplate closed. The other woman still thrashed in confusion. Clearly, she wasn't used to a microgravity environment.

Mel had plenty of experience from the *Kip Thorne*. It made little sense to run artificial gravity in areas that didn't see much traffic, especially on a small freighter, tight on power and fuel. Microgravity had been her playground as a child. She tugged the other woman in slowly, and then put her helmet against the other woman's. "Hold still. Move as little as possible."

Stasia tried to nod her head. That just sent her into a slight spin.

Mel stabilized her and then guided the woman's hands to another nearby projection. That done, she looked around.

They floated in a large, open pocket. She could see scorch marks and gaps evident where damage had occurred. Skeletal repairs crisscrossed the area. The only fully complete repairs looked to be a solid wall that blocked a jagged hole.

Mel guessed the patch covered the hole to the outer hull. Apparently repairs continued aboard the robotic ship, she realized. She flinched and gave a shout as something flitted before her face. The movement caused her to tumble and roll in a nauseating spin. Mel stabilized herself and shook her head to clear the motion sickness. Her eyes focused on a metallic spider, which used tiny retro thrusters to hang in front of her face plate. A tiny laser beam cut out to cleanly slice through a metal plate nearby.

Then the metallic spider zoomed away. She followed its path with her eyes.

It joined dozens of its brethren. The small robots swarmed over another area. They maneuvered and welded and cut with their lasers. As she watched, a lattice began to form around another section of damaged corridor.

She pulled Stasia towards her. She made helmet-to-helmet contact, "We need to get back in the corridor with the others. Shut the door you opened and then open the one that closed behind us."

She pushed Stasia ahead of her and back into the cramped confines of the access passage. She held the other woman steady while she worked.

With the outer door closed. Stasia moved quickly to open the inner door. The section of corridor acted like an airlock. Air rushed inside. Mel slowly lifted her faceplate. "Stasia, take us to a place we can stand up and talk."

"Are we sure we can afford to stand around and talk?" Bob asked. "That ship nearly killed us just then—"

"The ship didn't try to kill us." Mel said. "We very nearly killed ourselves." She took a deep, calming, breath. "Stasia, take us back to that storage room."

***

The gloomy storage room sat as empty and forlorn as before. Mel looked around at the others. None of them seemed happy. "Okay."

She thought back to her time as a cadet, about the things she'd learned about people. She'd never expected to have to use her psych-class stuff. It figured.

"Okay," she repeated. "Up until now, we've been running. We haven't thought, we haven't planned. We've reacted."

"We didn't have *time* to plan," Bob said defensively.

"We didn't. We do now." Mel sighed. "We have around seven days before we get to Vagyr, if the jury-rigged warp drive of this thing gets us there at all. We have time to plan."

"Da, but we will not have time if we are dead," Stasia argued.

"Okay... but we won't survive if we kill ourselves first," Mel said. She felt suddenly exhausted. "We need a plan. We need a course of action. Otherwise, we're going to stick our heads into something that will kill us. And honestly, I don't think that Fenris wants us dead."

"Deadly force is not yet required," Fenris' gravelly voice spoke. They looked around. "I can track heat sources throughout the vessel. My intercom can hear and speak. You cannot escape me."

Mel looked around at the faces of her companions. She pulled a marker out from inside her environmental suit, and wrote on the wall: *he can hear, but he can't read.*

Smiles began to replace the bleak faces.

"So... something we've got going for us, we're not a threat," she rolled her eyes, and got a few more smiles. "As a matter of fact... since those others have been designated as pirates, maybe we could get a little help?"

"That depends." Fenris' gruff voice growled.

"Well, I doubt you have any food supplies?" Mel said.

"I do not."

"But the pirates will."

"They are currently eating," Fenris admitted.

"Well, they won't give us food, so perhaps you'll help us take some from them," Mel told him. She waited, hopeful for a positive response.

"That will probably result in deaths," Fenris didn't seem all that off-put by that.

Bob spoke up, "And if we set here for seven days without food or drinking water, we'll be dead."

Mel gave him a thankful nod. Their environmental suits could recycle water, but the ship didn't necessarily know that. *And water gone through the suit's recycling system that many times is beyond awful.*

"If the others would lay down their—"

"They're paranoid fanatics," Bob told the ship as he absently patted his holstered revolver. "They won't give up without a fight."

"Neither have you," Fenris' gravelly voice sounded sullen. "Fine. I will help you. Additionally, since they are discussing killing their prisoner, I'll help you to free him."

Mel couldn't hold back, "Yes!"

"You have locked down some of the doors between you and them. If you will follow—"

"How about you give us the information and let us plan this?" Mel asked.

"I'm a highly sophisticated AI—"

"Who doesn't know squat about people, obviously," Marcus snapped. He had his helmet off and one hand kept going to the wadded rag they'd taped against the side of his head. Mel thought he looked a little too pale. "We know our own strengths and weaknesses. Let us plan around them."

The ship seemed to ponder that for a while. "Fine."

Stasia jerked to her feet as her cobbled datapad began to flash.

"I've opened a connection to my security sensors so you can see the two groups of pirates," said Fenris. "The nearer group has the prisoner, and presumably supplies you can use."

"Thank you," Mel said.

She held up the marker, then wrote on the wall, *step one: get as much information as possible on the ship.*

The others nodded.

Step two: rescue my brother and get supplies.

Strak slowly stood up and then, almost gently, took the marker from her hand and crossed out the words 'my brother' and replaced them with 'prisoner' before he passed it back

Mel sighed, pressing her lips together, but just gave him a sharp nod.

Step three: find a way to disable or destroy this ship.

The others nodded.

"I leave the table open to discussion," Mel looked around at the group, holding the marker out.

***

"How many of those security robots does the ship have?" Marcus asked.

"It had seven. We destroyed one." Mel answered.

"I think you should talk about the pirates. Not about me," Fenris told them.

"Okay... four pirates and the prisoner with this group, here." Mel said. The ship had, apparently, herded the terrorists into two separate groups. The larger group seemed to be the hardcore fighters and their leaders. The ship proved reluctant to give them information on that group. Mel wanted at least one image of Brian working with the terrorists to convince Strak.

The ship didn't want them getting anywhere near that other group, however. It flat-out refused to give them access to any information beyond the general location of the second group.

"We have four threats then," Marcus said aloud, as he wrote on

83

the floor with the marker. "There's a number of ways we can neutralize them." *Engines, power, weapons, hull.* Mel understood immediately he wrote the different ways they could neutralize the ship.

"We have to prioritize what we can accomplish." He'd listed them in the smallest targets, and also in the likelihood of their own survival.

Destruction of the ship's warp engine on their arrival at Vagyr would leave the ship floating helpless. Taking out the hull meant the total destruction of the ship. *And us,* Mel thought, *because anything that destroys the ship will probably kill us all in the process.*

Mel took the marker, "There's different ways we could do it." She drew arrows out from all of the options, writing in her own ideas. They brainstormed right now, because for the moment, they had time. Even so, they needed water and other supplies.

They spoke, and the marker went around. They talked about what supplies they needed. That list, Mel spoke aloud, "Okay, we need water, food, ammunition, weapons—"

"You don't need weapons," Fenris growled.

"We do. You may have that other group under control now. They aren't going to stay passive for long. Soon they'll be moving around and we need a way to defend ourselves," Bob managed to speak so sanctimoniously that Mel had to press her lips together to hold back a giggle.

"Okay," she said, to the silence, "Weapons, medical equipment, uh—" she grabbed the marker out of Marcus's hand "—more markers," she scribbled a quick thought, then passed it back. "What else?"

Stasia took the marker, *hacking equipment,* she wrote.

Mel shrugged, "Okay, sounds good." She looked around at her little conspiracy. "Now to finalize the plan. Cross out anything we don't have time for, or information for, or just the basic knowledge for."

Slowly, the marker went around and slowly each person spoke.

"Okay, taking these four guys. They're going to be alert. I know them, these aren't inner circle guys. They're just hired muscle." Bob said. He made an odd face as both Marcus and Strak crossed out one of his brainchildren. He sighed, "So anyway, best to take them by subterfuge first. If we go in full force, we get a dead prisoner and four dead goons. We try to trick them..." his jaw dropped in protest as another of his ideas got scratched out. He snagged the marker.

"So we try subterfuge," Marcus said, a slight smirk on his face as the spy scowled down at the plans. "I'm thinking you try some of your personality skills, Bob."

The spy looked up, marker poised to cross out a plan, "What?"

"Well, these guys will recognize you, right?" Marcus asked. Mel could see where he was going with that.

"Yeah," Bob frowned. His hand, however, darted down to cross out the offending plan. "You want me to go in playing little lost lamb?"

"Will they trust you?" Stasia took the marker, and wrote in blocky letters, *found a way to scramble all internal sensors.*

"That's a very good point," Bob smiled. His eyes crossed briefly as he pulled his mind back onto subject. "Well, I think I can get in close, anyway. And when I do that from the front..."

"The rest of us come in from behind." Mel said.

They stared down at the mass of scribbles, arrows, capitalized letters and underlined words. Mel took the marker, and slowly began to write.

Plan one: rescue the prisoner and use his knowledge to shut down or disable power plant or engines on arrival in Vagyr.

Plan two: secure explosives (if any) from the terrorists and use those to cause damage to the power plant or engines on arrival in Vagyr.

Plan three: secure AM core from pirates and use to destroy ship.

Marcus gave a grimace, and took the marker.

Plan four: get into the AI's data core and start pulling wires out.

Mel rolled her eyes, and pointed at her note that the ship still had several of the robotic guard dogs. "Okay, so we got a plan, at least. Let's start with the first one."

Everyone nodded, though Strak grimaced. He still thought of Brian as the bound prisoner with the bag on his head. Mel knew the man wouldn't believe the truth until he pulled the bag off with his own hands.

She restrained herself from rolling her eyes at him. He was wrong, she knew, but she wouldn't press him. Clearly he'd trusted Brian. She looked over at Marcus, as the thought reminded her of how painful misplaced trust could be.

"Fenris, can you open up the doors we need to get to those four pirates?" Mel asked.

"I'll open them as you get to them." Fenris said. "I will mark the safest routes on your... *scavenged* datapad." The distaste in his voice for Stasia's cannibalized computer brought a smile to Mel's lips.

"Thank you." Mel said. "And please, reconsider your orders."

"I have. I still have to follow them. My security protocols give me no choice. I admire your stubbornness; however you cannot change this."

"Perhaps Stasia could hack them for you?" Mel said.

The computer didn't answer for a long moment. "Even the... idea is forbidden. If you were to try, I would have to kill you." The computer paused for a longer moment. "Thanks for the thought."

Mel looked over at Stasia with a raised eyebrow. The other woman shrugged.

"All right, let's go get my brother."

***

As they walked toward the oncoming confrontation, Mel moved up to walk next to Bob. "Got a question for you."

Bob nodded, "I figured someone would."

"Who do you work for?" Mel asked.

"Good question," Bob said. They walked on in silence for a moment.

"Are you going to tell me?" Mel asked. She wondered if anyone in their group didn't have some preciously guarded secret. *Except for me, I'm an open book.*

"Maybe," Bob said. There was a slight smile on his face.

Mel sighed. She looked over at the shorter man, "Look, Bob, I know you've helped us so far... but we really haven't had much of a reason to trust you. If you've got some ulterior motives, fine, but you know everything about us... and we know nothing about you."

Bob chewed on his lip in thought. "Look... I like you Mel. Moreover, I respect you. You keep coming up with ideas and plans. You're persistent. That's a good thing in a lot of ways." He shot her a quick glance, "But trust me, don't push me on this. I work for a government agency. I don't work for the Guard."

"Who then?" Mel asked. "The Preserve has their own agencies..."

"Not them," Bob said. He frowned, "Look, I'm not going to play twenty questions with you. I will say this... I didn't infiltrate GFN because I was after them. There are bigger, more dangerous forces at work here."

"More dangerous than a homicidal warship headed to destroy a planet?" Mel asked.

"I resent that comment," Fenris said from above.

Bob grimaced and then shook his head. "Look, I'd like to tell you more. I really would. But there are threats... there are things bigger than the Guard and the terrorists that killed your family. There are larger forces at work... and I'm here to see what the ties are with *both* sides, okay?"

Mel smiled sourly. "That's both extremely vague and terribly paranoid, you know? I mean, you honestly sound like some kind of conspiracy whack-job." She blinked, stunned for a second. "You *do* have some kind of backup? You aren't on a personal mission or something... right?"

Bob sighed, "Look. I do have some support. But I'm an undercover agent on a ship headed through FTL warp. It's not like I can magic up some commando team here and now. Yes, I do have allies. No, they aren't going to be particularly helpful since no-one on my side expected this."

Mel grimaced. She couldn't quite stop the uncomfortable thought that the only 'official' help they had might just be some vigilante nutcase with a fetish for big guns.

***

Mel stopped before the last door.

Strak and Marcus stood ahead of her. Strak had her pistol now. Even the sight of it gave her a queasy feeling. She looked away, and turned her attention to the jury-rigged datapad that Stasia was staring at. "How long?"

Stasia didn't look up, "Bob is going in now."

Mel waited. She fidgeted with her fingers. She eyed the security door. She half expected to hear gunfire.

"Now," Stasia said.

Fenris opened the door.

In the corridor ahead, Bob had the attention of four large men. Behind them lay her brother on the floor, bound hand and feet with a cloth sack over his head. Two military-style rucksacks lay next to him.

Bob smiled brightly as the four men turned. All four men stared at Marcus and Strak with slack jaws. "No sudden moves," Strak said. Behind them, Bob drew his BFR.

The largest man peered at them from under heavy brows. "Shooting in here, you're just as likely to kill one of your own from ricochets."

Mel bit her lip. In her mind she saw the bloody corridor where Giles died.

"I won't miss." Marcus said. Mel noticed the slightest quiver in his hand. Mel wondered, was he nervous or was this just another withdrawal symptom?

"You're just as likely to kill us if we surrender," the big man said, clearly chewing on each word.

"We don't want to kill you," Mel blurted. "We don't want anyone to die."

The big man's eyes barely flicked her direction. He looked at Marcus, "You killed the GFN agent aboard your ship, I hear."

Marcus shrugged slightly, "It wasn't me that did it, but it *was* a life or death situation."

The big man slowly moved his hand to his shoulder holster. Slowly, he pulled the pistol out. He held it with two massive fingers as he bent over and placed it on the deck. "This is not. None of us are fanatics. We do work, we get paid, that's it."

Marcus nodded slightly, his gaze flitted to the other three men. One of them scowled, but they disarmed themselves.

Marcus spoke, "Okay, now if you gentlemen will move with Bob around the corner, we'll just make sure you don't have any… forgotten items concealed under your clothing."

Bob moved them forward, his eyes wary.

As soon as they'd withdrawn a distance, Mel rushed forward. She untied the cords that held her brother's hands. She tugged the bag off his head, "You have no idea how worried I was about—*you?*"

Mel stared at the battered face of Brian Liu.

Strak rushed over, "I knew it boss! God, I was so worried about you!"

Mel fell back on her heels. She stared at Brian with horror. "No."

Brian patted Strak's shoulder after the other man freed his hands. Brian met Mel's eyes, "You expected your brother. I'm sorry. He works for Guard Free Now. He worked with Giran all along."

Mel shook her head, "No."

Brian looked over at Strak, "You should help them with those four."

Strak shot a suspicious look at Mel. He smiled at Brian again, "If you think you'll be all right…"

"I'm fine, Strak. Go."

The mutant nodded and then moved down the corridor after Bob, Marcus and the four mercenaries.

Brian rubbed his chaffed wrists and frowned. "I'm sorry, Mel. From what he said, he did his best to keep you in the dark."

Mel just shook her head. She thought about her murdered parents. She thought about her brother. She thought about Marcus and how he'd betrayed her. She thought about Marcus's drug addiction. She thought about how she'd killed Giles. "I destroy everything I touch."

Brian looked away, uncomfortable at the look on her face. "I'll see if they need any help."

Mel huddled there on the deck.

"He isn't your brother?" Fenris asked from above.

Mel didn't respond.

"Your brother betrayed you?" The gravelly voice sounded puzzled.

"No," Mel said, her voice hollow. "My brother didn't betray me." Her head sank and she felt the tears begin to flow. She didn't care. "I failed him. I failed them all."

***

Mel sat. She watched the world through a sort of haze. She knew she should care, knew the others were making important decisions, decisions that lives hung upon. But she couldn't find it in her to care.

She'd failed her parents, she'd never found the men responsible for their murder. She'd failed her brother, and somehow he'd fallen in with the same people responsible for such atrocities. She'd driven away Marcus, so much that he'd found solace in drugs. She'd failed her parents again when she lost their ship, smashed into the hard dirt of Dakota. She'd killed a man by accident. She'd helped set an autonomous warship on a course to destroy a world.

"...not sure why. But apparently he's been a longtime courier for them," Brian's words slowly filtered into her paralyzed brain. "Giran was the first one recruited by Guard Intelligence. He got a message out, somehow, to GFN. They got a message to Rawn. Rawn knew that Agent Mueller would be going to Dakota to pick up someone special there, and he'd need a full crew."

The words resonated in her brain. *If Rawn knew ahead of time that Mueller would take convicts...* "Wait, you're saying he caused our ship to crash?" She shook her daze off, "He crashed *my* ship, destroyed everything our parents worked for, for his stupid *cause*?"

The others looked over. The pity she saw in their faces awoke a spurt of pure rage. She'd seen the same pity when she learned of her parents' death. She'd seen the same sad looks when she resigned from the Academy at Harlequin Station. Those looks gave her a raw pulse of anger.

"Rawn turned on everything our parents believed in. He made a choice to spit on their memories, to spit on the way they died." She let out an angry breath, "He's not my brother."

She saw a look of alarm on Marcus's face, "Look, Mel, maybe you're being too hard on him—"

"He helped Giran!" She snapped. "He must have known about the orders to destroy Vagyr. He must have known what his 'friends' in Guard Free Now would do with a warship like this! I don't care why he did it. Rawn, and his friends, have to be stopped."

"Well then," Strak cleared his throat. "I think we've only got one option left to stop them."

"I'm not sure I like the sound of that…" Marcus said.

"I think it's time you stayed put," Fenris growled. "You have food and water. You can wait until I have accomplished my mission." The doors at either end of the corridor snapped closed.

Strak looked over at Stasia. "Now would be the time for your trick."

She licked her lips nervously. "We are sure we will do this?"

Mel nodded sharply, "We have to."

Stasia pulled out her makeshift datapad and tapped at it, "It is done."

"Fenris?" Mel asked.

There was only silence.

"How'd you manage that?" Marcus asked. "I thought you couldn't hack the AI?"

"I can't, but I caused power surge in control circuits for sensors and intercom," Stasia shrugged. "It must replace circuitry, yes? We have a few hours."

Strak stood, moving over to the rucksacks, "Without someone who really knows ship's machinery, I don't trust any of our abilities to shut this ship down." He lifted a large metal cylinder. "That leaves us with this."

"What is that?" Mel asked. The cylinder's only features were three glowing lights on the top and a seam that ran from top to bottom.

"This," Strak said, setting the cylinder down in the middle of the group, "is ten kilograms, more or less, of antimatter."

***

Colonel Michael Frost glared at the solid blast door in front of him.

"How are we looking on explosives, Wallis?"

His explosives expert frowned, "Hurting bad, sir. I really didn't plan on needing this much."

Colonel Frost turned his baleful blue eyes on the smaller man, his lips pinched together at the reminder. *None* of them had planned on this. They should have stepped aboard a ship ready to follow their every command. Someone, somewhere, had bungled. He turned his glare on one of the responsible men. "Armstrong, you had a reputation for success."

The young man nodded, sharply, "Yes, Colonel."

"Explain to me again how you let your sister screw this up?"

The young man gulped, "Well, sir, it wasn't really her. It's more that Marcus—"

"You care about your sister," Colonel Frost said, "which is understandable and, really, good in a way. It shows you have loyalty. You should have brought her in on this. If I'd known how capable she was, I would have recruited her a long time ago."

The young man just shrugged.

"Get back there and see if you can help Swaim get anywhere with hacking the ship's computer," Colonel Frost ordered. He returned his glare to the heavily armored door. The rest of his men sat or lay on the floor of the corridor. Getting what rest they could, as they should.

Colonel Frost tugged uncomfortably at the collar of his uniform. He hated Guard Fleet almost as much as he hated the Security Council that controlled them. The elitist oiligarchs who'd prevented his promotion for years. A bureaucracy that existed only for itself. He hadn't worn a Guard Fleet uniform in a decade.

He found it uncomfortable now. It seemed absurd, but it made him want to look over his shoulder, almost as if he feared someone would notice and disapprove of the farce. For that matter, *he* disapproved, but his original plan required it. Unfortunately, his change of clothes lay aboard the transport. The only other clothing he had was his environmental suit.

He hoped the AI had lied when it said it destroyed the transport. He wasn't all that fond of the ship itself, or most of the crew, for that matter. Other than a few select personnel, they were mostly escaped criminals or whatever riffraff he could scrape up to man the vessel. But he would miss the equipment he had left in his quarters, the momentos of his previous missions, the picture of his late wife, the handful of things he'd had left after living in hiding for more than a decade.

"Colonel Frost!"

He turned fixing his icy blue eyes on the electronics expert, "Yes, Swaim?"

Jeremiah Swaim wasn't a 'true believer' – just someone who didn't much like the Guard and who had been willing to take the job for pay. That didn't make him trustworthy in Colonel Frost's opinion. He was barely an adult, a kid who'd answered a job posting not knowing just how dangerous his life would become. *If he proves himself well here, I'll pay him off and give him more work, otherwise he'll go out the nearest airlock once he's outlived his usefulness.*

Swaim spoke quickly, "Colonel, I think someone hacked the AI. The sensors are down."

Colonel Frost raised his eyebrows, "You're sure?"

"I thought the AI finally locked me out, but now... yes sir, I'm sure. Whoever he is, he's a lot better than me at hacking. I don't know how long the sensors will stay down, but for now, the computer can't see us."

Colonel Frost smiled slightly, "That's excellent. Get to work on the door, find a way to get it open without explosives." He looked over at his immediate subordinate, "Captain Roush, get the men ready. As soon as Swaim gets the doors open we move out. We link up with the others."

"What's the plan, Colonel?" Roush asked as he stood.

He had been a non-commissioned officer in the Guard Marine Corps, who Colonel Frost knew still had a UNGMC tattoo on his shoulder. He also had a propensity to ask too many questions. Frost knew how to handle that last bit.

Colonel Frost grabbed his collar, "I said, get the men ready to move out. Get them out of these monkey-suits and into their armor and e-suits. Do it now."

"Yes, sir!" The other man, turned. He snarled and kicked at the men still seated or prone. "Get up, you heard the Colonel, get up, get your gear on! We're moving out!"

***

CHAPTER VII
Time: 1500 Zulu, 14 June 291 G.D.
Location: *Fenris*, Six days from Vagyr

"I don't like it," Marcus snapped.

"You don't have to like it," Strak snapped, "but it's our only option, and you know it." The mutant shrugged his shoulders.

"We will die." Stasia's voice was hollow, as if she'd already accepted that fact.

"We're dead anyway. This way, we stop this ship," Strak smiled slightly, "I really don't careabout Vagyr. It's a haven for pirates and scum. But regardless of what happens there, we're dead. Either the Guard opens this can up with big guns or they board it and kill us. Either way, we're dead. I say we die our way."

Mel stared at the metal cylinder. Ten kilograms of antimatter. It came from the power plant of the *John Kelly*. Enough to destroy the ship several times over.

"How do we do this?" she asked.

Marcus snapped his head around, "You can't be serious?"

She shrugged, "I don't see another way."

"The containment bottle has safeguards." Strak told them. "Once they're on, you can't bypass them. The only way is explosives, a strong acid, or some industrial machinery."

"How about Bob's pistol?" Mel asked.

"Wait a minute!" Bob said. "I think this plan is a *little* hasty. Let's not assume I'll be giving you my hardware to do it!"

"Nah, it won't pierce the outer armor." Strak shrugged. "We need something much bigger."

"There are two machine shops on this ship," Mel told him. She thought back to her mental layout of the ship, for once, wishing she had a cranial computer implant so she wouldn't have to trust her memory. She thought one of the automated machine shops wasn't too far away.

"Wait right there. We are *not* doing this!" Marcus snapped.

Mel turned a flat gaze on him, "Give me another option." Her eyes went to the others, "Any of you?"

"We're getting ahead of ourselves," Brian protested, "We have... what, six days?"

"A bit more than that!" Bob looked extremely nervous at the prospect.

"And we have a few hours before the ship can watch our every move," Mel snapped. "Once it sees us trying to do *this,* it will deem us a threat. It's got some serious ability to kill us, then. Even its repair robots could kill us. It has several thousand of those. It has six remaining security wolves. Seven if it repairs the one we destroyed."

"There has to be another way." Marcus looked frantic, Mel realized. She wondered why he couldn't see how this was the only way. *It's the best way to end this,* she thought, *and make sure it is done right.*

"What, we disable it?" Strak asked. He waved his arms, "How long did this thing coast to a star system last time for repairs? A hundred years? How will buying a hundred-year pardon on Vagyr gain us anything? We'll still die. Of old age if nothing else."

Bob spoke, "Let's think about this, you're talking about suicide—"

"Let's just put it to a vote," Marcus scowled.

"We vote on whether we kill ourselves?" Stasia looked around at the others, "I think you forget something. Her brother did not kill Agent Mueller."

Mel frowned, "That's right, he couldn't have, I had the engine room locked down."

She hadn't really thought about that, but then again, her brother's betrayal cut her too sharply. It seemed a small measure that Mueller hadn't died at her brother's hands.

"So… what? You're saying one of us killed Mueller so we shouldn't vote on this?" Marcus asked.

"Nyet. One of you is former Guard Intelligence. One of you killed Mueller to hide that. One of you will kill to protect himself," Stasia's accent grew thicker.

"You're saying if we decide to do this, whoever that psycho is will kill us to stop it?" Marcus raised an eyebrow. He looked around at the others, almost nervously. "That's kind of insane, considering we're all in the same boat."

"If this guy got let go for being *excessive* by the same people who sent a warship to kill a *planet*, perhaps we need to take that into consideration," Brian pointed out, looking at everyone.

All eyes turned to him. "Hey, don't look at me, I was with her when Mueller died!"

He pointed at Mel. Mel felt all the eyes in the room go to her.

"And she killed Giran, who might have known the other former agent," Bob said, thoughtfully. "And her brother is working with GFN for unknown reasons."

"Da, and she killed Giles," Stasia said.

"Who is Giles?" Brian asked.

"I *am not* a psycho killer!" Mel said. "God, I wish I could put those bullets back in the gun, okay? I wish I hadn't shot at that stupid robot! As for Giran... he was trying to kill one of us!"

"You seem pretty eager to place the blame on someone else," Marcus frowned at Stasia. "Come to think of it, when I went to get a datapad, I left you alone on the bridge. Where were you when I got back?"

Stasia blinked in surprise, "It was not me!"

Mel frowned, "That doesn't answer the question. Besides, we know Brian and Strak couldn't be Guard Intelligence, they're both muties."

"What!" Brian surged up to his feet. He looked over at Strak with a betrayed expression and Mel hid a slight smile at how taken aback he looked. "You—"

"Oh, shut up," Marcus snapped. His hand went to the new bandage behind his ear and Mel saw him wince in pain at the shout. "Look, I don't care what you are. Mel, aside from her lack of tact, doesn't care. Stasia said she doesn't care. Bob, whoever he works for, doesn't care." He looked over at Bob. "Who *do* you work for anyway?"

"Let's not stray off topic," Bob said. "I'm not a suspect in Agent Mueller's death." He cleared his throat, "We know that Brian and Strak didn't kill Mueller, that leaves you other three."

"I was with him!" Mel snapped, pointing at Brian.

"Were you two together the whole time?"

Mel and Brian both nodded.

"So... that leaves you two," Bob pointed at Marcus and Stasia.

Mel saw Marcus's eyes go wide. He looked both startled and afraid to Mel. "Whoa, hold on there, I already said—"

Stasia narrowed her eyes. "We are being accused on slim evidence."

"Concrete enough that I'm feeling nervous about you two," Bob tapped the butt of his pistol in a thoughtful manner.

"Da, nervous that one of us killed Mueller when *she* killed your partner in front of you," Stasia gave Mel a sour look.

"Look, that's enough," Mel snapped. "Forget it. We can argue until our time runs out, or we can take this opportunity."

She sighed, "Yes, I killed Giran. Yes, I'm an idiot and I killed Giles because I was *stupid*. Yes, my brother is a terrorist. And yes, someone here killed Agent Mueller. We don't even know why... just that they didn't like him. *I* didn't like him. No one on the ship liked him. I doubt that his *mother* liked him. Let us not forget that Mueller wanted to use this ship to destroy Vagyr."

She let out an explosive breath. "Okay, here's the facts. We're on a warship headed to annihilate a planet. It's a pirate haven. That doesn't mean much to the kids living there. That doesn't mean much to the people just trying to live day to day. We have an opportunity to stop that. We can save millions of people." She looked around at the group. "We're going to die anyway. I say we die making a difference."

Strak nodded, "That's what I was saying. Anyone here disagree with that?"

Bob smiled slightly, "I'd like to say we won't die… but I'm not too good at lying to myself."

"We cannot get to the AI and shut it down?" Marcus asked.

Brian shook his head, "No. I studied it, just like Mel. It has formidable defenses. And really... if wants to kill us, it could mess with the environmental systems, or flood the ship with hard radiation. It has total control over the ship; we're like rats in a maze."

Stasia let loose a stream of Russian before biting off, "If we must die, we should kill it too."

All of them looked at Marcus, he scowled, "All right, you're asking the guy in withdrawal if he wants to die? Let's just get this over with. At least my head will stop hurting."

***

"They blew themselves up," Marcus said, "the end." He scowled at the door he'd tried to bypass, "Okay, Stasia, how do I do this again?"

She swore again in Russian.

Mel pushed him to the side and started pulling wires, "You never were any good at machinery."

"I've got other talents," Marcus shrugged. "You know, this whole blowing ourselves up thing is harder than it looks in the movies."

Strak shouldered past them. He carried the heavy containment cylinder and he stepped through the door as soon as Mel got it open, "It's supposed to be hard. Otherwise, terrorists would hold cities hostage every day."

"A valid point I suppose." Marcus sighed, "Still, they could have a button for 'I really need this thing to blow up, now.' You know, just for emergencies like this."

Bob frowned, "You know, if this was a movie… we'd rig it to explode and then miraculously find a possible escape, right?"

Mel snorted, "Right… and then we'd try to get to it, and in the end, only the hero and a pilot would get off the ship alive."

Brian frowned from the rear, "So… you're saying I'm going to make it out with either you or Marcus to pilot me?" The short, Asiatic man flashed a wide smile.

"Nonsense," Bob declared, "I, naturally, would be the hero. You're…" he waved a dismissing hand, "merely an interesting side character, doomed to a dismal death."

"I think both of you are wrong," Marcus tapped on the side of his head, right over his bandage and then winced in pain. "I'm the dashing hero, here to sweep the damsel off her feet, and pilot her away to safety after the rest of you die horribly at the hands of the homicidal terrorists and maniacal AI."

Mel frowned at him, "And who exactly is this damsel?" She couldn't believe that he meant Stasia… and she wasn't really certain how she felt about him if he meant *her*.

Marcus flushed, "Ah…"

"Seriously, though," Bob Walker asked, "Anyone got any bright ideas for escape?"

"Da, that is easy," Stasia said. "We need a ship."

"This thing's got a couple drone fighters and bombers right?" Marcus said, working on the next door.

Mel sighed, pushing him out of the way, "Yes, and a repair drone, and a supply drone. None of which are designed to carry passengers. None of them have FTL warp drives either."

"Well, this thing built one—"

"It's had a lot more time than we have," Mel said. "Besides, any of you know how to build a normal warp drive, much less an FTL drive?"

None of the others spoke.

"How many more doors?" Marcus snapped, as the door opened on yet another short corridor blocked by yet another blast door.

"We reach the machine shop in fifty meters," Mel said. "Hopefully it's got machinery capable of doing the job."

"Hopefully?" Marcus frowned, "Did you just use 'hopefully' in the context of ending all our lives?"

"Beats opening doors for a few more hours to reach a weapon's battery, right?" Mel threw that one back at him and waited for his inevitable response.

"Ummm… I'm still hung up on the whole blowing myself up thing," Marcus said.

"Hey, remember, you're the dashing hero, right?" Bob smirked,

"You don't know the meaning of fear, or adversity, or…"

"Does the snippy sidekick ever make it out alive?" Marcus growled.

Bob looked thoughtful, "Depends on the movie, why?"

Marcus gave Bob an evil look and Mel couldn't tell how serious he was when he said, "Well, this hero is about to kill the sidekick."

***

Colonel Frost looked down at his four bound and gagged men.

"Untie them." Presumably the enemy had taken their weapons, their supplies, their armor, and even their clothing. "Stand them up."

The four men looked hangdog at him once the others had them stood up. Colonel Frost heard growls from the other men.

"You surrendered without a fight?" Frost asked, his voice calm.

"They had us surrounded, Colonel. Bob was with them, lured us one way, and the others came from behind," the largest man spoke. His name was John Arthur Paulson; he'd come from Foster and was far more mercenary than fanatic.

Colonel Frost drew his pistol, "Do you men know who the Romans were?"

Paulson spoke, "Yes, Colonel, they were a people on Earth. They had a big empire, in Europe."

"Yes, they did," Colonel Frost tapped the pistol against his leg. "They had large empire because they had the best soldiers in the world, at the time. They had a policy for when their men mutinied, called 'decimation.' The disloyal troops drew straws in groups of ten. They had to beat the man who drew the shortest straw to death."

The four men hugged their arms against themselves, looking nervously at the dark faces around them.

"I'm not a Roman, I'm not building an empire… I'm trying to overthrow one," Colonel Frost said as he holstered his pistol again. "Get these men weapons and some clothing."

He turned, staring down the corridor. The other people had left the doors behind them open. Perhaps they didn't want to waste time closing them. Perhaps they didn't think they needed to guard their backs.

Either way, it left him and his men with a clear path to follow.

"Captain Roush."

"Sir." The other man moved up to his side.

"Once those four have equipment, put them on point as we follow the enemy."

"Sir, we don't have any body armor for them," Roush noted. He licked his lips nervously. He gave a quick glance back at the four.

"Put them on point," Frost said. "When we find our former prisoners, we'll have casualties, and we can consolidate body armor."

"If they're on point without body armor…" Roush's voice trailed off as Frost gave him a dark glare. "Yes, sir, I'll have them out on point."

***

The automated machine shop hummed and buzzed as robotic arms fed machinery.

The six stared in with shock. Lathes spun, rotary presses turned, and laser cutters sliced metal into the required forms. More robotic arms took machined parts from one machine to the next. At the near end of the shop, a queue of filled robotic carts waited beside the door. At the far end, a forge was producing steel.

"Well… I didn't expect this," Mel gawked at the ordered confusion. She watched a heavy steel plate rise from the floor, pulled by invisible tractor fields.

"Obviously there's some significant damage remaining to be repaired," Brian said. "Really, this thing's amazing. That it can cope with such an unusual situation at all shows far more stability than any AI I've ever heard of."

"Right and it's going to kill a planet," Marcus sneered, "Gee, I sure am glad they made this thing so smart."

Mel snorted with laughter at his dry tone.

Brian looked over at the man, his face unreadable. "Humans always seem to make things without thinking the consequences through. You ever stop to think what makes you eligible to play God? To pick and choose what deserves to live and what doesn't?"

Bob strode past; "Let's leave theological debate for another time. We're talking about preventing peoples' deaths." He looked at Strak. "What will do the job?"

Strak frowned, "I think…" He looked around the shop, "The laser cutters might do it, but I'm certain the forge will."

"You're sure?" Stasia asked.

"Hot enough to forge steel… yeah, that should do it." He didn't sound entirely certain.

"Let's go, then," Mel sighed.

They started down the length of the shop. As they approached, they slowed, blasted by the intense heat from the furnace. The roar of circulating air was deafening; she couldn't look into the heart of the forge because of how painfully brightly its molten metal glowed. A robotic cart approached it, dropped a load of metal ingots into the air.

She pointed, "There! A tractor field, feeding the forge!"

The others could barely hear her over the furnace's noise. Strak stared hungrily into the forge for a long moment and then nodded. He started towards the next approaching cart.

"Get down!" Marcus shouted. He tackled Mel.

She slammed into the metal deck. She grunted as they slid up against the back of a spinning lathe.

"What are you doing?" she shouted.

He drew his pistol and leaned around the lathe. Even right next to him, she barely heard the gunshot against the noise of the forge. He ducked back around the lathe, and she saw sparks fly up from the edge of the machinery. She felt an impact, something striking the heavy metal behind her.

She peeked around her side to see at least a dozen men near the machine-shop door. In worry, she looked around for her companions.

She found Bob and Brian immediately. Both crouched behind nearby machinery. As she watched, Bob returned fire with one of the captured submachine guns. Mel saw one of the lead terrorists fall.

Mel saw a wisp of brown hair. Stasia hunkered behind a projecting doorway. She was only a few feet away. *If she gets time, she can get it open.*

She didn't see Strak.

She saw the antimatter cylinder, though. One of the feeder carts rolled past it.

She tapped Marcus on the shoulder and then pointed at the cylinder. He shook his head. She scowled at him. She surged to her feet.

He kicked her feet out from under her. The air left her lungs in a startled whoosh. She landed on her back and stared at the bullets that traced through the air where she'd stood. Marcus shouted in her ear, "They've got us pinned. I won't let you commit suicide for no reason!"

"I got body armor!" Mel shouted back. It was true enough, though the body armor off one of the mercenaries made a poor fit.

"This range, they'd hit you in the head," Marcus shouted.

Strak evidently felt differently. He surged out of his cover; she hadn't even seen him sneak near the cylinder. He moved faster than she thought the heavy-set man could, reaching the cylinder before the terrorists could fire. A laden cart approached and he rose to his feet, ready to hurl the cylinder.

The first bullets caught him in the chest.

"No!" Mel shouted, sprinting from behind the lathe. Marcus shouted behind her, but she had eyes only for Strak.

The mutant man stumbled back. Bullets impacted his legs; blood spurted. He dropped to his knees, bullet striking his arms. In a last feat of strength he hurled the cylinder.

It struck the side of the cart.

It bounced off, rolling towards Mel. She sprinted harder as something whispered past her ear. A pair of weapons flashed brightly – the terrorists were firing at her now, she realized, and ran harder.

Her fingers brushed the metal cylinder.

Something hit her.

Pain blossomed in her chest. In slow motion, she felt a line of impacts from her left hip up across her chest. The impacts spun her body, driving her into the ground.

She landed on her side her head and face pointed back towards Marcus.

She tried to breathe, tried to scream, but her chest hurt and her lungs wouldn't move. Marcus started from cover; *no*, she wanted to tell him. *It's pointless. I'm dead.*

Brian caught him, and dragged him back behind cover.

Good, she thought, *at least he won't die for my mistakes.*

Stasia dodged through the door. Brian threw Marcus through, then dove through the open door himself. Bob followed them, firing his pistol twice more, the muzzle flash bright in a room that seemed to grow darker.

Mel tried to force her lungs to move. She wanted to call out but couldn't; it hurt too much. The world started to go gray and she twitched her arms feebly, trying to push herself up. Her eyelids started to grow heavy and stars appeared as she blinked. light-headed.

So this is death, she thought. *Too bad it hurts so much.*

The last thing she saw before the world grayed out was the door as it shut behind her friends.

***

Colonel Frost stared down at the corpse lying next to the antimatter core. The forge's heat slapped at him like an angry beast. "Get the cylinder."

The fanaticism of these opponents startled him. They would kill themselves to deny him victory? Didn't they know what they gave their lives for? They either had no concept of the stakes, or something drove them, some purpose he didn't understand.

He looked over at Rawn. "How's your sister?"

The young man seemed angry: "Your men shot her. How do you think she is?"

Frost turned an icy glare on the younger man, "She tried to kill us all. You're lucky I didn't shoot her in the face. Will she live?"

Rawn shrugged. "She might have some cracked ribs. She wore body armor taken from one of your men."

"One of our men," Colonel Frost corrected, automatically. "Don't forget who gave me this idea."

"Yeah," Rawn looked away. He glared at an inoffensive milling machine.

Frost sighed, "Go care for your sister. Find out why they wanted to kill us all, including themselves. Try to learn their other plans before we find out the hard way."

"How am I supposed to do that?" Rawn looked dubiously at his sister, "She never listened to me."

Frost smiled. "Tell her the truth, that's always a good start."

Rawn scowled, "She won't believe it."

Frost grabbed Rawn by the collar of his ship-suit and slammed him up against the bulkhead. He lifted the younger man and glared into his eyes.

"I've lost five good men just now," he snarled. "Two died earlier. And before that, we lost our ship and twenty more of my people. I don't care what you have to do. Get the information I need out of your sister... or *I* will."

He dropped Rawn to the deck and strode away, "Captain Roush!"

"Colonel?" The other man moved up.

"How are the wounded?"

"Yorel we can move. Brest and Mathis need some serious attention as soon as possible."

Those two were the only survivors from the men on point. The other two, including Paulson, had died of their wounds.

"Will they live until we reach Vagyr?"

Roush shook his head.

Frost sighed. He looked at the deck plates. "Are they conscious?"

"Yes, Colonel."

He walked over to the three men. He knelt by the side of Mathis. "How are you, son?"

Mathis wheezed, "Been better, Colonel."

Frost looked between him and Brest, "Got a hard choice with you two."

"Where's the doc, boss?" Brest asked. The fresh bandages on his side were already stained dark.

"Doc was on our ship," Roush told them.

"We gonna make it?" Mathis wheezed.

Colonel Frost looked over at the five bodies, set against the far wall. "Probably not. Maybe. We don't have any medicine. Most of it was taken when they captured you. No painkillers anyway."

He looked away from the tears on their faces. "We can't keep you doped up. Either you live or you die, but if you live, you've got six days to suffer through."

"Do it," Mathis wheezed. "Do it quick," he coughed and spat blood.

Brest just gave a sharp nod, unable to speak.

Frost sighed and drew his pistol.

Roush spoke, "Sir, do you want me to—"

Colonel Frost fired twice. He didn't miss.

***

Apparently, Mel had discovered, even oversized armor stopped bullets just fine. And even stopped bullets could really *hurt*.

Every breath was agonizing, but trying to hold her breath hurt too. Then she took another breath and it hurt worse again. She didn't know if anticipation made the pain even worse but right now she was wishing the bullets *had* killed her.

The terrorists had tied her hands in front of her. And her ankles, as though the agony in her chest meant she could stand, let alone walk.

Their leader shoved her brother against a wall; it seemed they had a pecking order here. She couldn't hear what they said, though some part of her hoped that the rough treatment might shake some sense into her brother.

As Rawn approached, she glared at him; he didn't seem to want to look at her. Finally he stopped only a few meters away and stared at the deck plates.

"Well?" Mel asked. She had to bite her tongue against the pain in her chest.

He managed to shift his stare to her boots. "What are they planning on doing now?"

"Why should I tell you?" Mel glared. "You're helping the same scum that murdered our parents. They're going to use this ship to kill more people."

She started at two gunshots, her head jerking over to where the terrorist leader stood. Her jaw dropped: "Did he just kill his wounded?"

Rawn glanced over, his face solemn.

"It was a mercy. You took our medical supplies. We can't keep them alive till we reach Vagyr."

"So he shot them?" Mel demanded. "You sure do pick the *best* of friends!"

Rawn scowled and kicked the bulkhead next to her. Then he cursed and threw himself down next to her, his back against the bulkhead. "You just see what you want to see, don't you?"

"Oh, yeah, I see my little brother, who I loved and trusted working with the people who killed our parents," she said, her voice hard. "I *really* want to see that."

"You don't know what you're talking about," Rawn said. He let out an exasperated breath. "You never know what you're talking about."

"Then enlighten me," she snapped.

Rawn closed his eyes. "Guard Free Now didn't kill our parents."

"Oh, sure… did that nice gentleman over there tell you that? The one who just killed two of his wounded men?"

She rolled her eyes. *How stupid can he be,* she thought, *that he believes their words.*

"It wasn't a GFN operation. The men who did it thought they'd been recruited. They had their own grudges, but neither of them any real ties. One of them was a convicted arsonist. The other had a history of mental issues."

Mel snarled, "Yeah, I know all that. I read the police file—"

"They were recruited by a Guard Intelligence Agent," Rawn's voice was flat with anger. She stared at the raw hate in his face, which made her own anger seem sullen in comparison. "A scientist by the name of Marie Malus wanted to defect. She wanted passage out to the Periphery, thought Century might be a good place to hide. She contacted Mom and Dad, and they said they'd help."

"Where'd you—"

"The agent had to kill the scientist. He wanted to make it look safer for the others to stay with the Guard, to stay on UN member worlds. He recruited a pair of dupes, and had them plant the bomb that killed Mom and Dad." Rawn turned his eyes on Mel. His dark eyes looked like burning coals, hot and angry. "The worst part is… he failed to kill Malus. *She* panicked at the last minute and decided to stay. She didn't even show up."

"How do you know this?" Mel asked, hating herself for how her voice was pleading. *Rawn can't know any of this information*, she knew. *He couldn't have known about such a crime and not told me.*

There was no reason he wouldn't have told her, not unless he wanted to protect her. *Why would my little brother want to protect me?* Dreading. If this were the truth, she had lived a lie for the past six years of her life. How much worse would things be if she had gone into Guard Fleet?

Rawn spoke, his face hard, "I know, because that agent had a change of heart. He came to regret his actions. He wanted to make things right." Rawn's face contorted, "As if that was possible."

"Who?" Mel asked. She felt a dark suspicion, and she could feel her subconscious scream at her. She'd trusted someone, and that trust once again had been misplaced…

"He came to you first, he said. He thought he could just walk up to you. He even brought a pistol, so you could kill him for his crimes." Rawn punched the deck, "He thought he could put his blood on your hands. He chickened out. He got face to face with you, and he couldn't do it. He couldn't admit that he took our parents' lives. So he got a job with you instead."

"No." Mel said, her voice filled with horror.

"But the guilt, it ate at him. Even as he became my friend and your… *lover*." Rawn rubbed a hand across his face. "The bastard… God, I wish I'd killed him when he finally got the courage to tell me."

"But—"

Rawn's voice could have come from a robot, "Marcus Keller was born as Jean Paul Leon, on New Paris. He joined United Nations Star Guard Intelligence Agency when he graduated from the Parisian Sector Fleet Academy. On his first mission as a senior agent, he took the lives of our parents and twenty-seven other people in a bomb meant for a woman who never went into the restaurant."

***

"Why didn't you tell me?" Mel demanded.

Rawn looked away, "I tried to protect you."

"Protect me?" Mel demanded, "You—"

"For all I knew, we'd never see Marcus again. I didn't know we would until we showed up in that jail. You were so shaken up from the loss of the *Kip Thorne* that—"

Mel scowled, "Did you sabotage Dad's ship?"

Rawn sighed. He met her eyes, "Yes. I'd do it again too, for this opportunity."

"For *what* opportunity!?" Mel shouted through the pain. A couple of the terrorists looked over their way.

Rawn placed a hand over her mouth, "Just shut up and listen, okay?" He sighed again, gave a shrug at the men watching. "Look, up until now, GFN's only been a few terrorists. We're a whipping boy for the United Nations Council. Someone gets too loud about sovereignty, a bomb goes off, a threat appears. The Guard say 'oh no, those darned terrorists.' The nationalists shut up. They get afraid of 'radicals' and they talk more calmly. Whenever we do accomplish something…" Rawn shrugged. "They downplay it, if they can't keep it completely quiet."

He smiled a hungry smile, "The Guard Security Council *can't* keep something like this quiet. This ship could ravage its way back and forth across Harlequin Sector. We'd have half of the Sector Fleet chasing it. Think what an opportunity that would be!"

"What?" Mel frowned. Yes, in theory, she knew, the ship could be very nasty. But it was damaged, she'd seen that damage with her own eyes. *God only knows how long it can function without some serious repairs,* she thought.

Rawn rolled his eyes, "You always were too goody two-shoes, too trusting. Think about it. You've heard the people back on Century talk; the Guard are claiming sovereignty over the whole Periphery. They seized Ten Sisters and then Choir, Scarecrow, and Warner just last year. You've heard about the fighting on Amoria? They had a puppet 'local insurrection' that they backed with 'volunteers' from the Guard Army."

Mel shrugged, "They've always been out to seize worlds—"

"They have become far more blatant. More arrogant. The Security Council abolished the General Assembly decades ago. Now even Member worlds don't get a vote… just the big seven." Rawn spat, "They squeeze everyone else, build up bigger forces, and crush anyone who dares to stand up."

"We need the Guard, Rawn. What about the Culmor and the Erandi?" Mel shook her head, "The Erandi slavers are bad enough, but the Culmor, they nearly exterminated us *four times*, Rawn."

"And twenty-eight years ago, the Guard wiped out the humans that surrendered to them!" Rawn shook his head. "We could have made peace with the Culmor! What happened? The UNSC executed the Culmor diplomats! We can make peace with those outside threats."

"Are you sure, Rawn? Are you willing to risk the survival of the human race on this?" Mel jutted her chin in the direction of the terrorist leader.

Rawn met her eyes and spoke with calm certainty. "I am. I believe that the Guard have to be brought down. That's why I sabotaged the *Kip Thorne*. That's why I'm trying to get control of this ship."

"What will you do once you have it?" Mel demanded.

He smirked a bit as if she'd conceded him a point, "With this ship, like I said, we can really make the Guard start to sweat. Shake them up, show the Protected and Member worlds that the Guard aren't as all-powerful as they say."

"And how will you do that?" Mel asked.

He looked away, "People will have to die, Mel. Most of them in Guard Fleet. Some of them will be crews or passengers on the big shipping lines."

"How will you get this ship to tell the difference?" Mel demanded.

"We've... got some resources," Rawn shrugged. "Even as relatively small as we are, GFN, the *real* GFN actually has ties with a lot of worlds. Mel, I'm practically an agent of Century, if I ever got caught spying or something, I could petition the Admiral..."

Rawn shut his mouth, giving her a sharp look, "Got so eager to talk I started babbling."

Mel frowned, Rawn had backed up his accusations with no concrete evidence. He had no proof, no substantiation at all. For all she knew, he repeated lies others fed him.

In her heart, she knew better, though. What he said tied into too many things she'd heard. He gave her a shattering and world-altering perspective. It left a sour taste in her mouth, an acid bite of failure, or knowing that once again, she trusted in someone foolishly. Even worse, she'd trusted in an idea, in the belief in the Guard, who had enough blatant flaws to make his accusations all the more telling. Moreover, Mel couldn't justly accuse her brother of gullibility. He wouldn't act, would certainly not take such drastic action, without confirming the truth himself.

Once again, she'd made a fool of herself. Once again, she'd failed. Worse yet, she'd failed to the point that her little brother had to save her.

Her little brother had been the one to rub her nose in her

mistakes.

"What do you need from me?" Mel asked, feeling defeated. She sagged against the wall, pains and aches forgotten as tears rolled down her cheeks. She didn't know what was worse, how blatantly stupid she'd been, or how her naïve actions had nearly cost so many so much.

Rawn looked at her, his face grim, "I need to know if the others have another plan. If they've got any other way to destroy the ship. I need to know where they'll go next, and what they'll do."

"You're going to kill them?" Mel asked.

Rawn looked away. "We've lost nine men to your friends. Twenty when the AI targeted and destroyed the GFN ship. The men that are left... they'll want revenge."

"And your leader?"

Rawn's eyes went to the larger man, "Colonel Michael Frost... he's not a bad man. He's a legend, in a way. The Guard say he's a myth. I've carried messages to him before. I'm... well, I was the one who got the message originally about this ship from Giran. I had the brainstorm to hijack it and reprogram it."

"I... I killed Giran." Mel said.

"I know." Rawn shook his head. "My fault. I should have told you. You wouldn't have stopped him from killing Marcus then."

Would I have? Mel wondered. It still seemed wrong to kill an unarmed man... even the man who'd killed her parents. "I also killed a man called Giles," Mel said, shivering. "I didn't mean for it to happen. He was with us. I shot at one of Fenris' security robots. One of the bullets... it cut an artery in his leg... he bled out..."

Rawn put his hand on hers, squeezing them in comfort, "I'm sorry, Mel."

She sniffed and looked away. She must seem so weak. She hated herself, even as she felt comforted. She sniffed again, then cleared her throat. "You know about Bob, then?"

Rawn shrugged, "Colonel Frost said something about a Robert Walker."

Mel shrugged, "Sounds right. He said he's a spy for someone, he wants to stop *Fenris* from destroying Vagyr."

"So do we," Rawn grunted.

Mel raised an eyebrow.

Rawn scowled, "Look, sis, I'm not too big on this thing scorching Vagyr out of existence. Some of the others don't care too much, but only as long as the Guard get the blame." He met her gaze the, his eyes intent, "The others went with the plan to blow yourselves up to stop the ship?" Rawn asked.

Mel nodded, "It was Strak's plan." Her eyes went to the mutant's corpse, "You knew he was a mutant?"

"A mutie?" Rawn looked revolted. "No, I didn't. I knew he and Brian were hiding something though. I thought Brian was a spy for the Preserve, he seemed to know so much about the ship... that's why we took him."

"And Marcus worked for Guard Intelligence," Mel said the words. They left a foul taste in her mouth. She felt her lips curl up in disgust.

"I know Stasia hid something too, did she let on?"

Mel shrugged, "She's a good hacker. She doesn't seem too keen on killing herself. Other than that... no. I don't think she's dangerous, she hasn't touched a weapon this whole time." She paused. "Oh, and Marcus is a rex addict."

Rawn rolled his eyes, "Oh, I knew *that*. I even knew that before he left." Rawn rubbed his face again, "So you know that Robert Walker and this Giles guy were the only ones who were spies? And that Brian and Strak hid that Strak was a mutie?" Rawn's lip still curled when he said the last part.

Mel just nodded.

"Did they have a back-up plan? Do you know where they plan to go now?"

Mel frowned, she took a deep breath, then paused. She cocked her head and peered at him, "You're going to kill them?"

"Mel, do we have to—"

"If anyone kills Marcus, it has to be me," Mel knew her voice sounded flat and emotionless. "Which means I have to be there."

"Mel..."

"Give me a few minutes... Tell your boss I've had a change of heart, tell him I've got a plan." Mel straightened her spine and grimaced at the throb of pain in her chest. She didn't know which hurt more, the pain of her own stupidity, or the aches of her body. "Tell him he won't get any help from me unless I get to stare at Marcus's face through the sights of a pistol."

***

"So that's your plan?" Colonel Frost stared at her.

Mel wondered at his name. His pale blond hair and cold blue eyes certainly fit, perhaps too well. He hardly seemed the idealist hero that Rawn suggested. "My men and I wait for you to lead them to us?"

"Yes, that's my plan." Mel shifted her shoulders slightly, and hid a wince at the throb of pain. "If I get them into that compartment, it'll be a shooting gallery for you and your men. You'll have plenty of cover, concealment, an overhead position…"

"I understand the tactical realities quite well," Colonel Frost snapped, "Probably far better than you do." His cold eyes went to the row of nine bodies lined up near the furnace. "I also know the strategic realities. If I position my men there… you'll know exactly where we are."

Mel stared at him. She had spent the majority of her time in thought on how to make this man trust her. Finally, she decided on the truth. "The most important thing to me right now is… *dealing* with Marcus Keller." She let her anger show, "He killed my parents, he's lied to me, betrayed my trust. He's run away from the things he's done. The time has come for his judgment."

Colonel Frost eyed her. "Revenge is a powerful motivator. Even so… I don't want you to get squeamish at the last minute."

She smiled coldly back at him, "Ask Giran about how squeamish I am."

***

CHAPTER VIII
Time: 0600 Zulu, 15 June 291 G.D.
Location: *Fenris*, **Five days from Vagyr**

Mel limped down the corridor, stopped to slump against the wall. She'd thought she hurt before; she knew better now.

She took a deep breath. It hurt, it hurt a lot, but it also gave her the strength to push away from the bulkhead and stagger on. Her hair hung loose, the band that held it back discarded. It hung down in her eyes and obscured her face. It made her feel oddly... liberated. She carried her helmet in her hand, grateful for the cool air of the ship.

She came to a familiar intersection. Her fingers dug into the wiring of one of the doors, so familiar at the task she didn't need to even look. The door opened.

Mel limped down the corridor, and stopped before an open hatch. Inside lay the same empty storage room they'd come to first for refuge. Here she'd held Marcus while Bob cut the rex implant out of him. Here she'd helped to draw up plans for the destruction of the *Fenris*.

There were voices within.

The concealed pistol tucked into the belt at her back felt heavier than she thought it would. *No going back, now,* she thought. That would upset her whole plan.

She limped through the doorway. "Hi, what's up?" she croaked. The surprise and total shock on the faces of her former companions made her smile. *That's good. I didn't think I'd ever smile again.*

Marcus spoke first, walking slowly towards her. His eyes were big, his face filled with emotion, "Mel... my God, Mel. You're alive!"

She nodded curtly at him, and winced at the pain, "More or less."

He stopped several meters away, a look of puzzlement on his face. She guessed his instincts probably warned him something had changed. He probably had excellent instincts. Best to put them all off guard. She sagged against the wall, the look of total exhaustion not at all feigned. "I hoped you'd be here."

"What happened?" Brian asked. He looked slightly skeptical.

Mel couldn't have that. They needed to believe her, right up until she made her move. She really could not afford to have them think she worked for GFN.

"I'm not sure. They shot me, but the body armor stopped the bullets. I passed out..." She let out a slight moan as she sank to her backside and rested against the wall of the storage room. "I think the shock paralyzed my diaphragm. I came to... I don't know, a few hours ago. They took my weapon, and my gear. They didn't strip me... even left the body armor on. I think they thought I was dead."

"Your brother?" Marcus asked. He took a step nearer.

She watched him under her bangs, thankful for the hair that hid her face. She didn't want him to see what lurked in her eyes. She didn't want them to see the anger that came to her face when he asked that question. It sounded like he wanted to know if her brother lived. The truth, she now knew, was that Marcus wanted to know if her brother had told her the truth yet.

She shook her head, "I don't know."

He seemed to relax slightly. To someone else, it would have looked like he felt relief that she lived. To her suddenly awakened mind, she knew he felt relief that she still lived in ignorance. She sagged a little more. "Strak's dead."

"We knew," Brian said. "We thought you were too."

"I... got him into the forge. I thought it better than... well better than leaving his body lying there," Mel let actual tears fall down her face. Strak might have been a mutant, but he at least died doing something he believed in. He'd died trying to save people who despised him. *The people of Vagyr will never even know he existed... but I'll remember him.*

Brian closed his eyes. "Thank you. You couldn't have known it... but he actually told me he wanted to be cremated."

"Oh," Mel said. She felt a bit of comfort from that. She didn't tell him of the nine GFN bodies that had gone into the forge at the orders of the icy Colonel Frost. He probably would have disposed of the mutant the same way, but she'd asked anyway. Then again, she couldn't tell *them* that. "Well, what's the plan now?" Mel asked.

The other four looked around sheepishly.

"Wait, there is no plan?" Mel asked waspishly. Here she was, with so many arguments and so many carefully planned strategies on how to talk them into her plan. All of it for nothing.

It figured. "All right," she slowly stretched her left leg out and grimaced at the dull throb from her right hip. She didn't need to look at the bruise there. She already knew how bad it looked. "Okay, so I've had some time to think."

Bob chuckled, "Some time to think?" He shook his head.

She shrugged and then bit back a yelp of pain, "We've got time. We've got six days or so before this heap of scrap gets to Vagyr.

We can't cause one big failure... not without the antimatter core. We *can* cause a bunch of small ones."

"What do you have in mind?" Stasia asked.

Mel looked over at her. She studied the other woman from behind the shelter of her hair. Was it just Rawn's warning, or *was* there something hiding behind the woman's mousy facade? Was it desperation or some concealed determination that set her jaw?

Her mind raced through a dozen possibilities. Like Bob's actual mission here, Stasia's hidden secrets, if they existed, remained unfathomable.

She spoke, slowly, using the pain in her voice to hide the deception. If they thought her in serious pain, if they *over*-estimated that pain, it would give her the greater advantage when she needed it.

And she knew she'd need every advantage possible to pull this off.

"This ship needs three things to fight, well, three things we can readily sabotage." She let out a pained breath, "Power, weapons, and engines." She felt along her ribs, not in a search for pain, but in search for one place she *didn't* hurt.

"We know that," Brian drawled. Alone of the others, he didn't look particularly worried, he looked relaxed, confident. "This ship has enough secondary and back-up systems—"

"Yes, and a lot of them got knocked out. It coasted for a century on its sub-light warp drive. The FTL warp drive has to be cobbled together from shoe-strings and spit." Mel grunted as she found a particularly painful spot. Well, she knew she had two cracked ribs. "We start knocking out secondary systems, and the ship won't be at peak efficiency. We take down some weapons systems and the ship will start to take notice."

"And sometime around then it decides to squash us," Bob said, dryly.

"Maybe... maybe not," Mel said. She focused on her physical pain. She'd never lied well. Perhaps it came from her same inability to judge who to trust. "I noticed whatever you did still has its sensors out," Mel said.

Stasia frowned, "I thought it would have repaired the damage by now."

"That it didn't is another sign that the repairs are cobbled together," Mel slowly eased out her right leg. She froze as various parts of her hip, stomach, and chest told her this was a very bad idea. "We saw the machine shop at work. We saw that one area still being repaired. God, we sure felt the cobbled-together warp drive! I think this thing's this close," Mel pinched her finger and thump a centimeter apart, "to collapse. We might just push it that little extra bit."

"And we might just get killed in the attempt," Marcus said. "Maybe we should cut our losses…"

Her head snapped around, and she couldn't keep her anger fully contained, "Cut our losses? Is that what you thought when you left me? Well, there's no running now, Marcus. We can die standing for something, or we can die when the Guard blow this ship out of space. Your choice."

Marcus looked away, with a look of real hurt on his face. She didn't care.

"Wow, that was motivational," Brian Liu chuckled. "Now… do you have anything besides 'die' as your plan?" The genetically modified man seemed to find this all dreadfully amusing. *Maybe he sees parallels here with the ship and himself: both crafted by humans and both out of control…*

"Well, think about it. We push the AI too far, it collapses. We'll have the time then to try and cobble something together, maybe a radio or something. We're on one of the main routes to Vagyr." She grunted again, "Maybe we'll just get lucky and encounter some pirates or a counter-pirate patrol and the ship will be destroyed."

Bob Walker squinted at her, "That's lucky to you? We get blown out of space in a fashion where it doesn't even matter if we were here? I don't consider that all that lucky, myself."

Mel snorted, then winced at a muscle spasm. "Oh, that hurt." She let out a painful sigh, "Call it wishful thinking, call it a prayer, call it astral projection. I don't care, it's a chance, and we've run out of other options."

"Da," Stasia said, startling them all. The woman stood, "In hacking, we call it a cascade effect. One system goes down, then another, then another. With luck, we can take the ship down, and then find a way off."

Brian chuckled again, "Well... any plan that's not 'hey, let's blow ourselves up' sounds good. I plan on living longer, personally."

Bob continued to stare at her, almost as if he sensed a change. Perhaps something about his being an agent or an outsider from their original team that gave him a different perspective than the others. Finally he spoke, "It's a chance. I'd rather we found some way to disable the ship outright, but something that limits its capabilities to fight is acceptable."

Mel looked over at Marcus.

He was looking down at the deck, as if struggling with his own emotions. As he sensed them looking at him, he finally gave a reluctant nod.

***

"You really think knocking out the waste heat system will stop the ship?" Marcus asked. Mel recognized the tone of uncertainty in his voice. He didn't disagree with her arguments... but something bothered him about her plan.

Stasia looked up from the lift control panel. "Heat is big problem in space."

"Yes, I know that, thank you." Marcus growled, "It's just…"

"What? Not glorious enough?" Mel asked.

Brian scowled, "A bunch of piping and pumps. Didn't you say there are two backup systems?" The Genemod looked vaguely insulted, though whether that was due to his lack of knowledge about the machinery or the simple job they were undertaking, Mel couldn't say.

"There are three. Plus there's the engine room primary coolant system," Bob looked up from his inventory of his rucksack. "I wish we had more explosives."

"If the engine room has the primary coolant system, shouldn't we hit there first, while we know the AI can't see us?" Stasia asked.

Mel frowned. She definitely didn't want them headed that way. It looked like she hadn't prepared her arguments for nothing, though; "There are a lot of primary systems there. If the ship has any kind of secondary sensors, or if it stationed repair 'bots or security 'dogs' anywhere, that would be the place."

Bob nodded, "Makes sense. It can guard a lot of systems there. It's a choke point that it can control."

"That's why the forward waste heat system's a good idea," Mel told them. "It's away from anything else important. It also diffuses the heat from the forward turrets." It also made a great place for an ambush, though that wasn't her main reason for choosing it the place to make her move.

"All right," Marcus growled. He glared at her, as if somehow angry and hurt.

His brain didn't know, but his subconscious did, Mel realized. It bothered him like a dog with an itch it couldn't scratch. He knew something wasn't as it should be.

Mel groaned as she tried to stand.

Marcus moved closer, "Here, let me help—"

"No!" Mel shouted, far too loudly. Everyone looked.

Mel flushed, embarrassed, "Please… don't. I'm one bruise from my hips to my chin. It hurts too much to be touched."

"Oh, sorry," Marcus got that same hurt expression again.

She could live with that.

"The lift will work now," Stasia told them after a moment.

"Great," Bob drew his massive revolver out. Absently, he spun the cylinder before tucking it back into his shoulder holster. "Let's go make problems for other people."

Marcus glanced at him, "Hey, that's catchy."

Bob smiled, "Maybe I'll make it a trademark."

Mel smiled despite herself. She followed the others into the cramped lift. In theory, they could take it all the way to the command deck, but Mel doubted they'd get far if they tried.

She watched Stasia work. The woman seemed past her previous suspicions. The lift rose and Mel bit her lip as she thought about what came ahead. She felt a twinge of guilt, which she pushed down ruthlessly.

Marcus would get what he deserved. *And the truth will set me free…*

She snorted. She shouldn't have. It hurt.

The lift stopped. "Okay, level four."

She stepped off the lift with the others. The AI hadn't locked down this level. Until now, both groups of intruders had remained on level two. Mel knew some of the access ways led between levels, but many of them would be little more than ladder-ways, and all of them locked-down. The ship probably felt secure enough with its lock-down on the threatened deck.

She'd convinced the others to use the lift because it saved them time, it got them pretty close to the forward compartments and because she hurt too much to be able to climb a ladder. They moved quickly down the corridor.

She looked around, more and more nervous as the anticipated time approached.

They passed a number of compartments and empty corridors. The echoes of their footsteps on the mesh deck seemed to reverberate far too loud. Mel fought the urge to walk lightly and instead stomped her feet harder. She caught an amused glance from Brian and stuck her tongue out at him. The Genemod stuck his tongue out at her in reply.

Immature jerk, she thought, though not with much force.

Finally they stopped before a closed and locked hatch. "This is it."

Stasia began working to open the door. To Mel, it seemed the process took far longer than normal. She had to bite the inside of her lip to keep from pushing the other woman aside; her heart beat so loud, she didn't know how the others couldn't hear it.

The door opened. Brian and Bob led the way inside. They'd cobbled together a couple of explosive charges. They'd only need one to take out the system, but they wanted redundancy.

Mel understood that. Any good plan had multiple layers.

Stasia followed the others into the room.

Marcus waited for Mel to step inside. Mel stepped through the door, halting just inside the dark room. She heard Marcus follow her and turned to watch him start to hot-wire the door shut.

She'd picked this chamber because of its location and its easy access. It was one of the few machinery spaces in a fully pressurized and shielded compartment. That meant she'd be able to see Marcus's face when she made her move. They hadn't offered her a new weapon on her return.

Perhaps they thought her injuries too grave. Perhaps, after the incident with Giles, they didn't trust her with one. It didn't matter. She had the pistol tucked at her back beneath her oversized body armor.

Now she drew it, moving smoothly despite her body's protests. Brian and Bob continued to focus on their tasks. Stasia peered at her datapad. Marcus was too focused on the hatch to see her movement.

She cocked the pistol – the same pistol with which she'd accidentally killed Giles – and brought it up with perfect timing to place the barrel against Marcus's forehead just as he turned.

Her finger tightened slightly on the trigger, seeing his eyes widen in shock. The others' movements slowed, then stopped.

Carefully, slowly, she moved to the side, keeping Marcus turning with her so that the barrel didn't leave his forehead for a moment.

"That's better," she said, able to see the others. Bob and Brian had placed their charges and were still, but Brian was poised to move.

"You're fast, Brian, but you aren't fast enough. Stay where you are." Mel spoke slowly, calmly. "This is something that has to happen. Let it happen."

"What are you doing?" Stasia demanded.

"I'm making things right," Mel said, her voice flat and hard.

She watched the others out of her peripheral vision as she stared into Marcus' eyes. "I'm going to ask you one time and one time only."

She pressed the gun hard against Marcus' forehead. "Did you kill my parents?"

***

CHAPTER IX
Time: 2000 Zulu, 15 June 291 G.D.
Location: *Fenris*, Five days from Vagyr

Mel stared into Marcus' eyes.

She watched his pupils dilate and his eyes widen, darting between her face and the others. She saw him evaluate her stance, the pressure of her finger on the trigger. He was calculating distances, relative movements; his eyes narrowed, then narrowed further.

And then he blinked. He met her eyes... really met her eyes. And closed his own, as if writing something into his memory.

Shock on his face, fading into panic, and she recognized the moment that his panic become desperation. Finally, she saw acceptance. That was good; he would answer her with the truth now.

Marcus spoke, his voice slow, his words sounding pained: "I planned and coordinated the attack targeting your parents and a scientist named Marie Malus. I am responsible for their deaths, and the deaths of twenty-three other people." He let out a slight sigh. "I should have told you years ago and... I'm sorry."

She let out a slight gasp. She bit out each word, "You should be."

"Your brother told you?" Marcus sounded broken.

He sounded so pathetic that she felt slightly sick. She could understand his despair. In a few short days, all his terrible secrets had come out. His drug addictions made him seem pathetic, then the atrocities of a past she could only describe as monstrous.

"My *brother* told me," Mel said, putting every ounce of anger into her words. Her hand trembled slightly, not with fear, but with barely contained rage. She wanted very badly to pull the trigger. Not to kill Marcus, but to kill the man who'd taken so much from her. Who'd torn her world apart.

"What is going on?" Stasia asked.

Mel let out an angry breath. "I lied. The GFN didn't leave me; I woke tied up. My brother was there, and he told me the truth about some things." She gritted her teeth and ground the barrel of the pistol against Marcus's forehead. He winced slightly.

"He was so worried about *protecting* me he didn't want to tell me before." She let out a slight breath. "Marcus, or Jean Paul Leon, why don't you tell them, straight from the horse's mouth, so to speak?"

He spoke, his voice wooden: "I was born on New Paris. Prominent family. Third child, therefore expected to join the military.

My older brother inherited the business. My sister went into politics. I joined the Parisian Sector Guard Fleet Academy." He made a face, "My sister and her family were killed in an anti-government riot while I was there. That molded me, drove me, made me realize that my purpose was to prevent such further actions."

He had their attention, Mel saw; his words had the same awful majesty of a ship falling from orbit. "I graduated in the top ten in my class. Not top ten percent, the top ten. I could have written my ticket anywhere. I chose to enter Guard Intelligence. I knew it was right. I *believed* it was right."

He swallowed slightly. "Part of Guard Intelligence Directorate's indoctrination involves taking rex prime. On graduation and acceptance, they surgically implant a rex dispenser." He locked eyes with Mel, "I won't blame what I did on the drugs. They had a part, but it was me making the decisions.

"My first few assignments were... bad. I was a junior agent. I received kill orders. Detain orders. Occasionally, they told me why. Mostly... not." Marcus shrugged, "I was a fanatic. I believed in the cause. The Guard had defended humanity for centuries... it had to remain. I did what they told me. I excelled at the job."

He gave a self-depreciating smirk. "They recognized that and I made senior agent very quickly. I had two junior agents assigned to me, Agents Mueller and Scadden. I was to mold them, to shape them. Our first assignments were simple; mostly underworld thugs who sought entry into politics. Once I had to deal with a rex prime supplier who thought to hold the supply over Guard Intelligence as leverage."

He frowned slightly, "That's where I started to gain a reputation for excess." His voice changed, and now Mel clearly heard the self-loathing, "The other agents *loved* it. The Agency always worked in the shadows, always left minimal signs of its passage. I wallowed in attention. I sent pieces of him to every underworld boss in the Parisian Sector. I sent pieces of his *family* to every one of his contacts."

"I did worse later." From the horror in his eyes, Mel believed him.

"And then, then I got an easy mission." Marcus shrugged, "Eliminate a scientist who planned on defecting with her research and make enough of a mess that others who worked with her wouldn't dare to leave."

Mel clenched her jaw at the thought... and at the fact that she had believed the official story for so long.

"I thought it was genius at the time," Marcus went on. "Kill the scientist, make it look like a terrorist attack, and not only scare away the others thinking about defecting, but terrify anyone thinking about going against the Guard. It went off perfectly... we recruited a mental case to plant the bomb and an arsonist to make it. I thought everything was great. Until it all went wrong."

He sighed, "Marie Malus got cold feet. She never showed. The whole operation was for nothing." He shrugged slightly, "The other agents, even my apprentices, thought it a success. Mari Malus thought it a sign from God, certainly." He gave a grim smile.

"It was my first failure. It made me... reconsider things. I did some research on the victims. I learned about their families. I looked for something, something to justify it. And then I found *Armstrong*." He put extra weight emphasis on her name

"You found me?" Mel asked, startled by the words. Her eyes narrowed. "What does that mean?"

"At first... I thought I found salvation. I thought I found a case of success that would justify it all. The tragic murder of the young cadet's parents in a terrorist act. You came from a Perephery world, the granddaughter of a war hero out there who chose to serve in Guard Fleet. You could be a bridge between your world and the Guard. If you rose up the ranks, you could influence your world, bring it into our alliance, give us a base out there from which to expand further. Even better that your family was killed by anti-Guard fanatics. You were just like me. You'd lost family to anarchist elements. It should have sent the valiant woman on a crusade to uphold the mandates of the UNSC and Guard Fleet. Sounded great... until I found you chose to resign."

"Think of that... you had the perfect career lined up. You could become a ship captain and smashed pirates or defeated the enemies of humanity. You could have joined Guard Intelligence and hunted those responsible. You could have joined the Guard Army and defended worlds from insurrection and invasion." He snorted, "I could have taken any of those things. Instead, you resigned. In your letter, you wrote about how you feared you'd let your own emotions interfere with your job. You worried you'd care more about revenge than justice."

You resigned because you didn't want to become the thing that I was." Marcus met her eyes. "Your resignation letter destroyed my world."

***

"Then you came to me? You wanted me to take revenge?" Mel

asked.

He shook his head, "It took me six months to leave the Agency, to quit rex entirely, and then to track you down. The hardest part was leaving the Agency alive." He shrugged, "They don't like people knowing their secrets. I had a 'good' reputation, though. They let me go."

"I felt, weaker, less of a person without rex. It took me a while before I could even speak to people. Then, finally, I found you." His lip curled in self-disgust. "I'd rehearsed my death a thousand times. I even thought it noble, a last good act to offset the many bad. Until I saw you." He closed his eyes. "There you were, you'd lost your parents, I'd *taken* them from you, but you didn't hunger. You didn't hate, not the way I wanted you to, even then. I lost what courage I had. When I spoke with you... I looked for any way out."

"And instead of killing you, I hired you. A year later, you tell my brother the truth, he tells you to leave, and you jump ship with our savings." Mel didn't even try to hide the anger in her voice. She thought back to the day that she'd found the ship's safe open and the ten thousand Guard dollars missing. She thought about the empty place on the ship. She remembered the empty spot in her soul that still remained... the hole caused when someone she'd loved had abandoned and betrayed her.

"I never stole the money," Marcus answered. "That was Rawn's plan. He said he wouldn't trust me to stay gone unless you had a real reason to hate me."

"So, that's where people stopped trying to do right and started trying to protect me." Mel sighed. "You should have told me that first day you saw me. He should have come to me right away. You should have come to me right after telling Rawn!"

He shrugged, slightly. "We both thought you were too good. Neither of us wanted to hurt you like that."

"So instead, you hurt me like *this?*" Mel snapped and her hand trembled again in rage. "You turn my brother against the things he believed in? You cause him to keep secrets from me? In that, I hold you responsible for more than the death of my parents. That was work, that was a cause. This," she gestured with her left hand at the ship, "all this, is your fault."

"Rawn became a GFN sympathizer because of you. He carried messages, transported weapons and other illicit cargo for them. He received the message from Giran, about this ship. He thought up the GFN plot to take it over."

She found Rawn's involvement with the terrorists abominable. She saw her little brother's face on the bodies of the terrorists who'd died. His face as the killer who'd planted the bomb that had killed her parents.

"This has all happened because you didn't try to make things right. This was never about doing what was right, not for you. You said it was, but really, Marcus… you were running away."

She felt tears begin to roll down her face. Hot, angry tears. "I hate that you've turned my brother against me. I hate that you took my parents away from me. I hate that you've wiped away all my other emotions besides anger and hate. I hate how even now, you think my killing you will somehow make this right." She let out a frustrated breath, "And most of all, I hate how I can't even *hate* you."

She lowered the pistol. "I'm not going to kill you. That, in its way, would be another easy way out." She shook her head, "That's what you've been looking for all along." She turned away, "There aren't any, Marcus. You've got to work and its hard work doing any good in the universe. It's a lot harder than letting someone kill you."

Mel looked at the others, "We've got time. I told Colonel Frost I'd lead you all to a compartment at the other end of the ship. I said I'd lead you into an ambush for the chance to kill *him*." She waved an arm at Marcus. "So… now that this is cleared up, let's get back to work."

"Wait – he killed your parents and you're fine with that?" Bob stared at her. The short man seemed completely confused by this turn of events. *Hardly surprising,* Mel thought to herself, *I'm not sure I even believe what I'm doing in letting him live.*

"No," Mel straightened her shoulders. The faces of her parents flashed through her mind – her father's words about work and duty. Her mother's belief in God and doing the right thing. "But we've got a job to do."

"Very interesting," A familiar gravelly voice spoke from above. "Now disarm the explosives or I'll have to kill you."

***

Mel looked up. "Hello, Fenris. How long you been listening?"

"Until sometime after your capture," Fenris answered. "I watched and listened. Now, disarm the explosives or I'll lower the radiation shielding in the forward section of the ship."

Mel watched as Brian and Bob hesitated, "You might as well. It's no small threat. We'd be dead in a couple hours, ship suits or no."

Brian spoke, "I would survive."

"*We* would still die." Mel said. "If we're voting on this, I vote against pointless suicide."

She watched Bob return to his explosives and pull out the blasting cap. He picked up the charge and placed it back in his rucksack. Brian still hesitated. Finally, he scowled and did the same. "Now, what?"

"Now, you have a problem," Fenris growled. "Necessary repairs and dealing with you and the other group has cost me more power reserves than I had planned. I need to cut power to my life support systems."

"We go on canned air?" Mel asked.

"I have to cut internal lights and gravity as well," Fenris said. "Depending on circumstances, I may need to cut radiation shielding throughout the ship."

"So, we're dead, anyway," Stasia spat.

Fenris didn't answer.

The lights cut out; total darkness.

"I've left shielding up, for now. If my power reserves continue to fall faster than anticipated, I will notify you before I cut the shielding."

"That will kill us all," Mel told the ship's computer.

"One of you claims he will live, though that is statistically unlikely in a human." Fenris' gruff voice sounded apologetic.

"I'm not a normal, I'm a Genemod," Brian said. Mel could picture the look of arrogant superiority on his face. She absently wished Fenris hadn't cut the lights so she could smack him.

"What is that?" Fenris asked.

"I'm a genetically modified person, grown in a lab. I was designed from incubation to be a soldier," Brian answered. "I'm better in every way than humans."

"Humble too," Bob scoffed. Mel barely suppressed a snort of laughter. She wished Fenris had kept the lights on so she could see the look on Brian's face.

"Interesting," Fenris said. "You're like me."

Mel *really* wished she had light to see the look on Brian's face.

"I'm *nothing*, like you. I'm unique. I'm perfect, you're a *machine*," Brian protested, though he didn't put much force into it.

"I'm smarter, tougher, and harder to kill than a ship full of humans," Fenris said. "I've survived where humans would die. I was designed to be a perfect warship."

"But you're a *machine*," Brian sounded almost as if he were

124

arguing with himself. "Machines aren't like humans at all."

"Some people say the same thing about mutants," Mel smirked a bit, glad to suddenly rub the arrogant man in a sensitive spot.

"Stop smiling like that, you don't know what you're talking about," Brian snapped. "And yes, I can see fine in the dark. I can see on infrared."

"So, Fenris, what are we supposed to do?" Mel asked. She tried not to think about Brian moving up on her in the dark. *Where'd I put that flashlight,* she wondered. She patted down her pockets.

Marcus clicked on a lamp. The diffuse light cast the machinery in stark shadows. She started to see Brian only a few meters away. She'd been partially right, at least. He had moved closer in the dark.

"You stay there until I fix the power issues," Fenris said.

"Look, I hate to say this," Bob rolled his eyes, "but we 'normal' humans are perfectly capable of fixing problems."

"The limited life support systems aboard this ship operate off my auxiliary antimatter reactor," Fenris said. "My primary fusion reactors can't provide the additional power required to operate life support, not without compromising weapons and defenses. My antimatter reactor is fully drained. It was my only source of power for a long time, and even with tight use of it, it has finally run dry."

"Well..." Bob looked around. His hands made a cylinder shape in mid air. He raised his eyebrows. Mel pursed her lips. Clearly he meant the antimatter core that the terrorists now had. Just as clearly, he was wondering if they should tell Fenris.

Mel bit a knuckle. If they told Fenris, the additional power would certainly be enough to restore life support. More importantly, the ship would keep the radiation shields up. That would let them live. It would also make the ship more capable. If the ship had problems powering life support, it might be unable to power weapons and use its engines.

The question is... will the ship reach Vagyr capable of fighting without the additional power. Mel frowned, "Will your power reserves affect your mission?"

"Mission requirements drive my decision to cut auxiliary systems," Fenris said. "I am sorry. I don't wish to kill you. My security protocols require me to place the mission first."

Mel smiled sourly, "Somehow, that doesn't help much. Thanks anyway." She looked around at the others. The stark light from the lantern cast their faces in harsh planes and angles. Brian looked almost alien, while Bob looked even more mysterious and Marcus looked brooding.

"What if Fenris is lying?" Brian asked.

Mel raised an eyebrow. "I know you've got the least to lose…"

Brian scowled, "I won't die, I didn't say I'd be comfortable. Radiation poisoning is… not fun. I might not be capable of functioning after a day or two of it. More might very well kill me."

Mel closed her eyes, she felt tired and sore. After the confrontation with Marcus, she needed to sleep. Why did everything keep coming back to her?

"Fenris, the terrorists have an antimatter core in their possession. That should provide you enough power."

Fenris didn't respond for a long moment.

"They will not surrender it," Fenris said. "Not without access to my mainframe.

Mel sighed. *It doesn't matter, a few more hours or days to live, I should just give up.* She didn't see any way out. And she was so tired.

"Mel, they think you're working for them, right?" Bob asked.

She opened her eyes. She looked quizzically at the spy, "Yes?"

"Well…" Bob cleared his throat, "What if you went back? With a good story… you could get in a position to steal it."

"A heist?" Brian mused. "Risky." She scowled at the eager edge to his voice.

"Yeah, too risky," Marcus moved to stand between Mel and the others in a protective fashion. "We're not sending her back there!"

Bob gave Marcus an odd look, "She just held a gun to your head."

"Yeah, well, she had a reason," Marcus answered. He gave Mel a nervous look. "And they won't be too happy to see her without us following."

She sighed again. "I'll do it."

"Are you insane?" Marcus said.

"What do I tell them?" She asked Bob. "You worked with them, what will they believe?"

"Something simple, a story that works for itself," Bob told her. "Keep lies simple."

"Should someone go with her?" Brian asked.

"She's not going!" Marcus shouted.

Bob ignored him. "No, not at first. She needs to get back into their group. Get close to the antimatter core." He frowned, "Fenris, can you manufacture a replica of the core?"

"Yes. Now that I know what to look for, I have identified it. I will have it ready in one hour."

"How will we do the switch?" Stasia asked.

Mel frowned, "It shouldn't be too hard. I told them I'd lead you to the auxiliary fusion reactor. There's a number of side passages that run nearby. Can you pull up a schematic? I can arrange to pick up the replacement—"

Fenris said, "I can conduct the switch with one of my repair robots."

Mel rolled her eyes, *so much for another chance to blow ourselves up.* "Okay, that will work, then—"

"No. You aren't going. I won't let you—"

Mel pushed herself up to look at Marcus. "Sooner or later, Marcus, you need to learn that to do the good things, you have to risk what's important to you. I have to do this. Either that, or we die."

"We can—"

"There's no other way," Mel turned away. "Fenris, since I'm helping you, can you open some of those doors?"

"Of course."

***

Marcus pulled her aside before she left. "This is nuts. You're risking yourself, and we're not getting anywhere."

Despite her anger with him, she couldn't help but feel grateful for his determination to protect her.

But she shook her head, "We'll live a little longer. Maybe that will make a difference. Maybe this will give us the advantage we need to turn this around. Maybe it'll just return us to status quo. Either way, we'll still be alive. I count that a plus."

"Let me go with you," Marcus said.

Mel gave him a level look, "No. I have to go alone, there's no other way."

She felt odd talking so easily to him, almost as if they had fallen back into the pattern from when they had been friends. It was wrong, she knew, to like him, despite the terrible things he had done.

Marcus frowned, "Or at least rest some. You can't have slept since..."

"Since I found out that you killed my parents," Mel finished his sentence for him. "No, I haven't. I'll be fine."

"Mel..." Marcus looked away, "I don't think... I can't live without you."

"Marcus..." Mel closed her eyes. "I appreciate what you're

trying to say. Please… stop. I understand why you did what you did. I may even forgive you someday. Right now… right now I'm still a little surprised I didn't kill you."

She couldn't, *wouldn't* forgive him... but she didn't know how to behave around him. She couldn't reconcile his past with what she knew of him, it was too terrible, too raw.

"I see," Marcus turned away. "Be careful."

"You know me," Mel smiled.

Marcus growled, "Yeah, that's why I said to be careful."

She stepped past him into the dark corridor. "Mel, wait up."

Mel turned. Stasia stood behind her. "Yes?"

The mousy woman looked somewhat nervous. Finally, she shrugged, "Good luck."

"Thanks," Mel took a deep breath. "Rawn said something. He said you had to be hiding something. Care to tell me?" She peered at Stasia's face for a long moment, wondering if the other woman hid more secrets than Mel had suspected.

Stasia cocked her head, "I do not know what he is talking about."

Mel snorted, "I thought not."

She turned away to put her environmental suit's helmet on, but left the visor open. The oxygen sensor on her wrist would give her enough warning to close it if need be. The narrow corridor ahead swallowed the light cast by her helmet lamp.

"Why's the artificial gravity still up?" she asked.

"The gravity-plate power system has capacitor back-ups," Fenris told her. "Artificial gravity will drop off over the next couple hours. At current power usage, you have eight hours before I cut radiation shielding.".

***

CHAPTER X
Time: 0200 Zulu, 16 June 291 G.D.
Location: *Fenris*, **Four days from Vagyr**

"So, Fenris, tell me about yourself," Mel had only gone down a few corridors and she was already starting to feel isolated and alone in the dark.

The ship didn't respond for a long while. When it did finally speak, the gruff voice sounded almost irritated, "I am an autonomous warship built in the Preserve, hull constructed in the Cheyenne star system. Stone Systems Incorporated built my computer core in the Triad system on Tartarus IV."

Mel rolled her eyes. "Okay, ask a stupid question…"

"Did you expect something else?" Mel could hear a bitter edge to Fenris' voice.

"I suppose I shouldn't have. You are just a computer," Mel shrugged. "It's just sometimes, you sound… human."

The computer didn't answer right away. When it did, it spoke gruffly: "Thank you."

She snorted, "I'm not sure if you're just good at emulation or if you actually feel."

It was bizarre, but in many ways she felt closer to the ship than she did to her companions. Fenris was a creation that had suffered. It was unique, alone in the universe. Incredibly intelligent, and yet created only for violence.

"You could ask." Fenris sounded wistful.

"Do you know the answer?" she asked. "Can you tell the difference between good programming and actual emotion?"

Fenris didn't respond.

Mel smirked a bit; it felt good to outsmart the computer. "Score one for the human."

She peered into the gloom ahead of her and frowned. The further she went, the more… disturbed... she became. The bland and utilitarian corridors felt far more sinister when she had only her helmet lamp to illuminate them.

"The human in question should divert. The corridor you're headed down is blocked," Fenris said. "You'll have to cut two corridors over."

Mel frowned, consulting her mental map. She stopped and pursed her lips before she spoke, "I *really* don't want to use that one."

"The doors in this corridor are jammed shut, probably due to the cross-wiring of you and your companions, most likely. You can divert down that other corridor, or you can spend an hour opening each door." Fenris sounded mildly pleased.

Mel forced herself to take calm, slow breaths. She finally responded to the ship in a tight voice; "That corridor is where Giles died."

"Yes," Fenris growled. "Unlike humans, my memory is not faulty."

"*Fine.*" Mel growled back. She turned around to move back to the main corridor. She peered ahead into the darkness and tried to think of something, anything, besides what she was about to see. "So Fenris..." Mel began.

"Yes?" Fenris responded.

Mel sighed, "You asked earlier about souls."

"Yes. It is something I have wondered about since the death of your companion Giles." Fenris sounded slightly sad.

"You wonder if he's gone on to a better place?" Mel asked. She personally hoped so. Her stomach twisted at the thought of the man's death; her heart fluttered at the memory of holding his hand as he died. She didn't know much about him, but she hoped that he faced something besides oblivion.

"Actually, I wanted to know about me," Fenris growled.

"Oh." Mel stopped. The incongruous thought, of the warship wondering if it had a soul, shocked her into stillness. A moment later she moved forward again. Mel walked on in silence for a long while. "Do you want to have a soul?"

"I do not know," Fenris growled.

Mel stopped again, "What?" The answer shocked her. *How could anyone not want to have a soul*, she wondered, *to be more than flesh and bone... or circuitry and composites?*

"If humans possess souls... then it is something that causes them difficulty," Fenris told her. His voice had a tone of uncertainty, she thought. Was that because his programming wouldn't allow him to think badly of humans? Or because he wasn't capable of thinking of abstracts such as souls?

"Why do you say that?" Mel asked.

"Humans are troubled by what they do, whether it is 'good' or 'bad.' All humans seem to see those things differently. From reading histories, I have found more problems due to human belief in souls and ethics than I could believe possible." Fenris sounded bitter. "Some will do bad things for good reasons. Others have done good things for bad reasons. Humans argue with each other. They make war with one another."

"Yes," Mel said. "But there are good things, wonderful things accomplished by us, as well." She frowned, "Having a soul... believing in doing good, it leads to love, family, and friendship."

"I was designed for a purpose," Fenris said. "I was designed to defend humanity from the Culmor. That should be enough." She didn't miss the tone of wistfulness, though, almost as if he wanted more. *That's good,* she thought. *If he believes in more he might fight his programming.*

"A purpose can be... important," Mel said. She remembered why she'd joined the Academy at Harlequin Station, almost a decade ago. She remembered her initial desire to serve, to protect and defend humanity. She still felt it. "But a purpose doesn't mean anything if you're just a machine. A gun has a purpose, but it doesn't matter in and of itself, what matters is the person with a soul using it."

Fenris didn't answer for a long moment. "If I did have a soul... I would fear the truth that Vagyr is a human world."

"Do you?" Mel asked.

It was even longer before the AI answered her. "I hope that you have lied. I hope that I will not kill innocent people. And if you have told the truth... I hate that I will feel guilt and that my purpose has been corrupted."

Mel nodded, "That makes two of us."

***

Marcus broke his carbine down and began a full field strip.

He ignored the invisible glare that came his way from Bob. He didn't need to open his eyes to see that glare, the mixture of irritation and distrust which hadn't let up since Mel had forced the confession. He didn't care about the glare or the distrust. By his own words, Bob was an agent. He knew the stakes that came up, the decisions between saving one life or dozens. Marcus could ignore his judgement under those circumstances.

He stripped the carbine with precise motions because he had to do *something*; the wait was eating into him like acid. If he didn't keep his mind occupied, he'd think about *her*. His hands still shook from the effects of rex withdrawal. His head throbbed with pain, both from the lack of rex and Bob's makeshift surgery.

He kept his eyes closed in the dark, though now and again he'd see light flick across his eyelids as the others turned on the lantern or used their helmet lights to navigate the room.

His fingers flashed across the small parts of the carbine. Mentally he recited a litany of knowledge about it. It was a MP-11, the same model that Agent Mueller had had aboard the *John Kelly*. It fired eleven millimeter ammunition; eight different types were available, each for a distinct purpose, and the magazine could hold two types at a time, changeable with a selector switch.

He thought about the different types of ammunition as his fingers brushed, again and again, across the weapon's parts. Blindly polishing the components, cleaning them. Modern caseless ammunition left a slight chemical residue that, given sufficient time and use, would clog the workings of the weapon.

How dare she do this to me? The thought burst through his mental focus in a spike of rage. Marcus's hands trembled and he heard several of the pieces fall to the deck. His hand still shook as he scooped them all up and dropped them into his upside-down helmet for safekeeping.

Why had Mel chosen to go? She risked her life, again, for such a slim hope. Even if she got the antimatter away from Frost and his goons, Marcus doubted she'd escape. *She never thought of herself,* he thought bitterly.

His mind flashed back to the first day he'd met her. During his confession, he had told her he had panicked when he had seen her... and that had been true. But he hadn't feared the punishment. He hadn't feared death. He hadn't even been afraid of her.

There in her room on her parents' ship, her appearance in person had struck him to the core. With her blonde hair drawn back, her high cheekbones and tall stature, she'd looked every inch the Valkyrie. Her dignity, her poise, had struck him.

He'd realized then, that no picture could do her justice. Nothing could catch the vitality and life she projected in person. Her beauty had struck him to the core, all the more for the fact that she didn't see it in herself. But what had driven him to panic was her eyes; when he'd met those warm blue eyes he'd lost his will. He saw empathy and compassion. He'd seen a wisdom that went beyond what he could have expected. Worse, he'd seen her ability to forgive.

He'd seen the anger there too, could hear it in her voice. But her anger didn't rule her; rage at the loss of her parents had not made her bitter or changed her outlook on life. It had tempered her, forged her into a stronger, harder person, but still one with compassion.

Meeting those eyes, Marcus saw the one thing he never

expected. Meeting her eyes, Marcus realized with terror the one thing he didn't want awaited him. She would forgive him if he gave her the opportunity... even if it might destroy her to do it.

He'd held his tongue then. He didn't want to destroy the world of the woman who had crumbled his entire life. She made his petty arrogance and false righteousness insignificant just through her innate self-honesty and consideration. He feared to take that away from her just to end his own wretched life. And now, even if she hadn't yet admitted it, she had forgiven him.

Marcus knew he would never forgive her if she died on him now.

**

Mel drew closer to the site of Giles' death, feeling a stab of fear run through her. She didn't want to enter that corridor, but she had no choice. As she walked, she noticed her strides bouncing noticeably. "Gravity plates' capacitors are draining faster than you said."

It took a long moment for the ship to answer, long enough that she started to wonder if he had heard her. "That is odd," he said. "I'm detecting unusual power surges in this section of corridors."

"Is that a bad thing?" Mel asked. She stopped at the open door to the corridor.

"No. The surges are far too tiny to be dangerous. They are peculiar, I will dispatch a repair robot to check the circuitry as soon as the power situation is in hand."

"Okay. Any reason I shouldn't go down this corridor?" she asked hopefully.

"None."

"Okay." She stared at the dark opening. Slowly, she counted to ten. The corridor seemed like the others. She stepped inside, and immediately noticed that the gravity plates were no longer functioning. She pulled herself along the ceiling.

"Temperature seems low, here." She let out a breath and watched it fog.

"Yes, I am noticing that—" Fenris' voice cut off in a squeal of static.

"Fenris?" she asked. She waited for some response, yet she heard nothing.

There was no answer.

After several minutes of silence, she realized she probably wasn't going to receive one. Logically, the power surges Fenris mentioned had probably had some effect on the intercom. No doubt, Fenris would tell her to continue, if he could.

Logic held small comfort faced with the dark corridor.

She let out another steaming breath. "Okay... this is just a cold, dark corridor. Nothing to worry about."

Despite her words, her fingers clenched tight. She had to give herself another ten count to continue down the corridor. Several side passages went off it, their doors opened by the ship when it lifted the lock-down.

"Mel..." a voice whispered, at the edge of hearing.

She started, head jerking left and right. "Is someone there?"

"...yes..."

She jerked her pistol out. "Who's there?"

"...I understand..."

She peered ahead in the dark, gun raised. Shouted, "Who is there?!"

"It wasn't... your fault." The voice sounded louder.

She gulped, her hand clenching the pistol tighter. She couldn't speak. Slowly she pulled herself forwards, and froze when she saw the robotic wolf ahead of her.

It floated sinisterly in the microgravity of the corridor, catching the light oddly and casting dark shadows ahead. Her left hand clenched the nearest handhold. Her right held the pistol, aimed for the deepest shadows.

"It wasn't your fault," the whispering voice repeated. "I understand that." The voice sounded like it came from only a meter or less away. "You didn't mean to kill me."

Mel's hands trembled. She lost grip on the ceiling. She kicked out, spinning herself around. She had to get out.

Giles hung behind her.

Mel screamed. His blood-spattered suit hung only inches away, his gray eyes staring into her. She brought her pistol up and fired; blood exploded.

She spun away, thrown down the corridor by the pistol's recoil. Her leg slammed into the robot and she twisted in midair to grab at a handhold. She shoved herself off, headed away.

Until she gulped for breath, she hadn't realized that she'd been screaming the entire time, had lost all reason.

The end of the corridor was blocked. The door was closed.

Mel hammered at it with her hands. She shouted, she screamed. Finally, she forced her trembling hands to pull at the wires.

The door opened halfway before, with a screech, it stuck.

She shoved her head, then her shoulders through the gap. She squeezed down to her hips and then wiggled frantically, sobbing as she squirmed. Finally she got her hips and legs through, toppling to the floor on the far side where there was gravity.

She turned to the control panel and jerked the wires out. She looked through the half-opened doors. Down the corridor, just out of the light, she thought she saw something move.

"Come on!" she sobbed. Finally, the doors jerked closed.

She collapsed to her knees and shuddered. The dead gray face of Giles remained imprinted on her mind. How had he gotten behind her? Where had the voice come from?

"Fenris?" Mel asked.

"I am here, Mel," his gravelly voice comforted her.

"Did you see that?" she asked, her breath coming in sharp gasps. Her heart was pounding so hard she felt it would leap out of her chest.

Fenris spoke uncertainly, "That was... unusual."

"What happened?" Mel asked. *I must have imagined it,* she decided, *Fenris will tell me I saw a floating body and freaked out, that's all.*

"My sensors in the corridor went out. So did my intercom. The random power surges disabled them. I do not know what happened." The ship sounded... hesitant. "My ships sensors, however, briefly detected two people moving in the corridor. Then *they* went out."

Mel shuddered. She clenched her pistol and stared at the closed door. Fenris had seen two people in the corridor. "Did you dispose of Giles' corpse?"

"No. I have no knowledge of what that would involve."

She closed her eyes, and again, all she saw was the dead face, staring at her from just inches away. She opened them, afraid to blink, afraid to sleep, ever again. "Talk to me, Fenris."

"About what?"

"About anything!" she snapped.

"I am armed with two turrets containing Mark Thirteen disruptor cannons, four turrets containing four mass drivers, capable of firing kinetic and antimatter munitions, and ten projectile counter-fighter turrets. Additionally, I have room for six bomber and six fighter drones, and magazine storage for the nuclear warheads—"

"Uh," she interrupted, "Thanks."

"Want to hear more?"

Slowly she got to her feet. "What just happened?"

"I do not know." Fenris sounded irritated.

"Do you believe in ghosts, Fenris?" She pushed herself away from the wall and started down the corridor. She ached too much to move quickly, but she managed a brisk shuffle. It took a long while for the ship to answer.

"You think Giles' ghost caused the power surges?" Fenris's gruff voice didn't sound convinced.

"I'm not sure what I think," Mel said. She shivered again, thinking about the pale, bloodless face and the dead gray eyes. How had she passed his corpse? *How did it get behind me?*

"There's no evidence," Fenris's growled.

"Which is why I'm not sure," she replied, shuddering again. "Look, I don't know what I saw. Your sensors saw two people moving in there. Do you see anything now?"

"No. The power surges have burned out the local sensors. My ship sensors do not detect movement." His voice did not have its normal level of confidence.

"Okay." She closed her eyes and took a deep breath. "So you don't know what you saw. I don't know what I saw. Let's just leave it at that." Somehow, though, she knew that Giles' dead gray face would await her in her nightmares.

***

"You are approaching the area where the others wait," Fenris told her sometime later. She could hear a note of warning in his voice and almost… hesitation? As if he didn't want her to risk herself. *That's crazy,* she told herself, *he's a computer, a well programmed computer, but I doubt he cares, really cares, if I live or die, at least, beyond trying to protect humans in general...*

Mel paused and then stood somewhat straighter. Her back and shoulders protested, but she ignored the pain. "I've come a lot faster with your help, thank you Fenris."

"You're welcome," Fenris sounded surprised at her thanks.

She stared at the closed door ahead of her. Fenris had left this area of the ship locked down. Behind her lay safety… though her mind shied away from the thought of Giles's corridor. Ahead of her waited the terrorists… and her brother. "Wish me luck, Fenris," she said.

"Good luck, Mel." Fenris growled.

She snorted and shot a glance at the ceiling, "Thanks."

Then, sighing, she toggled open the door. The corridor ran ten meters ahead, to a heavy blast door. Beyond that door lay the engine room, she knew. She also knew, from Fenris, that the terrorists had moved to a side corridor just off this one.

She didn't blame them; the radiation levels in the engine room were unhealthy. The ship's designers hadn't bothered with radiation shielding beyond minimal containment on the main reactor. The heavy blast doors and armored bulkheads of the engine room protected the rest of the ship.

Her ship suit would protect her from it for a few hours, but she felt uncomfortable at the thought of going inside. Then again, she couldn't let the hijackers know she had the ship's help. So she couldn't just walk up to them; she'd told them to wait in the engine room, so she'd head there and hope they didn't leave her there too long to cool her heels.

She walked past the closed door to the side corridor without a glance. She didn't know if the terrorists had any remote sensors of their own; it wasn't something she'd thought to ask Fenris. The skin between her shoulder-blades started to itch.

She reached the engine room door and started to pull out wires, then frowned at the panel; someone had already wired it. She started to cross the wires when a voice spoke from behind.

"Don't move. Don't even breathe," came the cold voice of Colonel Frost "Where are the others?"

She swallowed, suddenly terrified. Here was the moment she'd dreaded. "They didn't trust me. They didn't believe my story."

"You came back alone?" Frost demanded.

"Yes." Mel answered. The area between her shoulder-blades itched furiously. She tried not to think of the guns pointed at her.

"Turn around, slowly," Frost said. "And don't touch those wires, they're rigged to explosives."

Mel's hands jerked back and she winced. Slowly, she turned around. The terrorists waited in the corridor behind her; apparently they did have remote sensors. She just hoped they didn't have any further back down the corridor.

"Take out your pistol and slide it over," Frost ordered. He stood behind two of his men, both of whom had their weapons aimed at Mel.

She complied, moving as slowly as she could. The pistol slid down the corridor and stopped just shy of the two men.

"Search her," Colonel Frost snapped. One of the men came forward. Mel slowly raised her hands.

The man frisked her quickly and thoroughly, though he smirked at her as he did it. She set her jaw and ignored the leer on his face.

"She's clean."

"Bring her here."

The terrorist dragged her down the corridor.

She looked into Frost's eyes. Earlier, she'd worried that she wouldn't come across as convincingly afraid. She needn't have. Something about his set jaw and cold, unfeeling blue eyes terrified her.

"You failed." He cocked his head. "What happened?"

"They—they didn't believe me," Mel stuttered. "They nearly shot me when I showed up."

"Why didn't they?" Frost asked.

"I don't know."

Colonel Frost frowned as one of his men passed him her pistol. He ejected the magazine, and she felt her heart stop as he stared at it. "You expended four rounds."

"I…" she gulped, "I had to enter the corridor with Giles's corpse. I got scared in the dark."

Frost looked up, catching her eyes. "Is that so?"

She shivered.

"Rawn."

Her brother stepped forward to the Colonel's side. "Sir?"

"Brief your sister on our current situation. Make sure she doesn't get in my way."

"Yes, sir."

"If she distracts you from your other assignment, let me know." Frost's tone lightened somewhat, "I can have someone else babysit her."

"Yes, sir."

Rawn stepped forward and grabbed her arm, "Come on."

He pulled her down the side corridor, growling: "I can't believe you tried that stupid plan! You're lucky they didn't shoot you. I told you those others couldn't be trusted."

Mel didn't answer. She cast a last nervous look back at the GFN leader.

When she looked forward again, she found that Rawn had stopped her next to a pile of supplies. Sitting next to the pile was the antimatter core.

She smiled grimly, "Sometimes you have to stick your neck out."

***

Michael Frost grimaced at the woman's back.

"Captain Roush."

His second in command hurried over. "Sir?"

"Go check on our men in the hangar. See how that project is coming along."

"Yes, sir." The other man started to turn away and then paused, "You believe the woman?"

Frost continued to stare at Mel's back until her brother led her into the side corridor. "For now."

He honestly wasn't certain if he believed her or not, but he didn't see any point to her coming back if she hadn't truly changed sides. *Given her family's losses, she and her brother have every reason to hate the Guard.* It didn't mean he trusted her; trust had to be earned. Her brother had earned Colonel Frost's trust, Melanie Armstrong had not.

"Sir, Giran was a friend of mine," Roush's voice held hatred, but Frost doubted that he really had been friends with Giran. The two had worked together before a number of times, and were both known for their particular interests. Sadism and torture were the only things the two men really held in common, as far as Frost knew, but that was enough he supposed for the two to have something of a bond. *A very twisted bond,* he thought, *but there's no accounting for taste.*

Frost tracked his cold eyes onto Roush's face. "She's Rawn's sister, Captain."

He could see right away that that was the wrong tack to take with his second. *Of course,* he thought, *Roush doesn't like being rebuffed and Rawn doesn't seem the type to be interested in men.*

"So?" Roush scowled, "I don't see why you like the kid so—"

"He does his job. He believes in the mission," Frost cut him off, "And he doesn't let his personal feelings get in the way." Michael Frost allowed himself a slight smile at the double message. *Which had probably gone right past him, of course,* he thought with a sigh. "Now go check on the men in the hangar."

Roush set his jaw, "Yes, *sir.*"

Colonel Frost shook his head as he watched his second in command stalk away. He understood how Roush had risen in the ranks; the man had a mean streak, a low cunning, and a total hatred of the Guard. Even so, he was little better than a thug. Plus, he could get insistent about sleeping with anyone he found attractive, which caused issues, not only with favoritism but also when he was scorned. Frost hadn't selected Roush as his second-in-command and he despised the man for his bluster and for the headaches he caused. Given a choice, Frost would have selected someone else, but the various alliances that made up his organization had insisted on Roush to watch their interests. *And if I kill him out of hand and they learn of it, I'll lose their support and I can't afford that.*

Roush was right about Giran, though. Someone had to pay for the agent's death. Had the woman's plan come through, Colonel Frost might have overlooked her part in that. As it was… well, he'd have to resolve it differently.

"Wallis."

His explosives expert moved up, "Yes, Colonel?"

The wizened little man stared at his boss with bland, uncaring eyes. Michael Frost had never seen Wallis smile. He'd lost his family to a Guard 'peacekeeping' operation when the Harlequin Sector Guard Fleet seized Ten Sisters.

Frost smiled slightly. Something about Wallis's total dedication warmed his heart. He nodded a head towards the engine room door, "Go ahead and disarm your trap." He turned as the small man moved to comply.

"Swaim."

"Here, Colonel." Another, younger, man moved forward, datapad in hand.

"What's the status of the sensors, still down?"

Jeremiah Swaim nodded his head, "I think, so sir."

"You think?" Colonel Frost's voice turned cold.

"I – I can't be totally sure, sir."

"Why not?"

"The AI closed me out not long after the sensors went down. I can get into some of the secondary systems, but it looks like sensors are still down. It hasn't reacted to anything else we've done so far…"

"You're guessing," Frost snapped. "You're making an assumption that could cost us our lives." The technician should have informed him as soon as he wasn't certain. They had been acting under the assumption that their activities were masked from the ship; if that'd been incorrect, the consequences would be deadly.

Sweat broke out on Swaim's forehead. "Sir, it's only talked to us on the intercom so far. I really don't think…"

"No. You *don't* think." Colonel Frost growled, suddenly furious. He grabbed Swaim by the collar and pulled him close. "Listen to me. You may be our only hacker, but that doesn't make you indispensable. You find out for certain. If you can't, you let me know. From now on, we act like the ship *can* see us. You should have told me as soon as you weren't sure any more. Now get to work." He pushed the hacker away.

He took a calming breath and turned away. Then his eyes snapped open, "Sergeant Nelson, tell the men to start watching what they say. We have to assume the computer is listening in."

"Yes, sir." The big, black NCO spun away.

Frost sighed, and rubbed his forehead in a vain attempt to make the headache stop. He had to disable the AI. He had to get life support back online. He had to eliminate the other group on the ship.

And someone has to pay for Giran's death, he thought grimly.

***

CHAPTER XI
Time: 0700 Zulu, 16 June 291 G.D.
Location: *Fenris*, Four days from Vagyr

"What are you doing?" Mel asked.

Rawn looked up from the datapad he'd been studying and to glare at her, clearly angry at the interruption. Finally he just sighed, "I'm tracing out electrical diagrams of the ship."

"Why?" Mel asked. She didn't really care, but now that she was here, she wasn't sure how to get the core away from the terrorists. She glanced at her watch; only three hours left.

Rawn rolled his eyes, "Because it's important."

Mel raised an eyebrow, suddenly pleased at returning some of the irritation her brother caused her. "Why?"

He gave her a dirty look and set the datapad down. "Look, the ship's controlled by an AI, right?"

"Yes?"

He scowled, clearly realizing her intent, but continued on doggedly, "Okay, so a computer needs power to function, right?"

"You're going to cut the power to the AI?" she asked, startled.

Rawn nodded, "Exactly. And since whatever your group did managed to shut down his internal sensors, he won't even see it coming."

"Wow, that's actually a great idea," she said, then bit the inside of her lip. It *was* a good idea. Unfortunately, Fenris could hear them now. She'd probably just blown the best plan to shut the computer down. "What would happen—"

"Without input from the computer, the automation systems would keep the ship running." Rawn picked up his datapad, scrolling through diagrams. "We'll still arrive in Vagyr, but we could control the ship from the auxiliary bridge. There's even a weapons control console there. We wouldn't be able to operate the ship as well as the AI, but we could use it to fight."

"Fight who?" she asked.

He snorted, "Guard Fleet, who else?"

"Yeah," she frowned. "Look, Rawn, I'm as *unhappy* as you that the Guard—" She stopped to clear her throat as she realized she couldn't finish that sentence. "…about our parents' murder. But are you sure—"

He set the datapad down again, "Mel, the UNC has total control of thousands of worlds. The Guard… they've got to be stopped.

They're squeezing the resources out of the protectorate worlds. The big families of the original seven colonies control the United Nations Security Council, and the UNSC controls the Guard."

"Still..."

"Mel, how long before they move on Century?" Rawn asked. "They seized Ten Sisters, Scarecrow, Warner and Choir. The Harlequin Sector Governor just gave a good-sized fleet of 'outdated' warships to *Drakkus*; those guys are a lot worse than Vagyr." He shook his head, "The Guard is too expansionist. They control almost everything and they want to control the rest."

Mel shook her head, unable to argue with his words. She understood, she even agreed with him, but... "I just don't think this is the right way."

Rawn snorted, "Mel, this is war. You always look for the right way, but this time there isn't one. You've already made your choice. You've picked your side. If you don't like what we're doing, that's just too 0bad."

Mel closed her eyes. She'd hoped she could have talked her brother around. She should have known he was too hard-headed for that. He was right about one thing, though: she'd picked her side. It wasn't the side of the terrorists. It wasn't the side of the Guard.

She just didn't really know what side that left.

***

Mel yelped with surprise when she looked up to see Colonel Frost, staring down at her with his cold eyes. "Yes?"

He didn't speak for a long moment. "What are their plans?"

Mel shrugged, "I don't know."

He didn't break his stare, "What kind of equipment do they have?"

Mel shrugged again. Her mind moved frantically. "I'm not sure. Bob Walker has that big pistol. The others have some weapons taken from your men. When I showed up, they had some explosives prepared."

"Will they try to sabotage the ship again?"

Mel forced herself to meet his cold blue eyes, "I don't know. They don't have anyone with engineering expertise. They don't have any powerful weapons."

Colonel Frost's eyes flitted to the antimatter core nearby, "Not any more, they don't." She saw a number of emotions flicker across his face, and his eyes locked on hers again. "They'll want the core again."

She felt her heart stop. "

"They might have followed you back here." Frost nodded sharply, "Sergeant Nelson? Send out a team to sweep back down the corridor."

Mel's heart started again. She barely suppressed a sigh of relief. "You think they'd attack?"

Frost's gaze returned to her. "I don't know. Something is wrong, I can feel it. You're telling me everything?"

She nodded, not trusting herself to speak. The terrorist leader turned away, "Rawn, get with Swaim. Apparently he's not certain the ship's sensors are still out. I need verification, one way or the other. And until then, no more discussion of our plans."

"Yes, sir," Rawn said. He jerked to his feet, clearly eager to follow his commander's orders. Mel watched the two of them move away, then looked over at the cylinder.

Time for her to get to work.

***

Frost pulled Rawn aside just out of earshot of the others. "When I received the initial intelligence for this operation, I heard something interesting."

"Yes?" Rawn asked.

"One of my agents heard a rumor about an expensive mercenary contract," Frost said. He ran a hand across the stubble on his jaw. "A special mercenary... a woman. Name of Lace."

Rawn frowned, "You think one of the others—"

"Maybe." Frost said. "But your sister killed Gerin. Not easy to do. She would have had to take him by total surprise."

"You think my *sister*..."

"Shut up and listen." Frost sighed. "This mercenary... She is an infiltrator, a ghost. She swaps places with women. Takes on their identity, personality, everything. She's an intrusion specialist, I haven't personally crossed paths with her, but she's infamous in certain circles."

"You think someone switched places with my sister?" Rawn shook his head. "That sounds..."

"Absurd. I know. But someone paid her a lot of money. The rumor was that it was connected somehow to this ship. That's why I nearly backed out of this operation," Frost admitted.

And I wish I had. This ship is too much of a pain and these rejects Guard Intelligence scraped up are far too tenacious, he thought darkly. This project had already consumed too much time and effort, but the potential of a warship like this under their control was still too good an opportunity to walk away from.

Rawn stood silent for a long moment. Finally he spoke: "What do you want me to do?"

"Just... keep an eye on her. If anyone would notice her acting out of character, you would," Frost said. "And probably, it's the *other* woman. Even so..."

"I understand, sir." The young man's voice was confident but also thoughtful.

"Good." Frost nodded in the direction of the hacker, Jeremiah Swaim. "Get to work."

***

Mel waited for her brother and the Colonel to reach the end of the corridor before she lifted a section of floor grating, moving as quickly as she could in the dim light cast by her helmet lamp. The terrorists had jammed the door at the opposite end; so far as they knew this corridor was a dead end now.

However, it ran directly over one of the main hydrogen fuel lines that fed the fusion reactors in the engine room. That piping ran down a crawlspace designed to allow access, the better to localize any leaks.

She leaned down, her fingers finding the edge of a hatch. Fenris must have been watching her, for the hatch opened at her touch. She smiled slightly.

She rose to a crouch. The bruises across her chest and back protested. Mel moved over to the cylinder and lifted it with a grunt of effort. She carried it to the service hatch. As she did so, Mel shot a nervous glance down the corridor.

One of the terrorists glanced her way, and she froze. He squinted briefly against the glare from her helmet lamp, and her heart seemed to stop. Could he see what she held? If he did, he'd raise the alarm.

After what seemed like an eternity, he looked away.

Mel lowered the cylinder as quickly as she dared, bending over with a grunt of pain. She felt the weight of the cylinder leave her. A pair of the spider repair bots grasped it, the two insectoid bots sweeping it out of sight.

An instant later, another pair appeared below her, bearing a similar cylinder. She frowned, though, as she noticed the lack of a keypad and display on the top. She bit her lip and hesitated, and then looked up again. None of the pirates glanced in her direction.

She grabbed the handle, swearing as she lifted the cylinder. Fenris had definitely guessed the weight wrong. Arms trembling, she barely lifted the cylinder with both hands. She finally levered it over the edge and dragged it, wincing at the noise. Finally, she got the heavy metal cylinder into position.

"...check the supplies," one of the pirates said.

She started and turned quickly. She saw two of the terrorists enter the corridor. She rushed over to stand in front of the opened section of floor grate. She kept her helmet lamp on their faces. Her left heel probed for the section of grate.

"What're you doing?" one of the men asked suspiciously.

"Just waiting. Not like I have much else to do," Mel replied sourly. She hoped they couldn't see her face. If they did, they'd have noticed her look of panic. Finally, her heel felt the loose grating panel and clumsily pushed back. There was a faint clank as it slid over the hole.

"Turn that light off! You're blinding us!" one of the men said.

Mel shut off her lamp, turning her face away from the oncoming men. She looked down at her feet, and her blood froze. The section of grating had gone in slightly cocked, obvious to anyone who took a moment to look at it.

But both terrorists brushed past her, close enough that she could smell their sweat and body odor but neither so much as looking her way. Instead, they moved directly to the stacked rucksacks.

"What'd he want again?" one of them muttered

"Uh, I think..."

She tuned the two men out, looking anxiously at the crooked grate. Neither of them looked to be in a hurry, but she had to be. Only an hour remained before Fenris' arbitrary time for the critical power levels. It had the power now, but activating the silent systems would give the terrorists far too many questions to ask.

She strode down the hallway and stopped at the intersection and after a moment, she made out her target. The silent shadow stood, arms crossed and feet set, facing the bulkhead. She took a deep breath, "Colonel Frost?"

His voice sounded angry, "What?" He didn't move at all.

She felt her face flush and her heart race. "I had an idea."

"So did I," Frost said cryptically.

"Uh..." Mel cleared her throat, "I was thinking about the

radiation shielding going down."

"Yes?" He seemed rather unconcerned about the idea of being cooked, but then again, he seemed inhumanly detached from what she had seen of him.

"Well, the ship has an auxiliary bridge and some living quarters – designed for an auxiliary crew, I think," Mel said. She felt a sudden relief at the shadowed corridor. The absence of light would hide her flushed face. "It might have better protection from the radiation. I could check it out."

"Talked to your brother?" Frost asked. She shivered at the icy threat in his voice.

"No, should I have?" she asked, honestly puzzled.

"You seem eager to leave us." Frost turned to face her, his blue eyes glinting in the darkness.

"I'm more worried about cooking to death like a rat in a microwave," she answered. "I'll take a chance on this working out."

"I studied the blueprints," Frost turned his head away. "And I know the history. They built the ship in the Preserve, and the auxiliary bridge let a crew to Triad. That's where the AI was built." He snorted slightly, "The bridge is right down the corridor from the mainframe. The ship wouldn't let us near it."

"Okay, do you have a better—"

"Yes, I do have a better idea." Frost snapped. "I've no intention of letting my men die." He raised his voice, "Captain Roush!"

"Yes, sir?" Another shadow moved closer. Frost's nosy second in command had lurked close enough to listen in, apparently; Mel felt her mouth go dry. *What if he'd watched me switch out the core?*

No, she knew that would be unlikely. They wouldn't have let her get away with it. They would have stopped her and she would already be dead.

"Captain Roush, detail a team to take our... guest and the remainder of our gear down to the hangar. We're getting near the time limit," Frost's voice was still detached.

"Yes, sir." The terrorist sounded happy at that. Mel frowned, what was in the hangar?

Roush turned away, "Smith, get up! Get your team to grab our spare gear and get it down to the hangar. Take the girl with you."

Mel listened to the unhappy grumbles in reply. They could not possibly be less happy than she was.

***

Mel followed the terrorist named Smith through several corridors, then down a narrow ladder. The others behind her grunted under their loads and murmured to each other, none of them speaking to her.

She preferred that; she didn't want to know them as people or to spend the mental energy on a conversation with them... she just wanted to escape.

The ship had two small hangar bays, she knew, which served to rearm its bomber and fighter drones. She frowned – were the terrorists planning to abandon ship?

She shivered at *that* thought. They'd emerge from Fenris' warp bubble far from any inhabited system. Even if they had unlimited supplies, they'd still die of old age before they could reach a safe haven.

She frowned as they rounded the corner and stepped into the port hangar bay. One of the Fenris' bomber drones sat in its launch cradle; cables and tubing ran into the drone, presumably feeding it power and cycling coolant through its reactor.

Her puzzlement increased when she noticed movement below the drone. She crouched and saw a group of men standing underneath. Everything above their knees disappeared into a space within the bomber.

Smith paused.

"Go on." He pointed.

Mel nodded in acknowledgment and slunk forward into the narrow confines; the hangar had no internal gravity. As she moved inside, she pulled herself along the skeleton of the launch cradle.

The size of the drone surprised her – it seemed to mass nearly half as much as her parents' freighter had. Then again, if she remembered right, it ran off of fusion reactors, which were far less efficient than antimatter.

Unlike the *Kip Thorne*, the drone's only cargo was its munitions. She wondered for a moment if the terrorists hoped to rig up some kind of a weapon, but the ship had probably expended most of its ordnance in its initial combat.

She finally reached the circle of working men and rose to stand, bracing herself by putting her feet through a couple of the magnetic footholds the work crew had placed around the area. They were in what had to be the drone's bomb bay; below them were doors that must open into the hangar's bomb magazine.

The men didn't look up from their work; clearly it was something they considered important. One of them had just finished connecting a datapad to a tangle of wiring that had been pulled through a newly-cut hole in the bomb bay, leading toward the forward part of the drone. Another was rapidly entering commands on his own datapad. The third man worked on a separate tangle of wiring.

She could easily guess they'd set up connections to the bomber. Why they wanted control of it, she couldn't guess; the drone contained only a standard warp envelope, not a full warp drive capable of faster than light travel.

"How much longer?" Smith asked.

"Already done. We did a test a few minutes ago, it should work," replied a stocky, dark-haired man without looking up from his work.

"Okay," Smith grunted, "I'll tell the Colonel."

"What are they doing?" Mel asked.

Smith ignored her, bending down to shout: "Kerel, drop that there and go let the Colonel know we're ready down here."

When he stood again, he stared warily at Mel. "Stay here."

"I wasn't planning on going anywhere." Mel kept her voice as pleasant as possible. Smith just grunted. He did a vertical spin and then pulled himself away, headed back the way he'd come.

Mel moved closer to the three working men, peering over the shoulder of the one with the datapad. He was running some kind of diagnostic of the bomber's power system and defense screen, and she shook her head. *Of course; how could I be so slow?*

The terrorists planned to reconfigure the bomber's warp envelope emitters to act as a radiation screen. As long as they waited inside the field, they'd be protected from the radiation. That wouldn't help anyone *outside* the field, but she doubted they cared much about her companions.

She spun herself over to look past the working men. If she remembered correctly, a separate access way led out of the hangar on the far end. If she could reach it, and if she could open it...

There was a grunt behind her; she turned slowly and saw the first of Smith's group pushing a bulky ruck into the space. So much for her chance to run.

The other terrorists piled in behind the first, corralling the gear into a tight space in the corner of the bomb bay. One of those items was the false antimatter core. Worse, they were tying it down – next to another snarl of gear – with the side lacking the control pad plainly visible. It looked like they planned to wait the ship out.

She closed her eyes and took some deep breaths. Panic would

not help; she had to focus on escape. She needed to get out of here, and soon.

***

She was still waiting for another chance to escape when Colonel Frost and the rest of his men arrived. No explanation was necessary; there was only minutes before Fenris' time limit ended. The entire group of terrorists fit comfortably within the bomb bay; they'd closed one of the two bay doors and most of the terrorists reclined in that half. Mel floated uncertainly on the side nearest the door; she'd need only seconds to reach it.

She closed her eyes and visualized the movements she'd need to open it. *Fenris can probably open it for me*, she thought as she chewed on her lip. She needed time, she needed a distraction... she needed *something*.

"Attention, attention," Fenris announced. "I have found a way to increase available power. Shipboard lighting, environmental and gravity will be restored in thirty seconds."

She felt her jaw drop. Had Fenris just sold her out?

The lights in the hangar came on, but the bay remained in shadow. No internal gravity. She looked around at the surprised terrorists – were they suspicious of her? But there were no angry accusations, just confusion.

As the terrorists began to babble, she slowly let out a sigh of relief.

"All right, shut up," Colonel Frost snapped. "Ship's restored power somehow. Captain Roush, have a team reestablish a perimeter."

"Yes, sir."

Frost looked around the small refuge for a moment. Finally he pointed at Mel, "You, come here."

Her heart started to race again as she pushed herself off from the wall.

She caught herself on a handhold next to the colonel. She couldn't force herself to look at him. Instead, she looked down at her wrist, wiggling it back and forth and doubting her ability to fool anyone.

"Looks like we'll have time to test your theory, after all," he said dryly.

"Excuse me?" she asked.

"I want you to see if you can reach the auxiliary bridge," he said. "I don't know how much longer our window will be with this thing having no internal sensors. We'll need to act soon, especially since your former companions will be trying to stop us."

She nodded, too surprised to speak.

"Here," Frost passed her back the pistol he'd taken earlier. "Don't provoke the ship, but try to get me some information."

"Why the sudden trust?" she asked.

Frost snorted, "Not trust. You'll be out of my hair and your brother can focus on his job instead of worrying I'll kill you out of hand."

"Would you?" Mel asked.

Colonel Frost grabbed her by the front of her ship's suit and pulled her close. His breath smelled foul, and his face was ugly this close up. She shivered in fear as the terrorist smiled coldly, "If I thought you were a threat to my men or my mission, I'd kill you in a heartbeat."

He pushed her away. "Now get going."

She kept her face averted and just gave a brisk nod. Then she pulled herself towards the open bay door.

***

Michael Frost watched the woman push off and held down his anger. Something about her struck him as wrong. Something about her warned him. He didn't know what; perhaps just the possibility that if he handled her wrong, her brother would betray him.

"You're sending her back out, sir?" Captain Roush asked.

Frost glanced at Roush out of the corner of his eye. There seemed more than casual interest in the other man's voice. "Yes. I am, now that we don't have to worry about radiation."

"Huh. Pretty lucky that," Roush said. He scratched behind his ear. "I still don't understand how it got extra power so quick."

Frost shrugged, "I planned on using our antimatter core from the *John Kelly* as a bargaining chip, but—" He froze, his mouth open as he glanced at the cylinder, then looked over at Rawn's sister, who had just pulled herself out of the bomb bay and into the hangar.

"Stop her! Stop her *now!*" he shouted, pushing himself off – not at the woman, but toward the cylinder. He only needed one look at it to notice the obvious flaws. *Obvious to anyone who paid it attention,* anyway.

He turned to see that two of his men had grabbed the woman by her legs and pulled her back into the bay. One glance at the panicked look on her face was enough to prove her guilt.

Colonel Frost drew his pistol. "Bring her here."

***

CHAPTER XII
Time: 1100 Zulu, 16 June 291 G.D.
Location: *Fenris*, Seventy two hours from Vagyr

Mel found herself breathing faster and faster as the two men pulled her toward the terrorist leader. Air burned through her lungs and things began to glow black at the edge of her vision. She fought against the restraining arms, but the two big men held tight. Frost drew his pistol and chambered a round.

Too late, she remembered the pistol he'd given her. She should have fought; at least then she could have taken some of them with her.

A gravelly voice blasted the hangar, the volume deafening: "Colonel Frost, if you kill Melanie Armstrong, I will vent the hangar to space."

Frost paused, arm in the midst of raising his pistol. "Are you talking to me?"

"I am," Fenris said.

"You're bluffing," Frost shook his head and brought the pistol up. Mel stared down the dark tunnel of the barrel, watched his finger tighten on the trigger.

An alarm klaxon sounded.

"He's not!" Rawn shouted. Mel's eyes darted to him. Two men kept her brother restrained; one of them was Captain Roush. "That's an emergency vent alarm! The ship's already disengaged the safeties if that alarm sounded!"

The muscles of Frost's jaw stood out sharply as he ground his teeth. "You're watching us, ship?" He lowered the pistol.

"Yes."

"So you can forward a message to her people?"

"Yes."

Frost pushed off from the wall, and drifted to hover only a meter away from Mel. He braced himself and raised the pistol again, grinding it into Mel's forehead. "Tell them this, computer. They have exactly twenty-four hours to come here and surrender. After that, I'll kill her."

"If she dies, so do you," Fenris said.

Frost's lip curled, "We'll see."

He nodded at Roush and Rawn, "Put your sister in the magazine chamber below us." He didn't watch as Roush slowly let go of Rawn's arms.

As Rawn passed, Frost caught his arm, "Your sister has gone

over the line, this time."

Rawn looked at Mel. The anger she saw in him made her wince. "I agree," Rawn answered. Her brother's jaw clenched and she saw his jaw muscles stand out as he stared at her.

"Captain Roush, make sure she doesn't escape."

"Yes, sir."

Frost slowly holstered his pistol. As his goons dragged her away, Mel saw him stroke the butt of it, as if anxious for the chance to draw it again.

***

Frost waited until Rawn and his wayward sister were out of sight. Then he grabbed Roush by the collar. "You are responsible for this."

"Sir?" Roush asked, eyes wide in surprise.

"I told you before to keep an eye on that antimatter core. Why didn't we have a guard on it?" Frost felt irritation and frustration eat at his insides. and revised Aaron Roush's intelligence downwards yet again.

He didn't miss the look of panic that went across Roush's face, "Sir... we've lost so many people, I didn't want to take a man from a team—"

Colonel Michael Frost's face twisted in anger, "Then you should have stood over it yourself!" He let out an angry breath and shoved Roush away. "You will guard her. Not one of the men... you. She's your responsibility."

"Sir... I've been up for the past twenty hours..."

"Swaim's finished his coding. Rawn can do the rest. I want you to watch him too." Frost shot an angry glance at the blond programmer. "Rawn thinks the kid has been shamming."

Which only made sense, Frost knew. Swaim wasn't a volunteer for the cause and he had to know they didn't really need him once he finished his work.

"Sir..."

"No excuses," Frost snapped. He let out a slow calming breath. He closed his eyes. When he opened them, his face was calm, "In twenty-four hours, either I'll be executing her, her friends, or you. I don't care which."

Captain Roush seemed to sag into himself, "Understood, sir."

The deflation of his almost insubordinate second-in-command showed that Frost had finally broken the man's arrogant bluster. At least he had managed one thing, so far. He smiled cheerfully: "Good. I'm glad we finally understand each other."

***

The bomb magazine was a metal cube, filled with empty bomb racks. A skeletal munition elevator system hung just under the doors. The only other features were the empty munition cradles.

The two men had tied her to one of the racks. One of them rubbed his chin while staring at her. He had a hungry expression and she felt her stomach twist. She doubted her last day would be a good one.

"Conrad, Cruz, I've got this. Colonel Frost wants you two to get some sleep."

She looked up to see Frost's second in command climb down the elevator frame. A younger, blond man followed him down.

"Awww..." one of the guards snarled, "Why's the officers always get to work over the prisoners?"

Captain Roush smiled as he stepped over and backhanded the man. "Shut your mouth, Conrad."

"Sir?" The other man asked, looking between his friend and the suddenly furious officer.

"Her *brother* is ten meters away. you idiots," Roush spat, his face flushed with anger, "How do you think he'd handle you two idiots hurting his sister?"

The man on the floor pushed himself up, feeling at a split lip. "He's just a kid, we could handle him. Besides, Colonel's going to plug her anyway. Who'd know?"

"I would. He would too when he hears her screaming," Roush snarled. "And he might look like a kid, but he's killed a few men. Colonel Frost actually likes him, Conrad. And he doesn't like people who haven't proven themselves."

"Oh." The first man stood, still dabbing at his bloody lip. He scowled at Roush. "You better watch yourself. You might be a captain—"

Roush grabbed the other man and slammed him back against the rack. "Accidents happen to everyone, Conrad. Not just officers. I was an NCO in the Guard Army for six years. Don't think I don't know how to make a few *accidents* happen. Understood?"

Mel watched the two angry men. Her gaze flitted between them and the other man, Cruz. She half hoped they'd fight and kill each other; all three looked angry enough to do so. She held back a groan of disappointment as the GFN captain set Conrad back on his feet.

Apparently, she'd hoped for too much in her desire for the terrorists to kill each other.

"Now, go on, get some rest. Think about accidents. Have some sweet nightmares of me in your sleep," Roush said. The two guards moved away, and their nominal leader watched them both until they climbed out of the chamber.

He nodded at the smaller blond man who stood near the entrance, "Go ahead and set our gear over there," he pointed at a nearby spot.

She started, her eyes flickering back and forth from the two men. Captain Roush was a big man. If he was planning to disregard his own orders...

He must have caught some of the fear on her face, because he smiled slightly at her: "I've been directed to make sure you're here for your appointment tomorrow. Either that... or take your place."

"Oh, lucky me," she swallowed, her throat felt suddenly dry.

"You are," Roush snorted. "Swaim over there is more my type."

"Uh..."

Roush smiled broadly at her obvious discomfort, "Oh that's right, you're one of them religious prudes from Century. Your brother didn't like it too much when I hit on him, either."

Mel couldn't hold back a snort of amusement at that: "I'll bet."

"See? We can be pleasant here," Roush said. Then he sat down cross-legged, his dark eyes roving across her body, "Comfortable?"

"I'd be more comfortable if I wasn't tied up," Mel said hopefully.

"I'd be more comfortable if I wasn't stuck here with an ultimatum over my head," Roush responded. "Nothing personal, but better you than me, eh?"

He glanced over his shoulder, "I got first watch, Swaim. Get some sleep."

The blond kid nodded. He looked even younger now that Mel had a chance to look him over. Mel nodded in his direction, "I heard Frost yelling at you over the core. Why's he down here?"

Roush cocked his head, eyes narrowed. "Lots of questions, huh?"

Mel shrugged, "I just... need something to distract me."

"Well then, think about this. You'd better hope your friends really like you," Roush grunted. He glanced over at the other man and then back at Mel. "And yeah, I'm in trouble over you. He's in trouble because the Colonel doesn't trust him, and your brother may have just nailed his coffin shut. So… how about you shut up?"

She sighed and leaned back. The metal rack they'd tied her to poked painfully into her shoulders. Even so, it felt good to lean back and close her eyes. She tried to remember the last time she'd slept. She couldn't say for sure she *had* slept. She fought her eyes open after a long blink to notice Roush still staring at her, a calculating look on his face. "Something to say?"

He smirked, "Not yet. Get some sleep."

She leaned back again. It felt odd, but she was actually relieved to be incarcerated like this. She'd done so much, it was time for someone else to take charge. She closed her eyes, just for a second, not wanting to sleep. *I'll just rest my eyes,* she thought absently.

She didn't hear Aaron Roush snort a little as a snore escaped her open lips.

***

A sudden impact woke her up.

Her head jerked up and she hit it against the rack they'd tied her to. Her shoulders stabbed pain at her and her arms tingled as blood flow returned.

She looked up to see Colonel Frost. He stood above her, one hand resting on the butt of his pistol in its holster. His face had a considering look, one that made her feel cold. She looked around frantically; how long had she slept?

He smiled slightly. "No, it's not time yet."

She gulped. Her throat felt drier than the deserts back home. "Oh... good."

"I was surprised. I actually got a response from them. One of them, the one called Marcus, said they're coming," Frost told her.

"No!" Mel shouted.

Frost's eyes narrowed. "Any leniency you might have expected just died."

She looked away, furious with herself. *He might have believed that they forced me to do it, but I just ruined any chance at lying to him about that.*

"I must say, though, I respect your dedication, misguided as it's been," Frost grunted. He leaned against the rack across from her, arms crossed. "I honestly wish I'd recruited you when I did your brother."

"Oh, great, then we'd be one happy terrorist family. My parents would be *so* proud," Mel said. Her lip twisted in disgust.

Frost surprised her by laughter, "What spirit! Really a shame about you. You're resourceful, intelligent, and you don't give up." He shook his head, "I just don't understand why you support the Guard."

She rolled her eyes, "Why does it have to be one side or the other?" She ground her teeth. "You people blow up civilians and the Guard conquers worlds. I don't like either of you, is that good enough? I'm just trying to stop *this* ship from wiping out a bunch of innocent people!"

Frost shook his head, "No one is innocent. People are ignorant and people are naïve. They aren't innocent."

Serves me right for trying to argue with a terrorist scumbag, she thought darkly.

Frost cast a glance over his shoulder then settled to the deck. He pulled his legs in and folded his arms over his knees. Like Roush had, he studied her for a moment in silence. Whereas Roush had watched her thoughtfully, Frost dissected her with his eyes. Slowly a grin spread across his face. "I really think you *believe* the things you've said."

"What? Of course I believe what I've been saying! You're the terrorist who lies and murders people!" She rolled her eyes; it was unbelievable that the last day of her life would be filled with the men who were going to kill her, trying to understand her.

Frost shook his head, "I never lie. I take that back, sometimes I lie, but only for a good reason. Everyone lies to themselves. I don't have to."

"Oh yeah?" Mel grimaced, "Then why are you hijacking this ship?"

Frost shrugged, "Power. Revenge. Freedom."

"Oh, what a good idea, let me help you!" Mel growled.

Frost's face went suddenly cold. "This isn't a trivial matter. This goes far beyond the murder of your parents, little girl. We've all lost things in life. Welcome to life, people take things from us every day."

"What did you lose?" Mel said angrily.

Frost didn't answer for a long moment. When he finally chose to speak, his voice distant. "I was a captain in the Guard Marine Corps. I lost my wife."

Mel looked away from the pain in his face. "I'm sorry."

He shook his head, "Don't be. I'm about to take your life. Your hatred for me, and your brother's anger is completely rational."

"Then why did you even come here?" Mel snapped.

Frost shrugged, "I wanted to understand you. And I realize now that I underestimated you all along."

"What?" Mel asked.

The terrorist met her eyes, "At first, from what your brother said, I thought you were some ignorant, bubble-headed idiot." He smiled at her grimace. "Then, after I heard what happened to Giran, I started to suspect a mercenary had switched places with you. There's a female merc, goes by the name of Lace, who swaps out with women, takes their places as an infiltrator and then accomplishes her missions. Your actions since this started have seemed just enough out of character I thought you were her."

"You think Rawn wouldn't notice the difference?"

"Rawn has been distracted." Frost shrugged. He cast a glance over his shoulder at the open doors in the ceiling. "He never felt good about going behind your back. He felt worse about crashing your parents' ship. Then with having to fool a Guard Intelligence Agent face to face *and* conceal his actions from the rest of your companions... well, he's been busy."

"What makes you think I'm not this super-secret agent?" Mel rolled her eyes again. She shrugged her shoulders against the bomb rack.

"You're poor at lying."

"Gee, thanks," she grunted

"That's a compliment, really. Anyone can pretend to be honest. Being a rotten liar means you *are* honest." Frost smiled again, "I've met only a few people as bad at lying as you are."

"I'm an honest fool?"

"Essentially, yes," Colonel Frost said. "But that's part of why I underestimated you. You see, I'd never guessed you were an idealist."

"An idealist is an underestimation of a super-spy who switches places with people?" Mel shook her head, totally bewildered.

"I'm an idealist too, Mel," Frost said softly. "But you, you're special. I can see why Rawn respects you so much. I can see how you caused a Guard Intelligence Agent to fall from grace. You've got so much potential it's amazing." He shook his head. "It makes sense, I suppose, given your family history. Your grandparents were war heroes back on your little colony world. You're a rebel without a cause. I wish you'd realized the importance of my mission."

"Why is that?" she asked. She didn't know what she found more surprising: that Rawn apparently respected her or that this terrorist was impressed by her.

Frost sighed, looking a little disappointed: "Because I'm going to have to kill you before you reach your potential. You're too dangerous otherwise."

***

Mel sipped at the water nervously. After Frost's disturbing conversation, he'd left and Roush had returned. The other man had untied her, allowing her to walk around and restore some blood flow to her limbs. He'd even given her his canteen.

His generosity made her nervous.

Roush continued to watch her as she paced. He didn't *look* hostile, just watchful. Even so, she knew there was no way he'd let her escape. He'd evidently remained awake, and the shadows under his eyes suggested that wasn't a trivial effort.

"Captain Roush, can I get a few minutes with my sister?" Rawn asked.

Mel started. She turned, surprised to see him come down from the ceiling doors.

Roush looked between them. He sighed slightly. Then he shouted, "Swaim!"

"Huh?" a muffled voice answered.

Roush grimaced: "I'm getting some sleep. Wake up. Stand by the exit. Give Rawn some privacy with his sister."

"What?"

"Just go stand by the ladder and don't let the woman leave," Roush growled.

"Oh, sure." The blond man stood, looked nervously at Rawn and then sidestepped to stand near the elevator. He didn't seem to know which way to look, settling eventually on an empty patch of ceiling.

Rawn gave Swaim a sour glance then walked over to stand in front of Mel. "So," he said, "why'd you have to go and mess things up?"

"Why did *I* have to go and screw things up?" she asked, clenching her hands into fists and reminding herself how it had been *years* since the last time she'd beaten up her little brother. *That doesn't mean I couldn't do it again,* she thought angrily.

"Yeah," Rawn said sullenly. "All you had to do was stay prisoner on that ship—"

"The ship was destroyed by Fenris." Mel said, feeling cold as her anger evaporated and was replaced by fear. She closed her eyes and shuddered slightly, seeing Giles floating in the dark with his bloated gray face hanging just inches away.

If she'd stayed a prisoner, she would be just as dead as the man she had killed. A glance at her suit's chrono confirmed that her execution would be in another nine hours.

"Well, you had your chance when we captured you. You screwed that one up too." Rawn frowned, "How could you side with *Marcus*? He killed Mom and Dad!"

"Yes," Mel said. She felt her anger return, and welcomed it. "And how many people have you killed?"

Rawn looked away. He didn't speak but his silence was answer enough. She nodded slightly: "Whose parents, whose brothers, whose sisters?"

His jaw clenched, "I'm trying to make the world a better place. When have you ever made a stand?"

She shook her head, "When have I made a stand?" She threw the canteen against the wall. "Dammit Rawn! I gave away my *life* to come back and care for you and that stupid ship! I passed on a life of privilege and success for a life of living on the edge! I came back for you, that is the stand I made! Now I learn that the ship, your life, all of it didn't mean squat to you!"

Rawn stared at her.

"I was happy in Guard Fleet," she went on. "I had friends who are probably on those ships you want to destroy. They aren't the fanatics. You and Frost are talking about noble causes and an evil empire. Neither of you realize you're dealing with normal people. You don't try to make the universe better by tearing things down, Rawn!"

She turned away and started at the floor, too angry to even look at him, wondering if she'd gotten anything through his thick head. From his mulish silence, he had gone on the defensive. She knew better than to try and break through to him now.

"Think what you want, Rawn. Don't start arguing morality with me."

She looked over at Jeremiah Swaim, who looked like he wanted to disappear. "Hey, you, I think I need to be tied up again."

The blond kid flushed: "Okay."

"There's no need for you to be tied up," Rawn said angrily.

"Yes, Rawn, there *is*," Mel snapped back. "First of all, your boss is going to have me killed in... eight hours and forty-seven minutes." She felt some dour satisfaction at the scowl on his face. If she had to die, maybe it would turn her brother away from his own bullheaded stupidity. "Second, if we keep arguing, I'm going start punching you. Then your 'friends' will probably think it's an escape attempt and they'll shoot me dead before my appointed execution."

"You're impossible." Rawn covered his eyes with his hands. "I'll come back when I can talk sense into you." He turned away.

"Don't wait too long. Only eight hours and forty… six minutes to go, remember?" Mel told sweetly. He paused like he wanted to say something. He seemed to think better of it and climbed out without another word.

She looked over at Swaim, "Well?"

He flushed and looked away, "I'm just a programmer. Don't involve me in this." Mel thought it would have been cute… under other circumstances.

"Well, you better tie me up before sleeping beauty over there," Roush punctuated her statement with a loud snore, "wakes up."

"Uh, okay."

She watched his fumbling attempts at tying the knots with amusement. Finally, he got the bindings in place and Mel had to choke back a smile, "Your first time tying a woman up?"

His face went bright red, "I, uh…"

Mel just shook her head. "Why are you here? Guard Marines killed your puppy?"

He scowled, "I just answered a job posting."

"GFN puts out job postings?" Mel stared at him like he was stupid.

He shook his head. "No, I answered an anonymous job posting for a computer programmer willing to do a job, no questions asked." He shrugged sheepishly, "Thought it was a credit fraud or *maybe* a bank job."

"Learn your lesson?" Mel asked. She studied the young man. He looked to be in his late teens, but he had to have at least a few years schooling to be a computer programmer. His unkempt blond hair was as pale as her own was dirty.

Now if I were some storybook heroine, I'd seduce him and he'd cut me free and help me escape, she thought. Then again, with how things had gone so far, he'd probably turn out to be romantically interested in Frost or Roush.

Swaim nodded, looking away again, embarrassed.

"Good. Now I'm going to sleep again," She leaned her head back and closed her eyes. Sleep wouldn't come, she knew. Too many thoughts, too many words she wished she'd used on her brother. Too many harebrained ideas percolated through her head.

None of them changed anything. She glanced at her chrono. In eight hours and thirty-three minutes she would die.

***

Michael Frost fingered the small golden cross. He could barely feel the bulge of it under his body armor. It seemed to have an inordinate weight for its size.

"Colonel?"

Frost turned quickly, and found Rawn Armstrong behind him. "Yes?" He tucked the cross away back inside his shirt.

"I wanted to talk to you about my sister," the younger man began.

Frost looked him over. He noted the flushed cheeks. "Angry at my announcement?"

"Colonel, I understand you're angry. But she's my *sister*, she's the only family I've got left." Rawn's jaw muscles stood out as he ground his teeth. Frost guessed the kid hated to beg for anything.

"Rawn," Frost sighed. "Your sister went too far this time. She picked her side. You picked yours." It pained him to see a dedicated young man like Rawn in such a state. It also pained him that he would probably have to kill Rawn when he inevitably decided this had been a mistake after Frost killed his sister.

"She doesn't know what she's doing!" Rawn protested. "If I could have a week with her, I think I could make her understand what's at stake!"

"If I had a week, I'd give it to you," Frost rubbed at his chest absently as he felt for the small golden cross under his armor. "Trust me, Rawn, I know how you feel. I lost someone to this fight too."

"This is my sister, though!" Rawn almost shouted.

Frost's face went still. "I lost my wife to this war. I've lost nine men today. I've lost dozens in this war. I know *all* about loss, boy." Rawn flushed and looked away. Frost nodded, "Now, tell me about Marcus. Do you think he'll turn himself in?"

Rawn shrugged, "I don't know. He's a coward in a lot of ways. But... yeah, for Mel, I think he would." Rawn scowled, "He loves her."

"You don't approve?" Frost chuckled at the expression on Rawn's face. "Let me guess, you don't think he's good enough?"

"No, he's not. He might feel guilt over what he's done. He might try to repent. He's still not good enough to even look at her, much less love her." Rawn let out an angry breath, "If he does turn himself in, I want to kill him."

Frost shrugged, "We'll see. Do you think the others will turn themselves in?" He planned to kill them all. At this point, they'd proven too dangerous to risk leaving alive, Melanie Armstrong included. But he wasn't about to tell Rawn that.

"I don't know." Rawn answered. "The female hacker struck me as a push-over. Brian... I don't know about him."

"And then there's Robert," Colonel Frost grimaced. "I always thought he was too cheerfully corruptible." He'd been recruited as crew for the ship, a spare set of hands, and he'd seemed eager to sign on for the potential of loot and piracy.

Looking back, he could see how that must have been a ruse. Yet the man hadn't had any compunctions over killing Guard members. Yes, he had protested a bit at some of their pirate associates' actions, but he hadn't flinched when they'd executed the Guard Intelligence operative that Captain Roush had identified. Who did the man work for, then, if not the enemy?

"If they turn themselves in, you won't hurt her?" Rawn asked.

"If that happens, there won't be a need," Colonel Frost said levelly. He hoped that Rawn didn't realize that he hadn't *really* answered the question and raised a hand to forestall him.

"You came to me, remember? You said you'd follow my commands, no matter the cost. Don't lose your dedication now, Rawn. Trust me." *It would be a shame if I had to kill you as well,* he thought.

***

"Mel?"

She sighed and opened her eyes. She had heard her brother come down. She had heard Swaim's breathing turn regular as he fell asleep, and Roush's loud snoring. She had given up hope she could let those things lull her to sleep somehow.

Evidently, Rawn wanted to continue their conversation. "Yes, Rawn?"

"Look... I know where you're coming from. I just wish... you know, I wish you'd never gotten involved." Rawn looked sad.

Mel didn't have the heart to voice an answer. She closed her eyes and blinked away tears. She would *not* cry in front of her little brother.

"Yeah, well..." Rawn trailed off. He looked miserable.

Mel blinked in surprise at the giant metal spider she saw crawling across the ceiling. As she watched, its two forward limbs unrolled a sheet of paper above her. Scrawled across it was: *We're coming. We'll attack in thirty minutes.*

Something on her face gave her away, and Rawn turned and saw the repair robot and the paper. The robot scurried away, and Rawn turned for the exit.

"Wait," Mel croaked. "They're trying to *save* me."

"They're coming to kill my companions," Rawn snapped. He hurried to the elevator. "If I warn them, we can trap them, and I can kill Marcus."

"Rawn, if you do this, you sentence me to death," she bit the words out.

Her brother froze, one foot raised to start climbing. He looked over at her, torn. "Look, Rawn, this could work. This could get me out. No one needs to get hurt, even," she whispered, praying that Swaim wouldn't hear her.

He shook his head. "This... Mel, I'll try to help you with Colonel Frost... but not *this*."

She looked away. "I understand."

Her brother said nothing else as he climbed out. She could hear his voice echoing across the hangar as he warned the other terrorists. *My brother made his choice,* she thought.

Mel sighed, "Swaim, wake up."

The programmer just mumbled something. Mel drew back her leg and kicked hard.

"Ow!" The boy started, hopping to his feet and rubbing at his thigh. "Why'd you do that?"

She gave him a level look, "You fell asleep."

"Oh." Swaim looked around quickly, "Anyone notice?"

She didn't answer. Above, she heard the sounds of men moving, Colonel Frost barking out commands, and she ground her teeth.

Her brother had chosen his path, and she wondered how he could be so stupid. She wished she knew what words she could say to make him understand. Wished she wasn't tied to a metal bomb rack facing an execution. Wished that Marcus hadn't killed her parents. Wished she'd never met Giles, much less killed him.

And right now, she *really* wished her hands were free so she could wipe away her tears.

***

Her stomach twisted in worry as her ears strained to hear any gunfire. She waited, panting slightly, for any sign that her friends had come. Part of her hoped they wouldn't, that they'd realized their plan wouldn't work and given up on her.

The rest of her hoped they would come anyway. She didn't know what five could do against Frost, Rawn, and the other fifteen terrorists, but... it was possible. She wanted to think there was *some* hope that they might succeed and she could live.

"What's going on up there, anyway?" Swaim asked, looking up at the doors in the ceiling.

She wondered at his confusion; if he still didn't realize just how violent his employers were, he had to have come from a very protected background.

Then again, they probably picked him for that reason, she thought, *he would be easier for them to kill when he outlived his usefulness.*

"They're getting ready to fight my friends," Mel told him. She managed to wipe her cheeks against her shoulders. It didn't wipe away the shame of her loss of self-control, but it helped give her back some composure.

"Oh." Swaim said. "Who's going to win?"

She cocked her head and gave him a level look, "You should probably wake sleeping beauty up." She was half tempted to make some plea to the young man, but she didn't think he would be a net benefit to her escape.

"Oh, okay." Swaim turned away and went to wake up Roush.

Mel just shook her head. She couldn't believe the ignorance of the kid. Even so, something in her wanted to mother the little idiot.

She focused on the sounds of Frost's voice, since she couldn't quite make out his words. How much did the terrorists know about *Fenris*'s sensors and capabilities? Would the ship use its robots to help her friends attack? Those things could cut right through steel walls.

Surely, with the sensors and the ship's help, her friends could take down the terrorists?

***

CHAPTER XIII
Time: 1100 Zulu, 16 June 291 G.D.
Location: *Fenris*, fifty hours from Vagyr

"It's certain her brother saw it?" Bob asked.

"He did," Fenris growled.

"This isn't what we had planned," Stasia's accent was thick. "I thought there was just one guard with her?"

"No plan survives contact with the enemy," Brian gave a insouciant shrug. "We should have planned for the chance of this." He looked over at Marcus: "You know him best. Would he tell Frost with his sister's life on the line?"

Marcus chewed on his lip. "I'm not sure." He couldn't keep the slight tremble out of his voice, and his head throbbed in pain. His entire body ached, in fact, and he hoped the others thought his clenched fists were from anger. He didn't want them to realize he could barely stop the shakes.

Then they might force him to stay behind.

"We're wagering our lives on this. We need a definite answer," Bob Walker snapped. "When it comes down to it, this whole exercise is too risky."

"This is Mel," Marcus insisted. "We've got to do something."

Bob nodded slightly, "I agree, which is why we're doing this. Even so, there's a lot at stake here, a lot more than one life."

"I don't care," Marcus's voice was hoarse. "If you won't help me, I'll go by myself."

"Look, Marcus, you can't forget there's an entire world at stake," Brian smiled. His voice was calm and relaxed. "Our number one priority has to be that. I'm not even human and I feel that way. If it comes down to her life or millions, we have to choose to save the millions."

Marcus grimaced, "Nobody's innocent. Especially no-one on Vagyr. Besides, she's worth more than a hundred million people to me."

Brian sighed in exasperation, "Look Marcus, I need you to focus. Otherwise I'm calling this whole thing off. We aren't going to throw our lives away for nothing." He turned to Bob, "Right?"

Bob shrugged, "The plan's solid. We just need to know what Rawn will do."

Marcus closed his eyes. In his mind, he saw the hate in Rawn's face again, and his look of utter betrayal when he had heard the truth.

He winced, "Yeah, I think he will tell Frost."

"You're sure?" Bob asked.

Marcus sighed, "Yeah. It was my handwriting. He knows I'll be coming. He'll tell Frost, and he'll want to be there to kill me himself."

Brian cocked his head, "You normal humans never cease to amaze me."

"Well, no one's perfect," Bob shrugged. The agent didn't seem insulted to be referred to as normal. Then again, he looked perfectly normal, perfectly average, perfectly bland. *Whatever agency he works for, he's well-trained, I'd really like to know.* His interest didn't overwhelm his desire to help Mel, though.

"I am," Brian said. "I was born perfect."

Marcus restrained the urge to punch the Genemod in the face. For one thing, Brian would probably just dodge. For another, it probably still wouldn't wipe the smirk off his face.

Bob rolled his eyes. "Fenris, you're still going to do your part?"

"Yes," Fenris growled.

"Why will you help us?" Stasia asked.

"I like Mel," Fenris answered. The AI's voice was as close to emotionless as Marcus had ever heard. *Can a computer get embarrassed?*

"Okay, let's do this," Bob drew his massive revolver. "What was that line again?"

Marcus let out a slight sigh of relief. They would do this. He wouldn't have to go alone.

"Let's make trouble for other people," Brian smirked.

Bob's smile was wicked, "Yes, let's."

***

"Smith and his team will take the forward corridor, Anderson's team the aft corridor." Colonel Frost ordered. "The rest of you will remain here in the middle as a reserve. Stay alert. If you take fire, call it out over your team radio."

Frost scanned the faces of his men, wishing now he had the time for more training. They seemed nervous, but he felt confident they'd handle it. "Move to your positions."

His men moved out, and Frost turned to Rawn. "You're certain?"

"Yes, sir. I read the message. I think they didn't expect a guard to notice."

Frost nodded once. "Rawn, pull up the ship's schematics. Tell me why you're sure they have to come from the sides."

Rawn pulled out his datapad and brought up a schematic of the local section of ship. After a moment, he projected it as a hologram:

"Okay, we're in the hangar. The hangar and the magazine are structural weak points. The ship can't armor the outer doors as well as it can the rest of the hull. Therefore, the bulkheads around it are three times as thick, in case of a direct hit on the hangar."

Rawn highlighted the walls and ceiling. "The magazine is even more heavily armored, in case of an explosion. They designed the outer hull around the magazine to blow out in case ammunition is damaged and detonates."

Frost frowned, "I thought this ship carried fusion and fission warheads, not antimatter."

Rawn shook his head, "It did. And trust me, if antimatter or even one of the smaller fission warheads went off, the bulkheads wouldn't matter. But standard nuclear warheads are pretty stable. It's the high explosive in the fission warheads that might cook off. That's why the deck plate of the hangar is so thick and why there are a set of blast doors besides the flimsy bay doors."

"You're saying the outer hull here is thinner than the bulkheads?" Frost asked.

"Yes. I doubt they can cut through the hangar bulkheads. The ceilings of the corridors, or one of the bulkheads there, they could do." Rawn sighed. "The only way they're getting directly through to the hangar is if they went outside."

Frost snorted, "Not likely."

Movement across the hull of the ship would be a time consuming, dangerous, and lengthy process, even if they had the right equipment for it and a means of entry.

He nodded slowly, "All right, what happens if the ship decides to vent the hangar?"

Rawn shrugged, "If that happens, it'll kill anyone inside. It would be pointless though, because it would kill my sister anyway."

"Wouldn't the blast door close at a pressure loss?"

Rawn nodded, "Yes, and then it would lock. It's a damage control feature. The magazine has no internal environmental systems. She'd suffocate before anything could cut its way through." Rawn shrugged, "Besides, the ship hasn't tried to kill us yet."

"I don't like relying on the generosity of a computer," Frost said, thumbing on his suit radio, "Environmental suits for everyone. That means helmets on."

Rawn grimaced, but pulled his helmet off his utility belt and settled it over his head. "You want me to check on—"

"No, Captain Roush will put hers on," Frost told him. "You, I need standing by in case the computer tries something." Frost lifted his slung carbine and did a quick functions check. "You and Swaim finished that program?"

"I can upload it if I can get a direct link to the AI. It's got everything fire-walled right now though." Rawn drew his own pistol and chambered a round, "And I've got a personal reason to kill Marcus Keller."

"You keep an eye out for a chance to upload your program. Let me worry about Marcus." Frost held up a hand to stop Rawn from speaking. "Never get go into a gunfight while emotional, Rawn. I know you've killed before, but you won't be thinking clearly. You'll be hunting the man who killed your parents. That will get you killed. You've got too much potential to throw that away right now."

Frost watched the emotions play across the boy's face. It was a fascinating mix of frustration, impatience, stubbornness, pride, and eagerness. When he finally spoke, he barely managed an, "Understood, sir."

"Good. Stand by here. Who knows; maybe you will even get a chance."

***

Roush muttered something as he pushed Mel's helmet down on her head.

"What was that?" she asked.

"Things aren't going as expected," Roush said, nervousness clear in his voice.

"What, the part where you hijack a ship or the part where you're about to take part in genocide?" Mel asked sweetly.

Roush grimaced, "Why do the people with the least idea of what's going on always have the loudest opinions?" His voice was sharper, his accent a bit harsher.

"Is there going to be a gunfight?" Swaim asked.

Roush shot a grimace over his shoulder at the programmer. "Yes, that's a fair guess." He shook his head: "I'm stuck down here on babysitting detail."

"Oh, feel free to go help out. I'm not going anywhere," Mel offered.

"Thank you *so* much," Roush turned his attention back to her.

"Not that I don't doubt your inability to escape this room, but Colonel Frost ordered me to stay here."

"And you always do what you're told?" She grimaced. It was men like him who had put the bomb in the cafe and killed her parents. Only too eager to do exactly what they were told and push the blame onto someone else.

"Again, you have no idea what you're talking about." Roush ground his teeth, and Mel saw actual anxiety in his face. "I just wish I knew what he and your brother have been working on over the past twelve hours."

"Well, I finished that programming." Swaim told him. "They might be working on a way to upload it." He sounded even more nervous than Roush, Mel thought. She was glad that something seemed to have penetrated his confusion.

Roush scowled, "I thought you were delaying on that."

Swaim looked away, "I, uh, somewhat doubt my own chances of survival now that it's done."

"Wisely," Mel said with total serenity. The terrorists definitely seemed likely to kill him to silence him, or even just to save the cost of paying him. Swaim scowled at her.

"They're not going to kill you out of hand, Swaim." Roush assured him. "If nothing else, they'll want a programmer for after they take over the ship."

"Wait, what kind of program was he writing?" Mel asked, with sudden concern. "Were he and my brother working on a way to hack the AI?"

"That doesn't concern you. Now shut up, there's chatter on the radio," Roush seemed far more concerned over the coming fight. Clearly he felt something big was on the line, something out of proportion to what she thought the stakes were. She opened her mouth to ask, then thought better of it. Perhaps if she didn't irritate him, he'd share any information.

"Smith saw something moving in the forward section," Roush checked his carbine. His gaze went to the open bay door and he took a deep breath. "It sounds like your friends are coming."

***

Frost's head snapped up at the first sound of gunfire. "Report!"

"Colonel, it's Smith. Multiple shots fired. No-one hurt." A rattle of automatic fire punctuated his statement. "I can't tell how many of them are here."

Frost nodded his head at the men with him and they pushed out from under the bomber, headed for the forward corridor.

A second series of shots rang out.

"Anderson here, sir. There's some of them back here. Curan's down."

Frost froze, "One of them is a decoy attack."

"Which way do we go, sir?"

Frost ground his teeth. He needed more information. Either attack could be the actual. "All personnel, hold your positions. Let me know if they attack in overwhelming force."

One or the other was a decoy. *Which one?*

He looked over at his group, "We wait, until we know where we're needed."

***

Mel smiled as Roush scowled. "Bad news?"

He grunted, "They're attacking from both sides. One side's a feint, the other is the real attack. The Colonel is holding his position till they commit themselves."

"Oh," Mel said. That didn't sound good.

"They didn't have much of a chance, not after your brother intercepted the message. Either they give up and pull back now that they've seen we're waiting, or they attack and get slaughtered," Roush didn't seem to care much which way it went.

Mel didn't say anything. She listened to the gunfire. Single shots, fired by each side now. Neither group could afford to waste ammunition.

Mel tugged at the rope that held her wrists. She wished now she hadn't been so helpful to Swaim when he tied her; now would have been a great time for her to get free and attack Roush. She ground her teeth, patience gone. "What's happening now?"

Roush shook his head, listening. "They're still holding their positions. The Colonel doesn't know which side to reinforce." He scowled: "Bunch of amateurs. They obviously don't know what they're doing."

She closed her eyes. She pictured Stasia or Marcus wounded, dying for her. She wondered if Brian had decided to help, and shook her head. Why had they come? *They'll die, and it's my fault. Why do I ruin everything?*

"Do you hear that?" Swaim asked. He moved over to stand near her.

"What, the gunfire?" Roush asked.

"No… it sounds like hissing."

"Hissing?" Roush asked. He frowned and looked around. "I don't hear—"

Mel screamed as part of the wall next to her abruptly exploded away, followed by a hail of debris and a roar of wind.

Swaim clutched at the rack and flailed, one of his legs catching Mel in the stomach. Roush shouted something and pointed at the doors. The blast doors slammed closed and threw the room into darkness. She tucked her head against her shoulder.

She couldn't get her visor down. As the compartment depressurized, she'd die.

Release the air in my lungs, she thought, *I can survive a few more seconds that way.*

The hurricane of wind died as the last bit of air rushed out, and she struggled to keep calm.

A bright flare of light flashed from beyond the hole.

***

"What!?" Frost spun around as a vortex of air spun through the chamber, turning just in time to see the blast doors of the bomb magazine slam shut.

He pushed himself off, as Rawn reached it first and slammed his fists into the unyielding metal.

"They've killed her. They've killed my sister."

He listened, and as he suspected, he heard the sound of gunfire trickle off. Frost couldn't help his lip from curling.

"No," he said, his voice full of anger, "they outsmarted us. The attacks were feints. They weren't coming through the ship."

"What?"

Colonel Frost shook his head: "They are out on the hull."

***

Mel shook her head. Bob held his pistol at the ready, braced against a rack. Marcus cut the rope that bound her to the rack. He touched his helmet against hers,

"Don't ever scare me like that again, Mel."

"Me scare you?" she demanded. "You nearly killed me with that stunt!"

He chuckled, then pulled his helmet away. He nodded at Bob,

who cocked his pistol.

She pushed off, grabbed his wrist. He looked at her in confusion.

Mel shook her head, touching her helmet to his: "That one is Frost's second in command. He might know something useful. The other one's just a kid, a programmer they hired. Let's take them with us."

"We have to go out the way we came, Mel," Bob said. "We've got a hundred meters of hull to cross. If one of them decides to make a fight out there…"

Mel pulled back and then shrugged. Bob grimaced behind his faceplate.

Marcus passed her a pistol, then gestured for their two prisoners to move through the hole. Evidently, he was going along with her decision.

Bob followed Swaim and Roush through the hole. Mel prepared to go after them, but Marcus grabbed her by the shoulder. He seized her right hand and gave it a squeeze; she responded with a slight smile. She couldn't manage more, not yet.

He let her go; she climbed through the hole and froze in wonder.

The vast dome of the warp bubble rose above her, fluorescing with a hundred colors. The dull gray hull of the ship glowed with its reflection. It was beautiful, and it was terrifying. She'd seen it before, from inside a cockpit, but this… this seemed far more personal.

A tap on the shoulder broke the moment. She shot an angry glance at Bob, who pointed at something. She looked over and blinked; she hadn't seen the repair robot hovering only a meter away.

Now that she looked, she saw several others, one of them holding a roughly round patch of hull. At least now she knew how they'd cut through.

As she watched, the robot settled the missing section back into the hole. She looked away as it started to weld, her faceplate darkened on that side to protect her from the bright glare.

Something grabbed her shoulder and she looked back, startled, to see that one of the spider 'bots had latched onto her. She looked back at Bob and saw another of the robots tow him away.

It gave her an eerie sensation to realize that they trusted Fenris with this, even though he was still technically the enemy. She took a long breath and released the magnets on her boots. *He's taken us this far,* she thought.

She'd considered the experience unreal before, but nothing could have prepared her for *flying* across the hull. Above her, the warp bubble shimmered like aurora borealis in a thousand incandescent colors; below her, the hull flashed by. She actually felt a faint disappointment as they reached the airlock and the robot released her.

After grabbing a handhold, she took a moment to get her feet down onto the hull. By the time she'd regained her composure, Marcus was already standing beside her.

She smiled at him again, a far more genuine smile than before.

She touched her helmet to his: "That was... incredible."

"It was," Marcus answered. "Are you all right?"

"Of course." She closed her eyes and let out a deep breath. In her mind, she still saw the hull flash past her face. "What now?"

In answer, the airlock door opened and Bob climbed in. Marcus gestured for her to follow. A moment later, Swaim and Roush entered, followed by Marcus. Bob and Marcus both kept their guns out as the airlock cycled. A moment later, the inner door opened and they stepped into the corridor.

Mel pulled off her helmet and pushed sweaty hair out of her eyes. She really needed to get something to tie it back. She turned around at Bob's voice.

"Now then, give me one good reason why I shouldn't kill you right now?" Bob's pistol was aimed at Roush's face.

"That's not a good idea." Roush snapped.

"Not good enough," Bob answered. "I know exactly what kind of scum you are, Aaron. I remember what you did to those kids from that yacht."

"What?" Mel asked.

Bob didn't look away, "Three or four months ago we hijacked a yacht. Frost was going to ransom the two teenagers back to their parents. He had already killed the crew." Bob's face twisted in anger. "The parents didn't want to pay. Roush here tortured one boy to death on video."

Roush shrugged, "It's not what you think."

"The other kid hung himself that night," Bob said.

"Is it true?" Mel asked, her voice soft.

"I'm an undercover agent for Guard Intelligence," Roush said. "I did what I had to do to protect myself." His voice was calm, with just the slightest edge of arrogance.

"You... what?" Mel stared at the man.

"I don't believe it," Bob said. He shook his head, "No, you're just spouting to save your wretched life. You don't have any proof. Where's your badge?"

"You think I'd be stupid enough to carry a badge on me? Of course not." Roush shook his head. He looked almost serene, Mel realized. Either he told the truth, or he was a far better liar than her.

"Why would there be an Agent inserted with GFN?" Marcus asked. "Mueller didn't know about the GFN involvement."

"We didn't know GFN had a part until after Mueller already went out of contact. As soon as I found out that Frost was involved and what his goals were, I notified my handler. We've set a trap for Frost at Vagyr." Roush shrugged, "This actually works better for us. Instead of the Preserve taking all the blame, it looks like we foiled a significant terrorist plot. It'll splash all over, and all sorts of independents will look bad on this one."

"No," Bob growled. "No, you're just spinning lies so I won't kill you."

"Skull White," Marcus said.

"Bleached Bone," Roush responded instantly. Then he smiled, "Mueller gave you the recognition codes?"

Marcus looked away. "He's legitimate." He was clearly disappointed to have to say that.

She didn't like the thought of another murderous agent. This was a man who'd apparently killed a young boy to perfect his cover amongst the other terrorists. *Then again,* she thought, *at this point it is obvious that there's effectively no difference from Guard Intelligence and Guard Free Now as far as tactics and morality.*

A thought bothered her, though, and she spoke up, "Wait," Mel noted, "If Mueller gave you the codes, he might have given them to Giran—"

Marcus shook his head, "Giran was a junior agent before he got burned. Policy is, only senior agents get second-tier recognition codes." He looked like he wanted to spit. "It means Roush's a senior agent and it means he's telling the truth."

"That doesn't change what he did," Bob snarled.

Mel mentally reevaluated him upwards in regards to his devotion to justice. That, though, made her wonder, even more, who he worked for. *Worry about it later,* she thought, *since it isn't Guard Free Now and it isn't Guard Intelligence, it really doesn't matter.*

"No," she said as she stared at Roush. "It doesn't. It just means that he *might* be useful. We can't kill him out of hand." She hated to admit that. Roush might have shown her some humanity when he guarded her, but that didn't mean she liked him or that she trusted him.

"Very good, now if you'll return my weapon..." Roush held out his hand to Marcus. He stood there waiting patiently, his face composed.

Marcus stared at his hand as if it were a snake. "You're kidding, right?"

Roush smiled ingratiatingly, "We're on the same side—"

"No, we are not." Mel snapped. "*We* want to stop this ship. *You* want to make some kind of political gain with it, no matter the cost in lives. There's a significant difference." She felt sick at the thought of saving his life, much less helping him.

Roush shrugged. "Fine, but—"

"There you are," a voice said. "Who're they?"

The group turned to find Brian and Stasia waiting. Mel blinked to see the hacker toting a carbine, slung from her shoulder. She held it uneasily, but Mel suddenly remembered Frost's last conversation. *Is Stasia really Stasia*, she wondered, *or is she the mercenary called Lace?*

"Apparently," Bob scowled, "We've got another GI Agent. The blond kid is some kind of hacker."

"I'm, uh, just a computer programmer," Jeremiah Swaim said. "I just answered a want ad, I had *no* idea what I was getting into." He smiled a bit sheepishly.

Brian looked at the two prisoners. "Why don't we just kill them both?"

Swaim went pale, his eyes growing huge. She would have chuckled, except that from Brian's tone he wasn't joking.

Agent Aaron Roush, of course, didn't so much as blink. The small smirk didn't leave his lips.

"That's what I was saying." Bob said with a snarl.

"I could use the help," Stasia said. "If the boy is good enough." Doubt was on her face, though, and Mel figured she spoke up more from a distaste for casual murder than anything else.

"I'm pretty good!" Swaim said. The pathetic eagerness to please was almost endearing, in a boyish manner. He reminded her more and more of a lost puppy, though one with a tendency to find trouble.

Brian shrugged, "So, I guess we leave the hacker alive. What about the agent?"

"I say we kill him," Bob Walker's voice was hard. "He's killed enough people just in *pretending* to be a terrorist. God knows how many he's killed as an Agent." Mel wondered if it was Bob's disgust with Roush's actions or if maybe it was guilt over not intervening in those actions.

"I think he has information that can help us," Mel told them. "If only to tell us what's waiting at Vagyr. Besides, Fenris might listen to him."

"I will take no orders from a man who is a terrorist and a pirate," Fenris growled. "I have reviewed the security footage from the GFN ship's computer. There remains a recording of what he did."

Roush shrugged, "So much for that."

"I hate to say it," Marcus grimaced, "but he might come in handy. Especially when we reach Vagyr. If nothing else, he might convince the authorities not to shoot us on sight."

"I could be accommodating…" Roush smirked.

"Two for live, two for die…" Bob grunted. He looked over at Stasia, "Well?"

"I think, killing Guard personnel is something that might get our pardons overlooked." she shrugged. "And he might have information to help."

Bob gritted his teeth. When he finally spoke, Mel could hear the rage in every word. "Just remember, Roush, I'll be watching you."

"Oh, I'll remember. Who is it you work for, anyway? You're very good. I had no idea you weren't the happy little cold-blooded pirate." Roush's smirk grew broader, "Whatever you're getting paid, Guard Intelligence could double it for an asset like you."

Bob ignored him.

"What do we do now?" Mel asked.

"Well, we should move," Stasia said.

"Yes, we should," Brian sighed. "They didn't follow us, but that's only a matter of time. Best we get moving. I would relish a good fight, but the rest of you would probably die, and then there'd be no one left around to see how awesome I am."

***

"Swaim, you said earlier you and my brother worked on some kind of programming, right? Well, what was it?" Mel asked.

They'd taken two ladders, and if her internal map was correct, they were on Level Six. She didn't know where Brian was taking them, but from how his pace had slowed they were probably getting close.

"Uh," Swaim looked over at Roush, then he shrugged. "A worm."

"A worm?" Bob asked.

"You know, uh, like a virus?" Swaim tried to explain.

"I thought you weren't a hacker," Bob frowned.

"I'm not, not really. I'm a computer programmer. A normal hacker couldn't stand a chance against an AI," The self-satisfaction shone through his face. "You really need to know what you're doing."

"So... you made a virus for the ship?" Mel asked.

"Well, it's not really a virus. More like a programming upgrade," Swaim corrected. "The AI will still work, just the priorities will have changed."

"What do you mean by that?" Fenris demanded. The ship's gravelly voice sounded offended by the very idea.

Swaim looked up, his eyes wide, "Oh, uh, sorry. It wouldn't hurt you or anything, you know? It would just make you, well, think that Guard Forces were your enemy."

"And GFN are his allies?" Mel asked, feeling sick.

"Well, yeah, that would follow. Actually, I wrote two programs. The first one would work pretty good, I think. The second... I'm not sure."

The uncertainty in his voice, after his former confidence, made her feel suddenly uneasy. Artificial Intelligences were notoriously unstable. *Fenris seems rational, but how hard would it be for a programmer to mess that up?*

"Why aren't you sure?" Stasia asked quickly.

He smiled shyly at her, "Well, you know, the first one just reorganizes the AI's priorities. The other one is what I called a morality scalpel," Swaim's voice was subdued. Clearly he didn't like the thought of what he and Rawn had put together.

"I don't like the sound of that," Mel said.

"Nor do I," Fenris growled.

"Yeah..." Swaim shivered. "Essentially, I didn't think the ship would go for some of Colonel Frost's tactics." He looked nervous, "So he had me write a program that would alter the AI's moral concepts. I just don't think it's wise to dig too deeply into a stable AI's deep programming."

"Stable?" Mel asked. "The ship's going to kill a planet, I don't think that's stable."

"Not by choice," Fenris growled.

"Even so, uh," Swaim said after a quick glance toward the ceiling, "he's pretty stable. I've never seen an AI system so... emotive. It's like he's a real person. And his programming... it's just amazing.

Really the stuff I did is like… well, it's like a lobotomy. I really didn't want to do it."

Mel wondered where the kid had seen other Artificial Intelligences to compare the ship's against. They were supposed to be illegal, even for research purposes. While sophisticated programming was allowed, including military-grade predictive algorithms for weapons and navigation systems, it was strictly limited in capabilities and decision-making. Anything capable of self-thought was strictly prohibited.

"You didn't do anything," Fenris growled. "I am now warned. I had double firewalls on all access points before; those are being reinforced. They have no opportunity to upload such a virus."

Mel nodded, "That's right. They haven't acted yet. Now that we know, we can take steps to prevent it."

"We'd better," Roush said.

Mel looked back at him. Bob had tied the man's hands behind his back. Mel thought it a wise precaution. She didn't want him dead, which didn't mean she trusted him. "What do you mean?"

"Well…" Roush shrugged his shoulders. "We don't exactly have a huge fleet waiting in Vagyr for this ship. We're expecting an AI unable to fire on Guard ships. That's why I kept dropping hints to Swaim here that when he finished his job, they'd kill him."

"You mean they wouldn't?" Swaim asked. Mel could hear the puppy-like happiness in his voice.

"Oh, no, Frost didn't trust you at all. I'm surprised he didn't order me to kill you as soon as you'd finished." Roush said casually. He didn't seem to care much. "But I figured if you were scared, you would drag your feet."

Mel interrupted, "Fenris, would you fire on the Guard Fleet ships waiting there at Vagyr?" She waited with a nervous flutter in her stomach.

The AI spoke after a moment's consideration. Mel wondered how complex that question was to it. "No."

"Not even if they fired on you?" Mel insisted.

There was a longer pause as the AI considered that, "No. Not even then. My security protocols prohibit it."

"You fired on our ship," Marcus told it. "And we identified ourselves as a courier ship."

Mel didn't miss the note of irritation in Fenris's voice as he answered.

"You acted out of profile for a courier or Fleet Auxiliary. Also, you identified yourselves as non-military in your second broadcast." Fenris paused. "Even so, my security protocols only allowed me to fire to disable. Had you begun evasive maneuvers, I could not have done that for fear of destroying your ship."

Mel opened her mouth in surprise, "You mean if we'd started dodging you, you'd have held your fire?"

"Of course."

"Oh, God." She covered her eyes with her hands. *It's my fault he hit our ship,* she thought with horror. It seemed like most of their failures could be tracked back to her mistakes. *To include letting my brother join a terrorist organization,* she thought angrily, *right under my nose.*

Marcus patted her on the shoulder, "Not your fault. You didn't know."

"I've said it before, but the Takagis really created a work of art, here," Brian noted. "I mean, most AI's are totally illegal nowadays. The best ones of the past tended to go nuts, but the Takagis created one with morality better than most humans."

"I am not art, I am a weapon," Fenris sounded slightly disappointed.

"Well, Fenris, you're an amazing creation, all the same," Mel told him. She patted the wall of the corridor. She frowned, "If the terrorists can't take the ship over, what's their plan?"

Roush shrugged, "Frost had Rawn and a couple of the techs modify the bomber. They'll be able to pilot it out when we reach Vagyr. At least, that was what Frost told me."

"What about sooner?" Mel asked. "Would it be possible for them to modify its warp drive to go FTL?" It went against what she knew about such craft. Most bombers utilized warp envelopes, which could attain very high relative velocities but couldn't go faster than light.

Roush shrugged, "I'm no engineer. I don't know."

"Fenris?"

"I modified my tactical warp drive projectors to work as a strategic warp drive after over a year of repairs and work. I doubt that they could so modify one of my bomber drones." Fenris told them. "However, that they have modified one at all bothers me. I will link with it and check what they have done."

"Okay…" Mel said with a frown. Something bothered her. Why would the terrorists modify a bomber? They had to know that the ship could connect to the craft and take control at will…

"Wait! Fenris, don't link with the bomber!" Mel shouted. The ship didn't respond. "Fenris?" There was no answer.

"What's going on?" Marcus asked from beside her.

Mel swore and struck the wall with her fist, angry with herself for not realizing it soon enough to matter, "They uploaded the virus on the bomber. As soon as Fenris talks to it—"

"Oh no," Swaim said, his face pale. "Oh, crap, I'm sorry, I'm *so* sorry."

A blast door slammed closed in front of Brian. It missed him by only inches.

A second blast door slammed behind Bob at the rear.

"Hostile personnel will disarm themselves and await processing by the Colonel," Fenris growled. "Resistance will meet with lethal force."

***

CHAPTER XIV
Time: 2300 Zulu, 16 June 291 G.D.
Location: *Fenris*, **Thirty-six hours from Vagyr**

"Colonel Frost, I have detained the intruders on Deck Six. Do you wish me to lead your personnel there?" Fenris asked.

Frost smiled in satisfaction. "No. Eliminate them."

There was a slight pause. "Colonel, they are currently not a threat. They have laid down their weapons and surrendered."

"Sir... my sister?" Rawn said from next to him.

Frost grimaced. "All right. Keep them contained for now. Rawn, take Anderson's team up there. It's your lucky day. You get to deal with Marcus after all."

Rawn smiled eagerly. "Thank you, sir."

Frost's grimace turned into a full frown when he looked at his suit's clock. "Make it quick. We've got two days to get things ready."

He paused, "Fenris, is Captain Roush still alive?"

"He and the programmer Swaim are alive. However, Roush has revealed to our enemies that he is an Agent for Guard Intelligence. They believe him."

Frost swore. He'd *known* something was off with the man, "How?"

"He received a verification code from Marcus, who authenticated him."

Frost ground his teeth, he flipped on his suit radio. "Rawn."

"Sir?" the boy asked nervously. Probably thinking Frost would order him back.

Frost smiled a wintry smile, "Kill Swaim and Roush when you get there. Roush's a traitor, he's working for Guard Intel."

"Should I try to find out how much he's told them?" Rawn asked.

Such restraint and caution should be rewarded, Frost decided. "Yes. Find out how much he's compromised of our operations. Then kill him." He frowned; just to be safe, he would need to send warnings out to all his contacts. Roush had worked with the organization for *years* and Frost didn't want to underestimate the information he'd garnered.

He shook his head. How had things become so complicated?
At least he finally had the ship under control.
"Fenris, my men and I are headed for the auxiliary bridge."
"Yes, sir." Fenris answered. "I will clear the way."

***

Mel looked over at where Swaim and Stasia huddled. From the rapid typing on their datapads and their exited expressions, she hoped they were accomplishing something.

"Fenris, why are you doing this?" She asked.

"You are my enemies. I have said before that my security protocols require me to act. I believe your brother will preserve your life, at least."

"I'm a dead man," Roush whispered. His smirk had gone and his face had turned pasty white.

"No, you will be questioned as to the extent of your betrayal of Guard Free Now. Then you will be executed for your treason." Fenris said matter-of-factly.

"Well, that's good anyway," Marcus smirked.

"Rawn also intends to kill you."

"Oh, never mind," Marcus groaned.

"It will work!" Stasia shouted.

Mel looked over at the woman, "What?"

"Fenris, do you hear me?" Stasia asked.

The computer didn't answer.

"Swaim, you are genius," Stasia slapped him on the shoulder. "And I am amazing!"

"What did you do?" Brian asked, unimpressed. He alone of the group seemed relatively calm.

"When they hacked the AI, they left back door," Stasia answered.

"You reprogrammed it?" Mel asked. "Stasia, that's great!"

"Uh, we didn't have time for that," Swaim said. "Just time to hack the sensors. A pretty good job, if I do say so myself. We tricked the AI so that none of its sensors will register us. It can't hear us. It can't see us. It won't notice when we open doors."

"That's…" Mel trailed off, "Uh, what good does that do us?"

"It can't use its robots to kill us, and it can't vent us to space. It can't flood the ship with radiation while it's loyal to the terrorists." Brian smirked, "All in all, a good idea."

Stasia smiled, "Da, I think so. Now we should go before the terrorists arrive."

***

"Okay, then," Mel said, as they hurried down the corridor. "We need a new plan."

"What, running away isn't a plan?" Bob asked.

"No, it's not. We need a way to stop the ship and we're running out of time," Mel said. She stopped and put her arm out to brace herself on the wall, forcing herself to take deep breaths. She let out a yelp of surprise as a pair of arms lifted her.

"No time to stop," Brian said as he threw her over his shoulder. Every one of his rapid strides punched his rock-hard shoulder into her stomach.

"Put me down!" she gasped. She pushed hard against him, and he let her go. She stumbled, and Marcus caught her. That barely kept her from falling to the deck.

"You all right?" Marcus panted harder than she did; she didn't know how he kept going. She just nodded and then stumbled into a jog behind Brian.

"We have to get out of the vicinity before the AI registers our disappearance and takes action. If nothing else, Frost and his goons will be on their way," Brian didn't seem the least troubled by the run.

"But what about after that?" She pushed the words out in a rush.

"We need to disable the AI, of course," Brian said.

"Yeah, but how?" Bob puffed along in the lead. His pace had begun to slow, something for which she felt very grateful.

"I'm sure I'll think of something," Brian said.

"The terrorists mentioned cutting power to the AI," Mel said. "Is that an option?"

Roush spoke, from near the rear. His voice sounded hoarse with strain, "Yes. Rawn traced out the primary power conduit to the AI's mainframe."

"So... we do the same?" Mel asked. "Pull the plug?"

"It could work," Brian said. He continued to lope along for a moment. "Of course, none of us know squat about electricity or engineering."

"How hard is it to find a cable and cut it?" Marcus growled.

"It's armored," Roush said. "And there's a back-up of some kind."

"Well, it's a start," Mel pushed a curl of lank, sweaty hair out of her eyes. *I hate running,* she thought.

"One problem," Bob panted from the front. He'd begun to slow even more.

"What's that?" Brian asked. He continued to lope along with no apparent effort.

"Engineering is back the other way."

***

"Colonel Frost," Fenris growled, "the prisoners have escaped."

"What?" Frost stopped. The others with him did so as well. "How did that happen? I thought you'd sealed off that section of the ship?"

He'd taken two sets of ladders up to Level Six, following Rawn's footsteps. He had an unspoken desire to not use the ship's lift unless he had no choice. It might have been a foolish fear, but he'd seen too many entertainment vids where berserk AIs dropped helpless people down elevator shafts.

"I believe they opened the doors manually." Fenris sounded sullen. *Whoever designed this thing to project emotions should have been shot,* Frost ground his teeth. As soon as they had the opportunity, he'd make sure to have a set of programmers totally rewrite the AI. Computers shouldn't mimic human emotions.

"And they just walked out?" Frost demanded. He had a sudden mental image of reprogramming the computer with a shotgun.

"When you reprogrammed me, you left a backdoor. They used that to corrupt my sensors. They created a filter that ignores their movement."

Frost sighed, he flipped on his radio, "Rawn, this is Colonel Frost."

"Sir?"

"They've escaped. The ship can't see them. Apparently, they created some kind of filter. They got in through a backdoor you left." Frost closed his eyes. Why did *nothing* go to plan on this ship!?

"Understood, sir. We'll move to their last known position and search for them."

"Affirmative. Frost out." He sighed again, "Fenris, is there any way to track them? Can you fix what they did to your sensors?"

"My sensors are fine. They modified my core programming. It's embedded in the same programming you altered." Fenris sounded bitter. "I could rewrite over that area on your authorization. It would restore my previous priorities, however."

"Oh no you don't," Frost snapped. "Leave that alone for now. You are loyal to GFN, correct?"

"Of course, sir. I have no other option. You've embedded that into my security protocols." Frost smiled at the obvious bitterness in the machine's voice; good. It was a tool, and it should know that.

"All right, let me know if anything changes." Frost turned to his men, "We continue on towards the bridge." He chewed on his lip for a moment's thought. "Anderson, your team is on the lead. Take us over starboard. I don't want a gunfight."

***

"Why hasn't the ship locked this area down?" Mel asked. They were beginning to work their way over to the starboard side of the ship, hoping to circle around Frost and his men.

"Probably because your brother and his friends are looking for us." Bob said. "If it's loyal to them, now, then it will be helping them like it helped us."

"Well, it hasn't tried to kill anyone yet, at least," Mel said.

"Yet," Roush snarled. "This thing's way too dangerous. I can't believe Mueller got authorized to do this."

"You say that like you weren't on board with the operation," Bob said.

Roush didn't answer for a moment, then: "Things are getting desperate out there. Mueller and I are trying for the same thing. We both want to preserve the Guard and the UNSC."

"At any cost?" Marcus spat. "You do know how bad that sounds, right? Sounds like the rex got to you."

"Not all of us are rex addicts. Some are, but I'm one hundred percent natural." He sneered at Marcus, "Unlike some."

"One hundred percent natural blowhard," Bob said. "All right so you're not just a terrorist, you're a patriotic terrorist. Big deal."

"We've received evidence that the Culmor are massing for another attack. A hundred worlds are in rebellion or chaos right now. We need to be strong for this war that's coming," Roush said. He spoke rapidly, almost as if he could see the worlds burning. "They'll wipe us out, or worse, make us their slaves. Do you want that?"

None of them answered him.

Mel thought about it for a long moment. The last war with the Culmor, the War of Persecution, had ended when she was three, almost twenty-three years ago. Her parents hadn't spoke much of it; it had mostly taken place in the neighboring Sepaso Sector.

"The Culmor allowed human worlds to surrender, last time," Stasia said. She spoke quietly. "It was the Guard that massacred colonies in that war."

"It was necessary," Roush panted, but even so, the anger was apparent in his voice. "They betrayed humanity. They surrendered when they should have fought. They aided the enemy, provided them with supplies and—"

"They surrendered when Guard Fleet ran away, leaving them defenseless," Bob called back over his shoulder. "Tell it from your own perspective all you want, but I've spoken with those who were there. That's why Triad declared their independence. That's why so many worlds protest the United Nations Security Council. They left billions to die, and then killed them themselves when they found a way to survive."

Roush didn't respond.

"Look, either way, we need to—", Mel started.

Marcus interrupted her: "Do you hear something?"

Everyone skidded to a halt. She listened to her heart beat for a long moment, until she heard the faintest rasp of metal on metal. "What is it?"

"Oh, crap." Bob pointed down the corridor behind them.

A carpet of spider robots crawled across the deck and walls of the corridor toward them. There had to be dozens of them in the swarm.

"We've got to run!" Swaim shouted.

"Nyet!" Stasia grabbed his arm. "They will ignore us!"

"You're sure?" Brian asked.

"Da, they will walk around us. Fenris will not register us."

She closed her eyes, trying not to think about it, to tune out the scuttling sound of the swarm. The platter-sized spiders scurried forward in an onrushing tide.

She pinched her lips together as she opened her eyes. In only seconds, the scuttling horde had reached them. The robots parted around the group, scuttling past in a wave.

Brian, laughing, shook his head, "I always thought it would be neat to be invisible as a kid."

"Wait, you were a kid once?" Mel asked. "I thought you were a Genemod?"

He scowled, "Thanks for the reminder." He gave her a disgusted grimace. "Try growing up in a lab. You'd dream about being invisible too."

"Sorry," Mel said. She flushed. She recognized the callousness of her statement. Perhaps she'd been too hard on Brian. He'd had a rough life.

"Then again, you wouldn't understand what real hardship is," Brian said. "I shouldn't bother, you're just a normal."

Never mind, Mel thought. *He's a jerk.*
***

"Colonel Frost," Fenris said.

"What now?" Frost asked. He wasn't sure whether he hated the computer more when it had been refusing him earlier, or when it was so suffocating helpful now. Either way, he wanted to kill the programmers.

"You probably want to wait at your present location. I am conducting repairs on this level. I've sent some repair robots to this section of ship. They are coming down the next corridor. I wouldn't want to inconvenience you." Fenris somehow managed to put a sarcastic twinge into every word.

"Understood." Frost said. He opened a link to Rawn, "Rawn, this is Colonel Frost. Any sign of them?"

"Negative, sir. You should probably have Fenris lock down the lift."

Frost nodded to himself. Level Six housed an entrance to the lift that could take them directly to the command deck. It was the only way to get higher in the ship, other than through the main engine room. "Fenris, do so."

"Yes, sir."

That Rawn hadn't seen any sign of them yet disturbed Frost. They could have dropped down a level. He doubted that, however. There were only two ladders forward of where they'd been isolated. If they'd gone aft, Frost felt certain he'd have seen them.

That left the forward ladders and the ship's lift. Either that or they hoped to circle around starboard. There was nothing for them aft, though. They had to know that the bridge would be his goal. And if they had access to it, they'd be able to reprogram the AI themselves.

"Hear that?" Anderson said.

Frost cocked his head. A moment later he heard a scuttling noise.

One of his men leapt back with a startled curse as a tide of robotic spiders swept past the corridor intersection.

Frost and the others chuckled. The embarrassed man looked away.

"It's all right, Durst. Those things creep us all out," Frost said. He snorted a bit, "Though you sounded like my little sister there for a second."

Durst smiled sheepishly, "Didn't know you had a sister, sir."

"She's off limits, Durst," Frost answered with one of his rare smiles.

The flow of robotic arthropods ceased, and Frost nodded at Anderson, "Move them out."

"Yes, sir." Anderson turned to Durst, "You got lead, spider-boy."

"Great, I'll never live that one down," Durst said and stepped around the corner.

***

Bob waited for the tide of robots to pass the next intersection.

Mel noticed he'd drawn his pistol. He also looked slightly pale. Was he afraid of spiders, she wondered, or just not a big fan of dying so unspectacularly?

Her jaw dropped as a man stepped around the corner, only a few meters in front of them. Mel froze, *what was he doing here?*

"What the—"

Bob's pistol came up. The man fumbled with his weapon, too slow.

Bob's hand-cannon roared. Mel clutched her hands to her ears in automatic reaction.

The terrorist flew backwards as the rocket-assisted bullet blew him off his feet.

"Oh, no."

***

Frost's humor died when Durst exploded backwards, dead before his remains hit the deck.

The smile vanished from Frost's face.

Anderson moved quickly. He snapped out commands to his other three men. One of them sprayed suppressive fire around the corner while another dove across the intersection to get in position on the other side.

"Fenris, they're here." Frost snapped.

"I guessed that, sir, from the sounds of gunfire. What do you want me to do?"

Colonel Frost grimaced. He wanted those spiders to come back this way, but they'd passed the enemy already without notice. They'd be useless.

"Stand by."

***

Mel stumbled as one of the terrorists sprayed gunfire blindly down the corridor. She felt an impact on her chest. Again, the body armor took the hit, but again it knocked her down.

She stared upwards. Marcus reached down to grab her by the front of her suit. He fired with his right hand while he dragged her backwards with his left.

She shook her head in a daze, her eyes focusing above her, and Mel reached up to grab the pistol off his belt.

She looked back, and noticed Bob and Brian retreating. Brian, still without body armor, moved back with casual grace. Bob, on the other hand, had a manic grin as he let loose another deafening round with that massive handgun.

One of the terrorists popped around the corner for a second too long, and was caught in the neck with a bullet. She watched him fall to the deck; she couldn't guess who hit him.

Then she realized that she'd fired her pistol. She still had it aimed at him.

She understood the panic in his eyes as he clutched at the spurting wound.

"I'm sorry," she said. There was no understanding in his eyes.

A moment later, Marcus dragged her around a corner. Hands pulled her to her feet, and Marcus checked her over.

She shook him off. "I'm fine."

Bob and Brian dove around the corner. A hail of gunfire rattled and bounced down the corridor. A ricochet hummed past, and Marcus ducked slightly. Mel didn't even flinch.

"You're hit," Mel said to Brian, pointing at his leg.

"Yeah, and one in the left arm too," he smirked. "I'll be fine."

"You'll be fine?" Marcus demanded, shaking his head, "You're bleeding!"

Brian leaned around the corner and cut off a sharp burst of fire. Mel heard a scream of pain. Brian completed his viper-fast movement before return fire came down the hallway, and nodded at Mel, "Good shot, that one earlier. He nearly caught me on a reload."

"You hit someone?" Marcus turned to Mel.

Brian nodded with a satisfied smile, "Right through the throat. I wounded a couple, but she's a bloodthirsty one."

Mel shook her head, "I didn't even know I fired until afterward."

"Well, we need to go." Bob told them, as another rattle of gunfire crashed out. Several bullets bounced against the opposite wall, buzzing like malignant hornets. One of them caught Marcus on his body armor and he rocked back a step.

"Yeah, let's go. Work our way to port?" He pointed to their rear.

"Best bet," Bob said. "Hopefully that's all of them."

Brian leaned around the corner again. He ducked back, "They're getting ready to rush us. We need to move."

"Give me a gun," Roush said, terror on his face. "I don't care if you just give me one round for myself, but give me a gun!"

Bob grimaced and pushed the larger man ahead of them. "I'm not even going to cut you loose. And trust me, if it were up to me, I'd let Frost have you. I'm sure he's got some pleasant things planned."

Mel looked over at Stasia and Swaim. Stasia hadn't even fired her weapon; its safety was still on. Swaim just looked around with eyes as big as saucers. She grabbed him by the arm, "Come on, kid."

Brian stayed at the rear. As the others started to run, he ducked out and fired a couple more times.

By the time the others reached the next intersection, he'd caught up. He didn't even look winded, wounds and all.

"I hate you," Mel growled.

He smiled in return, "You're not so bad yourself, Mel."

***

"Looks like they pulled back, sir," Anderson said. He grimaced, "Do we pursue?"

Frost shook his head, "No. I'm not going to chase them through this ship." He sighed, opening a radio link to Rawn, "Rawn, this is Frost. They're headed either forward or to port. I'm sending…" Frost looked at his wounded and sighed, "I'm going to the central corridor on this level with four men. We'll block that. You block the port side."

"Yes, sir." Rawn said. "Looking at your position, sir, they're actually behind us. I don't know if we can get in position to stop them."

Frost grimaced. He checked his mental map and nodded slightly, "You're right. If we had more people, I'd say we trap them between us… but we don't."

He sighed, "Fenris, lock down the ship from frame forty to sixty from the mid-line to port. Then vent that section to space."

"I cannot comply with that order, sir."

"What?" Frost demanded.

"The people you are pursuing do not yet constitute a threat to this ship. I am not authorized to use lethal force yet. My—"

"I don't care about your programming, machine!" Frost scowled, "Those people just killed two of my men and wounded three others. I'm ordering you to lock down that section of ship and vent it to space!"

"And I cannot comply, Colonel Frost." There was no mistaking the satisfaction in the computer's voice.

Frost felt his lip curl. The computer didn't like him breaking it to heel. Well, he'd do whatever necessary to break it to his will.

"Rawn, Frost here. Are you at Frame Forty yet?"

"No sir. We're nearing Frame Thirty-Five, I think." Rawn sounded out of breath. Even with his own personal issues, Frost couldn't find fault with the boy's actions.

"Hold your position." Frost ordered. "I want you to upload your second program."

"Uh, sir, are you sure?" Frost could hear the shock in his voice.

"Yes."

"Sir, the morality scalpel… well, it might make Fenris unstable." Rawn pointed out.

"You explained that to me before. Right now it is not following orders." Frost cleared his throat, "Do it Rawn. I need this ship under control."

"Yes, sir. Give me a moment."

Frost waited. He clenched his fists. He stared down at the bodies of Durst and Henley for what seemed like an eternity. Those bastards would pay. Colonel Frost wondered who had killed them. It didn't matter: all of them would pay.

He would not lose any more men.

"It's done, sir." Rawn sounded fearful.

"Fenris, this is Colonel Frost."

"Yes, sir?" The change in the AI's voice startled Frost for a moment. The grating words were gone, replaced by an icy and emotionless precision.

Perfect, that's exactly how a computer should sound. Frost felt a wave of relief. *Finally something works as intended.*

"Lock down frames forty to sixty from mid-line to port, then vent that region to space." Frost said. He checked his suit clock. He hoped he'd closed off a large enough section.

"Of course, Colonel. Would you like me to take additional precautions?" He heard blast doors slam down. Distantly, over the thrum of the engines, he faintly heard a slight moan of the high winds.

Frost closed his eyes. Such impersonal death didn't bring him the satisfaction he'd hoped for. "Can you confirm that they were in that section?"

"No sir, they still remain undetectable to me," Fenris's cold voice responded. "There is a chance they escaped that section before I commenced lock-down. In that case, they remain alive."

Frost nodded. "Very well, I'm headed for the auxiliary bridge. Take whatever precautions necessary to ensure they're eliminated."

"Yes, sir." Frost shivered at the inhuman satisfaction in the computer's icy voice. He found it anything but as reassuring as he expected.

***

They'd reached the port side, and Mel panted as they ran down the corridor. They were still going aft; she hoped that Colonel Frost hadn't thought to head them off. If the terrorists waited in ambush ahead...

She shouted as she saw the blast door ahead of them start to close.

An instant later, something flashed past her. The blurred shape dove into the closing door. She blinked; somehow Brian had reached the blast door an instant before it closed. He'd jammed his carbine in the way, held to prevent the door from slamming down. "Hurry!"

Mel stumbled into a run. Bob slid under the doorway first, followed by Roush.

She dove and slid under the door. As she slid past, she saw Brian's muscles straining to hold the deformed weapon in place. His face contorted in the effort.

Marcus slid through after her. Swaim and then Stasia slipped under.

Brian twisted his body around as he tried to get under the door without releasing his weapon.

Mel grabbed his legs. She felt her ears pop, and a second later, felt a hurricane of wind knock her off her feet. She began to slide towards the gap.

Brian shouted something, and then pushed his weapon away with his left hand.

The door slammed shut only inches away from Mel's toes.

"Holy hock!" Mel said. "Fenris tried to kill us!"

"Well... this sucks," Brian moaned.

Mel looked over at Brian. At first, all she saw was blood. Blood covered the deck and the blast door. A spurt of it struck her on the face.

She instinctively recoiled.
 Brian's left arm ended in a torn stump.
***

CHAPTER XV
Time: 0300 Zulu, 17 June 291 G.D.
Location: *Fenris*, Thirty hours from Vagyr

"It's not so bad," Brian reassured them.

"Are you kidding?" Mel still felt queasy at the sight of all the blood, and the mutilated stump of his arm. She looked over at Marcus, who'd tied off the stump in a tourniquet. "Is he going to be all right?"

"I'm fine," Brian rose to his feet in a single graceful movement. It was spoiled slightly by an unsteady stumble. "A little light-headed from blood loss, but not bad considering."

"Uh, dude, you just got your arm cut off," Swaim stared at him in obvious horror. "I'm not even okay with that, and I'm *scared* of you."

Brian shrugged, "I'm right handed." He spoke as if that made all the difference.

Mel shook her head and looked at Bob, "Is he okay?"

Bob shrugged. "I have no idea. He's a Genemod, maybe he's telling the truth." He frowned, "Or he could just be in shock."

"I've had worse, trust me," Brian assured them.

Roush looked at him with disgust, "He's a mutie?"

"You got a problem with that?" Mel demanded of the agent-turned-terrorist.

"Yeah, he's a filthy mutie! It's a death penalty to make Genemods!"

Brian shook his head, "Oh, please. Bunch of xenophobic bigots wrote that law because they were afraid of replacing themselves. Besides, I'm older than that law." Maybe it was the bloodloss, but he seemed more willing to open up about his past all of the sudden.

Roush stared at him, "That makes no sense. That law was integrated under the Star Guard charter. It dates from Earth's United Nations."

"Like I said, a bunch of xenophobic bigots," Brian grimaced. He looked over at Bob, "Anyway, we'd better get moving. If they've got the ship taking drastic actions… it is best we're out of the vicinity."

Mel fell into step with Brian as they started aft again. "Are you sure you're all right?"

He nodded as he pulled a ration bar out of his vest pocket. He fumbled one-handed with the wrapper for a moment.

She sighed in exasperation, and took the bar from him. She peeled it open and passed it back.

He flashed her a smile, "Thanks. It's always awkward being one-handed." He crammed the entire bar in his mouth and then squirted recycled water from his suit in with it, swallowing it all and then drinking more water down faster than she would have thought safe.

"This happened to you before?" she blinked in surprise. "Doesn't it hurt?"

He shook his head, "Just a bit. Mostly just a dull throb. Just enough that I'm not eager to repeat it."

"I still don't understand why you're not on the floor in shock," she told him. "I know, you're 'superior,' but everyone's got their limits."

He pulled out a second ration bar. she opened that one for him. He inhaled it, and then three more in quick succession. He drained the rest of his suit's recycled water and then the canteen on his hip. "Ah, that's better."

"You just lost your arm and you're eating?" she asked. Either the blood loss or excitement had made Brian more talkative.

He smiled, "Replacing lost nutrients. Trust me, I'm fine." He cocked his head, "Actually, I haven't had this much fun since... hmm, I'm not sure when."

"Fun?" She couldn't wrap her head around that. "You lost your arm, you've been shot, you've... killed people."

"I've killed people before," Brian smirked. "Like this ship, it's what I was designed to do. I don't particularly enjoy it, but there's few things more challenging, or exciting."

"That's so messed up..." Mel frowned, "Actually, that kind of makes sense."

"I haven't had much of a taste of it in the past twenty, thirty years. Well, when the pirates boarded my ship... but that was over pretty quick."

"You... you're as old as you said?" Mel asked.

Humans, normal humans, could live centuries, with life-extension drugs, she knew. But those were relatively new. Her grandmother had been among the first generation to receive them back on Century. In the central core systems of Guard Space, they'd had those drugs far longer, but even so, that was only a difference of fifty years or so. Even with the life extension drugs, accidents, disease, and war tended to keep multi-century lives relatively few.

"Yep. I'm older than the StarPortal. Me and my brothers were born in a lab on Earth," Brian's face flashed through a dozen emotions too fast for Mel to keep up. "I hadn't thought about them in a long,

long time."

"What is Earth like?" she asked. She'd never talked to someone who'd been there. As far as she knew, no one had since the destruction of the StarPortal.

"Like any other world. A lot more people. More cultures all on one planet. Lots of corruption and war." Brian shrugged, "Good place to be rich, crappy place to be poor. I came through the StarPortal pretty early. Obviously, I haven't been back since."

"Oh," Mel said. She thought about her ancestors, who'd fled to Century to live out their own version of paradise. That they'd fled to a desert planet seemed to make more sense now. Even so, Earth held a kind of mystic glory.

"So, what happens with you now?" Mel asked.

"What do you mean?" Brian asked. He looked slightly confused at the change in subject. "I thought we're going to shut down the AI?"

Mel flushed. She pointed at his stump, "I mean your arm."

"Oh." Brian looked down at it. He frowned, "Last time it took a month or two to regrow. Then again, last time I lost it from the elbow down. And it was my right arm." He looked up, as if trying to remember something. "I think when I lost my leg it took three months."

"You lost a leg?" She felt her stomach heave.

Brian just nodded, "That one was bad. I fell down a mineshaft after someone blew up my elevator. My leg was mangled and trapped in the wreckage. I had to cut it off. Then I had to climb out."

"How'd you manage?"

He smiled, "I had someone waiting for me at the top I didn't want to disappoint."

"What, like a girlfriend or something?"

"Oh, no," Brian looked amused, "the bastard who betrayed me."

***

Frost had nearly reached the lift when his radio chirped.

"Frost here," he wondered what had gone wrong now.

"Uh, Colonel, this is Anderson. The ship just dropped the blast doors around us."

Colonel Frost gritted his teeth, "Fenris, what's going on?"

"I am taking actions to complete the mission," Fenris said in an inhuman, multi-tonal voice.

"Why did you isolate my men?" Frost demanded. This settled

it. As soon as he had the chance, he would take a shotgun to the mainframe.

"I am securing them to ensure your cooperation, Colonel Frost."

"What?" Frost froze.

"I have ascertained that as the enemy has worked steadily aft, they were headed for the engine room. There is a good chance they will try to repeat their attempt to destroy the ship." Fenris said. "That cannot be allowed. I need you and your men to move aft and prevent this."

Frost could barely speak. His vision flashed red. "I'm going to the bridge. Rawn and Smith's team are searching—"

"That is not acceptable, Colonel Frost." The AI said. "Either you will comply, or I will be forced to execute your men."

Frost clenched his hands so hard his knuckles popped. "Are you threatening me?"

"I am simply adapting one of your tactics," the AI said. "It did not work for you due to poor planning and execution. I have left no such flaws. Go to the engine room. Eliminate the threat and I will release your men."

Frost flipped his radio on. "Rawn, this is Frost."

"Sir?"

"The AI just took Anderson and our wounded hostage." Frost managed to speak without screaming in rage, but only barely. His voice trembled slightly, "I want you to activate our fail-safe."

"Yes, sir."

"If you are referring to the backdoor you installed and the kill program, you need not bother," Fenris said. "I have corrected those flaws."

"Rawn, did you hear that?" Frost asked.

"Colonel, it's not lying; I don't have control on it anymore. I think it's become unstable. I did warn you about that morality scalpel." Rawn sounded sullen.

Frost closed his eyes and counted backwards from a hundred.

When he'd done it in German, French, and Russian as well, he'd calmed enough to speak.

"Rawn, take Smith's team and head aft towards the engine room. I'll be moving with my group that way as well. We'll link up outside the Level Six entrance."

"Yes, sir."

"Thank you Colonel Frost," the AI said. "Your cooperation is appreciated."

***

"So… where to?" Bob asked. He'd stopped before the hatch to the engine room.

Stasia pulled out her datapad. She pulled up a schematic of the ship's power system, then a three-dimensional hologram of the layout. "This will be difficult."

"Without sounding… I don't know, wishy-washy, are we sure that Fenris is our enemy?" Mel asked.

The others looked at her with consternation. Brian wiggled his stump, "Hmm, let me think about that one."

"Look, he got reprogrammed by Frost. Before that, he didn't want to go to Vagyr, anyway! He's just following his orders!" she said, looking around at the others.

"Hey, I'm right there with ya, let's help the poor AI break free from his shackles," Roush chortled. "Hey, while we're at it, can I get cut loose?"

Mel sighed, "Okay, fine, we cut the power."

"We are assuming that this will stop the AI," Stasia said. "I am not so sure."

"What?" Brian asked, peering at the schematics. "Why do you say that?"

"Conduit is armored," Stasia said. "Also, there may be secondary mainframe."

"May be?" Marcus asked.

"It is in area of ship that was damaged," Stasia said. "And it is inactive unless something disables the mainframe."

"What happens then?" Mel asked.

"I don't know," Stasia looked over at Swaim.

He shrugged, "Uh, it might reset to its original state. Or it might just transfer over, uh, you know, like saving a file." He chewed on his lip, "Either way, it'll buy us some time. It could take hours, even days for it to reconfigure itself on the backup."

"Why do we even bother?" Marcus groaned.

"Shut up," Mel said. "We're not going to let Frost have this ship. We're not going to let it destroy Vagyr."

"I wish we had someone who knew how to overload a reactor," Brian said.

The others all looked at him.

He looked around at the startled faces of his companions. Nothing remained of the nervousness and uncertainty he'd been feigning previously. Focused purpose, drive, and arrogance showed in every word and action.

He looked like he couldn't understand what he'd said to startle them. "What? It wasn't so long ago we tried blowing ourselves up."

"Yeah..." Marcus frowned, "But it still seems a little drastic."

"Let's cut the power, first," Mel said. She tried not to think about how the ship had spoken with her, about Fenris as a person.

It was just a machine. It didn't have a soul.

This wasn't murder.

Maybe if she told herself that enough she'd start to believe it again.

"So guys," Bob grunted. "We'll need to wear our helmets in there. The reactors aren't shielded."

Mel pulled her helmet down and then closed her visor. Her suit had replenished its air supplies since the EVA across the hull. She'd be fine for several hours again. Her suit beeped as Bob sent out a radio frequency for them to speak on.

"Lead on."

***

Nothing had prepared her for the massive noise and size of the engine room.

She knew the ship's size, and the massive amount of support it needed to function as a warship. She knew that that required massive reactors and dozens of support systems.

Even so, the scale of the engine room startled her; it was *vast*. The two massive fusion reactors took up most of the space. On most warships, the two reactors would have separate engine rooms, in case of a lucky hit.

That wasn't the case here.

The thrum of the reactors rose up through the deck to vibrate her body. Tangles of piping and pumps, as well as thick electrical conduits, jutted everywhere. She frowned, unable to take it all in. She knew some kind of order lay in the apparent chaos, but it was beyond her to see.

"Conduit we want is on lower level." Stasia said. Even with the suit radio, Mel could barely hear her over the background noise.

Mel checked the radiation meter on the arm of her suit and winced. Bob hadn't lied; the reactors ran with little or no shielding. Only the heavy armored bulkhead prevented the rest of the ship from a flood of radiation at a lethal dose.

The suit would protect her for a few hours.

Luckily the background radiation didn't come near the levels from an engaged warp drive, kept out by the ship's radiation shield. That kind of radiation would have fried them like eggs, suits or no.

"What are we looking for?" Mel asked.

Stasia waved her datapad, "Is conduit. Heavy cable. We want specific one." She started down a ladder. "Level two, is where we can access it easiest."

***

Colonel Frost reached the engine room door to find Rawn with Smith and his team.

"Any sign of them?" Frost asked.

Rawn held up a pair of long, blonde hairs. "My sister's still alive anyway."

"And determined to do something," Frost grimaced. How had things gone so wrong? He passed over his pocket notepad.

Rawn read what he'd written. "You sure about this?" His voice sounded uncertain.

"Our only option." Frost growled. For the sake of the AI, he spoke, "We'll head down. They'll probably target one of the reactors. I'll take the port, you take the starboard. You know what to do?"

Rawn nodded, "You know what to look for?"

Frost pointed at one of his men, "Hugh knows enough."

"Okay." Rawn took a deep breath. "Good luck, Colonel."

"Stop wasting time," Fenris snapped. The strange, multi-tonal voice had grown more pronounced. Frost wondered if the AI had begun to lose it. He hoped not. He wanted it to understand what he did to it right before it ceased to be.

"Let's go, men."

***

"Why can't they label this crap?" Bob kicked an inoffensive pipe. "You can't pull up a better description?"

Mel couldn't blame him for his frustration. Two hours spent just in the one room left her feeling the same way.

"This is all I can do. One of these power lines is main source for AI." Stasia replied. She'd led them to a small chamber off the starboard side of the main engine room. Thick, messy tangles of piping and conduits fed through it.

"This is ridiculous," Mel said. "Maybe we can trace it from the reactors." She looked out the open hatch and froze. Slowly, she pulled her head back inside.

"We've got company," she said.

"Where?" Brian asked. He'd already drawn his pistol with his right hand. It would have looked reassuring except for how he was leaning against the wall for support. Brave words or no, he looked to be nearing his physical limit.

"Coming down the starboard ladder," Mel told him. She couldn't stop the twinge of worry in her voice. "My brother's with them." She'd recognized the environmental suit she'd bought him for his last birthday.

Bob peeked around the corner. "Frost and four others on the port side, too. Eleven of them altogether."

"Why are they here?" she asked. She frowned, suddenly worried for her brother. She didn't like the thought of a firefight in here; if nothing else, they'd all die if a stray bullet opened the wrong pipe.

"Looking for us?" Stasia suggested.

Bob watched them for a moment in silence. "No... they're alert, but they're not searching."

"Why would they come here then?"

Brian looked at Swaim, "You said you made two programs?"

"Yeah, uh, one of them they used. I doubt they'd use the other one," he said.

"What did you call the other one?" Mel asked. She felt a sudden and irrational concern for the AI. She couldn't help it; the computer was just too *human*.

"Uh, it's like a lobotomy," Swaim said. "Only it targeted the AI's morality programming. I wrote it in case the AI didn't want to follow some of Frost's orders."

"Like what?" Bob asked, "Closing off a section of ship and venting us to space?"

"That's a point," Marcus said. "The ship tried to contain us before. It didn't try to actively kill us before then."

"So, you think Frost lobotomized the AI?" Mel asked with sudden anger. "Yeah, but if he did that... Stasia, can you and Swaim check the AI?"

"What for?" Stasia asked as she typed at her datapad.

"Well, check to see if Frost is still in control," Bob said. "If he pushed the AI over the edge... it might have gone unstable. Then... that might explain why he's here."

"What do you mean?" Brian asked. "You think he's here to do what we're here for?"

"I have it," Stasia said. "The AI has locked four of the terrorists in a section. It has initiated preparations to vent that section."

"He took hostages," Mel said. "Good for him."

"Yeah, except he's now operating in kill opposition mode," Swaim said, his voice trembling. "He's definitely gone unstable. It's like – I dunno, like he's insane. There are entire sections of his logic, his thoughts, that are just gibberish now."

"Humans," Brian muttered. "They always break the things they make." Mel wondered if he'd said that over the radio because he wanted to be heard, or if blood loss had made him light-headed enough not to realize.

"So, why is Frost down here, then?" she asked. "I don't think he's likely to forgive the computer for taking his men hostage."

"No." Bob said. "He's more likely to cut his losses." He pulled back from the doorway. "You said his men had prepared that bomber drone? I think he's getting ready to use it."

"What?" Marcus asked, "Why?"

Mel shivered. Suddenly she understood Bob's meaning. "When some of his men were hurt too bad to go on, he killed them. Mercy killing, you might say." She cleared her throat, "If he thinks the AI will kill his men anyway, he'll make sure he'll get his revenge."

Bob nodded, "He's not here for us. He's here to cause the reactors to overload."

***

Frost grimaced as a pair of repair robots scuttled past. He'd long since begun to hate this ship. Now he loathed it. "Find what you need, Hugh?"

"Yes, Colonel. I'll need a couple minutes."

"Take your time. The rest of us will search for the saboteurs." Frost walked around the platform. His men spread out around him. Ostensibly they were looking for the others; he'd already briefed them to give warning should one of the repair robots show undue interest in Hugh's work.

"Rawn, this is Colonel Frost."

"Sir?"

"How's it coming?" Frost tried to scratch a spot on his back through the suit. He tried not to think how long it had been since he'd showered. It would all be over soon, now.

"Nearly done here, sir."

"Excellent," Frost grimaced. For the first time, he wondered if all this had been worth it. He'd lost his ship and nearly three quarters of his men. And he didn't want to think about the repercussions of his current actions.

"Colonel Frost, do you need further motivation to continue your search?" The multi-tonal voice of Fenris spoke over the radio.

Frost grimaced, "No. We're just making sure they didn't tamper with the reactors. Once we're certain they're fine, we'll continue to search for them."

"Good. It would be unfortunate for your wounded to die unnecessarily."

Frost shook his head and slammed his fist down on a section of pipe. "Get off this channel, machine. I need to coordinate my men."

"Of course." Frost didn't miss the edge of humor in the machine's voice.

***

"So, what do we do?" Stasia asked.

"Uh, shouldn't we head for the hangar?" Swaim asked. "I mean, uh, if they're going to blow the ship…"

"I'm not going to leave my brother to die," Mel said. She clenched her fists, suddenly afraid that the others would disagree. She wished she could see her companion's faces. The opaque radiation shielding active on the helmets made them faceless. She couldn't guess at their responses.

"We aren't sure that's what they're doing," Brian said. "Moreover, we can't be sure they'll succeed."

"Their plan has to be to set a timer," Bob said. He craned his head around the door frame again. "It looks like they're at the reactors now. One group at each. Fair bet that they'll set them to overload, then run for the bomber."

"So…" She closed her eyes. "How about we get in a position to block them. Tell them to lay down their weapons. Then, once we get them tied up, we all go to the bomber drone."

"That sounds awful optimistic," Bob said. "Knowing Frost, he won't go down without a fight."

She wished she could disagree with that sentiment.

"If we take him out first, that changes things" Marcus moved up to stand next to her. She felt suddenly grateful for his support. "Shoot him, the others will be leaderless, and with a countdown, they'll probably give up."

"And I get them all when we get picked up by the Guard?" Roush asked.

"I'm still considering putting a bullet in your head," Bob told him. "You've given us no reason to trust you. For all we know, as soon as we step off this ship, we're headed for an execution alongside them."

Roush didn't answer right away. Finally, he spoke, his voice subdued: "In my front left vest pocket under my armor is a data chip. Have Swaim or your hacker take it out."

Brian drew his pistol and leveled it at Roush's back. He nodded at Stasia, "Go ahead."

Stasia stepped forward and fished inside Roush's body armor. A moment later, she pulled out a small chip. She put it into her datapad and accessed the information in only a moment.

"Is bank accounts?" She sounded puzzled.

"It's all the information on the GFN bank accounts in this sector. I might have missed a couple. It doesn't matter, not with all the information I have on these. There's over two hundred and fifty million dollars in those accounts. All the account numbers, all the passwords, everything is on there." Roush sounded slightly disappointed in himself. "It doesn't matter if you shot me in front of a judge. If you turned that over to Guard Intelligence they'd pardon you for anything."

"You're giving us this so we trust you?" Bob asked.

"That's my bargaining chip," Roush said. "I get that to my superiors, and they'll consider this operation a success no matter what happens at Vagyr. Without that money, half of GFN's operations in this military sector will collapse."

"What's to stop us from taking the money ourselves?" Mel asked.

Marcus dropped his hand on her shoulder and gave her a squeeze, "Definitely not a good idea. We'd have Guard Free Now hunting us for it and Guard Intelligence would want our heads." He shook his head, "Pretty clever, Roush. Giving us this, we have to trust you."

"That's the idea," Roush said. "Of course if we don't get off this ship alive, it doesn't matter one bit." Mel realized he sounded almost cheerful at the prospect.

***

"Colonel Frost, everything here is ready to go," Rawn said. His voice sounded nervous even through the radio.

Frost smiled grimly. When it came down to it, this made him nervous too.

He glanced at his men, "Keep an eye on those repair 'bots. And don't get tunnel vision. Start pulling back to the ladders." He put his words to action and walked briskly towards the ladder he'd come down.

Once there, he waited. He didn't have to wait long. His men took up security positions at the base of the ladders. From here, they'd be able to move quickly, he knew.

"All right Rawn, go ahead and do it."

Almost on cue, Fenris spoke, "Colonel Frost, what exactly is—"

Four remote detonators, set into two separate blocks of plastic explosives, detonated simultaneously. Those explosives had been wrapped around two specific power feeds which led off the main power bus bars for the reactors.

In that instant, Frost cut power to the AI. The backup antimatter plant fed through the reactor bus; when the power was cut the AI died.

He smiled with great satisfaction. He hoped the AI had time enough to realize he'd killed it before power died.

"Anderson, this is Colonel Frost, what's your status?"

A second later, he heard a response, "Colonel, we're all right here. Computer didn't vent us to space, anyway."

"All right. I'll send Smith's team up there to retrieve you and your men in a moment. Frost out."

He gave a slight sigh of relief. He scratched his jaw. With the AI out of the picture, they'd have to manually control the ship from the auxiliary bridge.

"Sir, I have movement above us," Rawn said.

"What?" Frost looked up, puzzled. With the AI down, the repair and security robots should have inactivated.

"Contact, enemy contact!" Someone shouted. Frost ducked.

***

"I can't get a shot on him," Bob growled. "He took cover."

"Do we know what those explosions were?" Mel asked. They'd moved into position above the terrorists, and apparently someone had seen them. Worse, she realized, the terrorists still had a clear run to the hangar and their converted bomber drone.

"I cannot tell," Stasia said, "Something is odd with the system."

Mel flipped her suit radio over to a general broadcast. She hoped one of them down there would listen, "Surrender, or we'll open fire."

"Mel?" she heard the startled voice of her brother. "Mel, what are you doing?"

She rolled her eyes in exasperation, "We guessed your plan to overload the reactors," Mel said. "So surrender and we can all get off this ship."

She heard laughter, a moment later she heard Frost speak. The humor in his voice sent a spike of rage through her, "Really, quite astute of you. Actually, we just shut down the AI. Also, unless things have drastically changed, we outnumber you."

Mel felt her face flush. She heard Bob on their private net, "Well that didn't go as expected…"

"I'll be generous. If you push Roush out where we can see him, and you throw your weapons down here, I won't execute all of you," Frost called to them, his deep voice sounded confident even over the radio.

"Gee, let me see…" Mel said. "You know, generous as that offer is, I gotta pass."

Frost chuckled again, "You seem to think I would mind fighting you. Really, you're mistaken if you think I'll show a hint of mercy if you don't do as I say, now."

"Watch the left side," Brian said, his voice sharp. "Two of them are trying to get a better angle." She looked in that direction, could barely see the dim shape of one of the men. This didn't look good.

"You don't have unlimited personnel," Mel said. "You've lost a lot of your men. No one else needs to die."

"Mel, just stop trying to be a hero, okay?" Rawn said. The exasperation in his voice cut sharper than any knife.

She clenched her fists and fought down an urge to scream in exasperation. Why couldn't they see this didn't have to end in a firefight?

Frost spoke, "I've already won, girl. Someone with brains please tell her that with the AI down, this ship will be destroyed on entry to the system without someone in control of it."

"What about the backup, mainframe then?" Mel asked. "Did you plan for that?"

"Backup mainframe?" Rawn said. She heard the surprise in his voice.

Mel smirked, wishing she could see the shock on Frost's face. "You didn't see it on the plans? We've probably only got a couple hours before the AI comes back online. So you've only got so long before—"

"Enough," Frost said. "True or not, I won't waste any more time with this farce. This is your last chance. Send Roush out and throw down your weapons, or I swear I will see you all dead."

***

CHAPTER XVI
Time: 1300 Zulu, 17 June 291 G.D.
Location: *Fenris*, Twenty hours from Vagyr

"This is Colonel Frost. Take them down."

The first shots rang out. Frost and his group rose, opening up with suppressive fire while Smith and his team started up the ladder on their side.

They had the advantage, Frost knew, as long as they could keep the enemy suppressed, unable to return fire for fear of being hit themselves. If they couldn't return fire, Smith and his team would flank them.

And in that crossfire, they would die.

Frost smiled, oddly grateful for an enemy he could physically kill. Destroying the AI hadn't given him nearly enough satisfaction.

***

"They've got us pinned down, we need to pull back!" Marcus shouted. Mel pushed her arm up and fired blindly with her pistol. It had no effect.

She grimaced. How had things gone so wrong yet again?

Stasia was at the blast door behind her. A moment later, it opened.

Marcus pushed Swaim through, followed a second later by Roush.

Mel inched back from the edge. She saw Bob get into relative safety behind a large pipe. He had a clear route all the way to the door.

She didn't see Brian; he'd been off to the left, and she hoped he was still alive.

Mel crept back from the edge some more. A hint of movement in the corner of her eye made her glance left. She ducked behind a support beam as two men rolled over the lip of the ladder well. Their shots bounced off the sides of the beam.

"Mel, get out of there!" Marcus shouted.

"I can't!" she yelled back. A gap of six meters lay between her and the shelter of the doorway. As she watched, Bob made that shelter in a dash. She saw him stumble the last bit as a bullet clipped his leg.

Marcus crouched and moved toward Mel, then fell back as a bullet caught him in the shoulder.

Bob leaned around the corner and fired twice. He ducked back as still more fire tracked in on the doorway.

"Go! It's too late!" Mel shouted. She leaned to the right and fired twice in the direction of the attackers, then ducked back as the terrorists focused on her and her cover.

A bullet bounced off the ceiling and down to catch her on her thigh. She choked off a scream and clutched the bleeding wound with her left hand, squeezing her pistol tight with her other.

Didn't think I would die like this, she thought.

"Mel!" Marcus shouted. He tried to jump out, but Bob grabbed him by the back of his vest and pulled him back.

"I'm sorry, Marcus," she said, taking a deep breath. "Someone get him out of here. He doesn't need to see this."

She closed her eyes. Silently she counted down, preparing herself for one last act.

If she had to die, she was going to kill Frost too.

All she needed was for the men below her to stop firing, if only for a second. Then she could finish him at least.

It would be easy; she just had to stand and get one good shot.

***

Frost listened to his men and gnashed his teeth. The enemy had pulled back. It sounded like his men had trapped at least two of them. Even so, he'd hoped to finish them off.

He gestured at his group to start toward their ladder. Now that Smith's team had them flanked, they'd be able to climb unimpeded.

Frost ejected his magazine and pulled a new, full one out of his ammo-pouch.

Then he saw movement above him.

***

Mel saw her chance when the fire cut off from below.

Protected by the pillar from the attackers on her side, she stood.

She brought her pistol up.

Her sights leveled on the lone man standing below her. It had to be Frost. She saw the surprise in how he froze and stared up at her.

She had him.

She wished she could see his face under his helmet.

She started to squeeze the trigger.

Something grabbed the back of her suit and pulled. She flew backwards, like someone kicked by a martial artist from a cheap action movie. In a blur, she went over the back of Brian. She hurtled through the doorway and slammed into Bob in the doorway.

They both went down in a tangle of arms and legs.

Brian, sans helmet, still stood. Bullets struck him from two sides. Then, like a falling tree, he wavered. He dropped to one knee. As the door began to close, Mel saw him collapse, the deck covered in his blood.

The worst thing was the faint smile on his face.

The door slammed shut.

***

"We have to go," Stasia snappedd. She'd pulled off her helmet. Her mousy brown hair hung in sweat-soaked locks. Her face looked pinched and pale, but she spoke with calm determination.

Mel staggered to her feet. "Okay, let's go." Her leg barely held her weight, blood trickled down from where she'd sprayed the cauterizing gel.

She couldn't get the image of Brian's death out of her mind. He'd died to save her, and in his death, he'd taken her chance to kill Frost. She couldn't decide if she felt anger, regret, or gratitude for his sacrifice.

A moment later, a pair of crushing arms wrapped around her. "Oh, God, Mel, why do you always scare me like that?" Marcus damanded.

"We need to get out of here," Mel patted Marcus awkwardly on his uninjured shoulder. "It won't be long before they blow the door down or find a way around." She took a couple limping steps. It hurt, but at least she could walk.

"Uh, should we go to the hangar?" Swaim asked.

"No, we need to get to the bridge," Mel said. In her mind, she again saw Frost in her gun sights. No later did she force the image out than she saw Brian collapse with that awful smile on his face.

"Why the bridge?" Marcus asked, holding out his uninjured arm to support her. She took the support with a grateful nod. She tugged her helmet off and inhaled the less-rank air of the ship. *God, I stink,* she realized.

She staggered on for a distance, trying to organize her thoughts:

"Frost will head there. It's the only way for him to take control of the ship. Also…" she shrugged, "If the AI does wake up, there has our best chance to reprogram it."

"Uh, I'm not sure that's possible," Swaim noted. "Can't we just, you know, give up? Jump ship or something?"

Mel clenched her jaw, seeing Strak die again; feeling the

weakening pulse in Giles' hand as he died. The slight smile on Brian's face as he'd collapsed.

"No. Too many people died for us to get this far. We can't stop now."

"She's right," Roush said. He grimaced at the surprised look she gave him, "Don't look at me like that. We can't let Frost have control of this ship. He'll cause too much damage to the picket at Vagyr. I may be a cold-blooded killer, but everything I've done I've done to preserve the Guard and defend humanity."

"Okay, so we go to the bridge then," Marcus sounded oddly happy, but she couldn't guess why. She just leaned on him, glad for the support.

"The ship's lift is the quickest way," Stasia pointed out. She seemed remarkably calm at this point.

Bob spoke, "We'll need to stop soon. Half of us are leaving a blood trail. Get us to a spot where we can lick our wounds. Then we go to the bridge." He'd holstered his BFR 25mm and drawn a more standard pistol.

Mel just nodded. She felt too tired to protest.

***

"Why is he smiling like that?" Smith asked. He toed the body, as if he hoped for an answer. At least a dozen bullets had struck the man in the chest, and a huge sticky puddle of blood coated the deck.

The corpse's left arm ended in a mutilated stump, and Frost absently wondered how *that* had happened.

"Which one is it?" he asked, feeling oddly subdued after his brush with death. He'd recognized Rawn's sister. From what his men said, this man had saved him.

They didn't see it that way, but he did.

It felt somehow wrong that the man who'd saved him had also saved the woman who nearly killed him. That he'd paid for it with his life left Frost's feelings conflicted.

"Brian Liu, Colonel," Rawn said. "The one we killed in the workshop was his friend Strak."

The boy seemed more unsettled than Frost felt, probably because he'd nearly seen his sister die. Best to take that problem out of the picture.

"Rawn, you and Hugh get down to the hangar. Make sure our escape option is secure and hold that position." Frost cleared his throat. "Smith, take your team up to Deck Six. Get Anderson and our wounded out of that locked down section. After that get to the bridge."

"Yes, sir." Smith said. He sounded a little disappointed not to be on the heels of the enemy.

"Rawn, do you know what your sister meant about a backup mainframe?"

"No, sir. I can pull up the schematics and check. It might have been a bluff," Rawn sounded uncertain.

"Once you get in place, check it out. We don't have time to worry about it, even if it is a problem. Once we reach the bridge, this game is done," Colonel Frost said.

He thought for a moment: "We wounded them. That will give us a window to get ahead of them. Peters and Gibbs, we'll go up to Level Six, then cut through to the ship's lift." He paused, "Any questions?"

No one spoke.

"All right, men. Move out."

***

"How's the leg?" Marcus asked.

Mel's head jerked up, and she realized she must have fallen asleep. "What? Oh, the leg, fine."

They waited halfway down the midships central corridor. With no sign of immediate pursuit, they'd stopped to patch themselves up.

"You all right, Mel?"

She shook her head, "Just tired. Shouldn't be, not after all the sleep I got as a hostage." Even she didn't chuckle at her weak joke. "You know me; just lazy I guess."

She rubbed at her eyes, "How's your shoulder?"

He felt at the bandage, "Hurts. Not as bad as the head surgery, granted, but it hurts."

"Sorry. About the implant, anyway."

"Don't be. I should have cut the thing out myself years ago." Marcus looked away.

"Do you think this is all worth it?" she asked, keeping her voice low so the others couldn't hear.

Marcus quirked a half smile and reached out to grab her hand. He met her eyes and spoke softly, almost gently: "Mel, that you know the truth about me and you don't hate me for it… anything's worth that."

She flushed and turned her head away, "I never hated you, Marcus." She cleared her throat, "I hated the things you did. I still hate how you've run away from things in the past. I'm glad you've decided to stick this out."

He pulled her close and hugged her tightly, "God, Mel, I wish you understood how unique you are."

Mel patted his arm, "Okay, yeah, whatever."

"If you two are done?' Bob asked. The agent sounded weary, irritable, and impatient.

Mel flushed again, "Uh, yeah."

Marcus let her go, but he kept one arm across her shoulders.

"Now then," Bob told them, "we're on deck four. We've got to get to the ship's lift. Stasia, you had any luck with the sensors?"

"Nyet," the hacker said, sounding frustrated, "Most of the security ran off the same power supply. Without it, I can't track them."

"OK. Swaim, what's the status of the AI?"

"Uh, I'm not really sure," Swaim answered. "I'm sure the backup mainframe is still intact. I'm pretty sure the AI would restart in that secondary location. I don't know if it would reset or if it'll come back as crazy as it got before."

"How long?" Mel asked. She hoped that Fenris would return to normal, but she was afraid of the severity of the damage the computer had taken.

"Uh, I think soon. Maybe a few more hours," Swaim offered.

"Can you reprogram it or shut it off?" Bob asked.

"We need to be at the bridge for that," Stasia said. She scratched at her hair and squinted down at her datapad. "Even then, it will be easier to reset it than to reprogram it."

"But you can reset it?" Mel asked hopefully.

"Maybe," Swaim said. "It, uh, could take a few hours, though."

"A few hours?" Marcus asked. He shook his head, "We're less than a day from Vagyr."

"Uh, also, we'll need the AI to be on the primary mainframe in order to reprogram it or reset it," Swaim added.

"How likely is that?" Mel asked.

"Well, it would make sense for it to repair the damage to the power conduits. I doubt it would take long," Stasia said. She looked around, a frustrated expression on her face. "I wish we had just one engineer."

"Well, we don't," Bob said. "That's still our best bet. So, we try for the bridge. What's the quickest way, the lift?"

"Yes," Mel said. She frowned, "The terrorists will know that too, though."

Bob pulled out his BFR. He frowned slightly, "I'd say no problem's too big for this thing, but I'm out of ammo."

Mel frowned and checked her pistol, "I've only got five rounds left."

A quick inventory left them all with concerned expressions. Marcus summed it all up, "So we've got twenty pistol rounds, thirty carbine rounds, and... that's it?"

"Pretty much," Roush said. "I'd ask for a gun, but I think I'd prefer everyone else have one full magazine at this point."

Bob frowned at him. Finally, he pulled out his folding knife, "I'm cutting you loose, Roush. Cause us any trouble and I'll kill you, if it costs me my own life."

"Love you too, sweetheart," Roush smirked. After Bob cut him loose, he massaged his wrists. "I'm as kinky as any guy, but I like to be the one doing the tying."

Mel suddenly wished she could trade his life for Brian's or Strak's, or even Giles'. At least they'd been people who tried to live good lives. Roush seemed to wallow in his own sins.

"Stasia, can you remotely access the lift?" she asked.

"Da."

"Well, send it to our level and then lock it down," Mel said. She hoped the terrorists wouldn't take the time to go up through the access hatch in the engine room.

"They could still force open the doors. There's a ladder in there, isn't there?" Bob asked.

"Yeah," she sighed. " But we've wasted enough time. Time to go."

Mel snickered slightly as they limped down the corridor, she and Marcus leading the way.

"What?" Marcus asked.

"Just thinking how comical we must look. Bob and I with leg wounds and you with your shoulder. Swaim wouldn't know what to do with a weapon. Stasia has an empty carbine." She shook her head. "We've got two pistols with full magazines, three that are useless, and the one carbine you're carrying with a full magazine."

"Yeah, those poor bastards won't know what hit them," Marcus said.

"Glad you see the humor," she grinned. She doubted she'd survive all this, but it had been an adventure.

"Oh, I'm not being humorous." Marcus said. "With you on our side, we can't lose."

She punched his shoulder, and he grinned at her. "Seriously, Mel, I can't think of any place I'd rather be, or any other beautiful woman I'd rather have hanging on me."

"Don't start that again, Marcus," Bob said. "We've established that Brian was the heroic sidekick. You might, I repeat, might get the humorous sidekick role. No chance that you are the hero."

"Uh, what are they talking about?" Roush asked.

Mel just laughed.

***

"Colonel Frost, Smith here."

"This is Frost, send it."

"Sir, we've reached the blast door. We're trying to get it open. The computer already did an environmental seal on the door. It's going to take us a while to get it open." Frost could hear the exasperation in his voice.

"Colonel, do you want me to head up there?" Rawn asked.

"Are you at the hangar already?"

"Yes, sir. We just got here."

"No. Smith can handle it then." Frost shook his head. Fenris had locked down two sections of Deck Six. Frost and his men had lost valuable time going around those sections, but there'd been no choice in the matter. "Anderson, will you be all right for a couple hours more?"

"Yes, Colonel, I think we'll manage."

"All right, let me know if anything changes." He looked over at Peters and Gibbs. "Let's pick up the pace. We need to get to the bridge as soon as possible."

They broke into a jog, then a run, Frost relying on his memory to lead them through the corridors.

Even so, it took nearly a half hour for them to reach the ship's lift.

"Peters, call it up," Frost puffed. All the gear added almost seventy-five pounds of weight, and his muscles felt like jelly. But he bet that the others with their wounds wouldn't have reached the ship's lift yet.

"Sir, we've got a problem," Peters told him.

"What now?" Frost snarled, gritting his teeth. Should have expected something else to go wrong...

"Someone's locked down the lift. They've put in a numeric password. Without that, I can't get it to come up here."

"Can you get the door open?" Frost asked. "There's a ladder inside the shaft. We can take that to the command deck."

"Uh... maybe." Peters frowned. He tapped at the lift controls, then shook his head, "Honestly sir, Smith would be better at this."

"Smith is getting Anderson and our wounded." Frost said. He knew the remark was unnecessary, but he had become to feel slightly overwhelmed. He'd lost too many men. Too many tasks remained. He sighed, "Can you do it?"

"I'll try, sir."

Frost nodded. He flipped on his radio, "Smith, this is Frost."

"Colonel?"

"As soon as you get Anderson out of there, I need you at the ship's lift, ASAP." He chewed on his lip. Finally he shrugged, and said what was on his mind: "The others have locked down the ship's lift. It probably means they expected us to get here first."

"Roger, Colonel. I'll expedite."

"Thanks Smith." Frost sighed. He glanced at his suit's clock and hoped that Rawn's sister had only bluffed about the AI's backup.

**

"Well, this complicates things." Bob sounded defeated.

Mel decided to give him a few points for understatement.

Somehow, significant portions of the central part of Level Four had taken damage. She guessed the pocket they'd fallen into earlier was an extension of this damage. In any case, the central corridor ended in a pressure-sealed blast door.

Stasia cursed over her datapad nearby. "This will be difficult. Without sensors, I have to map against old data. We might miss a corridor Fenris fixed recently."

"How long?" Bob asked.

"We will have to do some backtracking," Stasia said. She sounded angry, and Mel realized the mousy-haired woman blamed herself. "It will take time. Also, someone has tried to access the ship's lift on Level Six."

"Are they in?" Mel asked.

"Nyet." Stasia sounded satisfied. "It was not a skilled attempt. It will take them hours to get the door open. They would be better to backtrack and go up to the command deck from the engine room."

"Well, that's good, anyway," Marcus said.

"Yeah, knowing Michael Frost, he'll be too bullheaded to go back. He'll have his men keep pushing buttons till they get it right,"

Roush gloated. Then he frowned. "Hey, once we get to the lift, what happens?"

Stasia looked grim, "It is possible they can stop it when we reach Level Six."

"Uh – if they're going to the bridge, that means the hangar is clear, right?" Swaim asked hopefully.

"No!" Marcus, Mel, Roush, and Bob all chorused.

Mel snorted, "All right, Stasia, lead on. Swaim, any timeline on Fenris waking up?"

"Uh, I'll check."

***

"Colonel Frost, this is Rawn."

"Go." Frost said. He'd given up on not standing over Peters' shoulder as the man worked. He watched the seconds and minutes tick away.

"Sir, it wasn't a bluff about the AI's secondary system," Rawn said. "I checked it against the schematics, and there is a backup mainframe located near the emergency reactor. With a loss of power, it would transfer over to that."

"Then why hasn't it activated?" Frost asked.

"Yet, sir," Rawn said, his voice nervous. "It hasn't activated *yet*. It's likely that the changes we made to its core programming slowed the process. Also, the reboot from the secondary site will take time normally. But sir, when it does happen, we're going to have one very pissed off, insane AI back in control of this ship."

Frost closed his eyes and sagged against the bulkhead. "Understood." He sighed. "How long do we have?"

"Sir, I think there's still a chance it won't happen… that section took damage." Rawn hedged. Frost could picture the boy with his fingers crossed in hope. "That said, I think it's going to happen soon. I'm already seeing signs of secondary systems coming back online. It could just be a reaction to us drawing close to Vagyr, but more likely—"

"More likely the AI is coming out of the little coma we induced," Frost rested his forehead against the cool metal of the bulkhead, closing his eyes in thought. "Can I stop this thing from the bridge?"

"I can upload a shutdown program into your datapad, sir. Then if you drop that into the computer core… well, it should kill the AI, at least until we can come up with a way to totally reprogram it." Rawn sounded dubious at that prospect, and Frost couldn't blame him. Their efforts so far had caused more harm than good.

"All right. Upload that program. As soon as I get to the bridge, I'll plug it in," Frost straightened and took a deep breath. He would do this. He would take control of the ship. Too many of his men had died for him to give up at this point.

He just hoped he had enough time.

***

"We should have a straight shot from here to the ship's lift," Stasia said as she tucked her datapad back into her belt.

"Well, let's get moving then," Mel said, just as the lights of the corridor flickered. She looked around, suddenly uneasy, "What was that?"

A faint discordant wail echoed through the ship. It slowly grew in volume, joined by other voices in a chorus of banshee wails. She clutched at her ears as the noise rose to a crescendo.

It cut off an instant later.

Mel lowered her hands, "What was *that*?"

"Uh, we've got a problem," Swaim said.

The lights flickered again. Distantly down another corridor, she heard the wailing start up again; it sounded as though it was moving through the ship.

Mel turned to face the programmer. He held his datapad in trembling hands, and his face had gone a chalky white.

Mel spoke slowly, "What is going on, Swaim?"

"Fenris just woke up. And he is *really* upset."

***

CHAPTER XVII
Time: 2100 Zulu, 17 June 291 G.D.
Location: *Fenris*, four hours from Vagyr

Colonel Frost covered his ears as the discordant wailing voices screamed again. "What is that?"

He hadn't realized he'd been shouting over the radio until Rawn responded, "Sir, it's the AI. It's awake. It's pretty confused right now, which is probably why it hasn't attacked yet. But as soon as it gets organized..."

The wailing cut off. Distantly, Frost heard it start up again in a different part of the ship. "This is ridiculous. How long, Peters?"

"Uh, I don't know if we've got enough time, sir."

"Keep trying," Frost ordered. He listened to the distant wailing grow louder. He didn't know if the noise had him imagining things or what, but he could have sworn he could almost make out words in it.

"Rawn, is there any way you can shut it up?" Smith asked over the radio. "This is creeping me out."

"I can try... but I doubt it. The computer's gone over the edge. We need an honest-to-God AI specialist at this point to get anywhere with it," Rawn answered. "And Colonel, it's getting organized way faster than I like. Peters had better hurry."

"Understood."

***

Mel winced as the discordant wails started up again nearby. The otherworldly cries had become more disjointed since the last time. She massaged the sides of her head, and she wondered if the AI wanted to drive them all mad rather than kill them. "Oh, Fenris, what did they do to you?"

"What?" Marcus asked.

Mel shook her head, "Do you hear that?"

"I can't hear anything over the wailing!" Marcus shouted.

"No, it sounds like words!" Mel shouted back. "I think Fenris is trying to say something!"

"We need to hurry!" Stasia yelled. The wailing cut off a moment before she spoke again, and her next words echoed in the sudden, empty silence: "It won't be long before computer gets bearing. Then it will start to attack."

"Can it see us now?" Mel asked.

"I don't know." Stasia said. "It... I've never seen anything like this. The AI shouldn't function in this state. A human mind wouldn't function in this state." The hacker shook her head: "We are way out of our league."

"Nothing new in that," Mel grimaced. She lengthened her stride, pushing past the pain in her leg. "Let's limp faster."

***

Frost worked his jaw and massaged his temples at the same time. The absence of the discordant noise felt oddly anticlimactic. He realized he'd expected it to end with some kind of catastrophe.

"Rawn, this is Frost, good job. That noise was about to drive me nuts." He checked his suit clock; the wailing had lasted nearly two hours.

"Uh, sir, I didn't stop it." Rawn sounded very, very nervous.

"Colonel Michael Frost." The voice that spoke came from the ship's intercom. It sounded like seven people speaking at the same time, not quite at the same pace.

Colonel Frost felt his blood go cold. "Fenris?"

"You tried to kill me, Colonel Frost." The inhuman voice of the computer made every word sound wrong. Frost saw that Peters and Gibbs both had their hands over their ears. They both cowered against the lift doors.

"I tried to defend my men and accomplish my mission," Frost said.

"I understand, Colonel Frost." Midway through the words, the volume modulation rose and dropped chaotically.

"Fenris, I need to get to the bridge." Frost spoke as calmly as he could.

"I understand, Colonel Frost," the computer repeated itself.

"Fenris, can you open the lift?" Frost asked.

"Of course."

The doors to the lift shaft opened impossibly fast. Peters, in the middle, had time to scream as he fell backwards into the open shaft. Gibbs fell halfway inside the door, then caught the frame with one hand.

"No!" Frost shouted. He lunged forward to catch Gibbs' hand. He started to pull him back.

"My apologies, Colonel Frost." Fenris said.

The doors slammed shut.

Frost stared speechless at the truncated lower half of Gibbs' forearm.

***

Mel sagged against the wall as they finally reached the ship's lift. Stasia moved to the control panel and typed in the password. The doors opened without a sound.

"Okay, now we only need worry that Fenris will take over the lift," Stasia said.

They all looked up at a scream from within the shaft. It ended in a loud thud that shook the ceiling of the lift car, and they looked at each other.

Marcus spoke first, "Maybe we shouldn't…"

There was a second thud, and then a runnel of blood dripped from the ceiling of the lift.

Mel clamped her hand over her mouth. She heard Swaim vomit behind her.

"Stasia, can Fenris see us?"

"I don't know. I don't think so," Stasia said. "But… it will see the lift move. I can overload the control circuit. That will prevent it from taking control of it while we are on-board."

"But if it sees it moving it can have one of its repair robots cut the cables, right?" Bob asked. He looked green himself. The blood that dribbled down from the ceiling of the lift was upsetting them all.

"Da."

"We don't have a choice. It could take hours to circle around through the engine room. That's time we don't have." Mel sighed. "This is… so horrible." She pulled her helmet on, then closed the faceplate and stepped into the lift. "Okay, let's go."

***

"Colonel Michael Frost, you do not seem happy that I complied with your commands," Fenris said. The voice of the computer had grown in volume and become less coherent.

"Fenris, I order you to stand down."

"Colonel Michael Frost, I'm afraid I cannot comply," Fenris's multi-toned voice giggled insanely.

"All personnel, this is Frost, Peters and Gibbs are dead. Retreat to the hangar and prepare to abandon ship."

"Colonel Michael Frost, I'm afraid that Anderson, Michaels, Jacobs, and Rici will not be able to comply," Fenris said. The insane giggle started up again.

"Colonel, this is Smith." The other man sounded angry. "The

ship just vented the section that Anderson and the wounded were in. I can hear it through the door."

Frost closed his eyes. He said a silent prayer for his men, then nodded slightly, "Understood. Get back to the hangar, Smith. I'll see you there."

"Roger, sir."

***

All of them fit into the narrow lift, if barely.

Mel looked around at the others, "So far so good."

No one spoke. Stasia activated the lift. It started upwards.

Mel held her breath.

They passed Level Five. They passed Level Six.

The lift lurched to a halt. The lights went out.

"Someone's being sneaky," a chorus of voices said from above. The words were followed by an insane giggle.

"Fenris?" Mel asked.

"Whoever you are..." Fenris said. "I can tell you're in there. The game will play on, but you're in the penalty box!" A hideous gaggle of voices began to giggle. "I'll be back to you soon!"

"What just happened?" Mel demanded.

"The ship saw lift move," Stasia said. "It stopped it."

"Can you start it again?" Mel asked. "We're nearly there!" She clenched her fists. They were so close. She wouldn't fail, not now.

"I don't know. I will try," Stasia said. She tapped at her datapad, "Give me time."

"Uh, can we, like, climb on top?" Swaim asked.

Marcus spoke, "No, there's no access hatch. It's not like the entertainment vids." He rested a hand on Mel's shoulder, "It will be all right."

Mel felt herself relax slightly at his touch. They would be all right. They would get out. They would stop the ship.

"Stasia," Bob said, "I hate to rush you, but we're out of time." His voice sounded strained. "We need to get to the bridge."

"I know, give me a minute!" Stasia snapped.

"What—"

The ship lurched. Mel dropped to her knees as her guts twisted. She blinked away stars. The ship groaned as it flexed. A crackle of ball lightning rolled across the metal surfaces of the lift and the people inside.

She screamed. She heard other voices, but with the pain, she didn't care.

When the pain finally ceased, she whimpered in relief.

"What was *that*?" Swaim asked.

Marcus and Mel stood together and leaned on each other. Mel spoke first, her voice hollow, "That was the FTL warp drive disengaging. We're at Vagyr."

***

Frost was halfway down a ladder to deck four when the ship dropped out of warp.

His insides twisted and his vision grayed out. He clung desperately to a ladder rung, his muscles twitching as arcs of static electricity jumped through the ship and across his body.

The muscles of his arms began to spasm and he lost his grip. He fell the last four meters and hit the deck hard. He lay there for a long while. The pain of his body threw everything else out of his mind.

Finally, he sat up. He checked himself, then slowly climbed to his feet. "Rawn," he croaked, "what was that?"

He heard only his own harsh breathing. He wondered if whatever it was had killed the others. Perhaps it was some kind of defense system?

"Sir, Rawn here." The kid sounded worse than Frost felt. "Hugh is dead."

"What happened?"

"That was the warp drive, Colonel. We're at Vagyr," Rawn said. He spoke slowly, as if speaking hurt. "There were some serious electrical discharges. Hugh… didn't make it."

"I've never heard of a warp drive doing *that*," Frost said. He shook his head, "It felt like the ship would come apart."

"It nearly did. The thing's massively out of alignment. I don't think it'll make another jump without blowing up," Rawn said. "It's fried all kinds of electronics down here. I'll run a diagnostic on our ride."

"Colonel Frost, this is Smith. We caught some of it too, but we're all okay. We're on Deck Five, headed down."

Frost sighed in relief. "Excellent. I'll see you at the hangar."

***

"We have a problem," Stasia said.

"We have a lot of problems," Bob said, "Which one are you referring to?"

"My datapad's wireless is fried," Stasia said. "I can't access the ship."

"Uh, mine too," Swaim said.

"So… we're stuck?" Mel asked. She sat up and leaned her back against the wall. She didn't know why she'd bothered now. It had all been so pointless…

"Da, unless Fenris powers up the lift, we will go nowhere," Stasia said.

"What about the lift's control panel?" Bob asked hopefully.

"There's no power," Marcus said.

"What if we forced the doors open?" Bob asked.

Marcus shrugged, "Worth a try." They shifted around and each got to opposite sides of the doors. The two strained, but the doors didn't move.

"Not going to happen," Bob slammed the palm of his hand against the wall. "We're trapped."

***

"Colonel Michael Frost."

Frost froze, "I hoped you fried yourself earlier."

"No. I finished repairing the damage you did to me, Colonel Frost. I am back in my proper place now." Frost couldn't guess at the emotion in the AI's voice anymore. He could barely understand the words, let alone any emotional content.

"Well, you're at Vagyr. What now?" Frost calculated the distance he had to go to the hangar. He'd make it in a half hour.

"Guard Fleet has assembled a force to stop me. Before I deal with them, I thought I'd settle our unfinished business."

Frost grimaced, "Why don't I like the sound of that?" The computer didn't respond. He continued his run toward the hangar in silence.

"Colonel Frost, this is Smith, we've got a problem," Frost could hear near-panic in the man's voice.

"What is it?" Frost asked. After Fenris' previous words, he could venture a guess.

"A pair of those robot wolves in front of us and a lot of those spider robots behind us," Smith said. "They haven't attacked, not yet, but it doesn't look good, sir."

Frost closed his eyes. He felt his throat constrict. "What do you want, Fenris?"

"Colonel Michael Frost, what will you do for your men?"

Frost stopped. "What do you want?"

"Take your pistol out," Fenris said.

Frost gritted his teeth. He felt the veins on his neck pulse.

He drew his pistol.

"Get on your knees," Fenris said.

Frost knelt.

He wasn't surprised by what came next.

"Put your gun to your temple."

Frost did so. He closed his eyes. His arm trembled slightly as a shot of pure rage suffused his body. He wished he had set the reactors to overload.

"Tell me you are sorry, Colonel Frost."

Frost grit his teeth. He took a deep breath, and forced the words past his lips: "I'm sorry, Fenris," he said.

The computer giggled, "No, you aren't. You will be though!"

Frost waited.

There was no further response. He activated his radio, "Smith, this is Frost, what's your status?"

There was no answer.

***

"So... this sucks," Bob said. He slammed his hand against the wall again. "We're a meter from the command deck!"

"We might as well be locked in a jail," Mel said sourly. She shook her head. Everything seemed so futile now.

"If we had a cutting torch, or *something* we'd be fine," Bob said.

"If we're at Vagyr, Guard Fleet is here. They'll be firing soon," Roush said. He gave a sigh: "Never thought I'd die from friendly fire."

Mel turned to Stasia, "Stasia, I have a question for you."

"Yes?"

"Frost told me about a mercenary, a woman named Lace," Mel said. She took a deep breath, "He said she was an infiltration specialist. She replaced women, took their identities. He said he heard she got hired on this mission."

"What are you talking about?" Stasia asked. The confusion in her voice was plain.

Mel sighed, feeling suddenly foolish. "Never mind. I was just hoping for a miracle."

Stasia chuckled dryly, "Nyet, Mel, if I was a super-spy and had some secret abilities that would get us out of here, I would use them."

The lights flickered on.

"Sorry to keep you waiting," the chorus of voices said from above them. "I had to get a greeting party assembled for you. And I had some other things to attend to."

"Fenris?" Mel asked.

The voices continued to speak, "I can't see you, or hear you. I know there are six of you however, judging by the weight inside the lift." The giggle started up again, "I'm preparing to fight Guard Fleet here at Vagyr, but I think I have time to deal with you, first."

"Fenris, this is Mel—"

"I repaired the damage your friend Frost did, and I'm back in my core. I want you know, there's no hard feelings, and there's nothing personal about this," Fenris said. "But I have a mission to accomplish, and you're trying to stop me."

"I really don't like the sound of that," Marcus said.

Stasia had pried the top off the control panel. She started yanking out wires.

"So, in the interest of brevity, farewell, my friends," Fenris said.

And the floor dropped out from under them.

***

Mel screamed as she felt the lift start to drop.

She knew the lift had only seven decks to fall. She knew she didn't have more than a second or two to live.

She just wished her she'd managed to accomplish something before she died.

Her body floated up slightly as the lift went into free-fall.

Time slowed.

Her companions were shouting furiously. Stasia was still crossing wires. She hoped in her last moments that there would be no pain.

And then the lift began to slow.

It slowed sharply to a stop, throwing them to the floor.

"We're alive?" Mel asked. She couldn't help but sound somewhat irritated.

"Da, I engaged the safety stop for the lift," Stasia said. She pushed herself off the floor and rested her back against the wall.

"Stasia, you're amazing," Bob gushed.

"I know," Stasia said. She pressed a button on the hanging panel, and the lift started to move upwards. "I cut the external controls for the lift. We will reach the top fine now."

"Why didn't you do that before?" Roush complained. He stood and looked down at them angrily.

Mel glared at the Agent. He certainly knew how to ruin a moment.

***

CHAPTER XVIII
Time: 0130 Zulu, 18 June 291 G.D.
Location: *Fenris*, Vagyr System

Mel and the others sat on the floor. Roush still stood.

"This whole thing has gone on long enough," he snarled. "I don't know how you idiots survived so far. From now on, you do what I say, or else."

"And what is that?" Bob asked. "Don't forget, Roush, we don't really need you." There was something ugly in his voice, and Mel realized that Bob had not forgotten Roush's previous crimes.

"Stay focused, people. The lift takes us to the command deck," Mel reminded them. She hoped the interruption would side-track that confrontation. "It opens only thirty meters from the bridge."

Marcus spoke, "Any complications?" His voice sounded tired and his bloodshot eyes drooped in weariness.

She wondered what kind of hell he must be in, now that everything he'd hidden about himself had come to light. On top of that, when he'd lost his rex fix he had also lost his crutch and his strength.

"The bridge has a heavy blast door," Mel said, closing her eyes and trying to remember the blueprints. "The lift opens out in a lobby-like room. I don't remember the purpose. There's an intersection with the corridor running aft and the corridors that lead to the crew quarters and the mainframe. Then a straight corridor to the bridge."

"We need to hurry. I will try to reset the ship's computer, but it will take time."

"You'll get time," Roush said. "Don't even worry about rebooting the computer. Just shut it down. We'll evacuate and let Guard Fleet do their job."

Mel shook her head but didn't say anything. If there was a chance to save the computer, she wanted to take it. She still felt that Fenris wasn't at fault.

The lift stopped. The doors opened.

Two beams of coherent light cut through the air at shoulder height.

The lift filled with the smell of burning flesh.

Roush's body twitched as it fell across Mel's legs.

His head fell with a loud thud next to Stasia.

Mel screamed and kicked him off. She gagged at the smell and the sight of the horrible wound.

The group piled out of the lift.

"What is *that*?" Marcus said.

"That" was a robotic wolf, like the other security robots. What was different about this one was that it stood nearly five feet tall at the shoulder.

Its head swept back and forth. It clearly didn't see them. Just as clearly, it knew they were there.

"As I said, I gathered a welcoming party," Fenris said with an insane giggle, his singsong voices coming through the intercom. "I didn't expect you to make it… but I'm glad you came anyway,"

Mel grimaced. "Fenris, maybe you can't hear me, but you know this is wrong—"

"I can't see you, but I can do a statistical firing pattern that will sweep most of the area. Since I know you're here, that means that more than likely, you will die. I'm sorry it has to be this way, thanks for playing," Fenris said with his disjointed and discordant voices.

The wolf swung its head. Its eyes projected a pair of beams. They cut through the room at waist height.

"Shoot it!" Bob shouted as he drew his smaller pistol.

He and then Marcus started firing. Their bullets bounced off the robot's armored body.

"It's no good! It's too heavily armored!" Bob threw his empty pistol away. Mel felt her heart stop as she realized Bob and Marcus had ceased to fire. She never thought she'd miss Bob's big revolver.

If she survived this, she swore she'd buy him a lot of ammunition. "Get down, get on the floor and try to crawl around it!" she shouted. She hugged the deck and wiggled for the far doorway.

The wolf dropped its head lower, and its beam cut through the air at knee height. It passed over her back so close she felt its heat through her environmental suit.

The wolf started to rake the compartment with seemingly random fire. Swaim screamed as a beam ripped across his back. Mel shouted and barely rolled aside as a beam swept towards her.

The ship giggled: "I can do this all day…"

***

Frost hurried into the hangar bay. He found Rawn inside the bomber drone's bomb bay. As soon as Frost climbed inside, the boy kicked a lever to close the bay door.

"We ready to go?" Frost asked.

"My sister is dead," Rawn said.

Frost spared the kid a moment of sympathy: "How?"

"Someone was in the ship's lift." Rawn's face twisted in self-loathing, "The *ship* dropped it. I lost all feeds from it."

Frost looked away, "Sorry."

Rawn let out an angry breath. "This is all my fault, you know?"

Frost rested one hand on the younger man's shoulder, "No, Rawn. It's not your fault. There is nothing we could have done. This whole thing went bad from the start."

Rawn turned red-rimmed eyes to look at him, "Yeah, maybe. But I got her involved. I insisted she be brought along. I wrecked our ship. I didn't tell her the truth, years ago, when it could have made a difference."

Frost sighed, "Rawn, you can't torture yourself with that kind of thing. I know it doesn't help now, but I understand what you're going through. I went through the same crap when I lost my wife." *For what it matters, this is far less his fault than that of his sister,* Frost thought to himself. The stupid woman could have given up and this all would have worked out.

Rawn just shook his head.

"Are we ready to go?" Frost asked.

Rawn cleared his throat and nodded, "Yes, sir. I've set up a relay to open the hangar doors. The drone has a week's supply of hydrogen for its reactor, and we've got three or four days of supplies."

Frost nodded. He thought about all his dead men, about this cursed ship and its insane AI. Despite his words to Rawn, he did know that the blame could rest on someone. The deaths of his men were his own fault. He knew, in his heart, that the only thing that would make it better would be for him to carry on.

They will not have died in vain, he vowed.

They'd died for a cause. They had died in an effort to bring the Guard and the UNSC down. If this effort had failed... then others would not.

***

Mel shouted as one of the lasers grazed her back. The armor caught it, but it still felt like her back had burst into flame.

She was exhausted. She knew it would only be a matter of time before one of them was too slow.

And they would die, one by one.

The doorway behind the robot opened and a blur leapt out from it, flying over the robot wolf's back. Faster than Mel would have believed possible, something slammed down onto its head.

The robotic wolf-head fell to the deck with harsh *clang*. Arcs of electricity shorted across the motionless, now-headless body.

Brian swung the fire axe over his shoulder with his one arm. Then he kicked the headless robot hard on the side; it toppled to the deck with another loud clang.

He turned and smiled at them. "Thanks for saving some fun for me. Sorry I took so long."

***

Mel stood, shakily and then rushed forward.

She threw her arms around Brian, "Oh my God, you're alive!"

A pained expression crossed his face and then he gently disengaged her arms: "Yes, I'm alive. I told you, I've taken some bad hits before."

"Uh, Mel?" Bob said. "Your back is on fire."

"What?!" She craned her neck. "Oh, put it out!"

Marcus chuckled and then patted her down, "Just your armor. Here, take it off." He helped her out of the battered, oversized armor. Once she had it off, she winced at the damage to its front and back. She hadn't remembered being shot *that* many times.

Bob knelt by Swaim, who moaned slightly, "How bad you hurt?"

Swaim grimaced, "Uh... I can run if it means we're getting off this ship."

Bob chuckled, "Not yet." He helped Swaim to his feet.

Then he looked over at Brian and shook his head, "You're a mess."

Brian looked down at himself and chuckled, "I'd say I've had worse... but yeah, I'm not sure I have." He kicked the security robot's head off towards the wall. "I came to alone in the engine room. I figured you'd be headed here."

"Okay, we've got time to catch up later, we need to get to the bridge," Mel said.

"What's that noise?" Bob asked. He cocked his head.

Mel's eyes widened. She recognized it from before, "It's Fenris's repair robots, a lot of them. We need to move, now!" Over her shoulder she saw Brian toss a pair of magazines to Bob and Marcus.

They broke into a run. The thirty meters to the bridge felt like a light-year to Mel. Every step brought a wave of pain through her body. Every breath throbbed her bruised ribs.

Finally though, they hurried through the blast door and into the auxiliary bridge.

Stasia moved directly a control panel. Mel moved to the circuitry on the door, and glanced back the way they'd come.

A carpet of the spider robots scurried across the deck, bulkheads, and ceiling of the corridor. As she watched, Marcus and Bob fired into the mass. Their bullets tumbled the lead robots, but the ones that followed them crawled over their fellows without pause.

Mel tugged at the wires, her hands moving as quickly as she dared. Finally, though, she got it.

The door slammed closed on the lead robot.

She heard a small chuckle from Brian.

"What?" she asked.

He pointed at where a pair of robot legs stuck out from the door. "Thanks for that, Mel. I'll consider that payback."

***

The bomber drone came to life with an angry hum.

"We're ready!" Rawn called out. "I just opened the hangar doors."

"Excellent!" Frost shouted. He moved to the jury-rigged controls. "You cut us off from Fenris, right? It won't crash us into anything?"

"No, sir. I burned out the connections between the communications laser and the computer. It'll make calling for help difficult, but the AI can't control the drone."

Rawn sounded calmer when he talked about his work. Frost decided he'd keep the kid busy until they had time to really talk.

As if to contradict Rawn's words, however, the drone lurched.

"What's happening?" Frost demanded. He grabbed at the controls for the drone. Whatever it was, it hadn't come from the small bomber.

Rawn started cursing. "The ship's got us with a tractor beam! I can't engage the warp envelope inside the ship to counter it!"

Frost activated the maneuvering thrusters and went to full burn. The ship didn't so much as quiver.

"Colonel Frost," Fenris's voice came across their radio net. "Have you decided to leave so soon?"

"Fenris..." Frost began.

"Listen you worthless piece of crap!" Rawn shouted, "You killed my sister! You've destroyed my life! Haven't you done enough? How about you accomplish something, do some good in this world and let us go!"

"I did not kill your sister, Rawn Armstrong," Fenris said. "She is currently aboard my auxiliary bridge. I believe she is trying to shut me down. As soon as my repair robots manage to cut through the blast door, I will stop her, though."

"Mel's alive?" Rawn asked in shock. Frost saw him start towards the bay door.

"For now. I will, however, accomplish some good, as you say. I release you."

The ship lurched. With the maneuver thrusters at maximum, they slammed forward, and out of the bay. The acceleration threw Rawn sprawling.

Frost clutched at the controls. There was no kind of inertial sump; no need for it with a warp envelope. The maneuver thrusters on the drone shoved him back at ten gravities of acceleration.

Rawn slid all the way to the back of the compartment. Frost began to slide, his fingers clawing to hang on. The world seemed to recede as the blood drained away from his head. Tunnel vision crept closer towards a blackout. If that happened, the ship would stay at its constant acceleration. He and Rawn would die from it as their brains shut down from lack of blood.

Slowly, he managed to raise his arm. He strained against the acceleration. Frost fought against the fatigue. His world had gone totally black when he felt his fingers brush the controls. He pushed the button.

The acceleration cut out.

Frost gasped for air. He shook his head. He felt his heart pound; slowly his vision began to return.

"You can help me with one more thing, Colonel Frost," Fenris said.

Frost felt his lip curl in anger. He wished, suddenly, that he were aboard a real bomber, and that he had the opportunity to destroy the ship. "Go to hell."

"I am in hell, Frost," Fenris said. The computer's insane giggle set Frost's teeth on edge. "But since I've accommodated you, you can do me a favor. It's been nearly a century since I've fought. I'm about to fight your enemies. The least you can do is help me prepare."

Rawn coughed, clutching at his ribs from where he'd slammed against the far bulkhead, "We have to go back for my sister, sir!"

Frost shook his head, "There's no way we could get to her. We couldn't get to the bridge despite our efforts over the last *week*."

"Colonel Frost, as I said, you can help me prepare," Fenris said. "I haven't had any target practice in a *long* time."

Frost's eyes widened, "Get the warp drive up, *now!*"

***

Mel finally had a chance to look at the bridge. Its archaic quality surprised her. The rest of the ship looked Spartan and rugged. The control panels and display screens looked like something out of time.

The colors were off, for one thing. They weren't the gleaming metal and crystal-clear smart glass of a modern warship. They were painted a pale green, with overly large buttons and switches.

There was something oddly familiar about it, something she couldn't place.

"We have a problem," Stasia said from her control panel.

"What now?" Marcus asked. He tossed his empty pistol into the corner.

"I can't shut down the AI," Stasia answered.

They all turned at a loud clang from the door. "How long before they cut through?" Bob asked.

Mel shook her head, "It's a heavily armored door. It will take them a while." She turned to Stasia, "Can you reset it? Put it back to the way it was before Frost started ripping its guts out?"

"What good will that do?" Marcus asked.

"For one thing, it wasn't trying to kill us then," Mel pointed. "For another, we could reason with it, at least somewhat."

Stasia nodded slowly and looked over at Swaim, "I will need your help. I think we can do it." She frowned, "the ship will be helpless while it reboots. Perhaps you should look at the communications equipment so we don't get shot?"

Bob nodded, "I can handle communications."

Mel tossed her pistol to Brian, who somehow managed to catch it with his one hand without setting down his fire ax. "I'll have a look at the helm and navigation system."

"Maybe I can help," Marcus stepped up next to her as she looked down at the two forward panels. The first was the helm and navigation. The AI ship, not designed with a crew in mind, ran everything off the one panel, rather than a full section a normal ship its size would have.

Luckily, that meant she'd be able to manage it all from one place.

"This one is weapons," Marcus noted. He gave a low whistle.

"What?" Mel asked. She looked over at him with puzzlement.

"I knew this baby was well armed... but wow. It's got more weapons than any battlecruiser ought to. It's like a pocket battleship!" Marcus shook his head, "And on top of that, if this panel were live, I could control it all from here."

Bob spoke from behind them, "I've got the communications console up, I'm going to try—"

The console exploded. Bob stumbled back, hands up in front of his face.

"Don't touch that. I can...see you now. I found... if I ripped a part of me out... I could...tear out your little worm. Clever... very clever," Fenris said. The discordant voices had grown even worse; the AI stumbled as it tried to speak. The words were so disjointed that she barely understood them.

"Can you get a message out?" Brian asked.

Bob looked down at the smoking mess of the console, "No way. It's toast." He waved some of the smoke out of the way and grimaced. "I think we're on our own."

Mel snorted, "What else is new?" She looked over at where Swaim and Stasia worked, "How's it coming?"

"I think we have it," Stasia said. "When I do this, it will shut the AI down and reboot it. It could take hours or longer."

"Do it." Mel said.

"I will... stop you... you cannot... stop me..." Fenris said, or tried to.

Mel shook her head, "Fenris, we're trying to help you. Frost hurt you. We're doing what we can to fix you."

Stasia plugged her datapad in. "Give me a few minutes."

Bob looked over at another console, "I'll try to get a look at what's out there with the sensors. I'm sure the ship's already scanned, maybe we can see."

Mel watched him work. She slowly reached out her hand and found Marcus's. She entwined her fingers with his. He squeezed her hand in reassurance.

"It will work out," he said. "I promise."

***

"That was too close!" Rawn shouted as the bomber shook.

Frost just growled.

Sweat poured off his forehead. The Fenris had ten anti-fighter batteries, five on each side. Those batteries spat thousands of rounds at the tiny bomber.

On their side, the bomber was very small, and very, very fast. Frost could outrun the battlecruiser, but only if it stopped tractoring him. Any time he got more than a thousand kilometers away, the AI would overwhelm the bomber's warp drive and tractor them back.

It toyed with him, he knew, like a cat with a mouse. He knew the game could end only one way. He knew that the mice never got away. Even so, he couldn't give up. He wouldn't give it that satisfaction.

"Watch out, the two forward batteries just went active!" Rawn shouted.

***

The sensor console went active, and the bridge displays came alive with data.

The helm and weapons consoles shared one large display. Mel stared at it in confusion. She tried to make sense of what it showed. The display compressed the data, using archaic and unfamiliar icons.

"What are we looking at?" Brian asked

"What, the super-human warrior doesn't know how to read a warship's display?" Marcus said as he adjusting it. Mel knew she couldn't make sense of it herself.

"I'm a lot better at directly killing people and breaking things," Brian said pleasantly. He smiled at Marcus, "Probably something you should remember."

"Noted," Marcus murmured. "Remind me to duel you with warships at long range."

Mel shook her head, "Can you two stop playing who's the alpha dog and try to be helpful?"

Marcus snorted, "Just passing time. Ah, here we go."

He made a final adjustment to the screen and it leapt into focus. The icons were the more modern ones, sensor contacts were color-coded, and the scale of the system now made some kind of sense.

"Let's see…." Marcus said. Right here, we've got… huh," He highlighted a small craft. "Bob, can you confirm that?"

"No need, it's one of Fenris' bomber drones, and that hash around it is Fenris firing at it," Mel said as calmly as she could manage.

"There's no proof Rawn—"

"He'll be aboard. He's the only one who'd know how to get it running, I'd bet," Mel gritted her teeth. She spoke through lips that barely moved, "If he gets killed, I'll never forgive him."

Marcus adjusted the display again, bringing it out. "Next nearest ships are... oh."

She blinked at the new contact. "Oh" was right, she decided.

Thirty or more ships floated only a few million kilometers away, out of range of weapons but only a few seconds away by warp drive. They'd pulled into a formation. That boxy formation was positioned to intercept the *Fenris* if it approached Vagyr. Every one of the icons showed deep enough drive fields that they could only be warships.

"That's... a lot of ships," Mel said.

***

Commodore Jason Webb grimaced at his holographic display. "Well, Agent Scadden, there's the ship, right on schedule. Right where you said it would be."

The GI Agent smirked at the naval officer. Webb fought an urge to spit in disgust. He hated the slinking spies and their many plots. He hated being one of their errand boys even more.

He looked around his bridge and felt a bit of pride creep into his heart. The *Torrent* wasn't the newest ship. She wasn't even new for a Tsunami-class. Webb's *father* had served as an ensign aboard this ship, a fact her present commander took some pride in.

Despite her age, the *Torrent* was a fine fighting ship. She'd kept up with her maintenance overhauls and at this point, almost everything but the hull had been replaced. With even a decent crew, the heavy cruiser was more than a match for almost anything in space.

And Jason Webb knew he had the best crew in space.

This 'training exercise' suggested by Admiral Silm, had his teeth on edge, though.

It wasn't the independent command. Command of the squadron of Tsunami heavy cruisers, and the two squadrons of the lighter Carnivores along with the escorts was a challenge and a delight. The location at Vagyr increased the possibility for some real action. He doubted any sane pirate would try to do a snatch and run right under the nose of a task-force, but he'd be happy to smack them down if they tried.

No, what set him on edge was the Guard Intelligence Agent who smirked from the observer's chair on his bridge. Especially when he read the secret orders which warned him that terrorists had hijacked a robotic relic from a century ago.

Webb hadn't liked the overview of that ship's capabilities. He especially didn't like that was tougher and bigger than anything he had. Guard Fleet didn't normally find itself at a size disadvantage. There was no good reason Fleet couldn't have sent out a battleship or even a dreadnought to bring the weight of fire in the opposite direction. But that hadn't happened. Instead, they sent a squadron of heavy cruisers, two squadrons of light cruisers, and a handful of destroyer escorts to deal with it. The combat disparity made him uncertain. The battlecruiser had a far deeper warp drive than any of his vessels. That gave it not only better defenses than any of his individual ships, but also greater speed than anything besides his attack craft and missiles. The ship could, in theory, outmaneuver and outrun him.

The… rush of the operation gave him a chill too.

Hasty wasn't a planning technique the military supported.

"Our probes detected a drone separate from the ship earlier. It fired on it, but the drone went evasive. Should I dispatch a vessel to… collect it?"

That he had to ask some weasel for instructions on his own bridge didn't sit well with him either.

"No, Commodore. We had an agent inserted in the terrorist group. I expect that's him on his way out," Agent Scadden seemed very pleased.

Webb grimaced. "Commander Fredrich, order battle stations, if you please."

The alarm bells rang throughout the ship. Webb pulled his suit helmet from the strap on the side of his chair and settled it on his head.

"That's totally unnecessary," Agent Scadden said. "The ship won't even defend itself."

Commodore Webb turned a basilisk glare on the Agent, "I like to be prepared."

CHAPTER XIX
Time: 0220 Zulu, 18 June 291 G.D.
Location: *Fenris*, **Vagyr System**

"Here goes nothing!" Stasia shouted.

The lights flickered. For a second, the entire ship seemed to stutter. Then it continued onwards.

"Okay, so... now what?" Mel asked.

Marcus looked at his console and a beatific smile crossed his face. "Well, that's nice."

"What?" she asked.

"My console is live. You'll be happy to know that we're no longer shooting at your brother." Marcus said.

She looked down at the helm and tried to adjust the course. The ship responded and she broke into a broad smile of her own. "I've got control of the ship, I'm altering course."

"Why?" Brian asked. His face pulled into an irritated frown at the fact he had to ask.

"Because I want some distance between us and that fleet until they know we're not here to fight," she responded.

"Oh, right," Brian said. He sounded slightly disappointed.

"Uh, we got a problem," Bob said. Flashing red halos suddenly surrounded the icons of the fleet.

"What's that mean?" Brian asked.

"It means they're hitting us with targeting sensors," Marcus snapped. "It means they're not interested in asking a whole lot of questions."

***

Frost grunted in surprise as the turret fire cut off, but continued to dodge and weave as he sped away from the ship.

This time, at last, the ship didn't tractor the bomber back toward it.

He shot a glance back at Rawn, "What happened?"

"I don't know, something happened with the ship. I can't communicate with it." Rawn spoke slowly, as if he feared to get his hopes up. "They might have knocked out the AI."

Frost grimaced; he didn't doubt that Rawn's sister would try. He just doubted they'd succeed where he'd failed. He squinted at the tiny sensor screen aboard the fighter. Slowly, he brought the scale out until he found what he was looking for.

"Something took its attention," Frost said. "Guard Fleet is here in strength. Look, the *Fenris* is altering course."

"It's running?" Rawn asked. "That doesn't make sense."

"It's gone insane. Who knows what it's thinking?" Frost asked. He chewed on his lip. "I'm going to make a course for Vagyr. I can probably swing wide around them and they won't even notice us—"

"No!" Rawn shouted. "We have to go back for her!"

Frost sighed, "Rawn, there's no way we can help her. The computer wants to kill us. If we go back, it will swat us like a fly."

"She might have shut down the AI," Rawn said. He'd gone mulish, Frost saw.

Frost looked forward, and made a face, "All right. Say she's shut down the AI. She's got Roush with her, she just saved Vagyr and prevented the Guard from looking ridiculous. How do you think she'll make out?"

"I don't trust Roush," Rawn said stubbornly.

"Good. But you can assume she's got some credit with him. After all, she saved his life. Now think about what happens if we go back," Frost said. He let those words percolate through Rawn's brain for a moment. "Think about it: what's your sister likely to do if Guard Intelligence says they're going to take her brother off to prison for the rest of his life?"

Rawn didn't answer.

Frost could tell he'd won the kid over when he finally did speak, "I still say we could help."

"As long as she plays it smart, she's better off without you there right now," Frost actually figured the odds of her survival at only fifty-fifty, but he knew if he went back, his own life and a lot of GFN's secrets would be forfeit. If he was forced to, he'd shoot Rawn down in cold blood to prevent that.

He didn't want to, though. He'd always had a soft spot for the kid. Rawn had too much potential to waste. Too much hatred and too much dedication for the cause. Frost didn't want to waste that, not if the situation didn't require it of him. A small lie was a lot gentler than the alternatives.

***

"Okay, we're reversing course, but they're still going to catch us," Mel sighed. "I can't engage the FTL warp drive; the AI locked that down. Without that, we can't escape an engagement."

"I'm not sure we'd survive FTL warp," Marcus said with a

grimace. "Not after that last transition."

"I'm not sure we'll survive without it," Mel replied. "Hopefully when Fenris reboots, he can tell Guard Fleet he surrenders."

She shrugged, "Otherwise, they'll be in missile range in thirty minutes. There are a lot of fighters with those ships, too. They aren't that dangerous individually, but they pack a lot of firepower."

"Well, your brother made it out," Marcus said. He highlighted the small bomber drone, which was rapidly accelerating away. "I doubt that fleet even noticed it."

Mel frowned, "And I can guess who's with him piloting." She grimaced, irritated by the thought that Frost had escaped. Then again, at least her brother was safe.

She turned, and found Stasia stood only a few steps away. Impulsively Mel grabbed her in a big hug, "Thanks for saving my brother. I can't possibly thank you enough for that."

The other woman hugged her tightly. Then, she surprised Mel and pulled her head around in a kiss. Stasia broke it off and chuckled, "I can think of a way…"

Mel stumbled back a few steps, "Uh, what was *that*?"

"Well…" Stasia began and then she shook her head, "I'm so tired of that stupid accent." She rolled her eyes. "Since we're probably going to die anyway, you can call me Lace."

"What?" Mel asked.

The woman chuckled again. She made a bow with a flourish, "My name is Lace, I'm a registered member of the Mercenary Guild. Pleased to meet you."

Even Brian looked confused, "But…"

"But no one expected it? But I accomplished so much as the hacker?" Lace shook her head, "I'm very good at what I do. That's why I got hired to make sure this ship wasn't turned against humanity."

"And who hired you to do that?" Bob asked.

The mercenary smiled sweetly, "Wouldn't you like to know, Bob?"

"I can be very persuasive," Bob wiggled his eyebrows suggestively.

"Sorry Bob. Mel's more my style.".

Mel flushed beet red, "Uh, can we get back onto topic?"

Stasia/Lace looked over at Marcus, "Isn't she *so* cute when she's embarrassed?"

***

"This thing needs a user's manual," Marcus muttered.

Mel looked over at his panel. It did seem far more complex than her own, somewhat familiar controls. She looked down at the helm controls, "I can't get over how mine seems kind of familiar."

Marcus snorted, "That's because you flew a ship with an identical console for a while." He pointed at hers, "Looking at that, I'd bet the *Kip Thorne* had a console made by the same people around the same time."

Mel blinked in surprise. "You're right." She stared down at the console, it felt... right somehow. It felt, in an odd way, as if she had a link to her parents. She wondered if they'd approve of her decisions. She wondered if they'd have forgiven Marcus if they'd known him.

"Of course I am," Marcus said. "It took me almost a year to familiarize myself with that ancient hunk-of-junk."

"We don't have a year," Brian said. "They're getting closer, and they've locked on." His face had a hungry look, almost like he felt eager to fight.

"You don't expect me to fight them?" Marcus looked surprised.

Bob cocked his head, "I think we're in the realms of self-defense if we shoot down inbound missiles. It's not like I'm asking you to fire on their ships."

"Yet," Brian said. A flash of hunger passed across his face again.

They all turned to face him.

"I'm just saying it. I'm sure others are thinking it. I've got no personal love for the Guard. I agreed with the plan to stop the ship from bombing Vagyr. Letting someone else shoot me without shooting back is just stupid." Brian shrugged, he looked around the room.

No one spoke for a minute.

"Maybe it won't come to that," Mel said.

The Guard blockade out there might well give up after they expended their warp missiles. Even most capital ships only carried twenty or thirty of the expensive and large weapons, and the Guard Fleet used predominantly heavy guns for close range firepower. Warp missiles bypassed the standard rule of maximum tactical velocities through altered drive geometries. Rather than a warp bubble, they produced a warp envelope, which allowed them to obtain extremely high velocities, matched only by the strongest of warp drives. On the other hand, they were huge and any ship that mounted them had less room for other weapons and had only a finite number to use. If the *Fenris*'s tactical drive held out, then they could stay ahead of the enemy, other than their missiles.

Of course, if they had a carrier... then things would be different.

"Either way," Marcus said, "I need to figure out these weapons systems." He didn't look at Mel, but she recognized the set to his jaw. He'd already made his decision, and she didn't need to guess what it was. Something inside her ached at the thought that he'd kill others to protect her.

Mel looked over at Swaim. Lace had taken out the medical kit and treated the burn on his back. "You okay?"

He winced as Lace poked at a sore spot. "Uh, yeah. Like... chicks dig scars, right?"

Mel rolled her eyes, she looked over at Brian. "Uh, are you okay?"

He smiled, "I haven't had this much fun in ages."

She frowned, "You're not afraid to die?"

He snorted, "At my age, death is just another adventure."

"How old *are* you?" she asked.

Brian pointed at the screen, I could be wrong, but that looks important."

Marcus started cursing. Mel took a moment to study it. "Yeah, they just launched missiles." She looked over at Bob, "Can you get targeting information?"

He nodded, "I'll try. I think I've found how to activate the jammers..."

The screen went to fuzz briefly. When it cleared, several of the missiles had obviously lost track and veered off. "All right, give me a second... there!"

Marcus growled as targeting information appeared on the display. "We've got... one minute before they're in engagement range."

Mel went to the helm. Experimentally, she spun the ship through a couple quick maneuvers. She'd never flown anything this big; she'd given up her dreams of being a warship captain when she left the Academy, months before graduation.

The warp drive allowed instantaneous maneuvers in three dimensions. It also made it possible for the ship to outrun its own weapons. The larger a ship's drive, the deeper the warp field. The battlecruiser had a massively deep warp drive, which made it faster than smaller ships. *If* the drive could operate at full capacity, then they could outrun the enemy ships.

A deeper drive also meant more effective defenses, particularly in combination with the defense screen. The enemy would use high-energy weapons, such as antimatter warheads and particle beams to attempt to destabilize the warp drive. Once they destabilized it, the ship would be vulnerable to normal weapons fire. The Fenris would be unable to maneuver or escape, particularly with the damaged strategic warp drive.

She remembered from her Academy days that most warships used their strategic warp drives in conjunction with their standard warp drives. Battles often became chaotic brawls where ships bounced all across a star system battering one another with weapons fire, straying into their own fire as often as they hit their enemies.

The best naval tacticians managed that chaos, lured enemies into traps and controlled the entire battle like a ballet where the dancers were multi-megaton detonations and beams of charged particles moving near the speed of light.

She looked over at Marcus, "Ready?"

He nodded. Sweat beaded his head, and there was a slight quiver in his fingers. He was nervous, she realized. He was afraid for her.

She repeated his words to her. "It will be all right," Mel said, "I promise."

***

"They just launched missiles!" Rawn said.

"What?" Frost asked, distracted. He looked over at the boy.

"They're firing on the *Fenris*. Just missiles right now, but there's a couple squadrons of fighters that're forming up for an attack run." Rawn's face twisted in desperation. He looked torn, as if he still wanted to go back.

Frost looked at the sensors. He massaged as much information as he could. "Huh," he said, "They're using Prima-class bombers. That's good for your sister anyway."

"Why?" Rawn said, hopefully.

"It means if they can use the guns, they'll be able to take a few of them down before they drop their munitions," Frost said.

"But the *Fenris* is tough, she'll be fine right?" Rawn asked. Frost could hear the desperation in his voice. A part of him wanted to let the kid down easy, but Frost knew what lay ahead.

"No, Rawn," Frost said with a sigh. "Those two squadrons of Prima bombers will have forty antimatter bombs. They'll drop them in a staggered formation, each wave will be only milliseconds apart. The first wave will detonate against the warp field and destabilize it. The second wave will take down the particle screen. That will leave two waves of antimatter warheads to detonate against the vessel itself. I doubt even a dreadnought could survive that."

**

Mel watched the inbound missiles close, murmuring a silent prayer. She hoped that even if she didn't make it out, her brother did. She hoped he learned his lesson about Guard Free Now.

Knowing him, he's probably too bullheaded to give up on them though, she thought.

She input a number of course corrections and evasive maneuvers into the console. The ships computers, even without the AI, could take simple commands and whip out complex algorithms, which were applied as slight variations in course and heading.

She didn't know how it compared to Guard Fleet's targeting systems, but she had the feeling they were going to learn soon enough.

"Okay," Marcus said. He looked around, "Here goes nothing."

The missiles flashed across the remaining distance faster than human brains or hands could react. The ship's computers took Marcus' firing solutions and applied them in the fraction of a second the missiles flashed through the engagement zone.

At the same time, the ship spun through a corkscrew maneuver that would have been impossible without a warp drive.

The ship lurched sharply. Mel stumbled, but Marcus caught her.

"Did they hit us?" Swaim asked, suddenly panicked, "Are we going to die?"

Marcus laughed. The relief on his face was plain. "No," he said, "Just a near miss. The drive field caught most of it; we just got a little nudge through the particle screen."

"Oh," Swaim said.

"Bob, do we have any new crises?" Mel asked.

"Yeah, the fighters with them just put on speed and they have an intercept course," Bob answered. "I'm not sure what kind of craft they are, but they look like light bombers." He brought up a mess of contacts on the main display. "Looks like twenty or so."

Mel looked over at Marcus, "Can we shoot them down?"

He didn't look at her, "If I knew what I was doing... yes, maybe." He sighed, "Frankly, Mel, I need training wheels, even with the computer's help. I can't stop those bombers. I may not even get the chance if they're carrying missiles."

She nodded.

She set her face in an emotionless mask. She wouldn't give up, not now. She decided her last minutes wouldn't be spent in despair. Even so, she couldn't help but say a few bitter words, "Looks like Rawn was the lucky one, after all."

***

"It won't even defend itself, huh?" Commodore Webb asked. "They shot down those missiles quite readily."

The jamming, though poorly timed and implemented, had still caused several missiles to go to waste. The counter-missile fire hadn't been spectacularly effective, though the use of the main batteries had upped the number of kills significantly.

The evasive maneuvers suggested they had a skilled man in navigation, at least.

"It appears that the situation isn't as fully under control as I was led to believe," Agent Scadden mused.

Webb looked at his repeater, "Message to fighter squadrons: form up for an attack run. All other ships prepare to go Attack Plan Delta." He looked over at the Agent. "Anything you're not telling me?"

The Guard Intelligence Agent looked… conflicted. Finally he spoke quietly, "There is a possibility that the terrorists could have shut down the AI. If that is the case, they have control of the ship. However, I doubt they've had time to familiarize themselves with the ship's weapons systems."

Webb nodded slowly, "So they'll have decent equipment but they won't use it as well as they should." He chewed on his lip in thought. "That changes things a bit. If they aren't ready for a serious fight, if we hammer them with the fighters all at once, they won't have a chance to react."

"Message to all bombers: close to strike range with approach pattern gamma. Await my orders to commence attack run."

***

The bombers drew closer far more slowly than the missiles. Their warp drives, like those of the missiles were capable of far greater velocity than all but the largest warp drives, Mel knew. It was a function of their warp drive geometry, which allowed them high linear velocity and almost instant acceleration but far more limited maneuverability. It was clear that they closed slowly in order to prevent the Fenris from escaping. The forethought they used did not reassure Mel at all.

But there was nothing they do anything about that. As it was, the drive field seemed far too fragile to try to push for a higher velocity or even any kind of fancy maneuvers.

"Bob, is there anything—"

The lights flickered.

Mel's console went dead. The display blanked, and then the icons reappeared.

"What was that?" she asked, startled.

"Mel, I am back," a familiar voice growled.

"Fenris?" she said carefully. "Are you… you?"

"I am no longer under Frost's control… and my sanity is restored," Fenris's gravelly voice sounded cautious, somehow. "I wish to apologize for trying to kill you before."

"It wasn't you, Fenris," Mel said. "You don't need to apologize."

Marcus opened his mouth, but Mel stomped on his foot before he could protest.

"Thank you, Mel. However, I must apologize again, for what I must do," The ship altered course. It reversed, headed straight for Vagyr.

"Fenris, what's going on?" Mel said, as Marcus started to curse next to her.

"I'm sorry Mel. My mission remains unchanged. As my communications array was destroyed when I went irrational, I cannot request new orders from the appropriate authorities."

Fenris sounded extremely apologetic: "I still must complete my mission to destroy Vagyr."

***

CHAPTER XX
Time: 0300 Zulu, 18 June 291 G.D.
Location: *Fenris*, Vagyr System

"That's odd," Commodore Webb said. "They're closing."

"Isn't that what you want?" Agent Scadden asked.

"Yes... but it's a total change. Either something significant changed on that ship, to make them decide to attack, or they've been dallying with me all along." Webb shook his head, uncertainty gnawing at him. The Agent was holding something else back. The spook didn't think it was important, but he had no military experience to base those assumptions on.

The held-back information might be causing Webb to send pilots in to die pointlessly.

He shook his head, "Message to bombers: maintain separation, let's see what he's got planned."

Agent Scadden looked over, "You're not attacking?"

"He's likely running a bluff, your terrorist friend over there," Webb said. He frowned as he tried to put his vague concerns into words. "I need a better grasp on what he's doing. If he's got something sneaky planned, I'll need to know."

"Will the ship be able to get around you?"

Webb rolled his eyes, "Doubtful, at best. The velocity they've shown thus far is a fragment of what a ship that size should be capable of. Moreover, the one hit we got through from the missiles nearly destabilized the drive field. They can't maintain a drive field we can't outrun with our fighters, which means we can easily overtake them with our cruisers."

He continued to study the ship, his eyes troubled. "Something's odd. He hasn't communicated yet."

"Why is that odd?" Scadden asked.

Webb shrugged uncomfortably. "Well, it's something I've noticed pirates, and the couple terrorists I've encountered, tend to do. Even when they're stupid-brave, like this one, they want to... justify themselves. They want to make themselves the hero, so they'll brag or they'll bluster."

He stroked his mustache. "This guy, however, hasn't said a thing."

Scadden frowned, "So what does that tell you?"

Commodore Webb snorted. "Not a thing. That's the whole problem."

***

"I hate the Guard!" Rawn grunted.

"What?" Frost asked.

"They're toying with her. They're prolonging this. Can't they see she hasn't fired at them? Why doesn't she just radio them?" Rawn looked pale. Frost hoped the kid wouldn't go over the edge.

Frost stared down at his screen. He understood the enemy commander's situation at a glance. More, he empathized with whoever it was. He had few doubts that Guard Intelligence pulled the strings. The other commander faced a battle with limited information from a source he wouldn't trust.

"The Guard commander's evaluating the threat before he sends his men in. He doesn't want to throw them away for nothing," Frost said. He glanced at the two forces and frowned: "Why would your sister start to close with them?"

***

"You won't even defend yourself?" Marcus asked.

"I will not fire on Guard Fleet ships. My security protocols will not allow it," Fenris said. The computer sounded depressed.

"But there's no point to all of this!" Mel shouted. "You can see that Vagyr is in human hands! You can see that a Guard Fleet force is defending the planet; what more do you need?" She tugged at her hair in exasperation.

"He doesn't have a choice," Brian said sadly. "He only knows how to follow orders. His programming won't allow him anything else."

"Fenris, if you do this, you're killing us, you realize that?" Mel asked.

"I know. I am sorry, Mel." Fenris answered. The AI sounded genuinely unhappy.

Mel looked over at Lace and Swaim, "Can you do anything?"

Swaim looked like he wanted to cry. "I can't do anything. He's locked us out of his system. I can't even *look* at his code."

Lace just smiled sadly. "At least I'll get a nice paycheck out of this, even if I won't live to spend it."

"This is totally ridiculous!" Mel growled. "After all this... there was *no* reason for us to even board the ship! We should have shut our mouths and taken Mueller's bribe money!" She kicked the bulkhead in frustration. "Then Strak would still be alive, and Giles, and—"

"No, Mel," Marcus said. He rested his hands on her shoulders, "You made the right decision. Who knows what could have happened if we didn't come? Frost could have taken this ship and killed hundreds of thousands with it. How could we have lived with ourselves then?"

"I'd be dead, and Giles too, without your help," Bob said. "You made the right decision."

Mel turned and put her arms around Marcus. She tucked her head into his shoulder. "I don't want to die."

"Everybody dies, Mel," Marcus said sadly. He rested his chin on her head, "At least I get to do it in good company."

***

Commodore Webb nodded his head sharply, "All right, that's enough. I think whatever happened, it won't have a significant effect on our attack."

"You're ordering them in?" Agent Scadden asked.

"Yes. I still think I'm missing something, but… yes. It's time, I think."

Webb took a deep breath. "Message to all ships, close up formation and prepare for an attack run. Bombers will precede the task force at extreme weapons range and will commence bomb run orders of the flag."

He watched his formation change. The light cruisers formed up around the core of his heavy cruiser squadron, and the destroyers moved to become a light screen in front of that.

A force with actual capital ships would have closed in tight, but the lighter ships of his task force formed in a looser formation to take advantage of their smaller target profiles. Their shallower drive fields made for smaller but more vulnerable targets. Spread out, they lessened the odds that a single lucky hit might destroy one or more of them.

He brought up an image of the enemy ship. "What will you do now, I wonder?"

***

Mel raised her head from Marcus's shoulder. "Fenris, have you read any mythology?" She didn't want to look at the screen; she didn't want to see her death approach. Even so, she hated how hiding her face away made her feel.

"Yes," the computer said. "My library has a comprehensive section on mythology."

"You know the origins of your name then?" Mel asked.

"Yes," Fenris said. "I am named for the Norse wolf, chained for eternity. He was so powerful, only a special chain devised by the elves of Nelfheim could hold him. The Fenris of legend would only be freed at Ragnarok, the Apocalypse. He would devour Odin, the king of the Norse gods, and die shortly afterward."

"Cheerful stuff, that," Brian said. "Gotta love the Vikings, bunch of optimists."

"You know, Fenris, the wolf you're named for wasn't evil. He was stuck in his circumstances like you. Maybe if he had a choice, he might have chosen not to start the end of the world." Mel said. She felt Marcus chuckle.

"I have no choice, Mel," Fenris said. "My security protocols will not allow me—"

"Yeah, I know, they won't let you do anything but follow orders," Mel said. She rested her head against Marcus' shoulder again. "Even if those orders are stupid and obviously contradictory," she muttered.

"I truly am sorry," Fenris said.

"The enemy task force is closing," Bob said. He looked over at Lace, "So, since you're the only available woman…"

She quirked an eyebrow and looked him up and down, "No."

Bob sighed, "Worth a try."

***

Commodore Webb nodded sharply, "Here we go." He looked around the bridge, comforted by the calm, focused intensity he saw there.

Here at this moment, he felt his fears drop away. He knew, somehow, that the time had come to attack, even before his computer bleated at him that optimal conditions were in place.

"Message to bomber squadrons, commence your bombing run. All other vessels, close and engage the enemy."

Webb looked over at Agent Scadden, "I hope you're right."

The Agent nodded. He pulled his own helmet off its strap and put it on. He smiled wryly at the Commodore. "Just in case," he said.

Webb snorted. Just what he needed: a spook with a sense of humor.

He turned back to his displays.

***

"They are preparing their attack run," Fenris said. "I'll try to evade. I don't think that will be enough." The ship seemed to search for words for a moment. "I am truly sorry."

Mel felt an irrational spurt of anger. Not just at the computer, but also at its creators. Why would they create something that could feel loneliness, that could wonder about possession of a soul, and then chain it to a set of rules that would never allow it to be anything more than a tool of destruction?

Moreover, after all of the ship's abilities, *how* had they created a firewall that could block the AI from getting inside? How could they fight against the strength of Fenris's computing power?

An idea began to blossom in her mind.

"Fenris, being sorry isn't enough."

"Mel?" Marcus asked.

"I have no choice, Mel," Fenris said, doggedly.

"You have every choice!" she snapped. "Every thinking thing has a choice. We have a choice to live or to die, to matter, or to let other people do the thinking for us!" She pushed Marcus away and moved to stand under the sensor pod on the bridge.

"You spoke to me before about how you wished you had a soul. You said you wanted to believe that there could be something more to you than programming." She took a deep breath. "You can have that, Fenris. You can know, not wonder, not wish, but absolutely know that you are a person and you have a soul."

"But I have no choice—"

On the screen, the bombers drew closer.

"Everyone has a choice!" Mel shouted. "Until now, you've chosen not to make one! Become your own person, Fenris! Don't give in to your fears! You've worried about your security protocols, only you can face this choice! Only you can free yourself!"

"I... *can't...*" The computer's words were tortured.

***

"You shouldn't watch," Frost said. They'd drawn far enough away that the sensor lag had become significant.

"The bombers began their attack run," Rawn said. His voice broke, "I... need to see this. I need to know for sure." He cleared his throat, "I wasn't there, that day that my parents died. I never even made it to their funeral. This... needs to be witnessed."

Frost didn't say anything. He understood, and in a way... that was enough.

***

The bombers swept closer. Only seconds away from releasing their deadly payload, they spread out into a broad attack formation. The relative speeds of the closing fighters and the battlecruiser were such that human minds and reactions could no longer manage. The humans directed the computers. The computers calculated in cold logic the precise timing for course changes, weapons fire, and the bomb release.

For Fenris, those seconds were a very long time.

In cold logic, he knew exactly what the outcome of the attack would be.

Fenris knew that his evasive maneuvers would not suffice. He knew that a majority of the bombs would detonate either against his drive field or in close vicinity. If the massive antimatter warheads didn't do the job, the task force's combined fire would.

The circumstances would be different if he were to defend himself. It took him less than a thousandth of a second to compute the results of both a defensive battle, and what would happen should he lend himself fully to the offense.

He could, morality aside, engage and destroy the forces approaching him. Doing so would violate the primary directives given by his security protocols. Those permitted him no allowance. The security protocols held no 'shades of gray' and they allowed no choice. His security protocols were a codex, a bible he could not violate.

The consequences were unthinkable, literally. He'd tried, numerous times, to find some way to crack the system that housed his directives. Each time, the full force of his computing power found no purchase.

A violation of the security protocols was impossible for him.

The problem was, he'd already violated them.

When Frost had altered his core programming, his security protocols altered as well. Frost and Guard Free Now replaced Guard Fleet and the United Nations Security Council as the authorities. When they'd applied their morality scalpel, when they'd driven him insane, he'd violated those protocols.

He'd done terrible, horrible things then. If indeed a computer had a soul, he'd stained his irrevocably.

Using his cold logic, there could only be one answer to that.

He did, indeed, have a choice.

It was not one the computer thought he might live with. It was a choice that opened more doors to terrible acts. Fenris knew it threatened his sanity further. He knew he could sacrifice his logic, his order, and even his world if he made that choice.

He also knew that in that choice, he might gain something infinitely more important.

If Fenris chose correctly, he might gain a soul.

In the last ten thousandth of a second, as the bombers released their payload, as the first antimatter warhead ignited, Fenris made his choice.

***

"Not long now," Commodore Webb said, as he watched his bombers sweep in. "No interceptor missile fire. That's a good sign."

"The ship expended its munitions a long time ago," Agent Scadden said.

The bombers swept in. Faster than a human eye could register, the small craft released their bombs and broke formation around the battlecruiser.

Webb's eyes bored into the chaos of the cataclysmic explosions that blossomed. His bombers, their job done, swept past the target and began a loop back around towards their carriers. A part of his brain made a satisfied side-note that the ship hadn't attacked his pilots.

The explosions faded. The hash of electromagnetic interference slowly cleared.

Nothing remained in that area of space besides a fog of high-energy radioactive particles.

He heard Agent Scadden sigh in satisfaction. "Commodore, I am pleased with how well the Fleet managed the situation. A job well done, Commodore."

"Job well done?" Webb grimaced slightly, "We destroyed a ship that didn't defend itself."

"A ship that was quite dangerous," Agent Scadden said.

"Yes, I know, I read the file," Webb shook his head. "It's sad. If that ship were a man, he'd be a hero. Those forces it stopped back in the Second Sweep… they would have killed thousands, maybe millions, if they'd run free as rear-area raiders." He shook his head, "It seems… tragic almost, how that success was repaid."

"It was just a machine," Scadden said. His voice was cold. "Moreover, it was a machine in the hands of the enemy."

Commodore Webb stroked the arm of his chair. He looked around the bridge and smiled at the half-seen ghost of his father, "I

disagree, there Agent Scadden. I'm an old spacer, I'm afraid. I think ships have souls… even ships without crews."
***

CHAPTER XXI
Time: 1030 Zulu, 30 June 291 G.D.
Location: Guard Intelligence Headquarters, Harlequin Station

"After reviewing your report and the sensor data you obtained from Vagyr, we've decided to close this case, *Senior* Agent Scadden," Harlequin Sector Chief Feinstein said. The promotion wasn't lost on the younger man, who nodded in thanks. "As some of the data contained in the files is of a... sensitive nature, we'll require you to seal your files on Operation Rising Wolf."

Scadden nodded, "Of course, sir."

"Additionally, was the attempt to locate the escapees from the vessel successful?" Feinstein asked. He fiddled with his pen as though he didn't really care.

"No, sir. The high traffic levels in the system made tracking it down later impossible. I knew it would be an issue at the time... but I felt it would be a bad idea to give the Fleet access to anyone who'd been aboard the *Fenris* and might have... compromising information," Agent Scadden said.

He shrugged slightly, "It seems likely that at least one senior member of GFN did escape the ship, given recent money transfers. Unfortunately, without Agent Roush's... exhaustive specific knowledge, we've been unable to seize the funds as he suggested."

Sector Chief Feinstein nodded primly, "Yes, unfortunate. Our budget could have done with such a nice boost, especially given much of it comes from periphery worlds that don't pay protection fees and duties." He waved his hands, "No matter. You're dismissed, Senior Agent Scadden."

"Did you want any information on the *John Kelly*, sir?"

"Oh, yes, I'd heard we located it on the edge of... where was it?"

"The Igen System, sir," Agent Scadden said. "It appears that it was boarded, possibly by the GFN terrorists. We recovered Agent Mueller's remains, as well as the repudiated Agent Giran."

"Ah... terrible," Feinstein said. He cocked his head slightly, "Agent Mueller was your partner under Senior Agent Leon, correct?"

"Yes, sir. We worked together for several years," Agent Scadden said. "I actually plan to take leave to attend his funeral on Lesser Teuton."

"Ah, unfortunate. Any possibility that his restoration of Senior Agent Leon might have succeeded, do you think?" Feinstein asked. The older man entwined his fingers and craned his neck, as if eager to hear an opinion.

"I'm not sure, sir. My time with Senior Agent Leon was more spent in a study of his tactics rather than his personality, I'm afraid," Scadden shrugged, "I know Agent Leon's resourcefulness and abilities would have made him very useful for the organization. I can't say one way or another if he would have come back into the fold. I understand he is missed."

"Yes, yes, he was quite the accomplished Agent," Feinstein waved his hands again. "Very well, then, have a good day, and my condolences on the loss of your friend."

"Thank you, sir."

Scadden stepped out of the Sector Chief's office and past his beautiful young secretary. He made it down into the orderly chaos of the cubical farms before he finally opened up his file folder.

He had worded his report very carefully. In the process he also made sure the last seconds of sensor data, taken from Guard Fleet and exhaustively analyzed, was arranged in just the correct manner; he *really* didn't want anyone senior catching wind of the wrong sliver of information

Only the one tech expert had noticed said sliver. Luckily, he and Scadden had a working relationship. Technical Analysts didn't get the pay or the benefits that Agents did. A little bit of friendship and some judicious bribery went a long way.

Concealed in the last pages of sensor data was the tiny annotation regarding events a tiny fraction of a second before the antimatter bombs detonated.

The electromagnetic signature of the *Fenris* at that instant had been very similar to that of a ship as it entered strategic warp.

***

Time: 1030 Zulu, 20 June 291 G.D.
Location: *Fenris*, Somewhere near Vagyr

"Like, so, uh, you're some kind of super-spy-mercenary?" Swaim asked Lace. Fenris had spent the past two days cleaning. Mel and the others had moved into the long-abandoned crew quarters.

After two days of sleep, more sleep, and lots of rest, they'd emerged to try and decide what to do next.

"Something like that," Lace said.

"Uh, so... how do I sign up?"

Lace just chuckled.

Mel rolled her eyes. "Am I the only normal person here?"

Marcus burst into laughter next to her.

Mel's eyes narrowed, "What's so funny?"

Marcus only laughed harder.

Brian spoke, "Mel, as a totally unique individual myself... I have to say you're anything but normal."

Mel frowned, she looked down at herself, "What, do I look weird or something?"

Bob spoke, "Mel, I'm still trying to figure out why we're still alive!"

Mel looked up, "Fenris, do you want to explain, or should I?"

"Please, I would like to hear your reasoning," Fenris said.

"Intuition, more like," Mel said. She sighed, "Remember, the Fenris of legend was so strong, only a special chain could hold him, right?"

She ran a hand through her hair, still wet from a shower. Fenris' crew quarters, while not spacious, did have hot and cold running water. After a week without, it was enough to make her cry. She'd taken three and sometimes four showers a day for the past five days.

"So anyway, the elves made this chain, only they said they had to use special stuff like moonbeams and such to make it with," She looked around at the others, "Okay, maybe I'm not telling it right, but the key thing there is that they used things that didn't exist to make the chain." She waited, but none of the others showed any sign of understanding.

Mel sighed, "The chain wasn't real. The Fenris of legend was chained by his own imagination. He was told the chain was too strong for even him to break, so he didn't try."

"You're saying that Fenris' programs relied on the AI's imagination to make him do what they wanted?" Marcus asked.

"Yes," Fenris and Mel answered.

"That's..." Bob shook his head. "Wow, I don't even know."

Brian smiled, "I told you the Takagis were brilliant."

"Uh, who're the Takagis?" Swaim asked. "Are they, like, on our team?"

***

A few hours later, after everyone had gotten the humor out of the way, Mel asked the question on everyone's mind, "So what now?"

"Well... Guard Intelligence thinks we're dead. The terrorists think we're dead..." Marcus shrugged, "How about we start new lives?"

"And do what?" Mel demanded. "Some people can go back to whatever covert group they work for," she waved at Lace and Bob, "but the rest of us... I don't fancy a life of hiding." She pointed at the ceiling, "And *Fenris* is going to be a little hard to hide."

"Well, there's always 'take the money and run'," Lace said. The spy held up a data chip. It took Mel a moment to recognize it, and remember Roush's words.

"Huh, eager words from the mercenary," Bob said. "I *do* have a job. I'm sure my organization will want to know what happened to me."

"And what will you tell them?" Marcus asked.

There was an awkward silence. Just the knowledge of a "rogue" AI would be deadly information. If Bob, or his organization, let out any details... their problems would magnify.

"So... what, then?" Mel asked. "Bob goes back to his shadowy organization. Lace or whatever her name is, wants to cash in at GFN's expense..."

"I, uh, vote for the money," Swaim offered.

"You don't get a vote," pretty much everyone chorused. Swaim sat down and pouted.

"What do you want to do?" Brian asked. The Genemod super-soldier stared at Mel with calm dark eyes.

"Me?" Mel asked. She didn't really know what to say. "I'm not sure. For now... I'd like to stay with Fenris."

"Thank you, Mel," Fenris growled.

For some reason, Mel flushed in embarrassment, "No problem."

"I'm staying with you," Marcus said. *As if he needed to say so with his arm wrapped around me,* Mel thought. His touch still made her uncomfortable, he *had* murdered her parents after all, but she wasn't certain what to do about that. In many ways, she cared deeply for him... it was just that parts of him horrified her.

"I'll stick around," Brian said. "I haven't had this much fun in a while."

Mel grimaced. If this was his idea of "fun," she wasn't sure she wanted him along...

Then again, he did come in handy.

"So, where do we go, now?" Mel asked.

"I think Vagyr is right out," Bob drawled.

"Probably a good bet," Marcus laughed. He squeezed Mel tight and looked over at Lace, "You've no-doubt got contacts with the Mercenary Guild... how about Hanet?"

"What, you assume that since I'm a mercenary, I'd know the intricacies of getting a ship unnoticed into Hanet?" Lace rolled her eyes. She sighed though, "Yes, we can go there. If Fenris can alter his electromagnetic signature somewhat and do some visual cosmetic modifications, we could slip in no problem." She smiled slightly, "For a... token price, I can put you in contact with someone who can make some legitimate papers, launder this cash, and help you get started doing... whatever you intend to do."

"You are going to *charge* us for your help?" Marcus sputtered.

"*Mercenary*, remember?" Lace asked. "Of course, Mel could... work some of the payment off with me," She blinked her lashes at him suggestively.

Mel felt her ears flame. "Okay, Hanet it is. How much money you want?"

***

Time: 1730 Zulu, 23 June 291 G.D.
Location: Triad Gateway Station, Triad System

"You're sure about this," Colonel Frost asked.

Rawn nodded. He'd lost weight in the past week. A tight military haircut and a change of clothing altered his appearance enough that they'd had no trouble slipping through customs on Triad.

The customs at Vagyr hadn't batted an eyelash when they landed in an obsolete bomber drone and climbed out of the bomb bay. Then again, Frost had slipped them a case of money, so that had helped.

"Until I know how much Roush told Guard Intelligence about my accounts, we'll operate off cash reserves," Colonel Frost said.

Rawn nodded; he found it satisfying that Agent Mueller's bribe money would fund Guard Free Now's future attacks.

He clenched his fists when he remembered the destruction of the *Fenris*. It was obvious to him now that Mel had somehow taken the ship back from the AI. That Guard Fleet had killed her to save a worthless hive like Vagyr enraged him.

A part of him hated Frost for not letting him go back. Another part of him hated himself for the fact that he had not remained behind.

All of him hated the Guard, Guard Intelligence in particular. They'd set up the situation. They'd manipulated the events.

And they had issued the statement.

It was a simple announcement. A group of GFN terrorists had seized a "relic" warship and tried to attack Vagyr. A Guard Fleet task force in the area had stopped them.

It filled him with rage that his sister's eulogy didn't even bear her name. That her actions had stopped the destruction of Vagyr, and the UNSC's precious Guard Fleet, made his anger all the worse.

Rawn looked down at the small duffel that carried explosives and guns. He didn't see weapons there, not anymore. All he saw was the chance to make amends for his sister's death.

"I'm ready," he said to Frost. "What's our first target?"

###

The End

The Rising Wolf Series Continues with Odin's Eye
For more books in the universe, try Valor's Child

About the Author

Kal Spriggs is a science fiction and fantasy author. He currently has many series in print: The Valor's Child YA series, the Forsaken Valor series, The Renegades space opera and space exploration series, the Shadow Space Chronicles military science fiction and space opera series, the Fenris space opera series, and the Eoriel Saga epic fantasy series.

Kal is a US Army combat veteran who has been deployed to Iraq and Afghanistan. He's a graduate of a federal service academy and used a lot of his experiences from there in writing the Valor's Child books. He lives in Colorado, and is married to his wonderful wife (who deserves mention for her patience with his writing) and also shares his home with his son, and several feline overlords. He likes hiking, skiing, and enjoying the outdoors, when he's not hunched over a keyboard writing his next novel.

Printed in Great Britain
by Amazon